This
Train
Is
Being
Held

This Train Is Being

ISMÉE WILLIAMS

Held

AMULET BOOKS • NEW YORK

PUBLISHER'S NOTE: This is a work of fiction. Names, characters, places, and incidents are either the product of the author's imagination or used fictitiously, and any resemblance to actual persons, living or dead, business establishments, events, or locales is entirely coincidental.

Library of Congress Cataloging-in-Publication Data
Names: Williams, Ismée, author.
Title: This train is being held/Ismée Williams.
Description: New York: Amulet Books, 2020. | Summary: Told in two voices, ballet dancer and private school student Isabelle Warren and poet and baseball star Alex Rosario grow closer after meeting on a subway, bonding over their parents' expectations and their own dreams. Identifiers: LCCN 2019033767 (print) | LCCN 2019033768 (ebook) | ISBN 9781419734939 (hardcover) | ISBN 9781683354871 (ebook) Subjects: CYAC: Dating (Social customs)— Fiction. | Social classes—Fiction. | Hispanic Americans—Fiction. | Family life— New York (State)—New York—Fiction. | New York (N.Y.)—Fiction.
Classification: LCC PZ7.1.W546 Thi 2020 (print) | LCC PZ7.1.W546 (ebook) | DDC [Fic]—dc23
LC record available at https://lccn.loc.gov/2019033767
LC ebook record available at https://lccn.loc.gov/2019033768

Text copyright © 2020 Ismée Williams
Book design by Siobhán Gallagher

Page 29: Excerpt from "Love Sonnet XI" by Pablo Neruda, from One Hundred Love Sonnets: Cien sonetos de amor (Austin: University of Texas Press, 2014). Page 254: "Hide-and-Seek 1933" by Galway Kinnell can be found in Strong Is Your Hold: Poems by Galway Kinnell (New York: Houghton Mifflin, 2006).

Printed and bound in U.S.A.
10 9 8 7 6 5 4 3 2 1

Amulet Books® is a registered trademark of Harry N. Abrams, Inc.

ABRAMS The Art of Books
195 Broadway, New York, NY 10007
abramsbooks.com

To Abuela and Abuelo,
who came from opposite ends of the island

ISA

The M96 veers around a stopping taxi before slowing as it approaches Broadway. The bus speeds up, then the driver hits the brakes, eases off, then hits them again. I don't fall because it's been jerk-stop, jerk-stop like this since Park Ave. It's OK. The driver's probably learning.

I push through the door to the sidewalk and dash across the intersection, the crossing signal flashing a countdown. My bag bounces against my shoulder as I double-time into the subway station. I run through my dance routine once more in my mind. Mom was home today so I couldn't practice.

The digital screen blinks zero at me. My train is pulling in. I dig out my unlimited MetroCard from my bag and swipe it through the turnstile. Below, brakes squeal. Doors thump open. My footsteps match the crescendoing opening rhythm of *La Gioconda*, the music of my audition, as I fly down the stairs to the platform.

I clear the bottom step as the conductor's signal chimes. I could call out, "Hold the train!" People do it all the time. Instead, I launch into the air, my front leg striking out as if for a grand jeté. The edges of the metal doors slice toward me. I'm almost through. But my back ankle is still outside the car. Mom once saw a lady lose part of a finger this way.

I throw my weight forward, snatching my leg in.

The doors snap open. They pause, then clang closed.

A boy steps back. He's maybe a year or two older than me, a junior or senior in high school perhaps. He must have held the door.

1

"Thanks," I say.

He slips his hands into his pockets then lifts his chin at me. A *You're welcome*, I guess.

The intercom scratches, informing us that holding the doors delays everyone and that there will always be another train. I press my lips together so I don't grin like an idiot. Mom says I do that when I get nervous.

I slide into a seat along an entire row of empties and check my bun for loose hairpins. It's the middle of the day so the train's not crowded. Across from me, a lady listens to music with her eyes shut. An Afro-Caribbean rhythm pulses from her earbuds. Even with the rush and rattle of metal wheels against metal tracks, I hear it. The boy who held the door for me hears it too. His head moves, ever so slightly, and the heel of his sneaker taps against a large duffel that he's pushed under the seats behind him.

The DJ woman's chin drops to her chest like she's fallen asleep. Her hand lies still, an uncurled fist above her multicolored patchwork skirt, the kind Merrit brought me back from Peru after he hiked the Inca trail in June. He called me at lunchtime today. I asked if he was leaving his cell in his dorm room like I told him so he'd meet actual people. The nerd flipped the camera to show students sitting in a circle on an emerald lawn, one of them holding a volleyball inked with the words *favorite food* and *best pet*. Mom, Dad, and I are hoping Merrit meets someone to help him forget Samantha, his high school girlfriend. The camera switched back to his smiling face. "Just wanted to wish you luck, both for the audition and for keeping it from Mom. Couldn't have done that without my phone." He winked and with a clipped "Ciao," signed off.

After, I found Mom in the library, reorganizing the books—by color this time. Her museum board meeting had been canceled. I wasn't sure if she'd be angry or happy about that. I often wasn't sure if she'd be angry or happy. I cleared my throat. "Hey, Mom? I'm heading out to meet Chrissy. We're going to rehearse a bit before class." I hate lying. It's different if you just don't tell the whole truth.

Mom tossed a thick, glossy book jacket onto a pile with the others she was sacrificing, then looked at me. I didn't dare look away, even when my palms started to tingle. I was in my standard uniform—hair up, tights under shorts. She couldn't have known about the audition, right?

Mom let out a long breath. She glared at the text in her hand, *Using Food to Control Your Mood*. The psychologist must have given it to her. The cover tore as she ripped it off, and I winced. At least she wasn't glaring at me anymore. I tip-toed to the hallway.

"Remember, no subways," she called out. "It's unhygienic. And unsafe. Forty-eight people were struck and killed by a train last year. Take a car. There are some twenties in my purse."

I like the subway. It's cheaper and often faster—even than a car share. And down here, it's like the real New York, with people from all over the city, not just the tiny slice of the Upper East Side where we live. Not that I would ever tell Mom.

I took the money, said thanks, and slipped out. It's harder to manage Mom without Merrit around but I try not to let her affect me.

I swing my bag to my lap and sink back into my seat. The song coming from the sleeping lady's phone changes to one with a faster beat. I tap my toes, warming up my Achilles and gastrocs. I lift one shoulder and lower the other, then switch sides. I'm swaying to the left then the right, trying to keep myself loose, as the train screeches into Eighty-Sixth.

My eyes close. I'm concentrating on the music. The deep hiss of mouth breathing hits me a second before a warm sticky thigh presses against mine. I jerk upright and stand. A guy with a receding hairline sits in the seat next to where I was. Even though the entire row and three-quarters of the one opposite are free. I move to the doorway, the music from the colorful-skirted

3

woman's phone following me. I flick my hips, trying to remember steps from that one class I took at a resort in Vieques. The man with no sense of personal space is staring at me. He adjusts the thin silver frames of his glasses then his hand goes to his shorts to adjust himself. *Whoops*, didn't need to see that. The man wipes the shine from his forehead with his arm. A phone rests on his leg. It's aimed at me. Wait—did he just hit Record? Umm . . . I think he did. Should I turn around? But then he'll have a perfect view of my butt. Maybe I should have worn more than my dance leotard and shorts. Maybe Mom was right. I should have grabbed a taxi.

The door-holding boy steps in front of the guy, blocking his phone. He's super tall—taller than Dad even, who earned the nickname GW—the Great White Hope—playing basketball in college. And the boy's fit. Really fit. Like superhero fit. Like I-wouldn't-want-to-face-off-with-you-in-a-dark-alley fit. After a long minute, the man tilts his phone toward a splotch of bright pink gum smeared into the rubber tiling. At the next stop, he rises with a grunt and tucks his phone in the pocket of his coffee-stained khaki shorts. He rams his shoulder into the boy as he gets off. I shrink back. I've seen fights start from less. With his broad shoulders and arms corded with muscle, the tall boy doesn't look like he'd tolerate disrespect. To his credit, he just slips to the side. His narrowed gaze follows the man out.

"Perv," he says under his breath as the train pulls away.

"Thanks," I say. "Again."

"Don't mention it." The intensity of his eyes startles me. They're a deep, rich brown, and yes, they're framed by impossibly long lashes. But it's not that. It's the expression in them. Like he's paying really close attention. Like he knows we're all here on this earth that's spinning a thousand miles per hour and he doesn't want to miss anything.

The boy eases back, crossing one foot in front of the other, placing the tip of his shoe on the ground. Black Chuck Taylors. They're scuffed and someone's taken a Sharpie to CONVERSE ALL-STAR, but the navy star is still there. Standing like that, hands tucked into his pockets, balancing on one foot though the train knocks us side to side, he could be a dancer.

The subway slows into a curve. Chuck draws a hand from his pocket. He makes a fist and touches his lips with the back of it. His mouth has the resting shape of a slight smile. It makes him seem content. And confident. Which makes sense given his looks. His eyes flick toward me though he's partly turned away, like he knows I'm watching him.

My cheeks grow warm. I feel like I need to say something. "It's probably my fault."

Chuck turns, brow shifting down just enough to communicate his confusion.

"I should be wearing something else. So, uh, people won't stare." I clear my throat.

He looks away again. "You should wear what you want."

"Yeah, well, it's because I'm in a rush." I'm almost always in a rush but I don't tell him that. "It saves me time not having to change."

He glances at me again. "You going to an exercise class?"

I don't normally talk to strangers. Especially not on the subway. But Chuck doesn't seem like a stranger anymore.

"It's an audition. I'm going to an audition."

One eyebrow shoots up. How does he do that? Merrit can do it too, but no matter how hard I try, I never can.

"It's a tryout," I add. "For a dance school." I don't tell him that even if I make it in there's no way my mom would let me switch schools. I don't tell him that I'm doing the audition for myself, to prove I could be just as good as the dancers who get to spend their day going from Pointe to Technique to Variations instead of just from precalc to chemistry. He'd probably think it's ridiculous.

Both of his eyebrows lift. "I know what an audition is."

"Of course. Of course you do." I need to stop repeating myself. "Anyway, that's why I'm dressed like this, which is why that guy was staring at me."

Chuck glances at my feet and then at my arm hugging my side. He swivels toward me.

"This dance audition. It's for salsa? For Latin dance?" He nods at the woman with the loud earbuds. He must have seen me moving to her music. She's awake, tracing the patterns of her skirt, kicking folds of it out from between her legs. The train brakes hard into Seventy-Second Street. The woman slides partway into the next seat. Neither Chuck nor I lose our balance even though we're not holding on.

"Nope," I say. "Ballet." I pop up onto my toes, just for a second. I shouldn't be doing that without my pointe shoes. Ms. Maria gave me an earful once when she caught me showing off to my friends.

My face heats even more. I can't believe I just did that.

The doors slide open. A bunch of people get on the train. I move to the other doorway, the one that will open at the next stop. My stop. Chuck follows.

He leans on the bar on his side of the entrance. "But you like Latin music?" He asks it like he's afraid of the response.

"What's not to like?"

He bows his head, which I think is him agreeing, but he's examining his phone. He fishes a headset out of one of his pockets and plugs it in. He offers me the earbuds. The beat hits me before I pick up the tune. Chuck is watching me, waiting. The song sounds like Vieques, fast and catchy like the music from the woman with the skirt, but deeper, richer somehow. I smile and forget to hide it. Chuck's lips part, revealing white teeth that gleam against his skin. I swish my hips. He nods along.

Ms. Maria's lilting accent rises over the music. *You execute perfectly, flawlessly, all the steps. But you need to feel the music. Why so stiff?*

Well, this music sure is loosening me up.

"What's so funny?" Chuck asks.

I didn't realize I was laughing. "Um... It's just... my dance teacher's always saying I'm too tense."

He shakes his head, still smiling. "I don't believe that." He shrugs. "You look..." He pauses, his eyes catching mine. "Perfect. You look perfect to me."

I move my feet, the dance from Vieques coming back. His shoulders sway, mirroring me even though he can't hear the music.

The doors open.

"Sixty-Sixth Street, Lincoln Center. Downtown local 1 train. Next stop, Fifty-Ninth Street, Columbus Circle."

I yank the headset from my ears. I clutch the strap of my bag. I've got to get out. I've got twenty minutes before my audition. Twenty minutes to stretch and lace up my pointe shoes. If I'm lucky, I'll be able to rehearse my piece one last time before I'm called. Is it ridiculous that I want to stay here, dancing with this boy I only just met? His smile is gone. The earbuds are swinging from his half-open hand. His gaze follows my face as I shift from side to side.

The signal rings. I still don't move. My legs are trained to do any dance step I want. They're frozen, like me, in first position.

The doors slide out from their pockets. A scuffed black Chuck Taylor catches them before they seal shut. They shudder open.

My stomach flutters as if I'm about to step on stage.

"Good luck," he tells me.

I leap out just before the doors slam.

THURSDAY, SEPTEMBER 1

ALEX

"Oye, chan. Your stepmom be the best." Bryan pushes a taco in his mouth.

Danny nods. He's leaning over his legs, two hands holding open foil. He's breathing like we just finished practice. But it's because he's chewing so hard.

I take a packet labeled CARNITAS out of the bag. I unwrap it only partway. I'm not going to waste any of this filling. I bite off half and close my eyes. My stomach screams at me to hurry up. But I got the bag. Ain't no way they're getting more than me. Don't care how fast they eat.

Bryan reaches for another. I slide onto the next seat, the bag tucked against me as if it has my lucky glove instead of twelve homemade bundles of meat. Bryan grunts. He kicks. I see it coming so mostly get out of the way. His cleats clip my knee. I don't even look at him. Instead, I toss an al pastor at Danny. I take out another carnitas for me.

Bryan's looking at me like I booted him from the lineup. He folds and unfolds his arms. His fingers tap the plastic seats. He jerks his chin up. "El Jefe was going to war today. He angry at you or something?"

I shrug. I peel back one corner of foil and then another. I inhale onion and cumin-spiced pork and hiss my approval. I take a slow bite. Papi couldn't be mad at me. I was three for four. He took my shoulder when we left, squeezed it like he always does.

Danny stops eating. He actually lifts his mouth from the tortilla. No way I could do that. "El Jefe always be at war. Nothing new there."

Bryan's eyes once-over me. Don't know if it's because I'm enjoying my taco and he's got nothing or if he's still thinking about Papi. Papi made us run the bleachers. And the pier. But that was because Danny was slow coming into home. It couldn't have been because of me.

Bryan shakes his head. "Coño. We got to get you a girl. Stop makin' love to your food and dame uno."

I grin and toss him a silver bullet of suadero. I wouldn't normally treat Yaritza's meals with such disrespect. But catching is Bryan's thing. He grabs it out of the air even though the train is slamming into the next stop.

Danny snorts. "Not like we gotta try hard. Kiara's been sniffing around since Memorial Day weekend when you hit those five home runs."

"Four homers. Not five." Bryan rips at the foil. "Kiara's been following after you since algebra with Mrs. Nolan. What was that? Two years ago? And besides Kiara, there's Franny."

"And Julissa," Danny crows. Bryan's cleats sink into his thigh. Danny yelps. What did he think was going to happen when he mentioned Bryan's ex?

I open the bag, show them the nine remaining bundles. "You don't both shut it, these gonna be mine." They stuff their mouths with what they got left but their eyes are still laughing at me. I don't need no girl. Not when my hand is gripping a mitt and I'm hurling a ninety-mile-an-hour ball. I reach for my water, gulp at the straw. "Anyway, you know what Papi says about las mujeres."

"Who says you have to tell El Jefe?" Bryan's cheek is balled up with taco. "It's not like you live with him."

I turn over the wraps, reading the labels on what's left. Papi has a way of knowing things, even if you don't come out and tell him. They don't call him El Jefe for nothing.

A woman with two boys gets on. One's about Robi's age. His mami sure is giving us the stink eye. Her nose hides in her sleeve. Yeah. Yaritza's cooking isn't shy in the smell department. But what are we going to do? We're starved from an hour and a half of drills. And a two-hour game.

The train swings into Dekalb. Danny hoots as Bryan stands and lifts one foot. The fool keeps his balance as he chomps what's left of his tortilla like he's a gator in some cartoon. I lean back in my seat, stretching my legs. Train's only going to get more crowded. The boy who looks like Robi digs into the shopping bag his mami's holding. He comes back out with a baseball cap. Not Mets. Yankees.

I lift off my own cap and push back sweat-drenched hair. I tug down the brim and meet the boy's smile with my own. My hat doesn't have an *N* or *Y* on it. The letters *AHH* are stitched into the navy fabric in the same font as the Yankees'. We're still in Brooklyn, not Washington Heights, so not everyone is going to recognize it stands for Alexander Hamilton High. But if you know about high school baseball and you recognize the names of two Hall of Famers and three Rookies of the Year, you will. The boy's mami stops fussing with the younger boy. Her eyes flit from Danny to Bryan to me. I know what she sees—three morenos in dirt-stained sweats taking up a row and a half of seats. She tugs at her son's sleeve till he looks away. Guess she doesn't know what AHH means either.

The doors crash open. Folks pile in.

"Muévete." I slide over the empty seats between us and push Danny toward Bryan. Bryan's standing, one cleat still off the floor, taco held high like he means to mash it into the ceiling. I rise and snatch it away. I hand it to Danny who downs it before Bryan can grab it back. Bryan knocks Danny's cap clear across the car. Danny dives for it. He pops back, hat pulled nearly down to his nose. The brim doesn't cover his upper lip, one side smooth, the other bumped with a red line snaking down from his nostril. But it hides his eyes so he can't see people looking at him. His abuela's still angry his mami didn't bring him to New York right after he was born. She's always going on about how if he'd had the surgery here instead of in DR it would look better. Bryan and I tell him it's not so bad. But still, he never takes off that cap.

"Y tú. Siéntate." I hold the last of the tacos. I don't hand them over till Bryan takes his seat like I asked. I keep the suadero for me. The boy who looks like my baby brother isn't there anymore. The mami's moved them to the other end, as far from us as possible. I concentrate on the warm fold of corn and grilled meat. I chew and close my eyes again. Bryan's telling some story about when he and Julissa went to some party. He reminds me if I ever went with him, Kiara would be waiting for me and I wouldn't have a girl problem. I take another bite. The top of a Yankees hat sticks above a cardboard box. The hat tips forward as if the boy is looking at his hands or his feet or the ground. It's just like Papi said. If that mami had seen us on the field, it'd be different. She'd be wanting her sons to be us instead of trying to keep them away. I could make a fist, stick out my thumb, then count on that one hand the number of times someone's met me not on the field, not in uniform, and actually respected me. Baseball is what makes people take notice of me.

● ● ●

"Alex, montro, come on!" Danny's calling me from the door. I snap up and follow him to the platform.

"What you dreamin' about?" Danny cranes his head back to me as we aim for the tunnel to the 1, 2, 3.

Bryan jabs me with an elbow. "Not what. Who?" He smirks. "Kiara, right?" I wave him off but show him a grin. They both start hooting. The local and the express come at the same time. Bryan goes for the express but I jerk my chin at the local.

We get on, the conductor screaming at us to wait till others get off. It's crowded, so we're stuck by the doors.

"Why you don't want the express no more?" Bryan's question is an accusation. "You do know it's faster, right? That's why they call it *the express*."

I give him my back. I gaze out at rainbow graffiti on concrete walls. I trace the curves of balloon letters on the glass. Bryan likes to argue. I don't.

"Manito, to 'ta frio. We got to change at Ninety-Six anyway," Danny says.

Bryan's reflection scowls. He likes to get his way. And he doesn't like to be ignored. At the next stop, Bryan mutters as he squeezes in tight next to me and Danny. At Fifty-Ninth, a couple people get off. None get on. Bryan rolls his shoulders and adjusts his cap. "Been meaning to ask, why don't you ever take El Jefe up on his offer to stay with him and Yaritza on the weekend? Bet Robi would love that. And maybe then he wouldn't make us run all those extra drills."

I have spent the night with them. Robi's mostly the reason I do it. But me staying over doesn't guarantee Papi'll be in a good mood. Plus, I don't like leaving Mami alone in the apartment all night. Unlike Papi, Mami doesn't have anyone else. Bryan lives with his abuela. Danny too. They'd understand if I told them. But I don't.

"What, and miss riding the train with you pendejos?"

Danny chuckles. Bryan barely cracks a smile. He's still angry about taking the local.

"Hey, Bry, how 'bout you and me head to Hood Park when we get back?" I nod at my ball bag.

"You kiddin'? We just finished practicing." Bryan rubs his thumb into his palm. "Yo, chan, I need a rest. Plus, I got someone to meet. And before you ask me, it's not Julissa."

Danny tsks. He bumps Bryan with his arm. "Don't you got work to do?" He peers at me. I have a science lab to write. But practicing the new pitch Papi taught me, showing Papi I'm serious, is more important.

I hold up the ball, two fingers on the red seams. My thumb cradles the bottom. "This is work."

Danny looks down and shrugs a shoulder. "I'll go."

He's not as good a catcher as Bryan. But I only need someone to toss the ball back to me. I wait for Danny to look up then give him my winner's smile. His face lights like he just got named MVP. We're coming up on Lincoln Center. I scan the platform, hoping Bryan and Danny don't notice. The door opens. I duck out, make a show of letting others in. Some girls with buns get on the car next to ours.

I jump back in. The train pulls away. I walk toward the next car.

"Hey! Alex!"

I ignore Bryan, even though he hates that.

I jerk the handle to open one door, do it again to open a second.

The next car is just as crowded. The three dancers hang close to the door. The one with blond hair is facing away. I hold my breath and wait for her to turn. She catches me staring and frowns. I look down. It's not her.

I head back to Danny and Bryan. Words on a poster confront me. I've seen this poem before. "Lost" is the title.

"What was all that about?" Bryan accuses.

"Nada. Thought I saw someone is all."

"Who?" Bryan presses.

There is only one name that'll make him back off.

"Kiara." I lazy-smile at them as they catcall and punch my arm. I stare out the window as patches of spray-can art zip by. The words from the poem fall apart. In my head, I reassemble them.

FRIDAY, SEPTEMBER 2

ISA

I'm holding five leotards (three navy for Technique, Pointe, and Adagio, and two white for Variations and Character class), twelve pairs of pink tights (they always run), one navy skirt, two white skirts, two sets of hairpins (I tend to lose them), two hairnets, and sparkle hair gel (whoever decided to add the sparkle to gel is a genius).

"Oh good, you saw the hair gel too!" Chrissy sashays toward me, her arms heaped with fabric. Her squeal makes a few customers turn. Chrissy drops the clothes in a chair, slides out her phone, turns the hair gel bottle upside down, and opens her mouth. She makes exaggerated gulping sounds and takes a selfie. She taps at her screen, no doubt posting the pic, then starts jumping up and down. "I am so pumped we get to take Variations this year! Aren't you?"

I nod. I should be excited. I mean, I am excited. It's just that Mom decided to come this afternoon instead of telling me to use her credit card like she did last year. Part of me grew a few inches and beamed when Mom grabbed her bag and followed me out. The other part is freaking.

I head toward the shoe section, glancing past Chrissy. My mom's still leaning against the wall next to the changing area. She's fingering the fabric of a leopard-print miniskirt as she talks on her cell. It must be Dad, because Mom doesn't look angry. If she were speaking with anyone from the boards of the Big Brothers Big Sisters program or the Art and Architecture Museum, I'd be able to hear what she was saying from across the room.

I stretch my neck, relaxing my back and shoulders. Mom can't get into too much trouble if she's on the phone. I drape an arm over my pile while I wait. I don't want anyone to think it's unclaimed. In sixth grade, I'd gathered almost my entire wardrobe and left it with Mom while I went to try on a different style of leotard Chrissy was raving about. When I came out of the dressing room, Mom and my stuff were gone. Mom had taken a call and wandered away. All the clothing and accessories had been reshelved. *Dance is your hobby and you have to take responsibility for it, Isabelle,* she'd shrieked. She was right. I shouldn't have let my things out of my sight.

"Size?" A woman with dyed black hair pulled into a severe bun peers over small square spectacles at me. Her hand juts out for the sample shoes I'm holding.

"Um." I give her the pointe shoe and the pink ballet slipper with the split leather sole. "I was a seven last year, but do you think you could measure me? Over the summer they started to feel tight."

"They're supposed to be tight." She has the slipper right up under her nose, trying to read the style number printed on the inside. Her accent is Russian. Or Ukrainian perhaps.

"Yes, but would it be OK if we just checked?" My Peds-clad foot is already on top of the metal measuring contraption. "I don't want to make a mistake."

The sales lady crouches beside me and adjusts the marker against my toes. "I will get you seven and half. And seven." She marches to the back, the ribbons from the pointe shoes trailing behind her.

"What's her story?" Chrissy puts her hands on her hips. She scowls as she climbs over the bench to sit beside me.

"I'm thinking failed trapeze artist." It's a game I made up to pass the time when Merrit was in the hospital. "She escaped a household of seven older brothers, three of whom ended up inheriting their mother's lycanthropy.

Before she found out if she was going to turn into a werewolf too, she ran off with the circus."

Chrissy's grinning. "So why did she fail? At trapeze, I mean."

"Well, in Paris, she was courted by a renowned acrobat from India and they started a torrid affair. Photos of them kissing midswing, knees locked around their own trapezes, plastered the city papers."

"Ooh! Like *Greatest Showman!*" Chrissy clasps her hands together and sighs.

I nod and pause, thinking of the worst thing that could happen to my character, who I've named Tatiana. "They were going to marry, but she made the mistake of telling him about her unstable family. Ajay left her and followed his troupe back to Mumbai. Poor Tatiana was heartbroken. She moved to New York and never touched another trapeze again."

Chrissy looks toward the open doorway that says EMPLOYEES ONLY. "No wonder she's such a bitch."

I go to smack Chrissy with a packet of tights, but she scoots out of the way. She turns over the shoe she's holding and makes a face at the price tag.

"Honestly, I don't know why you don't buy your shoes online. They're so much cheaper. And then you don't have to deal with Ms. Trapeze Wannabe Werewolf over there. What? You know the real reason she's so uptight isn't because she didn't get the guy. It's because she never got to throw her head back and howl." Chrissy puckers her ruby-red lips. She always wears that same lipstick, with thick black eyeliner and fake lashes. Otherwise strangers on the subway would still be asking her if she lost her mother and needed help getting home.

I nail her in the face with tights as a long "Arh-ooo!" comes out of her. I check to make sure Mom hasn't heard her. Chrissy's mom, Mrs. Mc-Callum, has cornered a sales associate next to the cash register. Thankfully, our moms haven't seen each other. A giant display of mannequins clad in tulle stands between them.

The lady who was helping me—"Tatiana"—comes through the doorway, a tower of boxes obscuring her face. Chrissy makes a noise that sounds suspiciously like a *woof* as the woman lowers the boxes to the ground. Tatiana removes the first shoe and holds out a hand for my foot, just as a voice booms behind me.

"Well if it isn't my second-most-favorite ballerina in the whole world. How are you doing, sugar? Stand on up and give us a hug." Chrissy's mother holds out her arms.

Tatiana frowns. "I have shoes here. Hug can wait."

"Goodness me, that can't be right. There's always time for a hug." Mrs. McCallum pats her ample bosom as she steps in front of the store lady. I rise and put my arms around her, bending my head a bit. My mom never hugs Chrissy like this. She never hugs me like this.

Tatiana click-clacks away to help someone else. Chrissy's eyebrows shoot up to her hairline.

"Ruh-ude," she warbles, giving the word two syllables. "Though maybe this is good. I'll take a pic of the pair you like and we can buy them online after all."

"Oh, yes. That is a fine idea," Mrs. McCallum whispers. "Isabelle, dear, is your mother here? I should go find her and say hello."

I nod. "She's over by the dressing rooms." I glance at Chrissy, worried. Mostly I want to protect her mom from my mom. But also, I don't want them talking about dance. I didn't tell Mom I'm taking ten classes instead of eight this year, because I don't want her to flip out.

"Mama?" Chrissy flashes her angel smile. "Could you find me some of those little sticky pads that go over your nipples? I'm almost out and I know you don't want me high-beaming everyone when I'm on stage."

Mrs. McCallum's eyes grow huge. "Oh no! That would be something, wouldn't it? Where do you think they are, honey?"

Chrissy points to the corner of hair accessories, even though the nipple pasties are next to the cashier's desk. Mrs. McCallum gives me a wave before wading through the racks of sequined dance dresses.

"Thanks," I whisper.

Chrissy lifts the cover off one of the boxes and wiggles a pointe shoe at me. "No probs." Chrissy insists she doesn't mind my mom. But we've been dancing together since fifth grade so she knows how my mom can be. "Mama will probably come back with a Pinterest post about how to make a tiara out of rhinestone bobby pins, *ain't that right, sugar?*" Chrissy grins as I laugh. She's good at that, attacking my family stress with humor.

I take the shoe as Chrissy tugs stuffing out of the other one.

"Are we almost done here? Oh, hello, Chrissy."

"Mom!" It's an out-of-breath gasp. I didn't see her coming.

"How are you, Mrs. Warren? Isa's almost finished. She just needs to settle on shoes." Chrissy puts a hand on each of the two towers of boxes.

Mom looks Chrissy up and down. I fight the urge to grab my friend and push her behind me. *Please don't say anything, Mom. Don't say a single thing.*

"Chrissy, you look wonderful! Your calves are so sculpted. And your arms . . ." Mom lifts one of Chrissy's hands, inviting her to twirl. "Have you been doing pilates this summer?"

Chrissy spins, her mouth stretching ear to ear. "Nope. Just dance."

"I've always said dancing makes the most beautiful bodies. Right, Isabelle?"

She's never said that to me. Not one time. I nod and smile anyway.

Mom's eyes come back to me and the shoe boxes. "Do you have to try all of them on?" She looks at her watch. "It's quarter to six and I have a board meeting at seven thirty. I'd like to see your father for more than ten minutes before I have to go."

"You know, Mrs. Warren"—Chrissy flips her auburn curls over one shoulder—"you could start checking out." She gestures at my pile of dancewear, then looks at me. "By the time they ring everything up you'll be done with the shoes, right?"

Mom doesn't wait for me to respond. "Where do I pay?" She's come with me to this same store at least four times, but Mom hates this stuff. She can't help not remembering it.

"I'll show you." Chrissy leaps up, grabbing the leotards, skirts, and tights. "Oh—I love these skirts! Don't you?" She holds up a hanger, letting the white gauze sway. "I'm so glad we get to wear them this year."

Mom picks up only the hairpins and follows Chrissy to the register.

I'm battling with a pointe shoe when Chrissy returns. "Thanks," I murmur, as I lace it up.

"Hey, what else am I here for? Any sign of my momster, by the way?"

I rise up on pointe and draw my knees to my chest in sharp, short jerks, turning in a slow circle. The added height gives me a good view. "She's over by the tutus."

"Ha! I knew she wouldn't be able to resist!"

Rising voices come from the direction of the checkout desk. Mom is arguing with the sales lady. I'm about to yank off my shoes and sprint over there when I notice a boy about my age standing by the windows facing Seventh Avenue. He's flipping through a rack of pants in the men's section. His white shirt hugs his body, showing the movement of his muscles underneath. An older woman approaches, speaking to him in Spanish. He laughs and lets out an, "Ay, Mami!" He turns and puts his arm around her. It's not Chuck, the guy from the subway. I'd thought maybe it was.

Chrissy takes the box of slippers from me. "These are the ones you want, right?" She eyes my right foot, then my left. "Those two feel the same?"

"This one is better." I hand the left shoe to Chrissy just as the boy and his mother pass in front of us.

Chrissy's voice drops. "Tell me you saw the fine piece of ass that just walked by." She makes the same noise she does whenever we go into the

Brazilian bakery near her for brigadeiros. "Hmmmm, hmmmm. Well done, Mother Nature. I commend you."

"Chrissy!" I hiss.

"Whatever. I saw you checking him out before." Chrissy peeks inside the shoe box, then snaps a photo. Her nose scrunches as her thumbs tap her screen. "Sending this now."

"I'll just buy this pair." The sales lady spent all that time with me. It wouldn't be fair to not give her the commission.

"Isa? You ready?" Mom starts toward us from across the store, head bowed as she rummages through her purse.

She runs smack into the dancer I'd thought was Chuck.

"Ah!" The bags fall from her hand. Her new phone hits the floor with a crack.

The boy's eyes are super big. "I'm sorry, so sorry. You OK?" His mother is saying the same thing in Spanish.

"Elisa? Are you all right?" Mrs. McCallum gets to Mom before we do. She picks up Mom's phone. She smooths the ruffled sleeves of Mom's silk blouse. "You're fine, just fine," she says. "It's just a phone. You can have it fixed."

The glass face is shattered.

Mom's hands draw into fists.

"You were looking at your screen, weren't you?" Mom shouts at the boy. He's holding a cell too.

I choke in a breath. "Mom, he wasn't—"

She silences me with a single enraged finger.

"You dancers are all the same," she spits, advancing on him. "Self-centered, thinking only about your art and not watching where you're going. What happens when you lose your youth and beauty? Are you even capable of thinking that far ahead?" Her cold eyes cut to mine.

My whole body burns. Like I'm on stage but there's no music and I've forgotten the steps.

"I'm so sorry, ma'am." The poor guy is on his knees, putting my dance stuff back in the bags. Even though none of it was his fault. He offers my mom a small smile.

"You think your charm will work on me?" Mom laughs, but it's too loud and too bright. "Well, it won't." Mom grabs her phone from Mrs. Mc-Callum, avoiding the fragments of glass on her cracked screen. "Isa, call us a car. I'll be outside." She whirls back to the boy. "And teach your grandmother English, for Christ's sake. This is Manhattan. You're not in the Caribbean anymore." She snaps it at him in Spanish, her Cuban accent clipped and furious. I've never heard her speak anything other than English in New York. Unless Abuela is visiting. Or Mom's on the phone with her family.

As soon as Mom's gone, Chrissy darts forward to help the boy. I'm right behind her.

"I-I'm sorry," I babble. In my head, I'm apologizing for all of it. For my mom running into him and blaming him for it. For the way she treated him, like he was beneath her, even though she doesn't know anything about him and his mami, other than what they look like and that they speak Spanish but aren't from the same island as her.

"No worries," he says, avoiding my eyes. Please, let him not go to the Academy.

"Her mom," Chrissy starts. "She has this problem."

Chrissy's trying to make it better. She's trying to give my mom an out. It's true. The therapist told me impulsivity is part of the disorder. But there is no excuse for the way Mom thinks. Just one for the way she's unable to conceal it.

I shake my head to make Chrissy stop.

Chrissy gives me a nod. "Here. Go." She shoves the bags at me and kisses the air in my general direction.

I take off after my mom, using my free hand to call an Uber. The stares of the entire store follow me.

ALEX

"I like your costume." Kiara nods at my uniform. She stands right up against me even though there are empty seats.

I shrug. "Didn't have anything else."

I almost said no to Bryan when he told me I needed a costume. Halloween is for pretending. This uniform? That's the real me.

Back at my place, Bryan was sweating. He scratched at the collar of his skin-tight suit. The pads of one of his pecs had shifted. He looked like he had una teta. "Por favor." He got down on his knees. I had to go, he said—he'd promised Julissa. And I had to wear a costume.

Brakes squeal. Kiara pitches forward.

I take her arm. "Cuidado."

She grabs on to my waist. There's more than just gracias in her smile.

I step back. "Eh, Black Panther, we takin' the L or the M?" I shout over the heads of a red-nosed clown and the Joker—we're not the only ones celebrating. Danny adjusts his Kylo Ren mask so he can see me better. Bryan's huddled into Julissa, talking real close. She's the only girl not showing stomach. She's dressed as Nakia. So everyone will know they're back together.

Black Panther lifts a cotton-stuffed shoulder. At least those pads are in the right place again. "The M?"

I nod. This party better be worth it.

"I love these." Kiara touches the buttons of my shirt. "They're the same as the Yankees', ¿veldad?" Her hand travels down like she's counting them. Behind her, Kylo Ren gives me a thumbs-up.

A 3 train pulls in across the platform. We should change to the express. But Black Panther is busy trailing his nose down Nakia's face. He kisses her jawline. Des . . . pa . . . cito. I almost holler it. But the train's getting too full to dodge fists. Julissa giggles. She leans into Bryan. Guess we're staying on the local.

There's a sharp clatter and the bark of a laugh. By the door, a tall dark-haired girl pulls up a shorter one. The blond must have tripped. She's got a hand clapped to her mouth. They've both got on tall-ass heels. And their dresses. ¡Guay! If Papi were here, he'd be whistling. I'd have to pretend I didn't know him.

Some guy dressed as an old Luke Skywalker stands to give them his seat. The short blond waves him away. They must have been drinking or smoking. Their smiles are too big. The blond whispers to her friend. The friend's gaze shifts to a guy sitting in the middle of the car. He's got a pile of papers on his lap, a pencil in his mouth and another behind his ear. One hand holds up a sheet. He traces small u's in the air. Is he some weird genius character from a movie I've never seen?

The shorter girl smooths down the black sequins of her dress. She says something that might be, "Wish me luck." She prowls toward the middle of the car.

The friend shakes her head, hands clasped like she's praying. Her smooth dark hair moves against her cheek. My heartbeat checks as if a batter's slammed my pitch out of the park. I recognize those bright eyes and that look—part fear, part thrill. It's the girl from the subway. The dancer. She's wearing a wig.

There's a *whoosh* of paper.

"Chrissy?" The weird academic guy stares at the blond. She's holding the sheet that was in his hand above her head. One of his pencils rolls under the seats.

She kisses him. She's so short she barely needs to bend down. Her arm is still up in the air, her hand gripping the paper. Her friend presses a fist to her mouth, hiding her grin. She did that before. On the subway with me.

The blond—Chrissy—pulls back. She gives the guy she kissed a little smile, like she's shy now or something. Wait, do they not . . . ? Ayyyyy, lo besó, and he wasn't even expecting it?

The guy stands. His papers scatter across the train. He fixes his glasses. He sways a bit, then grabs on to the bar above him. His other hand takes the blond's waist. He pulls her to him. He kisses her back. He's bent over, but her feet still leave the ground.

"Oh my." One old lady nudges another. An Elvis and some guy in a banana suit pick up the crumpled pages. Elvis is smirking at the kissing couple.

"That did not just happen." Kiara's arms cross in front of her. "Did that blanquita just accost that boy?" Her eyes flick to me. She licks her lips.

"He seemed to like it," I say.

The pencil behind the guy's ear slides free and hits the floor. It rolls toward me. I stop it with my foot, then bend to pick it up. When I stand, the dancer is staring at me. I show her the pencil and give her a small nod.

"Excuse me, do you know her?" Kiara swings around. She's standing way too close again.

I slide the pencil into my palm. "No," I say. It's true. I don't even know the girl's name.

Kiara examines my face. She pivots. "Oye, Julissa, you see that? These white girls are bugging, kissing strangers like it's some game."

Julissa extricates herself from Black Panther's arms. "¿Qué?"

The doors open. A couple with blackened eyes and red slashes painted across their faces get on.

The academic guy goes around collecting his papers. Chrissy leads him to her friend. The girls are like yin and yang, a blond with a black dress and a brunette in a silver one. The dancer glances at me. She looks away real fast. She nods at Chrissy, who's talking. I wish I could hear what she's saying. The girl smiles and nods again. She stops. Her face falls. She shakes her head, glances at me, and shakes her head again. The pink leaves her cheeks. She turns the color of the fallen papers.

Chrissy puts a fist on her hips. She stomps the floor with her massive shoe. "Isa, you promised!"

Isa. Her name is Isa.

Isa's fingers fold together. She nods and swallows. Her gaze meets mine. She steps forward.

"Qué no. Coño, no." The scream of wheels drowns Kiara's voice.

Isa's walk is not a prowl. But it's purposeful. Her eyes stay on me. There's mostly thrill in them, just a little bit of fear. The train goes faster. The clanking rhythm matches the beating in my chest. Isa keeps coming. She doesn't even wobble on those tall-ass heels of hers.

She stops in front of me. Her pupils shift, looking into one of my eyes and then the other. Flecks of gold dot the light brown of her irises. An escaped wisp of blond crosses her temple. She doesn't smell of alcohol. She smells like the flowers that grow in Mami's hometown. Like plumeria and jasmine. I can't help but breathe it in.

"Hi, Chuck." She smiles.

I don't have time to wonder about the name.

She reaches for my face. She's taller in the shoes. But not tall enough. I meet her halfway.

Her lips are warm. And soft.

I'm still holding the pencil. I slip it into my pocket. I take her elbow. My hand is behind her head. I crush her against me.

Heat floods my chest.

The doors are open. Passengers getting out bump us. I feel like I've been drinking.

Isa's breathing hard. Her eyes are dark, black eclipsing the gold. The fingers that were on my cheek are on my collar. She gives my chest a gentle pat. I want to grab her hand and keep it there.

"Sorry about that." She taps me once more. "Thanks for . . . being a sport." She pulls away. The fringe of her skirt is clumped together, showing almost her entire thigh. I want to fix it for her. But I don't know how.

"Your costume . . ." She brings the back of her hand to her mouth, hiding another grin. "I like it." Her chest rises as she inhales. Silver beads curve around her. Like water over pale sand. "You look good as a baseball player."

She walks to Chrissy. She teeters on her left heel twice, on her right heel three times. Chrissy jumps up and down. She's clapping.

A clawed hand grabs my neck. "Montro, what the hell was that?"

Kylo Ren gives me a fist bump. "Qué heavy."

"Seriously, who was she?" Bryan keeps looking from me to Isa who's laughing with her friends.

I shrug. I dig my hands into my pockets. My fingers close around the pencil.

Julissa takes a napkin from her bag. "Ven." She motions for me to bend down. She wipes my mouth. Red lipstick stains the tissue. Julissa whacks my side. "You look like Alex Rodriguez. You play ball like Alex Rodriguez. Now you're acting like him too, huh?"

She puts an arm around Kiara. Kiara's bottom jaw juts out. She pulls her jacket closed over her sports bra.

I trace the edges of the pencil in my pocket. I don't owe Kiara. All we've done is talk. I don't have time for more than that. I glance back. Isa's long leg, the slope of her shoulder, the tilt of her chin as she sneaks a look at me . . . I press my thumb into the sharp point of the lead until it breaks.

Kiara glares at me.

"Who was she supposed to be anyway? Madonna?" Julissa asks.

"Madonna has blond hair." Danny's voice is muffled through his mask.

"No." Julissa holds up a finger. "Not all the time she didn't. In the beginning, it was black I think."

There's an express waiting for us at Seventy-Second.

"¡Tu 'ta loco! You know that, right?" Bryan smacks my arm as we get out.

I touch my mouth. I give a slow shake of my head and try not to grin. Our trains pull away.

Isa's silver dress winks through the window.

ALEX

I carry a platter of roast pork back to the kitchen. The apartment smells of garlic and lime, crisped meat and baking. Brown grinds spill to the counter as I set the espresso maker on the stove. I clear rice and beans, fried yuca and mashed potatoes, turkey breast filled with olive and pimiento stuffing—Mami's version of the American holiday dish. I don't let Mami up from the table. She woke when it was dark to cook. She was still cooking when I came back from Papi's mandatory workout, a six-mile run with push-ups and pull-ups and crunches.

I leave her to talk with Sra. Hernandez, our neighbor whose family is all in DR. I store leftovers in old take-out containers, putting aside portions for Sra. Hernandez. Her arthritis makes it hard for her to cook. She made her tres leches cake anyway. It sits on the table, proud, next to Mami's pasteles de guayaba. I bring out cafecitos, heavy with sugar, just how they like it. Mami pats my back. She demands un besito and tells me she loves me. She piles sweets on my plate and scoffs at my fake look of horror. She knows I've got Yaritza's Thanksgiving dinner too. She's already packed a bag for them—for Yaritza and Robi—with her famous pasteles. They're one of the only things Yaritza doesn't know how to make.

Mami takes Sra. Hernandez back to her apartment. There's no way the old woman can carry all the food by herself. Mami returns to a clean kitchen and a dining table folded against the wall. She finds me in the living room, by the built-in above the radiator that knocks and hisses. Her scrubs are a light green with ducks on them. Her ID is already around her neck. I wish she didn't have to work. I wish she'd take the rest of the day to relax. She's told me a thousand times she's happy to go. She doesn't say what I know she feels. That it's better than an empty apartment.

"¿Qué busques?" she asks.

"Nada," I answer. But I tug out *The Geriatric Patient* and *Street Maps of New York* to get to a smaller book. The cover is a faded blue, the color of a baby's room. I show it to her, holding on to my unasked question.

Mami rubs my back again. "Books are for everyone."

On the train, I take out Mami's book by Pablo Neruda. I run my finger along the edge of the inside border. Unlike the cover, it's the vibrant blue of a Caribbean sea. I read the inscription that starts, *Para mi amor.* I flip to the first page.

I crave your mouth, your voice, your hair,

Silent, starving, I prowl through the streets.

Neruda's words are music and color. I read until voices fighting for attention interrupt me. I put the book in the bag with Mami's pasteles.

"Dímelo. Aver—where we meeting Caco?" A group of guys huddle at the other end of the car. Each wears a Yankees cap and a jersey. Two have red bandanas on the arms of their jackets. There's not enough passengers for them to not notice me.

"¿Qué lo que, chan?" One raises a hand to me. He goes by Pinchón. As they walk toward me, I shift back in my seat. There's five, not four, of them. The fifth one, hiding under his cap, is Danny. I keep my face still as I nod at him. I make eyes like Papi's, hard and disapproving.

"Alex, right?" Pinchón slouches into the seat next to me. "What you doing here?" He holds up his fist. I can't refuse him. We touch knuckles once, twice. Pinchón thumps his chest. I don't.

"Heading to see my papi's family. ¿Y tú?" My gaze shifts to Danny.

"We going out. Got us some things to tend to." Pinchón leans back. He puts his hands behind his head. He tips the brim of his cap up. "You ate?"

I nod.

"Second Thanksgiving, huh? Qué suerte. Some of us don't get even one. Ain't that right, Dannylito?"

It's been just Danny and his abuela since his brother landed in jail three years ago. Danny took it hard. You'd think that would have taught Danny not to get mixed up in this ratrería.

"What, your abuelita doesn't do Thanksgiving no more?" I ask him.

Danny's hands are in his pockets. He's still hiding under his cap. "Nah. She out at a friend's."

Out? And she didn't take him with her? I don't believe that.

"Men like us are not always welcome." Pinchón tugs the bandana until the knot is under his arm. "We make them uncomfortable."

Papi is going to make Danny a whole lot of uncomfortable when he finds out about this.

Pinchón grabs the edge of my bag. "Something smells good. What you got in here?"

I don't move. The pastelitos should be covering the book. "Mami made them. Can't show up empty-handed, can I?"

"Pues, no. Pero, you can share, right? Poor Danny here has got to be starving."

Danny's hand comes out of his pocket. Startled eyes come out from under his hat. "No, I'm OK. I don't need no—"

Pinchón gives him a look. Danny puts his hand down.

I lean all the way over the bag though it means I gotta take my eyes off them. I unwrap some pastries. I don't take the package out.

"Here." I give them each one. I'm lucky Mami made a double batch.

They're licking their fingers, smacking their lips. "Dame un más." Pinchón holds out his palm. I pass out another round. Danny shakes his head at me. I put the one intended for him in Pinchón's hand. Pinchón swallows it whole. "Diache, but that be good."

"Hey, ain't you the player who hit all those home runs in the tournament game?" The big guy, the one I don't recognize, wipes his hands on his pants and looks at me.

Danny nods. "We was playing against Lehman. We killed them 9 to 2."

"Yeah you did." Pinchón offers up his fist. Danny touches it with his own and smiles. Pinchón does the same to me. Again, I can't refuse.

"We?" the big guy asks Danny.

"I used to be on the team." Danny twists the sole of his sneaker into the rubber tiling. They're not what he usually wears. They're brand-new Nikes. Red and white.

Used to? What does he mean, *used to?* I keep my face still but my eyes . . . It's like I'm training to be El Jefe.

"Alex here is one of the best in the Heights." Pinchón slings an arm around me. "Ain't that right, baby A-Rod? You doing us Dominicanos proud. Keep it up. Show them what we made of. ¡Dios, Patria y Libertad!"

They all repeat the phrase and fist-bump me.

"Hey, you want un regalito?" Pinchón lifts his jersey, shows me an envelope. "Just a taste. A freebie. On account of your talent."

Danny steps back.

"Gracias. Pero no puedo." I keep it cool. I rise to my full height, move to the center of the car so I don't hit my head on the bar. I'm as tall as the big guy. But he doesn't look like he works out. "This body be a temple. Even off season, I train. Got to stay on my game, ¿veldad?"

Pinchón grins and nods. "Man's got a point. Tu 'ta roca."

"And his papi would kill him if he found out." Danny talks real fast.

They all look at him. I hold my smile steady.

"His papi don't even let him get with the ladies, if you know what I mean. Gives him power. That's why he's a power pitcher AND a power hitter."

OK, I know I said Papi was gonna give it to Danny when he found out. But he's gonna have to get in line 'cause I'm going to have at him first.

Pinchón is snapping his fingers, like he's trying to remember something.

"'Pérate, your papi, isn't he the one who used to play—"

The door at the other end of the car shoots open. The grating of wheels against track rushes in. Six dudes in baggy jeans and denim jackets move toward us. Their bandanas are black and blue.

Pinchón is up. He strides toward them. The big guy is at his side. The rest fall in line. Two remove blades from their pockets. They tuck them against their backs.

"Vete," Danny whispers. "Go."

I don't have a weapon. But I'm tall and I'm strong. If I go, they'll be outnumbered. Danny will be outnumbered. And those guys might not notice that my AHH cap isn't the Yankees.

I glance at my bag. I'd been thinking of bringing my new bat. But Papi said he had plenty. Coño, I should have brought it.

In the center of the car, Pinchón and the leader of the other group exchange words. Hisses rise from both sides.

"This isn't your fight. Get outta here." Danny's still whispering.

I grit my teeth. "It isn't yours either. What are you doing with them?"

"Just go. If you get caught, you'll be booted from the team. You'll be banned from playing high school ball. Your future—poof!" Danny fans his fingers in a mini-explosion.

"And what about your future?"

Danny shakes his head. "My future's not in ball and you know it. El Jefe sure does."

That's not true. OK, maybe it is true. But that doesn't mean he has to quit. It doesn't mean he has to run with these locos.

Pinchón is sassing the other guy. Blades come out of the denim jackets. We're pulling into a station.

"Go. Now." Danny's voice is desperate.

"I don't want to leave you alone."

Danny gives me a smile. The bump from his scar makes it look sad. "I'm not alone."

The doors open. There's a shout. A guy in denim lunges. Pinchón jumps back. The few other passengers on with us scramble out. The big guy with the red bandana knocks the knife from the denim guy's hand. Another blue bandana jabs. The big guy hollers and grips his arm. He nails the blue bandana in the head. Blue bandana goes down. He doesn't get up.

A lady holding grocery bags is getting on the train. She backs off and screams.

Everyone left standing is holding a knife. Except for me.

The doors are about to close. The lady on the platform is shrieking for help.

"Go!" Danny shouts it.

I grab my bag. I jump off.

The doors slam. The train pulls away.

I press my fist to my chest. I'm breathing like I've been stealing bases. Danny better be OK. He better not get hurt. Coño, what was he thinking?

The lady is running up the stairs to the station manager. She left her groceries on the platform.

Sirens wail in the distance. What should I do? If I go onto the street, they'll see me. If I stay here, they'll find me. That lady was white. I probably look just like those other guys to her. Even without my baseball cap and jersey, I look like them. And I was standing with them in the car.

Coño. What do I do?

"Chuck?"

I turn around.

ISA

I had a feeling he would be here. Every day since Halloween, a sense of anticipation has made me yank on my shoes and head out the door early so I can spend extra time on the platforms, on the trains, looking for him. But what are the chances of him being here today? At this time? Most everyone is still fighting over turkey with family.

He's wearing a baseball cap. And that's a jersey under his coat. He looks almost exactly like he did Halloween night. Bubbles of hope fill my chest. They pop and pop and pop as they hit against my too-eager heart.

Kissing him was hands down the wildest thing I've ever done. Chrissy's the one who's brave with guys. Ask the senior in coding to meet after class in the back of the computer lab? Sure. Tell the cute chess nerd playing in Washington Square Park a lie about meeting Kasparov? Why not. Kiss a stranger on the subway? Of course. It's always been easy for her. Never for me. But Chuck was standing there, in *my* subway car . . . I figured maybe it was a sign.

And here he is again.

I gnaw on the inside of my cheek. I can't be dreaming, not if I can feel that.

Chuck is staring at me. His eyes are huge, like he can't believe it either. He's not smiling though. Does he not recognize me?

"Isa, right?"

I bite my lip so I don't grin too big. "How do you know my name?"

"Your friend—Chrissy—she said it." His voice is how I remember, soft and deep, like the rumble of a train when you're up on the sidewalk. Chuck's gaze shifts to the steps behind me. He's still not smiling. Oh God. Is he angry with me? For what I did?

My face gets hot. I turn toward the uptown platform. What do I say to him? I've been this freaky girl stalking him and now I've cornered him in the subway where he has nowhere to go. If they made a movie about me, it would be called *Freaky Stalker Girl*. It would be a June release and I'd be played by some B-list actor. I pull up the hood of my coat so he can't see my cheeks.

Three police officers jog down the steps of the uptown track. Their handcuffs and keys knock together, throwing echoes against the tiled walls. One of the officers' radios spits static. Chuck yanks off his cap. He turns around to face the local track. Now we're standing next to each other, pointed in opposite directions.

Think, Isa. Say something.

I burrow my hands into my puffer coat. "Just missed one, huh?"

His face jerks toward me. "Sorry?"

"You just missed a train, right? You look like you were running. Are you in a hurry?"

"Ah . . . Yeah. Sort of." His hand is crushing his hat.

"Where are you going?" I can't believe I just asked him that. I *am* Freaky Stalker Girl.

"To my father's house in Brooklyn. My second Thanksgiving. My parents are split up."

"Two Thanksgivings? That's cool." *Witty response, Isa.*

A downtown local rolls into the station. Chuck closes his eyes and releases a sigh. He must really be late.

"Are you waiting for the express?" he asks.

I'm still facing the other tracks. "I can take either."

"Me too." He lifts a hand toward the local. "Why don't we take this one?"

I must look like I'm freezing, bundled into my coat with only my nose and eyes sticking out. I like that he seems concerned about me. That he wants to take the train with me. A few of those hope bubbles float into my chest and settle into nooks, safe from the wild beating of my heart.

We move to the middle of the car. There are only a few other people in the row. Chuck sits beside me but leaves an empty seat between us. Is he doing that because he's afraid I might jump him again? Or is he being polite and giving me space?

A crowd of students in blue-and-white football jackets bursts in. Chuck slides down to make room. His leg is almost up against mine. Two girls walk to Chuck's other side. They smile at him and giggle to each other. Chuck doesn't notice. He's scanning the platform as we pull away. I push back my hood and give the girls a hard stare. When I lean back, Chuck is watching me. The gray jersey under his coat rises and falls and rises and falls again.

Does he have bubbles in there too?

"Listen, I'm sorry about that night," I say. I don't want him feeling nervous about sitting next to me. "What I did, that wasn't cool. I shouldn't have, you know, touched you. Not without asking permission." If I were a guy, I never could have gotten away with it—I *shouldn't* have gotten away with it. With everything they've been teaching us in school about harassment and with what's in the news, I might even have been arrested. Wow, is what I'm doing now harrassment? At least Kevin knew who Chrissy was. We didn't know he did, but turns out he'd been watching her in Technique class for weeks, just as she had been watching his chamber performances.

"I would have said yes."

My gaze focuses back on Chuck. "Excuse me?"

"If you had asked permission, I would have said yes." His smile transforms his face. Sharp cheekbones. Straight, white teeth. Full lips. Square jaw. And those intense dark eyes and lashes. He's not breathing heavy anymore.

My mouth goes dry.

"When are you getting off?" Chuck shifts back and his thigh touches mine.

"Um ... Thirty-Fourth. I'm meeting my brother." I want to lean into him, put my arm through his. I remind myself I don't really know him. And he doesn't know me. I don't even know his real name.

"You have a brother?" He stretches out his legs. They're super long. And that's coming from somebody who also has long legs.

"Yup, he just got back from college yesterday. After brunch he went to see his ex-girlfriend. I made him promise to meet me so he can't stay all day. He's been kind of a stalker on her Instagram and Snapchat since they broke up." Yikes. Does being a stalker run in my family? I almost pull my hood up again. Instead, I slide back in my seat so he can't see my face.

Chuck's shoulder shakes against mine. He's trying not to laugh. "Stalker, huh? Why did they break up?" His grin makes the bubbles inside me multiply. I feel like I might float away. It's more powerful than my instructors' smiles. It's even better than one of my mom's, and those are pretty rare.

"They go to different colleges. You know. Long-distance." I don't mention how intense things got between them. How Merrit wanted to spend every moment with her. How he got angry if she did anything without him. "It wasn't Merrit's choice. He took it kind of hard."

"Would your boyfriend go for a long-distance relationship?"

"My boyfriend?" I squeak. Now my cheeks are really flaming. "No—um." I clear my throat to get out the rest of the squeaks. "No boyfriend. I don't have time. Because of dance." It sounds so lame. *I don't have time for a boyfriend.* Who says that?

Chuck sighs. "Yeah. Same with me. Baseball."

"Wow. You really do play, then?" Merrit wears sports stuff all the time even though he doesn't compete. "Are you any good?" I slap my hand over my mouth. I can't believe I asked him that.

He lifts a shoulder. "My father thinks I am, which is what matters.

He used to..." Chuck trails off. He's staring at something at the end of the car. A police officer—one from Ninety-Sixth—marches through, examining everyone.

Chuck turns to me. He closes his mouth. His eyes are huge again. Like he's scared.

I take his hand. I don't even think about it.

"What position do you play?" I hold his gaze with mine. He almost looks away, toward the police officer who's coming closer. I squeeze his fingers.

"Pitcher. Also shortstop." He's whispering.

"What team do you play on? Is it like a city league or something?"

He shakes his head. "School," he says. "Alexander Hamilton High. It's..." He pauses. The officer is in front of us. Chuck swallows.

"Oh, I know where that is. It's up near Fort Tryon Park, right?"

Chuck doesn't respond. He's gripping my hand like he's fallen off the subway platform and I'm the only thing keeping him from hitting the tracks.

"I love it up there. We're members of the Met. We go to the Cloisters every Mother's Day. My mom likes the unicorn tapestries. We always stop at this bakery up on 215th for guava pastries on the way home." I'm speaking a little loudly, trying to keep him focused on me. The girls on the other side of Chuck are too, about their hotel and their dinner plans. I don't know why he's acting like this—maybe he had a bad experience. I just hope I can help.

The police officer moves past us.

Tension drains from my shoulders. "That is so cool you go to school up there." I keep my words smooth and slow, like how I speak to Merrit or Mom when they get worked up. "So what are you? A junior?"

Chuck releases a breath. "Sophomore."

"Oh! Me too."

He runs a hand over his face. "You like guava pastries?" His whisper is hoarse.

"Love them. My dad sometimes makes a special trip up to the bakery around Christmastime."

Chuck watches the police officer exit to the next car. He bends down. He takes his cap and a small book out of the bag. He pushes the bag toward me. "Here," he says. "My mother made them." His eyes are kind of shiny.

I look inside. There's a huge foil packet, enough to fill an entire platter.

"I can't take these," I say. "Your mom didn't make them for me. I'm guessing they're for your dad? That's awesome that they're still on good terms."

He shrugs. "They're for my little brother and my stepmom. She and my mother get along just fine. My mother and my father, not so much."

"I can't take pastries from your little brother."

"How about I give you some? Please. It would make my mother happy."

"Your mom doesn't know me."

"If she did, she would want you to have some." His smile makes my heart miss a step. God, he is so beautiful. He unwraps the foil, tears off a piece, and makes a smaller package. He holds it out to me.

There's no use hiding my grin. "Thank you. Hey, what's your real name? I've been calling you Chuck because of your sneakers."

He laughs, looking down at his shoes. "Good thing we didn't meet today."

He's wearing white Superstars with black stripes. "I don't know, Adidas sounds pretty cool."

"Well, my name does begin with *A*."

"Adam?"

He shakes his head.

"Aaron?"

Another shake.

"Oh! I know!" I shoot up from my seat and clutch an imaginary microphone. "Alejandro, Alejandro..." I sway my hips a little. "Ale-Ale-jandro, Ale-Ale-jandro," I croon in my best Lady Gaga.

He uses his hand to wipe off his grin. "You're close. It's just Alex."

I plop back down, enjoying the jealous looks from the girls in the blue-and-white jackets. "Nice to meet you, Just Alex." I put out my hand. He takes it, gives me a shake. Instead of letting go, he turns my palm down. He draws my hand toward him, stopping just before it reaches his mouth. He gives me a moment to pull away. I don't. Of course I don't. He touches my fingers to his lips.

"It's very nice to meet you, Isa." His breath is warm on my skin. Our knees brush. I want to slide my leg between his, climb into his lap, thread my hand through his thick, dark hair and . . .

He releases my fingers. He motions toward the window. "Your stop."

Tiled pillars with the number THIRTY-FOUR whip by.

I don't want to get off. I don't want to leave Alex. But Merrit is waiting for me.

My throat tightens. When will I see Alex again? It took almost a month to find him. The fact that I found him at all is pretty amazing considering how many people ride the subway. I want to ask for his number. But what's going to come of that? We both said we were too busy.

Time's up. The doors open. I leap up and dash out. I don't even say goodbye. As the train pulls away, I glance back. Our eyes meet through the window. He lifts his hand in farewell.

● ● ●

I find Merrit where we said we'd meet. He's gazing through the window of the Sunglass Hut, hands cupped around his eyes even though the store is all lit up.

I sneak behind him, then bend my knee into the back of his until his leg buckles.

"Hey!" he cries out. But he's grinning. He reaches back with one hand and pulls me next to him, tucking me against his shoulder, his elbow crooked around my neck. I breathe in the leather of his jacket then burrow against him until I find the smell of freshly washed clothes. Magnolia-and-poppy-scented detergent always makes me think of Merrit. I remember the morning Merrit announced he couldn't stand the regular Tide our cleaning lady used. He claimed it made him itchy, gave him rashes, though I was the one with eczema. Instead of taking us to school, Mom took us shopping. Dad was out of town or else he never would have let her. We went to different markets, piling boxes and bottles of detergent into the carts. At home, we did load after load of laundry. Mom put on Celia Cruz and was dancing around saying instead of a taste test it was a smell test. Merrit and I lay on our stomachs and played Rummikub, jumping up every time the dryer dinged. The Whole Foods brand was Merrit's favorite. We've been using it ever since.

"See those glasses in the middle case? Second row?" he asks me.

"The horn-rimmed ones in purple?"

"Yup. Those. I've always thought I'd rock the rhinestone look." Merrit's arm tightens around my neck, just enough so I don't squirm away while he tickles my side. "I meant the aviators. Third ones from the left."

We go inside so Merrit can try them on. I have to admit, they look pretty good on him.

He bends to the mirror. His smile makes me smile.

"Can I get them for you?" I take out my wallet with my allowance money.

"You mean, can Dad get them for me?" His smirk is playful.

"Har, har." It's what Dad says when Merrit rides him.

Merrit wears the glasses out onto the street, even though it's dark. "Samantha has a pair like this."

I don't know what to say. We pass a window display of a little boy asleep under a plaid quilt, stockings hung over a fire beside a tree with gold and red ornaments. Letters made of ice spell the word *Believe* in a winter wonderland set just beyond the boy's room. "How'd it go?" I finally ask. "At her house?"

He shrugs. He shakes out chin-length strands of sandy hair, the same color as the sleeping boy's. "She said to say hi to you." We walk another block before he adds, "She has a new boyfriend."

Alarm burrows into my gut.

"I'm sorry," I say. What I think is, *Please be OK*.

We make it a few more paces before he stops.

"You know, it's not like I thought we were going to get married, at least the sane part of my brain didn't. I knew she'd move on. She's too gorgeous and perfect and brilliant not to. It's just that . . . the guy . . . His name is Connor. Connor Rhee. He's Korean, like her."

He takes off the glasses. His eyes don't settle on me. They dart through the crowd. "You think maybe if I were Korean, we'd still be together?"

Inside, I wince and think, *You're kidding, right?* Outside, I don't let my expression change. I want to tell him that his possessive behavior was probably the reason she broke it off and that it has nothing to do with what they look like or where their parents came from. I don't. I can't hurt him. Instead I say, "I think it probably isn't about that."

He lets out a sigh. He takes back my arm and starts walking again.

We stop in front of a Salvation Army. It's filled with funky old furniture, hats men used to wear in the fifties, and racks and racks of army-olive and camo clothes.

Merrit gestures to the window. "Come on. I need a purple jumpsuit to match my new shades." The teasing in his voice soothes the ache in my chest. He's not going to get wrapped up in Samantha. He's not going to let it strangle him again. I squeeze his arm and follow him in.

FRIDAY, DECEMBER 16

ALEX

"You sure she's gonna be there?" Bryan scratches at his neck.

"Por Dios! Yes!" Kiara presses her face into her sleeve. Even on her toes, she can barely reach the bar.

Bryan takes his cap off. He ducks to Kiara's level. "What exactly did she say?"

Kiara's head tips back. "¡Qué no!" She palms his face just as the train brakes. Bryan grabs hold of a guy's jacket before he hits the floor. Bryan lifts a hand in apology to the guy while Kiara rips it up, laughing.

I haven't seen Bryan much since the season ended. He's been with Julissa and I've been training extra. Papi got me a job at the Baseball Institute. He wants me in top shape for summer travel ball. I can use the BI facilities whenever I want, long as there's no class or party booked. Every day after school, if I'm not going to Papi's, I'm going there. It's the Saturday before Christmas and I already worked two birthdays, one for a bunch of six-year-olds. I planned to stay home after, work on a paper, and see Mami since I'm going to Papi's tomorrow. Then Bryan texts me Julissa's cousin's having a party. I told him I'd had enough of parties for the day. Figured he deserved it for disappearing on me all these weeks. Said I'd go only if Danny was coming too. Bryan and I, we need to talk with Danny about the company he's been keeping. Bryan texted sure, he'd take care of it. So here I am. But there's no Danny. There's no Julissa either. She sent Kiara instead.

Bryan's glaring at Kiara. "I don't get it. Why'd she go ahead without me?"

Kiara rolls her eyes. "No puedo." She twists to me. "Tell me a story, something interesting, so I don't have to listen to your annoying friend." Her voice is low, like there's a secret between us.

I shift back. Only, I hit against a backpack. Kiara watches me without blinking. What am I going to tell her? That a first-grader at the party dropped his cake and started howling? That the new setting on the pitching machine is bien chévere? Nothing interesting has happened to me since... since Thanksgiving. And I'm not telling her about that. I'm also not telling her about the Neruda book I got from the library even though it's chévere too.

Bryan tugs Kiara's jacket. "Julissa told you I treat her well, right?" His forehead is scrunched. He wouldn't be so worried if he hadn't done something.

I knock him on the shoulder. "Loco, what did you do?"

"¡Nada!" He flings out his arms. His mouth opens and closes like a fish trying to breathe air. Bryan totally did something. He wouldn't be denying it so hard if he hadn't.

Bryan glances at Kiara. "She see me with Franny the other day? 'Cause you know, we was only talking." The train screeches like keys over a car door.

"¡Eso!" I turn my face so Bryan doesn't see me laughing. That boy knows better. Bryan's had eyes for Julissa since the sixth grade. For him, it's always been Julissa. But whenever they break up, which is a couple times a year, she runs to some other guy. I told Bryan to relax. She probably does it to make him jealous. She always goes back to him. But Bryan thinks he's got to go out and show everyone he don't care that Julissa's not with him. He only ends up making it worse.

"'Pérate." Kiara holds up a finger. "You spoke to that bitch?"

"Julissa doesn't know, ¿veldad?" Bryan goes to grab Kiara's hand, only she won't let him.

People are piling on the train. I look away to hide another chuckle. That's when I see her. At the other end of the subway car, beyond a row of seats crammed with folks, is Isa. My heartbeat catches like a flooded engine. She's crowded against the door like I am, back to the window, long hair pulled up off her neck. She must have just gotten on. If she turns her head, she'll see me.

My hand passes over my coat pocket that hides Neruda's words. Would she know I think of her when I read those poems? Would she see it on my face?

People are gathered round her. That girl Chrissy is talking with her whole body, her hair an angry flare of red. She's got one hand on Isa and one on the guy with tiny glasses. Guess the glasses weren't part of a costume. An Asian girl with a green ski hat sticks her head close to Chrissy's, arguing back. A girl with streaks of purple in her hair grips Ski Hat Girl's coat. Isa lifts a hand to her mouth. Her face lights up with laughter. I wish I were closer. I wish I could hear what she said.

They all start laughing. Chrissy doubles over. The girl with the ski hat turns to the one with the dyed purple hair and kisses her. Isa's wiping at her eyes. The doors open. She flattens herself against the pole to make room for folks to exit. But still, she's pushed out onto the platform.

I've been resisting the shoves from people getting off. Now I give in to them. I step out onto the platform too.

Isa sees me even though there's another subway door spewing people between us. The leftover smile from her laugh freezes. Then it bursts wide open.

The door close signal clangs, though there's still a lot of people getting on. There's no time for me to make my way to her. We push back through our own doors. I find my spot next to the rail.

Isa's watching me. She tilts her head, like she's trying to say hi. Chrissy grabs her hand.

I want Isa to come over. I want her to say hi for real.

"You know she's going to dump your ass once she finds out, right?" Kiara takes my arm. "Can you believe what your friend here went and did?"

I lift a shoulder. I'm not getting into this. Isa's talking to Chrissy but her gaze lifts to mine. Her lips spread into another mega smile. I must be a mirror because I smile too.

I could go to her. I don't care that it's crowded. But why hasn't Isa come to me? She could wave. Do something more to acknowledge me. A chill blots out the heat in my chest. Maybe she doesn't want to. Not in front of her friends. Not when I have my friends. Not when it isn't part of some game.

"Don't you think so?" Kiara yanks my sleeve.

"Huh?"

"Bryan needs to fess up and tell Julissa. You agree with me or not?"

How am I supposed to know?

Bryan peers at me from under his cap.

"What you looking at over there anyway?" Kiara tries to see around me. I block her view.

"Sure," I say to Bryan. "Tell her. You don't tell her, it's like you're hiding something." It's true. Secrets aren't good between two people. To have a relationship, you have to have trust. That's what Mami says. It's part of why she and Papi broke up.

Kiara lifts her arm in an *I told you so* way.

The doors bang open. Isa and her friends get off. I wait to see if she looks back. She doesn't.

ISA

I was supposed to be home for dinner by now. My phone's dead, so I can't even text Mom. She's probably sitting in the kitchen thinking I got hit by a bus or a bike messenger, or that the chicken salad I ate for lunch gave me food poisoning. She'll get so worked up she'll insist on taking me to and from dance for the next several weeks. Dad should be home, thankfully. He's good at talking her off her mental ledges.

I tuck my phone in my bag. Even if I could call, I'd never tell Mom I'm on a train that's stuck between stations. She still thinks I'm taking taxis. I'll tell her Chrissy made me stay late to teach her the new floor routine since she went with Kevin for crepes on Monday and skipped Technique, which is true.

The woman next to me is playing *Candy Crush*, her finger tapping nonstop at her screen. The shopping bags next to her crinkle every time she hits them with her elbow.

"Excuse me, could I borrow your phone? Mine died and I want to let my mom know I'm fine."

She shows me her screen. No bars. "Sorry, darling." She adjusts her reading glasses before going back to her game.

By the door, a mom with a baby strapped to her chest scrolls through her phone. I leap up to ask her but stop halfway. Sitting across from the mom, a few seats down, is Alex. He's staring at the floor. I didn't see him before because of the lady and her bags.

I touch my hair, smoothing flyaways that escaped my bun. My lips are chapped. I should have reapplied gloss before leaving the Academy. I don't know why I care. Nothing's going to happen between us. But that's OK. Maybe we can just be friends who occasionally run into each other on the subway.

People look up, no doubt confused why I'm standing in the middle of the aisle. Alex doesn't. He tracks a line in the linoleum, back and forth, like he's Superman trying to cut the flooring in half with his laser vision.

I sit beside him. "Hi."

Dark brown eyes meet mine. My pulse skitters into my throat.

Alex looks away. "Hi."

I rub my bottom lip. "So . . . The train is stuck, huh?"

Alex leans back. He draws his arms to his chest. A few long seconds pass. "Just so I understand, so I know what to expect, are you only going to talk to me when we're alone?" His voice is quiet, like he doesn't want to upset the silence of the car.

I don't understand. "Uh . . . We're not alone." I gesture to the other passengers. "And also, what are you talking about?"

"Alone like not with friends. Not with people whose opinions you care about."

I go to wet my lips but stop myself because Mom is right and that only makes them more chapped. He must mean the time before the holidays when we saw each other in that super crowded train. Does he think I didn't want to go say hi to him? Because I did. I wanted to so badly.

"You were with someone else." I don't mean to sound angry. I'm not angry.

He shrugs. "Yeah. My friends."

Friends? "She had her arm around you."

One dark eyebrow rises as if to say, *And?*

I look down at the red bag by his feet. It says BB INSTITUTE in block letters. "You told me you were too busy for a girlfriend. I figured that was a line. I figured she was your girlfriend." I mean, who wouldn't? She was all over him.

Alex uncrosses his arms. "Nah. It's not like that. Kiara and I, we just hang out." He sits up fast. "We hang out with other people. Not alone."

He's kidding himself if he thinks that's all she wants. She was looking at him like she'd crossed a desert and he was a pool of cool water she wanted to slip into.

Alex touches the brim of his cap. "Anyway, Kiara's not my type."

It's my turn to raise an eyebrow, only I can't do only one so they both go up.

"And what I told you was truth. I don't have time for a girlfriend."

What he said should make me happy. The part about that girl, Kiara, does at least. Before I can stop, my mouth is shooting out the words, "What is your type? I mean, if you had time."

What's wrong with me? When I do that, when I talk or act without thinking, it makes me think of my mom.

Alex looks at me—thankfully not like my behavior is weird. He looks at me the way someone would look at a painting. He studies me so long my cheeks start to feel like marshmallows in a campfire. I swear they crisp and are about to catch fire when he says, "I don't know. Haven't figured that out yet." He rubs a hand over his knee.

"How about you?" he asks. "What's your type?"

I grin before I answer. "Oh, I know exactly what my type is. But I'm not going to tell you." Payback for the marshmallow cheeks. I scoot forward to his bag. "What's in here? More guava pastries?" Embarassingly, my stomach grumbles. Please let him not have heard that.

His eyes are on me, my face, my body, following my every move. Without looking away, he pulls the bag to his lap.

"Just my mitt." He shows it to me. "Why? You hungry?"

I shrug and make air fill my chest, hoping it'll calm the crazy hammering inside. I'm not going to tell him I'm so starved I could eat his BB Institute bag with the mitt in it.

He digs in his jacket. "Sorry, it's all I have." He offers me a protein bar. But I don't want to take his only food. Who knows how long we'll be stuck here.

Alex rips open the wrapper and hands me the bar.

"You'll split it with me?" Before he can answer, I spray my hands with sanitizer then break the bar in half.

He glances at the small bottle attached to my pack. "What, my hands don't deserve to be clean?"

The way he says it, like he's truly offended, makes me laugh. "Sorry. It's lavender scented. I didn't think—"

He holds out his hand. "I'm cool with that."

I unclip the bottle and squirt the sanitizer. A whole mountain of it comes out.

"Oops, sorry. Here." I swallow the rest of my laughter and slide my palm into his to absorb some. I suck in a breath. His skin is warm under the cool gel. Very warm. The deep curve of his hand is slick. It's so large both my fists could fit inside it. He has calluses at the base of his thumb and below his ring finger. I hover over them, tracing their shape. I slip to the outside of his hand and his broad knuckles flex, almost involuntarily. I circle up to his wrist, to the pound of his pulse. It matches the thrumming in my ears.

Alex's lips are fixed in a half smile. He's staring at our hands.

I don't pull away. He doesn't either. It's like when I kissed him. It just feels right. No, not right. Better.

The baby across from us lets out a squawk. The mother coos, and the little one settles down.

I draw my fingers away. "There. All dry."

I place his half of the bar in his palm. His eyes flick up. His half smile becomes a full one.

The bar is delicious, crunchy, like a Rice Krispies Treat dipped in peanut butter with chunks of chocolate shoved inside it. I could eat about ten of these for dinner. Shoot—I almost forgot . . .

"Hey, I'm sorry to ask this, but can I use your phone? I really need to text my mom, but mine ran out of battery. I'm so late and all she needs is another reason to hate ballet."

He hands me his cell. I shove the rest of the bar in my mouth.

"Thank you." I fire off a text and give it back.

"Your mother, she hates ballet?"

"Well . . . it's more that she hates it for me. She wants me to be this independent, modern woman. So cooking, cleaning, dancing—things traditionally done by women—she doesn't want me to do."

"A lot of famous chefs are men," he points out.

"A chef runs an entire restaurant. My mom might be OK with that. But she never even taught me to cook. She didn't want me anywhere near the kitchen."

"Wait"—he lifts a hand—"you don't know how to cook?" His eyes widen like I told him I was born on an alien planet and have five heads and a crocodile mouth. It makes me laugh again.

I lean over and whisper, "Actually, I kind of taught myself. Online cooking shows."

He lets out a huff that must be his version of a chuckle. "So why do you dance? If your mother doesn't want you to?"

I've been asked before why I dance. No one's ever asked the despite-my-mom part. I don't advertise that. Parents are supposed to be supportive of their kids.

I shrug. "I love the discipline. I love that if you work hard, if you do what they tell you, you'll improve and your teachers will be pleased. It's predictable. Also, I love that I can lose myself in dance. How everything except my body and the music just melts away. I can be flying across the stage, grand jeté to pirouette to grand jeté, my heart pounding, my muscles screaming at me that they can't possibly do one more leap. And then I don't do one more—I do five more, perfectly executed, and my teachers give me a smile. Yeah. It's pretty incredible."

Alex is smiling like he was in the audience in my mind just now. "You like being on stage."

He's right. I like being seen, being recognized for my hard work. I rise and, using the bar for support, lift my leg into a slow développé. A few heads turn to watch me. And, I can't lie, I like it. "My mom says I shouldn't want to be defined by what I look like," I tell him, coming back down into deep plié.

Alex's eyes are everywhere but on me—the floor, the ceiling, the other passengers. "Maybe you should tell your mother you want to run the ballet. Maybe then she'd be happy for you."

"The artistic director. I'd love to do that. Usually only former male principal dancers get the job though."

Alex shakes his head like possibly my mom is right about ballet. I don't want him to think that. I want him on my side.

"Maybe I'll tell my mom I want to be the first solo female artistic director of the New York City Ballet." I say this even though I know I could never confront her. Just thinking about it makes me tired.

"What is it that you like about baseball?" I ask at the same time he says, "You're sure you don't want all of this?" He holds up his untouched half of the protein bar.

"We had a deal." I wave at him to start eating. "Why baseball?" I ask again.

Alex takes a bite. He chews slowly. "I'm good at it. My friends play." He tucks the wrapper from the bar into his pocket.

"Your dad likes that you play, right? The one who lives in Brooklyn?"

His brow lifts like he's surprised I remembered. "Yeah." He picks up the mitt. "You into baseball?"

He's redirecting. I'm familiar with the move, especially when parents come up.

"No, not really." I'm embarrassed to tell him this. I mean, I've been to a few Yankees games. But that's about it.

He bends the mitt, working the leather. He looks like he's about to say something else but he doesn't. The hair at the base of his neck is wet. The collar of his shirt is damp. He must be coming from practice. I'm sweaty too. I realize I'm staring at him. I'm not sure if he knows because he's smiling down at his mitt, like the glove is whispering jokes to him. I pull my gaze away to a poem on the wall. They're all over the subway cars, a citywide attempt at making culture accessible to the everyday New Yorker. I squint, trying to make out the words.

"'Windswept.'" Alex reads the title for me. He reads the first sentence. Then the next. And the next. Only, he's not reading it. His eyes are on mine as the words tumble out of him. He recites the entire poem.

"You know that by heart?"

He shrugs. His knee swings back and forth.

"It's beautiful," I tell him. "Thank you."

His leg stops moving. "You like poems?"

"Yeah. It's like music. Or art. Or dance."

His mouth looks like it's about to smile. His lips remind me of our kiss.

I lean back, tucking a foot under me. "Hey, you want to play a game?" I've got to stop staring at him. When I do, it feels like we're the only two people on the train.

He coughs then clears his throat. "What kind of game?"

"Just something to pass the time. I make up a story about someone around us and you have to guess who I'm talking about."

"OK." He puts the mitt away. He turns to face me. It's hard to think when he's looking at me like that.

"My cats don't like it when I leave them in the apartment alone. It's not like I'm gone that long—only the four or five hours it takes to hit my favorite stores. I can't help myself. The word *sale* is like a drug to me. But I bring them treats, so they don't stay angry for long."

Alex is giving me his you're-an-alien look again. Maybe it's because of the Boston accent I used.

He scans the car. He tilts his head toward the woman with all the bags. "Her."

"Yup."

"You really think she's a cat lady?" He studies the woman. "She looks more like a dog lady to me."

"Your turn," I say through my laughter.

His gaze sweeps away from me. "I'm tall, but I hate basketball. I'm into golf. I grab every chance to take my convertible out of the city to my club where my golf friends and I stand around in V-necks and drink martinis."

I'm covering my mouth, trying not to lose it. He sounded like a British guy who swallowed a frog. "Wow...That's—um—pretty good for a first-timer."

"Any guesses?" His long fingers stretch across his thigh.

I search the car for someone tall.

"It's not me, by the way." That half smile is waiting.

"It's that really tall guy at the other end with the red jacket."

"Nope. Too old."

There's only one other guy who's younger. "Navy coat, brown loafers."

"Yeah. You know him?"

I shake my head no. The guy has thick dirty-blond hair, a scarf around his neck, and is wearing the same type of watch Merrit got for Christmas.

"I thought maybe you went to the same school." Alex pulls a sports drink from his bag.

"How do you know which school I go to?"

"I don't. But I bet it's on the Upper East Side. And I bet that guy goes to school on the Upper East Side too."

"Well," I point out, "most of the schools are on the Upper East Side. That's not hard to guess."

Our train inches forward, just as an announcement comes on with a full dose of static. The conductor apologizes for the delay and says something about track work.

I watch Alex's face. Is he glad we're not stuck any longer? Or does he wish, like me, we had more time? We pull into Eighty-Sixth Street. The next stop is mine.

Alex smiles down at his cell. "You on Instagram?" He says it quietly.

"Yup, of course."

"I bet your account is all fancy."

The way he says it makes me want to nudge him. I don't. I don't trust myself to touch him and be able to stop. "Why would you say that?"

"Because of your fancy Upper East Side private school."

"I never told you I went to private school."

He lets out another chuckle-huff at my expression. "You said most schools in the city are on the Upper East Side. Most *private* schools are. There are publics schools all over the city."

I'm taken aback—he's right, of course. How stupid of me. I trace a run in my tights, not knowing what to say.

"I bet you live in a fancy apartment in some sweet building on Park Avenue too."

I cover my face with my hands.

"Wait, you live on Park Ave? For real?" There's a note of mild panic in his voice.

I nod, still hiding behind my hands.

"Hey." His fingers take mine. He pulls them away from my face. "I'm only joking. I wish I lived on Park Ave." He keeps my hand in his. There's that warmth again, only now it's filling my chest. "It's pretty over there. I bet there are good views. What floor are you on?"

"Fourteenth." I don't tell him it's the highest one. "My Instagram isn't fancy though." I want to change the subject. "I pretty much only post about dance."

"Show me?" His eyes gleam as he leans into the light.

My heartbeat startles. If Alex can find me on Instagram, he can contact me.

"Phone's dead, remember? Give me yours."

I open the app on Alex's phone and type in my handle: @BalletBelleIsa, and press Request. "Don't get too excited. I don't post a lot."

"You probably have more than five." He shows me his: @ARos0133.

"Wow." He wasn't kidding—there are five total posts on his page. All baseball-related.

The train breaks with a sharp screech. It's my stop. "Thanks," I tell him. "For letting me use your phone. And for the snack."

"Hey, there's a good taco truck right on Ninety-Sixth and Broadway. If you're still hungry. If you like Mexican."

"I love Mexican." I wait, wondering—no, hoping—he'll suggest getting tacos together. But he doesn't.

The doors slide open.

"Bye, Isa."

I'm almost out but I turn back around. "Goodbye, Alex."

Later, when I'm tucked in bed, my phone charged, I open my Instagram. I accept his request. Tomorrow, I'll post a selfie in front of the taco truck, a secret message just for him.

ALEX

"Diablo, bro, habla con ella. Just talk to her already." Bryan's standing over me. He won't sit until I give him what he wants.

I rotate the ball in my hand. I don't say anything.

Danny's sitting five seats over. His thumbs attack his phone. He's the one I need to talk to. He's the one missing practice. Sure, he's coming with us to Papi's to take advantage of this crazy fifty-degree January day. But Papi's not the coach of the high school team. Papi can't save him from being cut. Instead, I'm stuck with Bryan and his telenovela love life.

"Kiara'll listen to you." Bryan ducks, trying to see under my brim.

I look down. Cap hiding works. So what if Kiara will listen to me? I'm not getting involved. Already got enough hate for siding with Kiara about Bryan fessing up to Julissa.

Bryan sneaker-taps me. "Come on. You owe me. I'm dying here."

I sit up. I lean all the way back. "No te debo nada. You grown. You made your own mess."

His mouth opens. His hands fly up as if I accused him of being a Mets fan. Bryan does that move so much I bet he does it in his dreams.

"Alex." He says it the way Mami and Papi and everyone who wasn't born here say it: *Ále.* "Friends gotta help each other."

Danny's phone is still out. His thumbs have gone quiet.

I stand. Bryan gives me room. "Ven, we gotta talk to him. Come on."

"Now?" Bryan takes in the passengers around us.

"You want my help?" I say. "Danny comes first. We put this off long enough."

Bryan's eyes get big. He nods five times. "So you'll talk to Kiara?"

I stop and turn back around. "What did I just say?"

"Yala, OK. Pero, dime—does El Jefe know? About Danny?"

I'd thought about telling Papi. Only, Papi's big on tough love. He might kick Danny out of our training sessions. Might make me promise never to talk to Danny again. That's not what Danny needs.

"Qué no," I say.

Bryan nods. He rubs at his chin with his sleeve. "Oye, Danny, we need to talk." He goes right over to him. "Those tigueres you been hangin' with? You gotta cut them loose. They up to no good."

If Bryan weren't so close, I'd hurl the baseball I'm holding at him. He's not playing it cool. It's like he just shared our pitch signs with the other team.

Danny looks up from his phone. He flattens his mouth, to hide the scar. It's something he does when he's nervous.

"To 'ta frio," I tell Danny. "It's just . . . we been missing you."

Danny's staring at those shiny red Nikes on his feet. "Well, I been around. Ain't going nowhere else."

"Well, your nowhere should be the weight room Monday, Wednesday, and Friday." Bryan grabs Danny's bicep. "Else you gonna lose all this, flaquito."

"Oh, I been lifting," Danny says. "No te preocupes."

Bryan's hands do their thing. "With who?"

The doors open.

Bryan's stopped looking at Danny. He's not looking at me either. He's looking at whoever's standing behind me.

"Alex?"

Not *Ále*. Alex.

My stomach bottoms out.

I always take the same car now, fifth one from the front. I pretend it's the best car, least crowded, closest to where I'm going. Even when I have to walk half a platform to get on and off. I pretend not to hope.

I can't pretend away this feeling.

"Hi! I was wondering when I was going to run into you again." Isa's smile is pure light. Her bun is a crown of gold on her head. Her coat's open, because it's so warm. She's wearing a sweatshirt with a ballet shoe on it, tights, and leg warmers. That's it.

Bryan's mouth is open.

"Hi," I say back to her. I keep my eyes on her pinked cheeks. I don't look at her thighs or the curves of her calves. I blow out a breath. That sweatshirt is from her Instagram feed. All her posts, except the one in front of the food truck, have ballet shoes in them.

"Eyy, why is this Barbie talking to you?" Bryan's words are whispers through his teeth. He's looking at Isa like she's the last taco Yaritza will ever make. I shift until my arm, my shoulder, my back, are in front of him.

"Are you heading to dance?" I sound different when I talk to her. It's not just my voice, which I keep low and calm. I talk to Isa like I talk to my teachers. My coaches. The parents at the Baseball Institute. I don't care if my boys notice.

"Yup." Her teeth glow behind glossed lips. If she heard what Bryan said, she doesn't show it. She doesn't seem to notice his staring. Or Danny's.

"Coño, do you see those legs? What I wouldn't do to have those beauties wrapped around me at night, eh? I mean, Julissa is fine and all. But this one . . ." Bryan shakes his head in surrender.

I close and open my fist. Bryan deserves a toletazo upside the head. He's speaking Spanish, gracias a Dios. Still, what he's saying, the way he's looking at her . . . I ignore him. It's not worth turning away from Isa.

I should have done more than just "like" her posts. I should have sent her a message. Or at least commented on one of the pics. I was afraid my words would come out all wrong. They don't sound like how I feel, like how she makes me feel. Neruda's words are close, but they're not right either. Because they're not mine.

"And you thought I was the one holding out." Danny hoots. "La reconoces, ¿veldad? She's the girl from Halloween. The one who kissed him."

Isa's watching me. Her mouth still has that smile—the one that makes me feel like I've done something worthy of a trophy without even picking up a bat or a ball.

"Hey, Don Juan, why you haven't shared this?" Bryan thumps my shoulder. He continues in Spanish. "No wonder you're not into Kiara. ¡Guay! A dancer! Does El Jefe know you got yourself such a fine woman? He'd bend the rules for this one." Bryan makes kissing sounds.

I grit my teeth. Isa's eyebrows lift.

Bryan's breath is hot on my neck. "This is what it's for. All the work, the training. You become a star, this be your prize. Show this princesa how Dominicanos dance. You get her hooked, ¿me escuchas? Give her my number when you move on. Te lo juro, she's gonna be the first of many."

I want to slam him into the wall. Instead, I shrug him off me. I give Isa a tight smile so she knows everything's fine. I've got to pretend this isn't a big deal. That Isa's not a big deal. Otherwise, they'll never let it rest. "Tranquilo, montros. Just don't say anything to Kiara. Hear me?" I'm talking in Spanish too. They howl. They call me a jodontón. A stud.

Sure. Let them think I care what Kiara'll say to this. As long as they don't think I care about Isa. As long as they stop staring at her.

Bryan called Isa a princess. She's more than that. So much more that at night I lie awake and think of what I'd do to fit her into my life. It's stupid, all the imagining. Even if Isa had time, why would she spend it with me?

Isa's waiting for my eyes. Her lips close, making her smile different. She reaches for the rail next to me as we skid into a stop. She puts one foot between both of mine and leans in.

"You think you can dance better than me?"

So she understood some of what Bryan said. She probably takes Spanish in that fancy school of hers.

Isa slides her long leg between my knees. I draw a sharp breath. She's so close, I smell her tropical flower smell. My heart revs and catches, and revs and catches. Her golden-grass hair glints warm under cool LED light. Is it her shampoo that smells so good? Perfume? God help me if it's just her.

Isa's eyes look like they've got glitter in them too. Like she knows I'm doing everything I can to distract myself from how close she is. She glances at Bryan's phone. "Got any Prince Royce?" She takes my hands. My heart speeds up and out from under me. She presses my fingers to her hip, the others to her shoulder.

Bryan and Danny are mouth-open silent. Isa glances at Bryan again. He fumbles with his phone.

"Oh, wait." She takes off her coat. She hands it and her bag to Danny.

I must look like Bryan with my hands up in the air. I don't care. My heart is long gone. It's up in the front car, racing us to the next station.

Isa places my hands back where she wants them.

"Culpa al Corazón" comes on. It sounds tinny through the cell speakers. We hear it well enough.

Isa's hips roll under my palm. She steps back. She pulls me with her.

"You can dance bachata, right?" Her voice is teasing. I need a few seconds, but I catch her rhythm. Her hips do another crazy roll. Not just side to side either. Por Dios. Behind me, Bryan—or maybe Danny—lets out a whistle.

Isa grins up at me. She takes my hand and slides it up to her waist. "I should take off my sweatshirt, so you can really see my moves. But I don't think your boys could handle that." My arm is holding up the bottom of her sweater, showing off her lower half. I let go of her waist and grab hold of her hand.

Isa makes a fake pout. "You're no fun."

I clear my throat and cover it up with a chuckle. "You're right. Bryan and Danny can't handle this." I let go of her hand and gesture at her hips that are rolling like hurricane waves. She takes the opportunity to spin. Bryan and Danny have backed up to give us space. We have the floor to ourselves.

Isa laughs as she comes around to me.

I catch her outstretched fingers.

"OK, maybe you're a little bit of fun," she whispers.

I move us out of the doorway before we hit Seventy-Second Street. A few people get on. They barely look at us as they find a seat.

"You're not bad." Isa's mouth is right under my ear. "But you need to practice. You're light on the dips." She throws her head back. She swings it around to my shoulder. She presses right up to my chest, letting my moves move her. My hands go back down to her hips.

The song ends. Her head is still on my shoulder. She laces her fingers in my hand. She lifts it up and away from us then does another spin.

Danny claps. Bryan's still holding his phone. Hold up—was he just videoing that?

Isa extends a pointed foot. She bows, one hand still in mine, the other raised over her head. Her smile is so big her cheeks crowd her eyes. "Cuidado," she says. "Wouldn't want Kiara to get ahold of that." She tips her head at Bryan's cell.

Did she just tell me to be careful in Spanish?

The train brakes hard into Sixty-Sixth Street.

Isa takes her coat and bag from Danny. "Gracias. And just so you know, mi mamá es Cubana. I understood everything you said."

Danny's scar flushes bloodred.

Bryan flings his hands in the air. "How is this blondie a Cubana?" Bryan gives me a what-the-hell-just-happened look.

My heart crawls back to my chest. I don't think it's beating at all. Isa heard everything? Her mother is Cuban? Coño.

The doors open. Isa waves and steps out.

On the platform, she looks at Bryan. "Oh, and thanks for the offer, but I'm like him." She points at me. "I don't have time for anyone special. So unless you're going to come and take classes with me . . ." She points to the ballet shoe on her sweater. "You'll be waiting years before I move on from even my first novio."

If I were her, I'd be umpire-made-the-wrong-call mad. I'd be throwing down my cap and kicking dirt on the base. But Isa's still smiling as she backs away. I give Bryan and Danny a look that says I'm coming for them later. I grab the door as it's closing.

"Isa!"

She looks over her shoulder.

"You're not angry?" I ask her.

She runs back to where I'm stuck between the two halves of the subway door.

She brings her nose right up to mine. The gold flecks in her irises twist and twirl, just like her dancing.

"Not at you. You made it up to me with that dance." She kisses my cheek. My skin, where her lips were, burns. "Hasta luego, jodontón." She whirls and runs through the turnstile.

I can't let her leave. She's smiling. But she can't not be upset.

"You better cover for me," I shout. Danny and Bryan are crowded around Bryan's screen, grinning like fools. "And don't you dare share that video." I don't care anymore what they think about me and Isa. I don't care who knows. But I'm not letting others watch that clip—watch Isa dance—the way those two are.

I catch up to Isa on the subway steps.

"I'm sorry. For what went on back there."

"Listen, I have a lot of cousins back in Miami. I'm used to that sort of talk—not that it makes it OK. At least you weren't talking like that." She gives me a smirk. "Anyway, I heard what they said about you not being interested in Kiara. So not all of it was bad."

I look down at my feet. I don't want to show her my smile.

"But I meant what I said about not showing her the video." Isa's boots are soundless on the stairs. "Kiara definitely wants more from you than just friendship."

We're almost at the top, at the street. I want to ask Isa what *she* wants from me. But her answer won't matter. She just told Bryan what she told me before. She has no time for anyone.

"Can I walk you to practice?" I can't help asking.

"Sure. But we call it class. Don't you have to practice?"

"They can start without me."

"That's right, you're the awesome star player who's going to get all the girls." She throws out her hands like she's holding down an enormous balloon.

I deserved that. My silence makes her laugh.

"You're cute when you're shy," she says.

I refuse to look up from the sidewalk. My heart is ticking like mad.

We stop for the light. "So, your mother's Cuban?"

"Yup. Hard to believe, right? My dad's from Indiana. But you know, my mom's blond. Her great-grandparents came from northern Spain."

The light changes and we cross.

"How'd they meet?" I want to keep her talking. I want to hear her voice.

"In college. Mom couldn't wait to get out of Miami. Of course she fell in love with the most Nordic-looking guy she could find and never let go."

"Your father's a Viking?"

My heart trips at her laugh.

"No. Dad's family's from Scotland and England. Total WASP. He's like the opposite of a Latino, except he can sort of dance. I think Mom wanted someone as different from my abuelo as she could find."

I glance up from slate-gray stone.

Isa takes a deep breath and lets it go. "Yeah, my mom hated her dad. He left her and my abuela a bunch of times. She blames him for them not having money when she was growing up. They could have gotten out of Cuba earlier, but my abuelo was in the middle of another affair. He didn't want to leave his mistress."

"I'm sorry," I tell her. That must suck. To lose everything and blame your papi for it. We've stopped in front of a poster for *Peter and the Wolf*, the symphony.

Isa shrugs. "It's OK. But it explains a lot about my mom. Don't ever tell her I said any of that, though."

The look she gives me, like she's delighted we're sharing this secret, sends a jolt into my gut. She touches my arm and I almost take her waist. I don't need Prince Royce. I could dance with her right here on the street.

"Hey . . ." She hesitates, glancing away. "I'm not like my mom. I don't put people in boxes based on where they came from or who their family is. I mean, my friend Chrissy's dad has had affairs and he's from Georgia."

I don't like to put people in boxes either. Only, that's what Bryan and Danny just did to Isa. They assumed she didn't speak Spanish because she's white and blond. And I let them do it.

It's my turn to cup my hand to my mouth. "I hate tostones. You Cubans cook platanos much better with those thin chips."

"Oh, I know, right? Tostones are so dry. But you know what I hate?" She widens her eyes again. "Flan."

"Flan? You kidding? That stuff's great."

She presses a hand to her forehead. "I know. A lot of people love it. My abuela used to make it for our neighbors. They'd come knocking as soon as the doorman told them she was in town. But I hate the consistency, you know? Anything pudding-like is just—yuck!"

I start walking again, even though I don't know where we're going. I don't want her to be late for class.

"Yeah, well other than the tostones, I'm kind of a poster for a Dominicano. I'm really good at baseball. I love my mother. I love bachata."

"But I don't know. Mr. Alex Ros doesn't sound very Dominican to me." She extends her hand toward the fountain we're passing, as if asking the pigeons to weigh in.

"My last name isn't Ros. It's Rosario."

"Oh! I just thought, because your Instagram said *ARos*..." She laughs at herself. It makes me want to dance with her even more. "But yeah, Rosario, that could be Dominican." She double-winks at me. She runs over and jumps up on the ledge around the fountain. I follow but stay on the ground. In case she needs help to balance.

She twirls on the ledge, keeping herself in a perfect line. She stops and puts a hand on each of my shoulders. She's taller than me now.

My heart thumps a rhythm that's not the bachata. The bachata's too slow. My heart is merenguing against my ribs.

"You so could not fit into a box, Mr. Alex Rosario. You're different. From everyone I know." She glances at the building as a girl, also in tights, runs through a door.

"Shoot! I've got to go." She hops down. She skips toward an entire wall of glass doors. She never bothered to close her coat. It flies out behind her like a cape.

I stay where I am, next to the fountain that's been drained for the season. I want to follow her. But I know I can't. She's like a bird, swooping with joy and life. I want to write about it. I take out my phone and snap a pic.

All that I do, with baseball, with Papi, is so folks see beyond what their eyes tell them when they look at me. Isa did that all on her own. She doesn't even care about my ball playing.

Isa yanks open a door. She waves at me with her entire arm. "See you on the subway!" She disappears inside.

I sit on the ledge as if it's a bench. I'm already late for practice.

I pull up Instagram. I comment on Isa's first post, the one she put up almost a year ago. I comment on her second and her third posts too.

I type in a private message. A few lines. Something I've been working on. I read them over. They're rough. They're not my best. I stand, press Cancel instead of Send. I pocket my phone and head back to the subway.

ALEX

I lunge to my left, holding the thirty-pound disc to my chest.

"Más por abajo." Papi grunts the command. "Bring your butt to your heel."

I come back to standing. I drive down to the right.

"Again." Papi leans against the tower of weights as he watches me. His muscled back is reflected in the mirror.

"Otro," he tells me. I'm on set three of four. The door opens. Robi comes down and sits on the steps. He was at the dining table, cutting hearts out of red construction paper when I came. In elementary school, I had to bring valentines for the class too. Only, I got mine from a box. I was going to tell Robi how cool it was he was making them. How his friends and teachers were going to be impressed. Papi closed a hand on my shoulder, steered me toward the basement before I could. He yelled out to Yaritza, asked why his son was playing with paper hearts when he could be watching his papi's old games.

Robi slides a valentine from behind his back. Loopy black letters spell out my name on white lace. I give Robi a nod. I try to smile but I'm gritting my teeth. I sink as low as I can. Papi rolls a medicine ball under his foot.

"Good." Papi opens the small refrigerator and tosses me a protein drink. I take the towel Robi holds out and wipe sweat from my face.

"Looking good." Robi always talks to me with a smile.

"Thanks." I drape my towel over his head and ruffle his hair. I pick up my valentine. Robi's drawn a picture of what could be a papi and an hijo holding hands. Only, the bigger figure's wearing a jersey with a thirty-three on it. That's my number, not Papi's. "This is great. I love it." I tip my drink to him, offering him some.

"Toma." Papi tosses the medicine ball at me. I catch it, but just barely. The drink would have spilled over Yaritza's carpet if Robi hadn't taken it. My valentine drifts like a leaf in October. It settles on the bottom step.

"La jaqueta." Papi shoves open the door before I can shrug my jacket on. I slide Robi's card into my bag. Mami's going to want it on the refrigerator.

"Can I come too?"

Papi's already outside, walking toward Sunset Park. He doesn't hear Robi.

"Go get your coat." I'm rewarded with a mile-wide grin.

Doesn't matter that it's thirty degrees. As long as there's no snow or ice, Papi will run me through drills. And Robi will try to join.

Papi's waiting by the streetlight half a block away. I jog past him, my sneakers crunching grass that's winter-brown. I squat, the medicine ball hanging between my knees. Cold air scrapes my throat. It ice-picks my chest from the inside. I clench my jaw, shoot up, and hurl the ball as far as I can. I sprint to it, pick it up, and do it again.

"Más rápido."

I do as Papi says. My legs burn. I didn't think I could go any faster. But Papi was right. If I push myself, I can.

Robi kicks around a rock. He stays on the other side of the walkway. Papi's yelled at him for getting too close before. I don't want Robi getting hit by the basketball-size weight. I don't like him getting yelled at either.

Papi takes the medicine ball from me when I finish ten reps. He hands me a water bottle.

Robi's hanging from a tree branch. His legs swing in the air. He sees me get down on the ground. He drops and sprints so he's behind Papi. He gets into push-up position too. Papi's marked off ten yards with a red ribbon.

"Go!" His stopwatch clicks.

I spring up and pump my legs until I'm past that ribbon. Papi frowns at the timer. I've got thirty seconds before the next one. I pace. I remember Papi's words. I shut my mouth and force air through my nose, warming it before it hits my lungs.

On the other side of the green, Robi mirrors me, hands on hips, stomping down dead stalks of weeds.

At Papi's nod, I get into position.

Robi does too.

Click.

"¡Pa'rriba! Knees to chest! Knees to chest!" Papi chants.

I barrel toward the ribbon. I pull my legs as high as they'll go.

"¡Eso!" Papi's not frowning anymore.

It's hard to smile when you're catching your breath.

Robi's skipping sideways, arms pumping the sky. If I had my phone, I'd take a photo.

When Papi takes two gloves from his bag and a ball from his pocket, Robi bounds over to us.

"Can I throw too?" It's impossible not to hear his hope.

"Más tarde." It's what Papi always says.

"But I want a chance to throw with Alex." Robi shouldn't whine. It just makes Papi dig in.

"I said later. ¡Vete pa'lla!" Papi points to a rock under a tree.

Robi hangs his head. A drop hangs from the tip of his nose. Instead of wiping it away, Robi snorts it back in.

"Come on, we can do a few tosses all together. There's time, right?"

They both look at me, surprised I've spoken. Robi's eyes light up. Thunder gathers in Papi's.

"Time?" Papi says. "We have just four months until travel team starts. When you here, I train you. Es todo. ¿Me escuchas? This is not a game. This is your life."

When we get back inside, Yaritza's waiting. Mami called. She wants me home for dinner.

"Qué no." Papi smacks the wood banister. "You said you'd spend the night. We still have game strategy to review. Y mañana tienes que practicar más."

I haven't seen Mami all week. When I get home, she's already at work. She was supposed to work a double shift tonight, which is why I agreed to stay. But now . . .

"This is most important." Papi shows me the baseball in his fist. "This is what makes you more. What do people see when they look at you, eh? Un moreno walking the streets."

He stomps toward the display case in the living room. Behind him, Robi's eyes are twin full moons. Papi swipes the key from the top ledge. He wrestles the glass open. With two hands, he takes out his cap, the one he wore when he played for the Yankees. He comes back to me, slips it on my head. I want to tell him to stop. My hair is a mess of sweat and dirt.

He pulls me to the mirror. "Now what do people see?"

I tip my chin up. The cap fits me. It fits me perfect.

"A baseball player." I know what to say. I've said it before.

"Eso." Papi grips my shoulders. "People don't see color when you're wearing this. And you, you're better than I was." He tugs the brim over my eyes. "This will be yours one day."

In the mirror, Papi's smiling at me. It makes everything worth it.

Behind us, Robi's looking at the floor.

"Pero, mañana it will be en los teens. You said, less than twenty-five is too cold." Yaritza sidles up to him. She knocks her hip against his.

"And why do we have the room with the weights and equipment?" Papi jabs his hand toward the floor.

"So you can look good." She squeezes his thighs. "And all this doesn't turn to fat."

Papi's hands find her butt. "Ah, sí? I look good, eh?"

Robi clomps up the stairs. He doesn't give me a smile. I don't know if it's because I won't be spending the night or because of what Papi said.

Yaritza's whispering to Papi. He closes his eyes and tilts his head back. She leans into him. She drags her hands down his arms.

"He'll come back tomorrow, won't you, Ále?" Yaritza looks over her shoulder at me. She waves me to the kitchen where I find a foil packet of what smells like tortas.

Papi's eyes are still closed. They're swaying together, dancing to music I can't hear.

"Gracias." I plant a quick kiss on Yaritza's cheek. "Nine o'clock good for tomorrow?" I sling my bag onto my back. On the weekends, it takes a good hour and a half to get here.

"Eight," Papi calls out as I shut the door.

TUESDAY, FEBRUARY 14

ISA

"Gods be damned, my trap is killing me." Chrissy's whispering through her teeth. She extends over her leg, reaching for her pointed toe, an exact mirror of me and the five other girls at the barre. Madame Toussane, our Adagio teacher, claps her hands, stopping the piano. Chrissy rubs her shoulder as we reposition ourselves for the final combination. Madame Toussane nods at Mr. Richards, the pianist, and the music starts. She snaps her fingers to the beat, calling out the steps.

There are two sharp claps and the music stops. "Non. That is incorrect. Isabelle, venez ici. To the center."

I bow my head and step away from the barre. Did I do something wrong?

"Now, everybody watch. Isabelle, please, again." Madame Toussane glances at Mr. Richards and notes fill the room. She chants the moves.

"Plié, tendu. Plié, développé. Plié, now the grand rond de jambe . . ."

I stretch my leg as I lift it in front of me. I imagine it growing longer from my hip to my heel and toe as I swing it slowly, ever so slowly, behind me.

"Front, second, now écarté, écarté, écarté . . . then to arabesque. Yes! Excellent! Now let's see it with some movement across the floor. Isabelle, please." Her praise is like air to a balloon inside my chest. I feel pumped up and light on my feet. She gives me new steps. I take my place in the corner. I sink into a deep plié, one foot pointed behind me, my arm reaching up as if to the branches of a tree dripping fruit. Music begins. I drag my foot forward, lift the leg into développé, transfer onto it for the pirouette, arms forward, chest out, then slow into the grand ronde de jambe, ending in arabesque with another deep plié. My hand reaches now not for the tree but directly in front of me, toward the door of the room. I imagine Alex there, watching me.

"Beautiful. Well done. We will all work on that next class. Dismissed!" Madame Toussane gives a final clap.

"You are so getting a lead part for the spring performance." Chrissy prods me with her elbow as we walk to the locker room. I duck under the arm of a dancer whose leg is being lifted by a young man in dance shorts and a T-shirt. He's helping her stretch, but the way they're facing each other, her foot in his hand, her ankle above his shoulder, their pelvises inches apart, seems awfully intimate. I think of Alex doing that for me and my cheeks flame.

"We'll see," I say to Chrissy. I don't like to hope for things that might not happen.

Chrissy scoffs. "Madame Toussane hardly ever compliments anyone. And she loves you. *Excellente, Mademoiselle Isabelle. You are the most perfect dancer who has ever graced my classroom! Come, let me have you dance for the entire school!*" Chrissy's French accent makes me laugh. It comes out with a tinge of southern twang. She's not making fun of me. Or being jealous. She just likes to make me laugh.

"Meet you downstairs?" She grabs her bag and runs to find Kevin. Like she does each day after class. She's so lucky Kevin is in the same building as her every single day.

Ten minutes later, Chrissy comes down the marble steps. Her arms cradle pink roses tied with a satin ribbon, but there's no Kevin. I'd forgotten it was Valentine's Day. I scheduled an e-card for Merrit a few days ago, but he hasn't responded. I give Chrissy a supersad face. "Did you lock Kevin in the janitor's closet? Sorry, I meant to tell him about your thing against flowers."

Chrissy hates them. She's always thought giving something that's going to die is a stupid way of showing affection.

Chrissy shrugs a shoulder. "Perhaps my antifloral attacks were too vicious. I've never gotten roses before." She buries her nose in the petals, then sighs. "Kevin's stuck in rehearsal for another hour. Guess it's just you and me, chica!" She flings her arm around me then grimaces in pain. She rubs her neck as we push out into the frosty air. When we get down to the subway, I massage her shoulders.

"Thank you . . ." Her growl is eclipsed by the screeching of our train pulling in. "You. Are. The. Best. Man, *Coppélia* is the worst variation ever. My body's not meant to be stiff like a doll. I'm meant to be pliable and loose, in the arms of a lover." She wags her eyebrows and I laugh as we get on.

"How's it going with Kevin, by the way?" I think of Alex again. Ever since Alex walked me to class and uploaded a picture of me to his Instagram—you can't tell it's me because it's just my back, my coat sailing behind me—he's posted almost every day. The photos feel like they're for me: shoes, all types, not just ballet shoes. Anything to do with dance. And then there are some that are just plain beautiful. The sun hitting the George Washington Bridge. An old lady on a park bench, her smile wide as she feeds the pigeons. I can't wait to see what he posts today.

Chrissy swings herself around the pole, like she's in a Broadway musical. "Kevin is perrrr-fect." Chrissy purrs like a cat. I try to keep a straight face.

"Well, he can pick up where I left off." I gesture to her shoulders. "His fingers have to be pretty strong from all that keyboard banging."

"You have no idea," she replies, looking up at me from under lowered lids. "He's got the best hands. Long and slender, and quite, quite agile." Chrissy leans in. "Do you know he can span eleven keys? That's only one less than Rachmaninov, who had possibly the biggest hands of any composer." Chrissy shouts over the train's rattling. "And since you mentioned banging, I should tell you, we're not going there yet. This time, I'm taking it slow. I'm enjoying myself. Kissing can be really fun. I mean, really, really fun. Did you know all the things your tongue is capable of?" A woman in an orange puffer coat and bright purple snow boots peers over the top of her *New York Post* at us. "Kevin's got the tongue of a bassoonist," Chrissy continues, oblivious to the woman's gaze. She should know—she met one at camp last summer. I never met any of the other guys Chrissy hung out with before Kevin. They weren't really boyfriends.

"This is me, chica." Chrissy kisses my cheek as the doors slide open at Seventy-Ninth. "I'm meeting Glenda for dinner. Well, Kevin and I are both meeting her, but Kevin's coming after apps. You know how hungry my momster gets."

"Wait, you're introducing Kevin to your mom? For Valentine's Day?" Chrissy's never done that before. Ever.

Her face flushes. She backs out to the platform and shrugs. "Yeah. Guess I am. I really like him, Isa. I hope I don't screw it up."

"See you tomorrow," I call. "Use a heating pad on your neck. In case the wonder hands don't do the trick!" The newspaper beside me rustles. Snow boot lady pretends she wasn't listening but she's smiling.

"Attention, passengers, this train is being held in the station due to a red signal. We should be moving shortly."

I check my phone. Still no message from Merrit. But Alex posted a pic of an open subway door. In the background, a sticker that reads KEEP CALM AND DANCE ON is slapped to the wall, below the tiled numbers SEVENTY-NINE. I stand and move to the open door. There, on the other side of a row of benches, is the same sticker. Is Alex here?

I scoot out onto the platform and slip into the next car.

Alex is at the other end. He's leaning over, writing, his baseball cap pulled low on his forehead. Adrenaline bursts across my palms and dives into my fingers.

Every day on the train I close my eyes and dream about our walk. And our dance. Sometimes I see his friends' faces as I tell them my mom's Cuban. I try not to think about what they said. It's exactly why Mom hates ballet. Sometimes I rehearse words I'll never say to her. That there are plenty of people who don't judge only on appearance, even when appearance matters. Alex has never made assumptions about me because of ballet or the way I look, even if his friends did.

"Stand clear of the closing doors, please."

I make my way to him as the train lurches forward. The tingling is in my belly now. He's sitting in a two-seater against the wall. He's so intent on his notebook, he doesn't look up. Even though it's cold out, his jacket's open. His pants and his gray jersey—with the letters *AHH* embroidered in blue—are splattered with dirt. I tap his sneaker—not Chucks, but Adidas.

His eyes dart to me and widen. The edges of his mouth lift. "Hi."

I show him my screen with his post. "I was in the next car."

"Really?" His smile makes me smile even more.

"Coming from practice?"

He gestures at his clothes. "What gave it away?" His hand slides over the paper and he scoots toward the wall, pushing his bag under him.

I sit, turning to face him.

"You coming from practice too?" he asks.

"Yup! Well, *class*—not practice."

He chuckles at the faux-fierce look I give him.

I sit back and pretend to wedge my shoulders next to his. He moves to give me room. I don't need any—I was just being funny. I lean all the way into him as we brake into the next station. I throw my weight into it then bring up my foot and push against the bar until he laughs. The feel of him along my entire side sends a rush of heat through me. He frees his arm. His wide hand settles on my shoulder neither pushing nor pulling me away. It just rests there. I stop and lie against him. I want to tip my head onto him like I did when we danced. I wish I could. I wish we both had more time. I've never missed having a boyfriend. But seeing him, feeling him, makes me realize I miss *him*.

I give Alex space as the doors open. He doesn't take his hand away.

A small man with silver hair peeking out from a frayed cowboy hat gets on. His fingers whirl over the keys of an accordion as soon as the doors close. A fast-paced tune heaves out of the machine as the man compresses and unfolds it. I glance at Alex. We smile at each other. The music isn't bad. I tap my foot, knocking my knee against him.

The old man moves toward us. His weathered face squints as he starts to sing. Alex presses his lips together. He takes his hand back to cover his mouth and turns to the wall. The man's singing is awful. Alex shakes with laughter he won't let out. Luckily, the poor man's singing with his eyes closed. I don't understand all the words because of his accent. I tap my fingers on Alex's leg, marking the beat. It makes him go still.

The song finishes. The little man takes his hat and flips it over. He murmurs gracias to the few who give him money. I take a twenty from my bag.

"You're not serious?" Alex's eyes are wet from trying not to laugh. "You know he's scamming you, right?"

"How do you know? We have no idea what's going on in his life. Maybe his wife died of cancer and the hospital is suing him for bills he can't pay. Maybe he lost his apartment. He can't get a job because he's too old and he doesn't speak English."

Alex sighs. "Most people who ask for money are either druggies or alcoholics. You're just enabling him, preventing him from seeking the help he needs."

"That little grandpa is not an alcoholic."

Alex's eyebrow rise. "He was slurring his words."

Hmm. Maybe that's why I couldn't understand him.

The man shuffles over, holding out his hat. There's not a single bill, only a few scattered coins. "Please, please," he says. "Anything, anything." His eyes, almost swallowed by the folds of his face, shift from Alex to me. He smiles wider, revealing dark gaps where teeth should be. I drop the bill in.

"Ay, gracias. Dios te bendiga." He backs away.

"De nada," I reply. "Un placer."

Alex watches me, his head cocked to the side.

"My mom wants me to take taxis. I prefer the subway. She'd ask questions if I gave her the money back. And I feel funny keeping it."

Alex's hand rests on his leg. A bit of paper from the notebook peeks out from under his thumb. "Is that the real reason?" Alex doesn't look away.

I shrug. "It makes me feel good. To help. Even if he does need more help, like doctor help or AA help, at least he won't be hungry tonight."

Alex nods. "OK. I can understand that." His fingers curl over the paper. It disappears into his fist.

"What's that?" I ask.

"What's what?"

I laugh. "Under your hand. What were you writing when I so rudely interrupted you?"

"Nothing." He folds the paper and tucks it into his coat pocket. The notebook disappears into his bag. "And you didn't interrupt me."

"I see." I remove a few pins from my bun. My scalp aches. "You stole some kid's parakeet and now you're crafting the ransom note." I drop the pins in my palm. Alex's mouth is fixed in that uneven smile. "That's not it? Oh, I know." I lift my arms again and remove the rest of the pins. "You're creating a hit list for all your rival baseball players." Alex lets out a soft chuckle. I unwrap my hair and let the ponytail fall down my back. "Perhaps it's your abuelita's recipe for asopao. Don't want to share the Dominican secret with a Cuban, even a half-Cuban, huh?"

"My abuelita is dead. Both of them are."

I drop my hands and face him. "I'm so sor—"

He cracks a grin. "They're not dead. One's in Santiago, the other's in Santo Domingo. I couldn't resist."

I go to swat him. He grabs my wrist. He slides the piece of paper under my fingers.

He doesn't say anything as I unfold it, as I read the words scrawled onto a ripped piece of yellow lined notepaper. Some are scratched out and written over. Some I can barely decipher. But it doesn't matter. Because it's a poem. About me. He wrote a poem about *me*.

> **Your feet rap a rhythm**
> **of beauty and power and rhyme,**
> **faster than the gallop of train beneath us.**
>
> **I struggle to follow.**
> **You slow.**
> **You pour your hip into the cup of my hand**
> **showing me my thirst.**
>
> **What takes my breath isn't your body.**
> **It's your eyes.**
> **They stayed with me**
> **though I could barely keep up.**
>
> **Though the floor lurches and sways,**
> **though you continue to move to the beat**
> **of "no me culpes a mí,"**
> **the calm earth of your eyes tells me**
> **it doesn't matter what my hands, what my feet can't do**
> **as long as I'm with you.**

"What do you think?" His voice is quiet.

I read it six times. I want to read it six hundred more.

I finally look up at him. "I . . . It's . . ." I don't have any words that can match his.

He gives me a stiff smile. He reaches for the paper. "I know it's not very good."

I take his hand, wrap my fingers through his. "It's beautiful," I tell him. "Can I keep it?"

His eyes, soft and brown, blink at me. "It's for you."

"Will you sign it?"

He blinks again.

I offer the paper. He lifts his pen. He signs *A* at the bottom.

"How did you learn to write like this?"

He looks away. "I don't know. I just picked up the pen and started."

"One day one of your pieces will be up there." I motion to the MTA poem framed behind the glass.

He scowls at his shoe. "Nah. I'm no poet. I'm a ballplayer."

"Why can't you be both?"

He's silent, considering.

"Hey, I know neither of us has time what with my class and rehearsal schedule and with your baseball, but do you think you could message me when you're riding this train? If we happen to be heading in the same direction . . . ?"

"I'll let you know my schedule," he says. "But I'm on varsity. Our away games are mostly in the Bronx." He doesn't have to tell me that means he won't be riding this line. It was stupid of me to suggest. Stupid of me to dream.

He takes my hand back. "But I'll still be going to Brooklyn on the weekends."

My fingers brush against the poem in my pocket. It's like a nugget of hope.

Alex rises when I do. He walks me to the door. We stand there for a few seconds, me on the platform, him still in the subway, our hands bridging the gap. He doesn't let me go until the light above us turns red and the bell rings out.

TUESDAY, FEBRUARY 14

ISA

"Good rehearsal today, Miss Isabelle?" Gerry holds the lobby door open for me. The thick rings on his fingers shimmer in the light from our awning. I've always been fascinated by those rings. On my sixth birthday, Gerry let me try the one with the amber stone. It fit over two of my fingers together. Even then I had to make a fist so it wouldn't fall off.

"Always," I reply.

"Toes no bothering you?" Gerry is convinced my pointe shoes are going to give me bunions.

"Not yet!" I sing it to him.

His laugh is a deep rumble. "Is good you're home. Your mother, she could use your smile."

I feel my grin deflate. My hand closes around Alex's poem, tucked safely in my pocket. Even if Mom is in one of her moods, I have this.

Gerry walks me to the elevator, reaches inside and hits the button for my floor. "Good night, princesa." He tips his hat. The elevator closes with a quiet *thump*.

Voices reach me as soon as I open the door. Strange. Mom and Dad are usually at the other end of the apartment, in the eat-in kitchen or the library. Even Dad's office is all the way in the back.

I kick off my shoes and hang my coat. I'm halfway down the hall when I realize the vase of two dozen long-stemmed red roses that Dad always gives Mom on Valentine's Day isn't on the entryway table.

A crash of glass makes me jump. I run for the kitchen. Mom's shrill voice mirrors the smashing of crystal.

"What are we going to do? What are we going to tell people?"

"We'll figure it out. Let's just take it one step at a time." Dad's words are calm but strained.

I lean against the wall, my heart pounding. My parents never argue openly. Sure, Mom yells. But her outbursts have nothing to do with Dad.

Mom swears in Spanish. Another bad sign. Merrit's face smiles down at me from our family portrait from five years ago, his mouth full of braces. He'd seen a new psychiatrist right before the photo shoot. Later that night, I overheard Mom crying in the master bedroom. Dad was saying over and over it wasn't her fault. By then at least, I knew Mom was different. I'd never heard the words *bipolar disorder*, though. In the portrait, our smiles look carefree and happy. I'm not looking at the camera. I'm looking up at my brilliant, bigger-than-life big brother. I hope this doesn't have to do with Merrit. I hope he's OK.

I backtrack down the hall to the door. I open it, slam it shut, then cry out, "Hello! I'm home!" I hum as I make my way to the kitchen. "I'm starving. Is there anything to eat?"

Dad is leaning against the stove. His glasses are on the counter next to a huge package of unwrapped flowers. Mom's watching him from where she stands on the other side of the island, clutching a glass. It's not her usual sparkling water. Her dad had an alcohol problem, something she brings up every year to make sure Merrit and I never forget it. But next to her is an open bottle of wine. Remnants of a broken goblet sparkle in the sink.

"Sorry, we haven't gotten around to thinking about dinner." Dad rubs his eyes.

"Want me to call for sushi?" I keep my tone light. Pretending everything is OK is the modus operandi in our household. "Oh, that's right." I slap my hand to my forehead. "The dead fish won't hear me. I'll just run out and pick some up." Dad jokes are a good technique too, though Dad's much better at them than I am.

Mom turns to the window. She takes a long sip as she gazes at the Empire State Building. It's lit up blue and green tonight.

"That's a good idea, honey. Here." Dad hands me his credit card.

Mom whips around. She slams the glass down. Drops of wine splatter like blood across the granite. "What are you doing?!"

I drop Dad's card.

"We need to have dinner," Dad says quietly. Why isn't he joking with her, making her laugh like he usually does?

"Sushi is expensive. We'll make do with whatever is in the refrigerator." She slides by me, picking up the platinum card and chucking it back at Dad. She drags out cheese and grapes and hard salami. Leftovers from her book club.

I take small breaths. Mom gets like this when she's stressed, all crazy frugal even though we don't need to be. It's like a flashback from her childhood. Dad always stops her. He wraps her in his arms, puts on the Buena Vista Social Club, and makes her dance with him. He starts out dancing badly, to make her laugh. Sometimes she cries. But he always promises he'll take care of her and that she'll never have to live like that again.

Tonight Dad just takes out some plates. He reaches for a tumbler and gets down a bottle of scotch. I've only ever seen that bottle when their friends the Rosens come over after a show.

I try to swallow but my mouth is too dry. "Is it Merrit?"

Last I talked to Merrit, he mentioned a new app he was developing. The campus sports teams were loving it. It was spreading "faster than an STI." He'd been talking so fast, I couldn't help but be nervous—I know all the signs of a manic episode now. But Merrit promised he'd been sleeping and taking his meds. So I assumed he was just excited. What if I was wrong?

Dad puts down the scotch. "Merrit's fine." His hand comes out for emphasis.

I relax my fist, loosening the nails digging into my palm. Whatever it is, it can't be that bad, then.

I get out three placemats and arrange them on the banquet. Mom shakes her head.

"I'm not eating. It's just you and your father."

"Elisa," Dad starts.

"You think I can eat at a time like this?" Her accent thickens, hardening her words.

Dad looks down at the polished stone floor. I'm thoroughly confused. Mom turns back to me. "How's your school going? Any homework tonight?"

"It's all fine, Mom. I have a paper due tomorrow on *Franny and Zooey,* but I already have a draft."

"Bring me your laptop. I'll read your paper while you eat."

"Why?" She doesn't usually go over my work.

"This has nothing to do with Isabelle," Dad interrupts.

The look Mom gives him is so vicious it makes me step back. "It has everything to do with Isabelle. It's even more important now that she gets good grades."

I'm used to Mom being overly dramatic. But she's starting to freak me out. "Dad? What's going on?"

"Nothing, sweetie, everything's going to be fine."

"How can you say that to her? God, and with that smile on your face?" Mom marches over for her glass of wine. She grabs it but doesn't take a drink. "Your father lost his job. He was fired." Lost his job? But he's not a trader. Dad's the chief risk officer. His job is secure.

"I just don't understand why you signed off on a deal you knew wasn't sound." Mom glares at him.

"Elisa." Dad sighs. "The MD made it clear he only wanted my approval."

She waves an arm. "Do you have proof? An email? Something to demonstrate you're not accountable?" Dad doesn't answer. "You don't, do you? They would never be so foolish as to put something like that in writing."

Dad comes over to the table and rests a hand on my shoulder. "I don't want you to worry. I can get another job."

Mom makes a mild shrieking sound. "Why would you tell her that? It was a multibillion-dollar screw-up, Isabelle. And now the SEC is investigating." She starts muttering in Spanish. "You don't know what will happen. You don't." She's gripping the glass so hard the tips of her fingers are white.

Dad reaches for Mom. She doesn't step away. He rubs her arm, his voice dropping to a soothing drone. "There are plenty of other banks in the city. I'll find work at one of them."

Mom takes a long drink of wine. "You just told me you might be blacklisted."

Dad glances at me. He ducks down to find Mom's eyes. "That would be a worst-case scenario," he whispers. "We'll have to make adjustments. You're right. We don't need to eat sushi every week. At least not from Takai." He tries for a smile, and Mom leans into him. His nickname for Mom's favorite sushi place is the word *expensive* in Japanese.

"We can sell the Hamptons house. We hardly ever go out east anymore anyway."

Mom's mouth opens.

"And there are other ways we can cut back," Dad murmurs. "Isabelle's been begging to attend the Manhattan Ballet Academy full time since she was twelve. It's a specialized city school. Free tuition."

Mom's finger slices the air. "No. We are not sacrificing her education. Deerwood has one of the best college acceptance lists in the city. Merrit graduated from there. And their STEM curriculum is excellent, not to mention the special mentorship program they have for women who want to go into medicine."

Dad sees me chewing my lip. He knows I don't want to be a doctor, that I hate the sight of blood. He sighs. "What do you think, Isabelle? If the Academy will honor your acceptance from last summer, would you like to go there?"

I give the faintest of nods. Dad knows I would kill to be able to dance full time. But I don't want to get my hopes up. They might not accept me. I'm older than most candidates for transfer. Mom is looking at me like I'm holding a knife and I'm about to stab her.

"Mom, there's this one dancer, Mia, who got into Columbia early decision from the Academy. She wants to be an OB doctor."

Mom's lips pinch. She doesn't believe me.

"David Jeffries is on the board there," Dad says. "I can ask him who the right person to call would be. This is a good idea, Elisa. The savings would be significant."

Mom doesn't say no. She doesn't shout and stomp her foot. That means there's a chance.

"Come on, we can talk more about this later. For now, let's sit and eat together. I've been craving"—Dad squints at the plastic container—"almond cilantro hummus all day." He wheels Mom into the seat of honor, directly north of the Manhattan skyline. Dad sits next to her, tapping the cushion of the bench on his other side. I slide in.

"It will work out. It always does," Dad says. It's our mantra, his and mine. I say it to myself as we eat, as I clean up, as I head back to my room.

When I'm on my bed, I take out Alex's poem. I read it over and over until it blocks out Dad's promise, until it's all I see, all I think about. Before I turn out the lights, I open Instagram. Alex's account is right up top. He's posted a photo of our two hands. It's blurry—the train must have been moving—but still, I make out the curve of his fingers under mine.

FRIDAY, MARCH 3

ALEX

I don't know whether to sit or stand. If I sit, Isa might not see me. If I stand, I'll pace. I don't want her to see that. I'm not in my usual spot in the middle of the train because I want to see her as soon as she comes down.

I unzip my jacket. There's dirty snow and brain-freeze wind on the streets. Down here there's only tracks of muddy slush. Two little kids take the stairs, lowering one foot at a time. Behind, a mami clutches a metal cart filled with groceries. It clangs on each step.

I push off the post.

"Can I help you?" I motion to the cart. The woman jumps, like a pigeon scared by a bear.

"No, no is OK. We OK. Thank you, thank you." The mami bows her head and shoulders to me again and again. The cart smacks onto the next stair. A carton of eggs wobbles on top. The mami's eyes dart from me to her kids, like she thinks I might do something to them. I've been keeping my eye on them. They're too small to be on the platform by themselves.

"Alex!"

Isa's running down the steps. She doesn't stop until she's in front of me. "Alex." She grabs my hands with both of hers. She looks at me like I'm hidden treasure she's finally found.

I try not to smile too big. "You're breathing hard," I say. Her face is flushed.

"Oh." Her light-brown eyes bug. She rises onto her toes then drops to her heels. "I was so excited to see your message. I can't believe it's been two whole weeks and we're finally making this work! I couldn't wait to see you." She whispers the last part.

I'm glad for my sweatshirt. An extra layer to hide the pounding inside me. It's been two weeks and three days. But who's counting?

Her fingers squeeze mine. "How are you? Are you ready for your first game? It's in two Saturdays, right?"

I hide my surprise. "You been checking up on me?"

She ducks her head. "Your team's schedule is online. You're playing Morris. Are they a good team? Will you still play if there's snow?"

"We'll see about the weather. And yes, Morris is good." I don't tell her that AHH is better, that last year we crushed them 11–4 and then 10–5. I don't want to talk about ball. "How's your rehearsing?" Isa's hair is in a bun again. Tiny flecks of pink light up in it as she moves.

"I've got big news." She goes on her toes again. It brings her eyes about level with my nose. I bend my knees to see her better. "I might go to the Manhattan Academy of Ballet full time!" She's jigging up and down. Like she's on a trampoline, about to launch into the air.

"Wow!" I tell her. "That's great!"

"I'm still waiting to hear if they'll accept last year's audition. I'd start over the summer. I had to promise Mom it doesn't mean I'm going professional. I told her I'm still considering medical school."

"A doctor, huh?" I fix the collar of her jacket. She must have thrown it on fast. "You'd look good in a white coat. A stethoscope hanging here." I trace a line down the side of her neck. Her skin, where I touch her, colors. I tug at my hoodie. Coño, I'm glad I'm wearing it.

Her eyes look straight at mine. "Yeah, well. I'm actually kind of scared of blood."

"Maybe you should tell your mother that."

She leans close. Her breath smells like fruit, like orange and mango. "That guy over there?" She's whispering again. "The one staring at us? He looks like one of the lion statues in front of my building. With his jowls and frown." Laughter trickles out of her.

I go to turn but she stops me.

"Wait. Don't make it obvious!"

I give her a look that tells her I know how to do this. I push back my hood and search the ceiling for the next train's estimated arrival. The family with the cart and the two little boys watches us. The mami smiles at me and bobs her head. Sure, now that she sees me with Isa, I deserve a smile.

Farther down the platform is a white man with droopy cheeks. *Jowls* Isa called them. Yeah, I can see why she thinks he looks like a lion. It's his attitude. I know guys like him. Guys who look at me and decide they're more important than me, 'cause I'm nothing.

I face the man. He looks through me. He adjusts his tie. He turns to the approaching train.

It's because we're standing together, Isa and I. I'm still holding her hand. He doesn't like it.

The heat in my blood goes from simmer to boil. I get that feeling again, that no matter what I do, I can't win. I exhale, nice and slow, like I'm preparing to take the mound. What Lion-man and that mami think of me doesn't matter. They're like a heckling crowd, trying to shake me. I won't let them.

"Come on." I tug Isa with me, down past the man with the necktie and loafers, toward the middle of the platform.

"What?" she asks.

"You'll see."

The train rushes past. Wind hits the back of my arm, my neck. A wisp of Isa's hair flutters onto her cheek. She presses against me. Words swirl in my head. My hand itches for a pen and a piece of paper.

I count the cars as they roll by. "This one," I say as the doors open.

"It looks empty." Her bright gaze slides to mine. "Is that why you want it?"

The sly curve of her mouth punches heat into my gut. I try to keep my expression cool. "No, no, it's just . . ." I go to wipe the sweat that's coming on my forehead but stop myself. "I'll show you."

She follows me in.

Ofrescome. I nearly gag at the smell.

Isa turns to me, her eyes bugging again. She slaps a hand to her mouth. Her fingers cover her nose. I'm not sure if she's trying not to laugh or not to breathe.

The car's not empty. There's a homeless person at one end. Ratty blankets cover his shoulders. Ratty sneakers, tongues hanging out like desert dogs', sit beside him. He's got a piece of cardboard under his feet. They're bare and red.

I drag Isa into the next car.

Laughter pours out of her as soon as the door shuts.

"I'm sorry," I say. "I didn't know he was in there."

Her hand seizes my arm. "I'm not laughing at him." She points at my face. "I've never"—she snorts—"I've never seen you look so surprised. I thought . . ." She covers her mouth as she hiccups. "It's just, you're always so calm, so in control. I like that you can be caught off guard." She tips against me.

"What are you talking about? I get surprised." She thinks I'm calm and in control? That's good though, right?

Her lashes are damp. They're clumping together. "Yeah? When?"

"Well." I think for a moment. "Halloween. When you . . ." I nod at her. "You know."

She stops laughing. She wets her lips. Her eyes drop to my mouth.

I can't help it. I wet my lips too. Inside, my heart taps a merengue beat.

"You didn't look surprised." Her voice is softer. "You didn't feel surprised either. It almost felt like . . ." She traces her smile with a pink fingernail.

"Like what?"

Her gaze swings back to me. "Like you knew I was coming."

I close my mouth. I remind myself to swallow.

"So why did you bring me into that car?" she asks.

"Doesn't matter. Just . . . I was going to show you something."

"Show me what?"

The other day, on the train, I almost didn't show her what I'd written. I've never been more nervous. A bottom-of-the-ninth playoff game with bases loaded, us up one run and me on the mound, has nothing on that afternoon. I felt naked, watching Isa read. She smiled. And what she said? Her words were like robes of fur and velvet, making me feel like a king. Making me feel like I could do anything. Be anyone. Not just what everyone expects.

Isa bumps me with her arm. She's waiting for an answer.

I shrug. "Something I wrote."

Her mouth makes a small O shape. "But how?" she asks.

I tell her how I spoke with a conductor who was from La Vega. How he confirmed how long it takes to run the whole line, how many trips a day a train can make. There's still luck involved. Some trains get switched out on the weekend. I tried to account for that by planting extras.

Cool fingers burrow into my fist. "Come on," she says. She tries to pull me to the door.

I don't budge. "No. I don't want you going in there again."

"Listen." She's smiling at me. "I don't care about that. I've smelled worse."

"You have? Like in dance school? Dancer feet, they smell like that?"

She ignores my joke and bounces on her toes. "I want to see what you wrote." Her fingers tap against my palm. "Please? Show me?"

I take her arm. I draw an exaggerated breath. I wait for her to do the same. I yank open the first door, and the second. I rush us inside. The poem I left for Isa is at the other end, tucked under the seat beside the framed poem by Enrico García, a thirty-eight-year-old Nuyorican with a wavy website.

Isa's eyes glow. She doesn't look away from me.

I reach down and feel along the edge of the two-person bench. I untape the folded note. I hand it to Isa. I try to pull her out, to get her into the next car.

"Wait." She snaps it open. The paper covers her face as she reads.

I look away. The homeless guy is checking us out. He has reason to be suspicious. Bryan and I once saw some dudes with blue bandanas beating up a homeless person. We were only in seventh grade. There was nothing we could do. And I was too afraid of the cop outside the station to tell him what was going down beside the tracks. I should have told him though. I think about that homeless person sometimes.

I give our fellow passenger a nod. As if to say, "Hey. You cool, I'm cool." He nods back.

My eyes are watering. ¡Guay! Maybe we're cool but that be a powerful smell. It's like dead fish and dead mice are having a zombie party.

Isa's eyes are teary too. Her lip shivers. Is she cold?

"How?" she says. She draws a breath through her mouth. "How do you write this?"

I'm afraid to ask. But I need to. "You like it?"

"Look at me." She rattles the paper at her face. "You made me cry." Her lip shivers again.

"Here." I draw her hand around my back. My arms close around her shoulders. She's going to feel the thudding in my chest. But I don't know what else to do.

Her nose rubs against my hoodie. She sighs, and I dip my face to her hair. She's like a breeze off the ocean. "You smell good," I breathe. "I can barely smell the stanky feet."

She laughs against me.

"Come on." I tow her to the door. Push us through to another car.
She's still leaning against me. I can't see her face. But I hear her smile.
"Read me the poem?" She passes the note into my hand. I don't take it.
I recite from memory.

I LOVE

The oiled leather of my glove
    baking in my full-sun window,
The untouched pages of a new book,
The tip of a freshly shaved pencil
    you hand to me,
My madrastra's cooking,
Papi's rare not-frown,
Your hair,
    wet or dry or in between.

Cool cotton sheets
    on legs sore from sprinting and sliding,
Snow drifting
    onto eyelids and uncovered cheeks,
Shavings of coco-flavored ice
    on outstretched tongues,
Your hand melting in mine
    on an ever-moving train.

Arms tighten around me. Fists bury into my sides. "Can you do it in
Spanish?"
I can.
She tilts her face up. Her smile hits me like a ninety-five-mile-per-hour

ball to the chest. I was downed by one last year. At a game against JFK High. I couldn't breathe. I couldn't move. I couldn't hear what Coach and Papi were shouting at me. It wasn't until they brought that heart-shocking machine next to me that I gasped and pushed the paddles away. This time, I wouldn't push them away. I need that machine. Because it aches too much.

Isa's hand slides off me. My heart shifts into a panic step. I don't want her to take it away.

She doesn't. She touches my face. She draws a line from my cheek to my jaw to my chin.

There's no way she can't feel my heart. It's fighting its way out to her.

"Alex," she whispers. Her fingers slide to the back of my neck.

Her hands are cool. But her lips, on mine, are warm and wet. She makes a small noise. I can't help myself. I reach under her. I lift her to an empty seat. Her arms wrap around my shoulders, my head. She makes another noise, and I almost lose it. I grab her to me. Her leg is around my waist. Holy God.

The side door opens. The homeless guy shuffles in. "Get a room! Get a room! Get a room!" he shouts at us.

Isa pulls away. She keeps her forehead pressed to mine. She's laughing.

The train doors open.

"Hold on." I pick Isa up.

"My bag!" she cries.

I snag it from the seat. She still clutches my note in her hand.

I don't put her down until we're on the platform.

"Kiss me," she says.

I do.

People stream by us. We're like rocks in a river. Isa pulls me toward the wall. Behind a column that says SIXTY-SIX. Coño. That homeless saved us. We would have missed her stop.

Isa's hands are on my back. At the waistline of my pants. I bring her fingers to my chest. They slide to my face. I can't breathe. I don't need air. All I need is her. The roar of the passing express is distant. I don't want to stop. But she's going to be late.

"Your class is at eleven?"

"Yes," she gasps.

"You need to go."

"No!" Her lips find mine.

I kiss her then pull back. "It's 10:55."

"Can't be. We met at ten." She sinks against me, ear to my shirt. Like she's listening to a secret.

I show her my watch. Her eyes get round. She bites her lip. It's red and swollen.

The train ride is fifteen minutes, tops.

"No way!" She hides her smile.

I kiss her again. I fight my body and release her. I step back. "Go!"

She doesn't move. "When will I see you again?"

"Tomorrow." I blurt it. I'll leave for Brooklyn later or come home earlier. I'll figure something to tell Papi. "You have class?"

"Nope." She beams. "Just breakfast plans with Chrissy." She comes toward me again. I hold her at arm's length. "You're going to be late." I won't be able to let her go a second time.

"Hasta mañana," she says. She turns and runs. She stops at the gate. "Thank you!" She removes the poem from her pocket and presses it to her lips. Then she's gone.

FRIDAY, MARCH 10

ISA

I push open the door of the Capezio store and take off down Amsterdam, a bag with brand-new pointe shoes inside slapping against my hip. The air is cool on my face. I burst through the crosswalk at Sixty-Eighth just before the light changes. The weather gods have been kind these past few days, sending rain to wash away snow piles that looked like slushies covered in Oreo cookie crumble, and then sun to dry it all out. The weekend should be good too, which means Alex is going to get to play. I'm wearing my Chuck Taylors today because of him, though mine are tie-dyed pink and army green. I can't wait for him to see them. I can't wait to see him.

It's been seven days since he showed me where he's been hiding his poems. Six days since we last kissed, when I rode with him from Lincoln Center all the way to Riverdale and then he rode back with me down to Ninety-Sixth Street. *Kiss* doesn't seem like the right word though. A kiss shouldn't be enough to turn my insides into warmed honey. It shouldn't be enough to scramble my thoughts so all that's left is wanting more. But with Alex it is.

I only ride the fifth car from the front now, so I can search underneath the two-person seats for a small fold of paper. This afternoon, I found one. The poem is about his mami—about her noticing a difference in him. He describes her clever smile, her knowing eyes. Passing a gentle hand over his head, she asks when she's going to meet the girl responsible. Soon, he answers. Soon.

I swing my arms for speed, then fling out my hands and sail into a grand jeté right on Amsterdam Avenue. I clear two full squares of sidewalk. An old woman with a walker pulls up short as I land beside her.

"Sorry!" I don't stop. I can't. Alex will be coming back uptown when I'm done with class. I feel like Stravinsky's firebird in the "Infernal Dance," like I have no choice but to keep moving, even though I know in the end I'll die.

A bunch of guys in baseball caps circle a lamppost. They stop talking as I soar past. One separates from the others. His lip, split by a scar, lifts in a smile.

I smile back, my face warming. He's Alex's friend—Danny, I know his name from one of Alex's posts. I land in perfect fifth position. I twist around, my arms still moving to the music inside me.

"Danny, right?"

He nods, but steps back. One of the other guys punches his shoulder. Danny shoves him. He says something low in Spanish. I catch Alex's name and the threat to leave him alone—no, to leave me alone.

"Want to walk me to class?" I ask between breaths. "It's just a few blocks."

Danny's eyes grow big. One guy whistles. Another hoots. They can think whatever they want. I'd just like to get to know Alex's friend.

Danny glances to the boy leaning against the light, hands buried in his jean pockets. At his shrug and smirk, Danny tugs his cap down, buries his own hands in his pockets, and ambles toward me. I wait until the end of the block before asking how he is.

"Good?" His answer is a question. "You remember me?"

I don't know why he's surprised. "Why wouldn't I?"

He winces. "Sorry. For before. On the train." The scar on his lip darkens.

I shrug, showing him I've gotten past it. "Thanks." I don't tell him Alex already apologized plenty. "Great day, huh?" I change the subject just as he asks, "You seen Alex recently?"

"Yup." My hand strays to my coat, to where I've tucked the latest poem. I face Danny, walking backward, deciding I don't care if he sees my blush.

"You really like him." It's a statement, not a question.

I nod, unable to suppress my grin.

Danny nods back. He doesn't look away. "You're not going to hurt him?"

I laugh so loudly, Danny's friends from down the block turn around. "How would I do that?"

Danny shifts. The brim of his cap tilts down. He must be looking at my fist in my pocket, closed around Alex's words. "You're not just using him because of baseball?"

I mash my lips together and shake my head. I don't even know what that means. Would Alex be able to get me tickets to the Yankees or something? I don't ask because it doesn't matter. It's cute, what Danny's doing. It makes me like him—and Alex—even more. That they're watching out for each other.

I glance back at Danny's friends. A couple of the guys have broken off, and are walking in the same direction we are, on the other side of the avenue.

"Can I tell you a secret? If you promise not to tell Alex?"

Danny stares at me, saucer eyes blinking again.

I lean toward him. "I don't really like baseball. But I do like your friend. A lot. That last bit you can tell him." Danny grins. We turn on Sixty-Fifth and walk up the steps to the Library for the Performing Arts. "Hey, how come you're not in Brooklyn this afternoon training with Alex? Don't you guys usually go together?"

Danny stops abruptly. His face disappears under his hat as he examines the ground. He shrugs, glancing back to where his friends are waiting at the corner. "Yeah, I told those guys I'd hang with them."

"Isabelle?"

My breath turns to tacks in my throat. My mom stands above us, right beside the reflecting pool. She's clutching her leather bag against her jacket. A silk scarf flutters around her neck.

"Mom! What are you doing here?"

She taps the toe of her boot. Her narrowed eyes are pinned on Danny. "The Dean of Faculty invited me for coffee. I had some questions about the academic curriculum."

My heart beats like a thief who's been caught. Mom went to speak with Mr. Fairchild? Alone?

She comes down another step. "He invited me to observe one of your classes." The idea of Mom sitting in on a class makes me dizzy. Her sharp gaze swings to Danny. She draws her bag closer. She glares at Danny as if he's a monster, a murderer, an alien. She doesn't introduce herself or ask me to introduce her. I'm not sure if that's better or worse.

Tears prick my eyes. I fight them back and glance at Danny, offering him a silent apology. I've got to get Mom away before she embarrasses me more.

Danny gives me a faint nod. He lifts his fingers in a salute and backs off the steps. "If you see Alex before I do, tell him hi from me." He says it so quietly, I'm not sure Mom heard him.

Mom's heels stamp onto stone as she makes her way down to me. If lightning bolts could come from eyeballs, they'd be shooting down every single person around us. "Who was that?"

"No one. Just a friend," I answer.

"Is he a dancer too?"

"No. Just someone I met." I almost make the mistake of adding "on the subway."

She's glaring at Danny and the guys who are slapping his back and the top of his head. One of them yanks off Danny's cap and races away. Danny, laughing, takes off after him.

"You can't be friends with him. I don't want you talking to him or spending time with him again."

I swing back to my mom. "What?!"

"You know what he is, right?"

I stare at her, wondering what word she could possibly be thinking. A cheater, like her papi? If she says it, I'll scream.

"Those bandanas. They're all wearing them." Mom tracks the flash of red tied around Danny's arm. They're almost at the corner.

I frown at the implication. She thinks Danny's in some gang? Because of how he dresses and how he looks? A white-hot fire sears my chest.

"Boys like that are dangerous. Do you hear me? You're forbidden from seeing him again."

I nod. To let her know I heard her. I'm not agreeing to her ridiculous demand.

"Good," she says.

I stop breathing. Suddenly I'm terrified she heard what Danny said about Alex. I don't want to have to lie about him; I hadn't thought that far. But I don't see an alternative after this.

Mom digs in her bag for her cell. She squints at her screen. "I've got to go. I'm meeting a broker back home."

"Broker?" The word comes out as a croak. "We're selling the apartment?" I lean on the railing, clutching it so I don't fall. You'd think I'd be used to Mom's emotional whiplash by now.

"Yes," she sighs. "Your father doesn't think we need to, but—don't get me started. I'll see you later." She air-kisses my cheek as if we're girlfriends instead of mother and daughter. As if we were talking about shopping instead of leaving our home. As if we weren't just talking about innocent boys and racial profiling.

She clops down the steps. "Oh, and I meant what I said. I don't want you near that boy or anyone like him."

She doesn't wait for a response. Which is good. I can't say anything. I feel like a hand's closing around my throat. I sink down on the steps and take out Alex's poem. I lay the paper flat on my thigh and smooth out the creases. I read it until my tears dry. Until all I can do is smile.

SATURDAY, APRIL 8

ISA

I wait in my regular spot, under the ESTIMATED TIME OF ARRIVAL sign, right where the fifth car will stop. My stomach feels like Mother Ginger's skirt from *The Nutcracker*, squirming with children ready to leap out and dance. I bend to touch my toes, stretching the backs of my legs. The digital readout says 3 MIN. Three more minutes to wonder. I never know if the train I'll get will have one of Alex's poems.

He's been writing a lot, he says. It helps him focus for his games. I love finding the secret notes meant just for me. Whenever Alex gets on the 1 train, either to or from Brooklyn, he leaves me a poem. If there's already one there, if I haven't found it yet, he gets off and waits for the next train. The other week he sent me a DM showing him in front of three different cars. He wanted to know if I'd stopped taking the subway. I told him about our rehearsals for the spring performance. Chrissy, Kevin, and I have been riding home together, and I'm not about to look for Alex's poems when they're with me. I've been spending time with Mom too, looking at apartments. But Alex doesn't need to know that.

The shriek of steel announces a train. I count the cars that pass, just to be sure.

Students crowd the entrance. They're singing "You Don't Know Me," Leo Xiao's hit single. They're probably going to Leo's free concert in South Street Seaport, the one Alex suggested we meet at since he only has a Sunday game this weekend. But I have rehearsal.

"Excuse me. Pardon me." My heart is doing its own sautés as I push into the car. I make my way to the bench by the MTA poem poster. Two ladies, one with white hair, one with magenta, are having a full-body conversation. They're Dominican—I can tell by their accents. They don't look like they're getting up anytime soon.

I have a plan for this. I take out my tiny notebook, along with the fancy pen Dad brought me back from a business trip years ago. I pretend to write. I drop the pen. It rolls under their seat.

"Oh, oops! I'm so sorry. Lo siento. May I?"

It's an odd request and the women regard me with weak smiles. One moves her shopping bag, and I squat and peer behind their legs. The pen is way back there. The other woman's leg is blocking where the note would be.

I straighten and ask, in Spanish, if they wouldn't mind standing for a moment at the next stop. They give each other a look but nod and then go on complaining about their hairdressers.

At Eighty-Sixth Street, the women rise. I duck under the bench, murmuring apologies. I snatch my pen and feel behind the hard border of plastic below the seat. My heart pitter-patters as my fingers press against tape. I rip off the note, tuck it into my palm.

"Thank you!" I show the ladies the pen and wedge myself into the corner, where fewer people can see me. I unfold the note, careful not to tear the paper.

"Would you like me to read it to you?"

I crumple the poem to my chest, stifling a gasp.

Alex is in front of me, lips lifted in that half smile. His eyes dance with amusement.

I thought he had practice this morning. I want to ask how he got here and why he didn't text he was coming. Something inside me shifts. The stress of Dad always in the apartment on his computer, of furniture being appraised and marked for sale, of our car being sold—it all just goes away, like it no longer belongs to me, like it was never there in the first place.

Alex steps closer, and tugs the paper from my fingers. I don't wait for him to take my hand. I press against him, foot to foot, knee to knee, cheek to his chest. He smells like fresh air and pine-scented soap. I forget about yesterday's rehearsal, when I stumbled out of the fouetté en tournant and almost fell. I forget about the shouting coming from Mom and Dad's room as I left this morning.

Alex recites the poem, whispering near my ear.

"Thank you." I breathe him in.

His hand settles on the back of my head, just below my bun. "For what?" he asks.

"For finding me. For the poem. For this—" I lift onto my toes until my mouth meets his.

Alex kisses me until my hands are sliding under his shirt. He takes my wrists, puts my hands on his face. His smile blinds me. "You're welcome," he murmurs. "Creative, by the way. Getting to the poem."

I grin back at him. The women are still talking, but they're both watching us. I wave at them. They wave back. One of them gives me a thumbs-up. At the next stop, they shuffle off, the other giving two thumbs-up.

"I think they like you," I say as Alex leads me to the now-vacant seats.

"And they didn't even read my poetry."

"Darn, I should have showed it to them. Speaking of which, did you submit to that online literary magazine I sent you?"

He runs a hand down his leg. His other hand clasps mine. He gives a noncommittal tilt of his head.

"Come on, you have to! Your work is amazing." I've been telling him this all along. I'm not sure why he doesn't believe me. Alex leans down and touches his lips to the tip of my nose.

"I know you think they're good. It's just . . . you're biased."

"I may be biased. But that doesn't mean I'm wrong. If you're not going to believe me, we need external validation."

"How about we make a deal?" Alex tucks his arm around my waist. "I'll submit to the magazine after you come to Brooklyn and the Heights. And after you show me Park Ave. I've always wanted to see a fancy Upper East Side apartment." He gives me a playful wink.

Alex has invited me to meet his parents before. He's hinted about meeting my family too. We'd be able to spend more time together if it overlapped with family time. But I don't want him to see a room that doesn't look like mine anymore, the pictures on my desk and the figurines on my bookshelf moved by the realtor for the people traipsing through. I don't want him to see my dad stressed and rumpled. And I don't want him to meet my mom at all. If he knows about everything that's going on with my family—everything that's wrong with it—it will become part of us. I want to protect what Alex and I have. I want to keep it separate. And I can't meet Alex's family if I'm not going to let him meet mine.

I keep my smile steady as the deep bass of a speaker takes over the car. Four guys in sweats skip down the aisle, asking passengers to pull their legs in and pick bags off the floor. The guys move together, shoulders and knees bouncing to the beat, until they form a straight line. Arms jut out, necks roll. They side-kick in unison. I recognize the routine from a Beyoncé video, but they're dancing to Drake's latest hip-hop track. One breaks off, runs and does a flip in the air, narrowly missing the bar. The crowd *ooohs*. Another dancer drops to the floor and windmills right in front of the doorway. The Leo Xiao fans holler. Drake stops rapping and the guys run through the car, caps out, collecting money.

"Is that a no?" Alex is leaning over, elbows on his knees. He's watching me as I watch the guys rack up a good amount of change and bills. I open my wallet. All I have are some singles. I hope Alex doesn't notice.

Alex's thigh knocks mine. He wants me to look at him. I'm afraid if I do, he'll see right through me. He'll know everything at home is a mess. And I don't want him to.

The song starts over. I stand and pull myself into a long stretch, hands to the ceiling, fingers glued together. I sway to the side. My arms swing, snap together. I turn, thrust my hips, pump my arms, just like Beyoncé does it. I'm better than those guys. I've been classically trained. My eyes stay on Alex. I ignore the rhythmic clapping that surrounds me. I ignore the guys beside me, doing the moves, copying my technique. My blood roars in my ears. Sweat drips down my chest, my back. I keep dancing. For Alex. For me.

I'm doubled over in front of him when the music stops. The car goes crazy. Alex pulls me up. He isn't smiling. A few of the performers pat my back. I hear, "Damn, you good, girl." And "Who said white girls can't dance?" They do another round of collections as Alex leads me off the train onto the subway platform.

I'm still pumped from the music, from the dance. This is what I want to feel. This is how he makes me feel. At the gate, I kiss him hard. He doesn't stop me. But he doesn't kiss me back. Not the way I want him to.

I know I've hurt him. I know a little dance, a little fun, isn't going to make it right.

"Will you come to see me? At my performance?" I give him the date. "I don't have a big part, just a semisolo. But it's famous ballet—a great story, you'd love it. My parents will be there, and you can meet them ... if you want to, I mean—" Alex cuts me off. He kisses me, the way I want him to.

SUNDAY, APRIL 16

ALEX

I raise the glove to my chin. The leather smells warm, though the air's cold. Red seams dig into my fingers. I huff out a breath. My knee comes up. I pivot and reach for the catcher as if I can grab his hat. The ball thumps into Bryan's mitt. Papi nods at me. I smile before I can stop. The batter drops the bat and walks off the field.

Papi's friend, the other coach, mutters something I can't hear. He stays behind the chain-link fence. Papi asked him to bring his best hitters, the ones he's considering for the travel team this summer. I've struck all four of them out. And the sun's not even above us yet.

Papi waves me in. Bryan stands and stretches his legs. He keeps looking toward First Ave. He's wondering if Danny's gonna show. He'll be an hour late if he does. Danny doesn't have to come. But he does if he wants to stay on Papi's team. Danny hasn't been playing well for AHH. He's missed too many practices. At least he's been playing. At least he's trying to stay part of one team.

I glance at First Ave too. Someone's coming. But it's not Danny. It's another of Papi's friends. He's got three players with him.

Papi's hand goes up for the new coach. He walks past me to meet them. Robi runs onto the field. He's been practicing swings behind the fence this whole time. Robi drops into the dirt beside Bryan, legs as wide as he can get them. Bryan ribs him a little, then tosses him his glove. Robi sinks into a squat. He does the drills Bryan taught him. Robi's always wanted to pitch.

Papi won't let him. This spring he started following Bryan around, learning all he could. He's asked if I could pitch to him about a thousand times. I only ever do it when Papi's not watching.

"Yefri! ¿Cómo tu 'ta?" Papi knocks the coach's shoulder. Yefri introduces his players. Papi shakes their hands.

"Oye." The other coach, the one still hanging on the fence, calls me. He shows me his fist, taps his chest with it, and nods.

I nod back.

Bryan's watching. He turns so the coach can't see him. He grins and sticks out his tongue. He's probably swinging his eyebrows but I can't tell because of the mask. He's been in a good mood since he and Julissa patched it up.

Robi snatches the mask off Bryan and drops it on his own face.

"Throw me one!" He runs toward first.

Papi's coming our way. He's got an arm around Yefri. I shake my head at Robi.

"You heard from Danny?" Bryan creeps close.

I shake my head again.

"You think he's with—"

"Not now." I tilt my head toward Papi. He's still chatting with Yefri about which positions to put us in. They can hear us.

I check my watch. I got to be on the train by four if I want to meet up with Isa. She's been practicing nonstop since she was named understudy for one of the leads. She's probably backstage right now, sewing ribbons on her shoes for her tech rehearsal. It's crazy that dancers do that. They've got these rituals to prepare their shoes, kind of like what we do to our mitts. Isa's eyes got this crazy glint when she told me about it. Like she'd just had a double espresso. And an energy drink. They get like that whenever she talks about dance. Or her brother. I wonder if that's what they look like when she talks about me.

"¡Ále!" Papi's shout jabs me in the back. The players are fanning out to the field. "What you waiting for? Let's go. Yefri will play right field."

I turn toward the pitcher's mound.

Papi's yelling at Bryan about his mask. Robi is flying back from first, kicking up dust. He calls, "Papi! Papi! Papi! When Bryan hits, can I catch?"

Papi says something I don't hear. Robi scuffs to the bench.

I raise my glove. I watch Papi's hands, changing my grip to what he wants.

A white and blue car rolls by. It stops as I wind up to pitch. They can't rattle me. Not when I've got my mitt and a ball in my hand. One of the cops nods as I strike the first batter out. They're cruising for Saturday trouble. They won't find any here. We just playing ball.

Out of seven hitters, only one makes contact. It's a foul. Bryan straightens. He takes off his pads. He's the last in the lineup. Papi takes Bryan's mask and props it on his head. Robi barrels out from the bench. He jumps up and down. His hands pray against his chest. I jog to home.

"Come on, let him catch. It's only gonna be three throws." I give Bryan my wicked smile, but he's looking at First Ave again, waiting for someone who's not coming.

"Please! Please! Please!" Robi hops like a toy with too much battery.

Papi ignores him.

"Pedro! ¡Déjalo!" Yefri shouts from right field.

"Yeah. Let's see your other boy play." Papi's friend, his players call him Mr. Jhonny, rattles the metal fence.

Papi hands the mask to Robi. He doesn't look at him. I grab the pads. I get on my knees to strap Robi in. I make sure the mask fits good and tight.

"Remember what I told you?"

"Yup." His braces shine in the sun. "Toes out. Chest up. And don't forget to widen your feet."

I tap the side of his head with my glove.

Papi comes up as I back away. "Just 'cause it's your brother, I don't want you easing off your pitches."

"What about Bryan? He *is* my teammate. Hitting a homer would be good for his confidence, no?"

Papi sniffs. He doesn't like humor. He takes his place behind Robi and I go back to mine. He wants me to throw a fastball. For the first time, I don't do what he asks. I throw a changeup, and not just because it'll be easier for Robi to catch. Bryan can't hit them.

The ball cuts through the air. It drops into Robi's glove. Robi jumps up and hurls it to me. Light flashes off his smile. He did it just fine. But Papi's on him, telling him his chest was too low, his feet were too close.

A couple of moms with babies pass by. They're frowning at Papi. The strollers pick up speed as they power walk away.

Why is Papi always so hard on Robi? He's hard on Bryan, on Danny, on me. But never as hard as he is with Robi. I like that Papi saves time for me. He didn't when I was little. It wasn't until I hit my first ball past that dented orange garbage can beyond the outfield that things changed. I was nine. A full year younger than Robi is now. I keep wondering when Robi's gonna hit his ball out of the park.

Papi strides toward me.

"What did I ask for?" His jaw is clenched.

"It was the wrong call," I mutter.

"What you say?"

I drop the ball into my mitt. I palm it then drop it again. "Bryan didn't hit it, did he?" It's not like this is even a real game. We're all trying out to be on the same team.

"When you here, I'm coach. You do what I tell you." Papi storms back to Robi. Robi's grinning, already in position.

Bryan taps the bat to the base. He swings it into position.

Papi's fingers dance. He wants me to do the four-seam. Fine.

I draw my knee to my chest. I hinge forward. The ball shoots from my shoulder, from my arm, from my fingers. It cracks against the bat. The ball rockets upward. It's in front of home plate.

"Go! Go!" Papi yells.

Bryan streaks for first.

Robi staggers off his knees. His mitt is out. He's peering up. Sunlight and metal flicker from his teeth.

The ball plummets. It bounces off the pad at Robi's shoulder.

Papi curses. He's so loud, Bryan turns around.

Papi pushes Robi. It's like a truck pushing over a paper stop sign. Robi hits the dirt with an *oomph!*

"¡Levántate!"

Robi gets up as Papi asks.

Papi's hand is on Robi's chest. He's driving my brother backward. They crash against the fence.

I drop my glove. I run for home. I get there just as a man with a badge rounds the corner.

Papi's yelling. His fists are out. He's not going to hit Robi. He's just angry. The police don't know that. All they see is a brown man losing control.

"Papi! ¡Tranquilo!" I put myself in front of him. I take his shoulders with my hands. Bryan gets to Robi. He brings him to the other side of the fence.

"You know how to catch the ball! I teach you that! I no teach you to drop it!"

"He's just learning." My voice is low.

"You never did anything so stupid." Papi spits into the dust. "Even when you were five."

"Is there a problem here?" One cop is at my side. The other, a lady, is talking to Robi.

Papi's chest is like a train engine without a brake. I shake my head. Papi better keep quiet.

"Good afternoon, officers." Yefri arrives from right field. His chest is going pretty quick too. "How can we help?" He has no accent when he speaks. Unlike Papi.

The officers say other parents in the park have issued complaints. They want to take Papi to the precinct to ask him some questions.

Papi can't go there. He's not good in those situations. He's not good with authority unless the authority is him.

"You baseball fans?" Yefri asks them.

Of course they are.

Yefri puts his hand on the back of Papi's neck. Papi's looking at the water. He squints against the glare. His mouth is like a line between bases.

"Well this here's a former Yankee. He and Jeter were rookies together."

I see it happen. The change Papi always talks about. When folks learn to know you as someone more than what their eyes tell them.

The creases on the officer's brow relax. He smiles an openmouthed smile. "No way, man. What's your name?"

Papi's still gazing out at the harbor. "I only played one year."

"Eighteen months and twenty-six days," Yefri corrects. He doesn't tell them how many games Papi played. He's trying to inflate what Papi did. Yefri whips out his wallet. Papi's rookie card is tucked behind his driver's license. Papi's got a few in his desk. I've never seen anyone else with one.

What would Isa think if she were here? Would she see why baseball is important for someone like me? That it makes folks see me as more than just another moreno?

"Wow. That's cool, man." The officer gives Papi a fist bump.

"You see, my friend here's passionate about the game, ya know? Sometimes a little too passionate when he's coaching his own kids." Yefri's smiling like he's got tickets to give away.

The officer glances at me, at Bryan, and Robi. The other players know enough to stay away. "These are your kids, sir?"

Sir. The cop didn't use that word before.

"The little one, and this one here." Yefri pats my shoulder. "This one's got a future. They call him Big Papichulo because of his hitting and because, well, look at him, he's a handsome guy."

That nickname makes me want to gag. But I smile at the cop like he's my favorite teacher.

"And he can pitch too. Did you see him play?"

The officer nods. "His pitching isn't bad. Can I see him hit?"

All eyes turn to me. At least they're off Papi.

What would the cop think if Isa were standing with me? If she were holding my hand? Would he still look at me the way he's looking at me now? The way he did when he saw me pitch? Or would his look be different? Like the lion guy with the suit on the subway?

Yefri hands me the bat. Mr. Jhonny gets out his glove and takes the ball from me. Yefri signals him to throw a regular two-seamer. Something easy enough to hit. Mr. Jhonny nods, but he does something different. He throws me a slider. No matter.

I slam it like it's the part of Papi I want to get rid of, the anger he holds inside.

José in left field turns and runs. He passes the dented orange trash can.

Papi's not looking out at the water anymore. He's looking at me.

• • •

It's after two when we get back. Yaritza meets us at the door.

"How'd it go?" Her eyebrows lift over her smiling eyes.

Robi walks up the steps and into her arms. He hides his face in her shirt. His shoulders shake like he's cold. Yaritza glances at me. She doesn't look at Papi who goes to the kitchen and opens the fridge. She purses her lips at the sharp *snap* of a can opening.

I pick up the glove Robi dropped on the stairs. "It smells delicious. Tamales?"

Yaritza's smile comes back. But only to her mouth.

She takes my sleeve as I go by. "Did you ask him yet?"

I shake my head. Her eyes narrow as she strokes Robi's hair. We're both thinking the same thing: *Later.*

"I found one that would work. I pressed it for you," she whispers.

I kiss her forehead. I kiss Robi's hair.

After I shower, I set the table and help put the food out. Robi pokes at his meal. He eats enough to not draw attention.

When Papi's belly is full, and Yaritza is sprinkling cinnamon on his café con leche, I ask if he has a suit I can borrow.

Papi puts down his cup. He looks at Yaritza. She turns her back and walks dishes to the sink. "What's it for?" he asks.

"A dance performance," I say. "Of a friend of mine."

Papi's eyes slide closed. He sips his coffee and grins. "A dance performance, eh? ¿Con una jévon?"

Isa isn't just a pretty girl. I don't want to tell him how much more she is until they meet her.

Yaritza slaps Papi's arm with the dish towel. "Déjale. The boy needs proper clothes. His old ones don't fit. Look at him, he grew un centimetro while we were eating."

"Es como su papá. Big and strong. Takes after me in other ways too, eh?" He winks.

"Está guapérrimo. Súper handsome. How they say—you'll have to be beating them off with the sticks?" Yaritza beams at me as she scrubs a plate.

"What do you mean, beating them away?" Papi drawls. "The way to deal with flies is to give them a taste of the honey."

Yaritza swats him again with the towel. Papi grabs hold of the end and pulls her toward him. She falls into his lap, giggling. Papi makes wolf noises as he kisses her neck. Robi brings his plate to the counter and leaves. I want to go after him. But I need that suit.

"Remember, only a taste." Papi tickles Yaritza. Her shrieks make him smile. "You need to save up for lo más importante, your games. Te lo prometo. They will be falling over themselves to get to you. Like this one here was." He kisses Yaritza again. "You'll get your reward. You'll see."

I shift in my seat. When his hand goes under her blouse, I look out the window. A father plays catch with a little girl in the yard next door. Her ponytail swings as she throws. I wonder if she and Robi are friends. I've never asked him about his friends. I never see any around.

Yaritza whispers in Papi's ear. Papi pulls her upright. He stands, one hand around her waist, the other massaging her back. They move to go upstairs.

"You know that's not why I do it, right? That's not why I play ball."

Papi stops and looks at me. Yaritza slips out of his grasp. He spanks her bottom as she scurries up the steps.

"Of course not. You play because you love it."

The stairs groan as he follows her up.

I go to check on Robi. He's curled on his bed, asleep, a manga under his hand. *Ace of Diamond* is written below the Japanese characters. I slip it out without waking him. I flip through animations about a boy who's a gifted pitcher. Papi's scrawl is on the inside cover. *For Alex.* It's dated the year I was in fifth grade. I don't remember getting it.

Robi's clock, a baseball player holding a bat and a glove, shows the glove near four, the bat at ten. I go to get my bag. I'll have to come back before Saturday to get the suit. I also have to tell Papi I won't be able to spend the night next weekend. I'll be with Isa.

A garment bag hangs on the front door. Below it is a bag with foil-wrapped tamales, enough for me to share with Bryan and Mami when I get home.

Yaritza is the best.

SATURDAY, APRIL 22

ISA

"He really is the hottest pianist. Don't you agree?" Chrissy peers through the curtain. "Remember that guy we had last year? The one who looked like he had measles on his face? I mean, come on. Ever heard of a dermatologist?"

I give her a distracted smile. "Yes, Kevin's skin is much better than that other pianist's." I'm running through the steps of my duet for about the fortieth time since finishing my makeup and trying to ignore what this performance means. Mr. Jeffries, Dad's connection on the Board of the Academy, said my acceptance would almost certainly be honored. But Monsieur Thibault, one of the directors, gets to make the final call and he'll be watching today. And then there's Alex. And my parents. I edge closer to Chrissy and glance through the curtains. None of them have arrived yet. I press my hand to my burbling stomach and pat my lips together to make sure my lipstick is still smooth.

"Don't do that. You're going to make it clump. Your face is perfect. Don't touch anything, not even an eyelash," Chrissy says.

Now I have an itch on my eye. I blink to make it go away.

Chrissy lets go of the curtain and glances at the backstage clock. She smooths out her skirt. "Hey, I've been meaning to ask you something. About me and Kevin." Her voice has dropped. She doesn't meet my eye.

"What? All's not paradise in the land of Chrissy and Kevin?" It's a thing Chrissy started. How in the land of Chrissy and Kevin there are no missed notes or false steps and everyone's breath smells of cinnamon Tic Tacs.

117

"No, everything's good." Chrissy fiddles with a piece of tulle. "Well, actually, maybe too good. We're, you know, at that point where we're ready to take it to the next level."

I do not know this girl who beats around the bush instead of saying exactly what she means, especially not in this department. I put a hand on my hip. I fake whisper, "You mean *S-E-X*?" I'd assumed she and Kevin were having sex already. Chrissy's the one who taught me all there is to know, including using double protection—she's been on the pill since she was twelve when her gynecologist prescribed it for massive period pains. I've only ever had time for two things besides dance: family and school. Chrissy's two things have always been boys and more boys. I never wanted to be like Chrissy. I never thought I was missing out. Until now. Until Alex.

Chrissy motions me off the stage. More dancers pass us, rolling their heads and stretching their arms as they walk. Chrissy draws me to the pulleys in the back that control the skrims. Bert, the props manager, isn't in his chair.

"OK, spill it," I say. "Don't tell me you're not attracted to Kevin. I see the way you look at him."

Chrissy's peeking around, maybe to see if we're alone. "That's just it. Have you ever seen me look at another guy the same way?"

"No." It's the truth. The longest Chrissy was with a guy before Kevin was a week. "So, what's the problem?"

Chrissy shakes her head. She picks at her fingernail. "It's just. He doesn't know about my party past. He thinks I'm a *virgin*." She says the word like it's a swear.

I try not to laugh. Chrissy grabs my arm. Her nails dig into my skin.

"It's not funny," she says.

"Sorry, you're right. So, what are you going to do?"

"I don't know! What do you think I should do?"

"Has he asked you? Have you told him you're a"—I look around for Bert—"a virgin?"

"No. It's like the idea that I'm not never crossed his mind. At first I was offended. Did he think me a novice based on my kissing? But then he was like"—her voice gets all gruff—"'I can't believe someone with such little experience knows how to handle—'"

Bert walks by.

Chrissy's words become a hiss. "Certain anatomic parts that sound like *peanuts*."

I press my lips together so I don't laugh.

"I just never corrected him," Chrissy continues.

"Ten minutes, ladies," Bert calls to us.

Chrissy pulls me toward the front of the stage.

"So don't tell him," I say. "Kevin clearly has some cute little maiden perception of you in his head. Why take that away from him?"

Chrissy faces me. "You sure? You don't think I should just tell him?"

"You can, but it might backfire. Not that your sexual history is something to be ashamed of, because it's not. You know I support you and you're my hero—" I take a breath. "But . . . do you think Kevin will want to hear about all of that?"

Chrissy's hands circle her tiny waist. "No, I think hearing about it will hurt. That's why I haven't told him."

I shrug. "So, listen to your gut."

Mia, the senior who's playing Giselle, whisks by, holding her voluminous skirts off the floor. "Are you ready to jump in? Should I twist my ankle or anything?" She makes a face like someone bonked her on the head. We've spent a lot of time together these past weeks. She even stayed late two nights to help me with some of the more difficult transitions. Just in case.

I blow her a kiss. "Merde!" I call out. Mia taught me that. It's what all the French ballerinas say instead of "Break a leg."

"OK," Chrissy breathes. "I won't tell him." She leans forward to sneak another glimpse at the audience. "Oh, there's my mom. I don't know why she insists the balcony has the best view. You're so far away. Where are your parents sitting?"

"Center orchestra." I don't tell Chrissy about this morning's breakfast argument over apartment bids. Or that I left for the theater without anyone even noticing.

"I don't see your parents," Chrissy says. "But I do see Thibault."

I grab the edge of the curtain from her. The man who will decide my dance and academic fate for the next two years strides down the aisle.

"Don't worry," Chrissy says. "You'll make it in. I can't wait to be able to pester you during precalculus *and* pointe."

I don't answer her.

Alex is behind Mr. Thibault.

The fluttering in my stomach rises to my throat. I've never seen Alex in a suit before. I almost tear through the curtain, run across the stage, and leap off it. Alex would catch me. I know he would.

He's holding tulips, red with a blush of yellow at the tips, and reading the ticket I left for him at will call. Why didn't the ushers seat him? Two women, both in Chanel jackets, follow him down the aisle. They ask Alex something. Whatever he says makes them laugh. They point him to row G. As they walk to their seats, they turn to check him out again. I don't know why it makes me jealous—they could be friends of my mom's—but it does.

Alex waits for an older couple to stand. He dips his head, apologizing for having to slide by them. Alex is supposed to sit next to Dad. His seat is in the direct middle of the theater. The best spot in the house.

I told Dad last night that a friend might be coming. He assumed Alex is from Deerwood. I didn't correct him. I didn't tell him that Alex is more than a friend either, but I think he knows. Dad understands me that way. I didn't tell Mom anything. Dad guessed that too. He agreed she'd probably get worked up and ask a million questions. He knows I don't bring friends, other than Chrissy, home. I think he feels bad about it.

I'm banking on Mom being late, so they won't have a chance to talk much with Alex before the show. Alex is supposed to find me at intermission and afterward Alex and I are going out with Chrissy and Kevin, so there won't be time for a scene. Just a quick introduction. Still, I don't know how Mom will react. I never do. But the run-in with Danny showed me how bad it could be.

"Wait a minute, that's your man, isn't it?" Chrissy leans next to me. She lets out a low whistle. "My, but doesn't he clean up nicely. Even Monsieur Thibault is a fan."

I nod. My heart's thumping too fast for me to speak. Monsieur Thibault smooths down his goatee as he admires Alex. It all makes me want to go out there and throw my arms around Alex to show everyone he's taken. I don't even care if my parents are watching.

"How are things going in Isa and Alex land?" Chrissy's looking at me sideways. With her lips so red, her grin is like a superhero's.

"Good," I gush. "Very good." Alex is the one thing that's *all* good in my life right now. "His mom's making dinner for us next Saturday. And then he's taking me to Brooklyn on Sunday to meet his dad and stepmom and brother." Provided my family doesn't scare him away.

"Ooh. That sounds nice. Kevin and I will be in the Catskills at his parents' house next weekend. His parents won't be there, of course." She arches an eyebrow, then smiles as I glance back at Alex. She takes my hand. "I'm looking forward to tonight. Thank you for arranging for your dearest friend to spend more time with this boy who's stolen your heart."

SATURDAY, APRIL 22

ALEX

Coño, these seats are tiny. My knees are halfway up my chest. This would be a good stretch if I were a catcher. Next time I see Bryan, I'll tell him I know where he can go before the game. He'd love this place. Everybody looks so fine. He'd likely make a fool of himself panting after some of these ladies. Not that he'd make a move. He is so lost over Julissa. He was complaining about all the weeks we'll be away this summer traveling to upstate New York, New Jersey, Ohio, Pennsylvania, even Georgia, all in that big Chevy van Papi bought a few years back. I haven't told Isa about travel ball. I don't want to think about all that time apart.

I rest Isa's flowers below my seat. The sleeves of my jacket ride up. I tug them down. Being bigger than Papi should make me smile. But everyone who looks at me has got to know this suit isn't mine.

There are still empty seats on either side of me. Two have to be for Isa's parents. Isa apologized she wouldn't be there to introduce us. I told her not to worry. I know how to introduce myself. I open the program. Prints from my fingers mark the glossy cover. OK, maybe I am a little nervous. Maybe I wish I'd met her parents earlier, when Isa was with me. I flip through advertisements for watches and cars and cruises until I find the part that lists the cast. I find Isa's name. She would like to thank her family for their support, her mom, her dad, and Merrit. She also thanks *A*, for everything. I shut the program. I straighten my tie and make sure my coat is covering my shirt, covering my heart that's beating mad fast. Isa's parents are going to read that. They're going to know I'm *A*.

A man and a woman come into my row. The woman is tiny with dark hair piled on top of her head. She could pass for Cuban, but Isa said her mom was blond. The man is blond, tall and good-looking. The only things that keep him from looking like a Viking are his glasses and suit. A suit that doesn't pull tight across his shoulders. A suit that looks like it was made just for him.

I wipe my hand on my pant leg and stand. I watch their faces, but they're not looking at me.

"Hello," I say. The man gives me a curt nod. The woman looks at me then looks away. She doesn't say anything either. I sit back down when they sit. They don't speak, to each other or to me. They can't be Isa's parents, right?

I clear my throat and lean forward. "You know anyone dancing in the show?"

The woman doesn't look up. The man puts a hand to his mouth like talking to me has to be a secret.

"Our neighbor's daughter, Cecilia, is a Wilis."

I don't know what that means but they're not Mr. and Mrs. Warren. Isa's parents must be on my other side.

A family passes in front of us, the boy grumbling as he takes his seat. The mother hushes him and says she expects him to behave. He's got braces, just like Robi. Only none of them look like they could be part of my family. They could be descended from Vikings too.

I look down at my program to see what a Wilis is. I don't want to think about Robi asleep on his bed, tears staining his cheeks. I don't think about the phone call with Papi, the one where I thought he was going to apologize but instead he told me I'm easy to coach because I take direction and have natural talent. Robi, he said, is stubborn. Robi doesn't listen. And he's just not good enough. He told me my little brother is trying to be something he's not, something he's never going to be.

I reread the first two lines of the synopsis. Some great lord, who's already engaged to another lord's daughter, falls in love with a peasant, Giselle. The lord disguises himself so he and Giselle can be together. In the Middle Ages people didn't marry between classes. Even now, giving up all your riches to be with someone you love would be impressive.

A chime rings. The lights dim halfway. People hurry to their seats. My pulse pounds in my palm where it grips the empty armrest beside me. Two of those people have to be Mr. and Mrs. Warren. I make myself read the rest of the first act. The disguised lord is outed by another peasant and is forced to admit he's a fraud and is promised to another. In a fit of grief, the beautiful Giselle dances until she dies. The heroine of this supposed romantic ballet *dies*. In the first act. At least in *Romeo and Juliet,* Shakespeare doesn't kill off the lovers until the end.

"You must be Alex." A man sinks down next to me. He holds out his hand. His smile is a smaller version of Isa's.

I go to stand but the lights disappear. "Hello. Nice to meet you." I shake Isa's father's hand while sitting down. It's difficult seeing as I can barely move.

"I'm Clifton. Glad to meet you," he says in a low voice.

The woman beside him has yellow-gold hair. She's frowning but still, I see Isa in the shape of her face, the high cheekbones and small chin. I want to introduce myself to her. Only she's not looking at me. She's looking at the stage.

"Mrs. Warren?"

She turns. The curve of her mouth deepens to a full-on grimace. She stares at my extended hand. Her forehead wrinkles and she shrinks back, as if I'm offering her something unclean, like a dirty tissue.

The music starts up.

Mr. Warren leans forward, putting himself between us. "It was so nice of you to come watch Isa." He's so quiet I can barely hear him.

My stomach clenches. Did Isa's mother really just not want to shake my hand? I pull at my jacket. I straighten my shoulders. Fabric creaks. Coño. Did it just rip?

A phone lights up Mrs. Warren's face. She stares at her screen, then stands. She pushes past the other people in the row.

"Elisa?" Mr. Warren calls after her. Isa's mother strides out of the auditorium.

Isa's father's cell vibrates. He juggles it out of his pocket. As he reads, he gets this pained look. Like he's sliding a mitt over open blisters.

"I'm so sorry, we have to go. I hope to see you again." He follows his wife out before I can say anything. Their empty seats look like black holes. Sweat pools in my palms. The inside of my mouth is dust and sand. I can't even swallow. The people behind me must be wondering what I did to scare Isa's parents away.

The curtain rises. The huts have real hay for roofs. A donkey and two sheep are tied up beside them. Behind a tree, the lord—his name is Albrecht—changes out of red pants and a navy hunting jacket into the dull brown clothes of the other peasants. The assistant takes the lord's sword and his fancy clothes and hides them under some hay. Albrecht walks out and joins a village dance. He pairs himself with Giselle. It's a complete joke. Even in the clothes, you can tell he doesn't belong. The way he moves, the way he smiles. He's as different from the peasants as the donkey that's chewing hay from the roof of one of the huts. Giselle doesn't see it. They kiss and she leaps the length of half the stage. She twists, her head and arms extending back to him. How can she think they could ever be together? They can't be something they're not.

It's like Isa and me. Isa didn't want me to meet her parents—it's clear now. She didn't tell them my family's Dominican and that I'm not from Park

Ave. It was plain in their faces. The usher and the dark-haired woman in my row looked at me and turned away. They saw nothing worth their time. And what about that lion-faced man and all the others on the subway who saw me with Isa? Were they looking at me like I'm looking at Giselle and her lord? Like they know it doesn't matter what we feel for each other because it's never going to work out?

The rich folk appear on stage. Albrecht hides. Giselle bows to a woman in a red gown. Two peasants rush to the center to dance for the lords. Isa is one of them. Even in her brown smock, she shines. Legs, impossibly long, lift and spin. Her arms are wings, wrapping air around her as she leaps and pivots. She lands soft as a bird. She's rare and remarkable—an eclipse, the sun coming out from behind the moon. I should look away. Or at least put on shades. I don't. I can't. I'd rather burn.

How could I have thought someone like Isa could belong with me?

The stage lights go down. Isa is gone. Giselle is dancing for her mother, trying to convince her the peasant she loves is true. I loosen my collar. It's hard to breathe. Isa and I, the story could be about us. We're too damn different.

"Excuse me." I duck through the row. I only step on three or four feet. I jog up the aisle. I burst through the doors as applause crashes around me.

SATURDAY, APRIL 22

ISA

I'm back in the dressing room, the one all the girls from Second Intermediate share. Lipstick and wands of mascara wave around heads angled inches from mirrors. Exclamations of "Did you see Mia's grande jeté?" and "Even Thibault was smiling!" peal like bells. A knock interrupts it all.

"Is everyone decent? Males entering." Kevin's question is met with shrieking.

Chrissy grabs me. "Come on!" she squeals. "He said males—plural!"

I shake free so I can secure my headpiece. I dash into the hallway after her. My semisolo is done and the director seemed pleased. I should be relaxed. But my gut is still quaking like I'm about to run on stage for a piece I haven't rehearsed.

Chrissy's holding Kevin at arm's length. She doesn't want him to mess up her skirt or her makeup. They're smiling like they're in a toothpaste commercial. There's no one else in the hallway who's not in tulle or dance tights. A salty taste fills my mouth. I've chewed my lip too hard. Is Alex still out there, cornered by my mom? What is she saying to him?

A figure steps into the light.

Alex!

I reach for him. The palm that meets mine is cool and clammy.

He studies our joined hands. His thumb strokes a slow line down my finger.

"Well? What did you think?"

"Amazing." Alex's voice is rough. Like he's been shouting at a game. "Really?"

He only nods. He's still looking at our hands.

"Did you like your seat?" I wonder if he knows he had the best one. I wonder if he knows what I'm really asking.

His eyes find mine. He's still partly in shadow so the brilliance of them doesn't show. "They left. Your parents. Before the show even started."

I take a step back. "What?"

His hand squeezes mine. "I think it was because of me."

I shake my head. That can't be right. Dad promised he'd make everything OK. "Hold on." I leave Alex standing in the hallway. I go back into the dressing room. I pull my bag out of my locker, my phone out of my bag. There's a message from Dad.

Merrit's school called. He's fine but something's happened. We have to pick him up. Don't know more. Sorry.

Merrit's supposed to be studying for finals. It's why he couldn't come for the performance.

I make myself take a breath. And another. And another. Dad wrote that Merrit was OK. But this can't be good.

I put on my smile like I'm about to go back on stage.

Alex stands where I left him.

"Something came up. They had to go get my brother from school." It's not a lie. I'm just not burdening him with the whole truth. "It had nothing to do with you." I take his hand to prove it.

Alex's head is bowed, his chin resting on his chest. "Did you tell them what I look like? Before? Did you tell them I'm Dominican?"

"No! I would never do that. Why would that matter?" I mean what I say. He's got to know that.

Alex's eyes are fixed on me now. I can see the fire in them. But also, I see hurt and disappointment.

"Alex . . ." I try to thread our fingers. He doesn't let me. He removes his hand from mine.

He reaches in his jacket and passes me an envelope. My name is written on it.

"For after." His words are so curt, they feel like a slap.

I look back up at him. I bite my cheek again to hold back tears. "You're not staying? For the second act?"

He shakes his head. "Something came up." He doesn't look at me as he walks away.

SATURDAY, APRIL 22

ALEX

I punch my key into the lock as if it's my fist and the lock is the whole world. It sticks. I batter the door as if it's the world against me too. Mami comes running from her room. I didn't think she'd be home.

"¿Qué te pasó?" Her hand is on her chest. Her eyes widen at my ripped-open shirt. The collar was too tight. I couldn't undo the buttons.

She takes three quick steps. Her arms come around me. She holds on tight.

I drop my head onto the top of hers. The keys and my tie fall from my hand. I close my eyes.

I don't want to tell her what happened.

After a plate of coconetes from Sra. Hernandez and a cup of café, she asks me again.

I chew my cookie. I get up for a glass of milk.

I tell Mami about the performance. I pass her the program with Albrecht and Giselle. I tell her about Isa's parents and about people trying to be what they're not.

Mami listens. She flips through the photos.

"What about Isa?" she asks. "What do you feel about her?"

I don't answer. I inhale and exhale slow.

Mami sees my wet eyes. She goes to the living room. She returns with Neruda's book. She shows me a page. Poems, not just printed but written in the margins, at the top and the bottom. My words next to his.

"Does she feel the same about you?" she asks.

I swallow and look away.

"Falling in love, it is easy. Fighting for it, that is hard." Mami turns to the beginning of Neruda's book, to the inscription that starts, *Para mi amor.*

"Sometimes it is too hard." She waits for me to look at her. "Your papi, he wrote that. He gave me this book when I was nineteen. You were born a year later. And your papi, he was traveling. He was doing things he shouldn't. It was too hard for me to fight. I had to protect you."

I take the book from her. I thought it came from a used bookstore in Santo Domingo. That's what Mami had told me. Maybe it did. She never said who bought it.

I read the inscription again. He loved her. He really loved her. And she loved him. I know it because her eyes are wet now too.

"No sabia." I didn't know. I take her hand. I cover it in mine.

She lifts a shoulder, sniffs and looks at the ceiling. She waves as if to scatter smoke. She used to love cigarettes. Once, when I was little, I got a cold and wheezed. No more cigarettes after that, doctor's orders. Something else she gave up because of me.

"I'm sorry," I tell her.

Her fingers tighten. "Don't be sorry. I made my choice. You have to make yours."

She pulls away. She slides the ballet program in front of me. It's folded open to the dedication page. To where Isa thanks *A,* for everything.

"It is work, Ále. Only you can know if it's worth it."

SATURDAY, APRIL 29

ISA

I sit on the floor of my room, cross-legged. It's been a week since the performance, and I haven't heard from Alex once. I DM'd him two days ago, asking if he was OK. He didn't respond. I read the beautiful poem he gave me, and Chrissy found the tulips he forgot under his seat. I wish he hadn't left. I wish we'd gone to dinner as we'd planned. I would have convinced him my parents leaving wasn't because of him.

Papers lie around me, organized into three piles: what to keep, what to store, what to toss. They're mostly old school projects. In my hand is an acrostic poem about my brother from the fourth grade—Marvelous, Exciting, Righteous, Resourceful, Inventive, and Trim—decorated with flowers and hearts. I can't believe *trim* was the *T* word I used and that my fourth-grade self didn't think of *trustworthy* or *thoughtful*.

Someone knocks on my door.

"Come in." It's Dad—he's the only one who ever waits for my reply.

Dad pokes his head from behind the cracked door. He looks at the mess on my floor and runs his hand over his stubble. It's been four days since he shaved.

"How's it going?" he asks. He comes in and surveys my "toss" pile. It's about four times larger than my "store" pile and ten times larger than my "keep." He plucks up the report on top. His mouth widens into a smile under the blond and silver scruff.

"I remember this one. It made your mother and me crack up during your parent-teacher conference. I loved your use of exclamation points." He flips through some pages. "'*Your eye can work during the day and at night! A little hole, the pupil, opens and closes to let in the light!*' Poetic, informative, and very demonstrative of your unique voice. Mom took this as a sign you were meant to be a doctor. Look at this detail." He holds up the cover showing a cross-sectional diagram of the cornea, the lens, the retina, and the optic nerve, in crayon.

"Your mom loved these. Where are the rest? Your drawings of the inside of the stomach might have been the most disgusting ones you ever did. Are they still here?" He flips through the pile.

I shake my head. I don't remember the others. But I remember making books and bringing them to Mom. She always liked them. The predictability of her response was a relief. The voices she used for the different characters were always fantastic, actually. She was like a professional actor when it came to books, any book, not just the silly ones I made. It wasn't until eighth grade when I stopped asking her to read to me. Sometimes I wonder why I stopped. I wonder if things between us would be different if I hadn't.

"You know, I used to worry about you. You were always so grown-up, even as a little kid. You did a lot of things to try to please Mom, to keep her happy. You had that one friend, what was her name? With the curly brown hair and glasses?"

"Susana," I tell him.

"Yes! Susana! When the two of you were together, you would tear around the apartment for hours. Then one night at dinner Mom said she didn't like Susana. Was it because her hair was never combed?"

I lift a shoulder, even though I remember. It was because Susana threw her coat on the floor, and her socks didn't always match. Mom said not paying attention to your appearance and not taking care of your belongings showed lack of character.

"You never asked for a playdate with her again. Which was too bad, because with her, you acted like what you were—a little kid. Instead of trying to be a grown-up. Not that I'm saying anything against your mother. I'm sure she would have let you have playdates with Susana if you'd wanted to."

Dad's right. The problem was, I didn't want Susana to come over anymore. I was afraid Mom would say something to hurt her. And embarrass me. Even though Susana always loved my mom. Because she was funny. Because she said the most outrageous things.

Dad thumbs through the drawings. "Then in fourth grade, you wanted to try out for preprofessional dance at the studio. When Mom told you you'd have to give up swimming and gymnastics, you said you liked dancing more. Even when Mom made all those comments about how it's important to be well-rounded." Dad puts a hand on my head. "That's when I knew you were going to be OK."

I nod. I'm not sure what to say.

Dad's foot knocks the throw-away pile and papers slide across the rug. He bends down. "Awww. You can't get rid of this. *The Story of the Lost Cat* by Isabelle Warren." Dad starts to read. "'*Cleo was lost.*'" He shows me the pictures. "'*She called everywhere for Ella, her owner.*' I like how you got the comma correct here. Though you did spell everywhere with an extra *h*."

"I think I did that on purpose. For emphasis. Everywhere-eh."

Dad nods as if he never thought of this. "'*Ella looked everywhere for Cleo.*' See here, you spelled it correctly. No actually, you made it into two words. Every. Where."

"Dad!"

"'*Then Cleo saw Ella! Ella saw Cleo! They were together at last! The End.*'" He clutches the tiny book to his chest, his fingers framing the crayon drawing of Ella and Cleo hugging with hearts floating above them. "You can't throw this away." Dad draws a hand over his face. "It made me cry the first time I read it too."

"Dad, you did not seriously cry." I go to snatch the packet away. Dad steps back.

"It made me tear up. Really." He walks to the window. The sill is bare. The porcelain figurines of ballerinas, one on pointe, one stretching along a barre, and one doing a pirouette, are gone.

"Dad, I can't keep it. My 'stay' pile is already too big."

"My 'stay' pile isn't. I'll keep it for you." He doesn't turn around. I wonder if he's looking at the Chrysler Building. The Empire State is Mom and Merrit's favorite, but Dad and I love the arcs of triangular windows atop the Chrysler. At night they light up, each one a toothy beacon shouting out that this city is the greatest on earth. Because it doesn't matter where you come from. If you work hard enough, you can do anything. Become anyone.

"Isabelle," Dad says. "I'm sorry we have to move. And I'm sorry about our new apartment. That there are only two bedrooms."

I know what building he's looking at. It's not the Chrysler. It's the MetLife Building. His old offices are there.

"It's OK, Dad. I understand." It wasn't his fault he got fired. It wasn't his fault the stock market tanked and interest rates are rising. Or that the New York real estate market has softened and we're selling the apartment for much less than Mom wanted, so much less that we're barely getting anything back from the bank. And we've gotten no offers on the Hamptons house so we're stuck renting it out at cost for a year. Mom's told me all of it. Every gruesome detail.

"We're only moving ten blocks north," I add in my most cheery voice. Dad doesn't call me out on trying to sugarcoat it. We both know there's a huge difference between Park Avenue south of Ninety-Sixth Street and Park Avenue north of it where the Metro-North trains run aboveground. There's also a huge difference between a prewar co-op with doormen to get you taxis and bring up your bags and a rental with no staff other than a live-in super.

"Well, I should have prepared." Dad looks at the carpet. "I should have saved for a rainy day. Or better yet, a rainy year." He lets out a gruff chuckle. It's so forlorn, tears leak into my eyes.

"I was thinking..." Dad goes back to staring out the window. "It's important for you to have your own space. Despite what your mother suggested, with the divider, I'm going to ask Merrit to sleep on a pullout in the living room."

I wipe at my eyes, careful not to let Dad see me. "Dad. I don't mind. Really. We'll have a plastic wall between us for privacy. And Merrit's going back to college in the fall anyway. I'm sure of it."

"I hope you're right." Dad raises his head. Papers crackle as he unrolls the little book. He comes over and lowers himself next to me. "May I?" He motions to my "toss" pile.

I lift my hands. "Sure."

I take out the last set of files from my desk. Dad reads through the stories of my childhood, one by one. None make it back into the "toss" pile.

"Hey, how's that friend of yours? Alex?" Dad asks.

I pretend to scan the old *Pointe* magazine articles I'd ripped out and saved. "Um... He's good." I'm not going to tell Dad what happened. I don't want him to feel guilty about something else that isn't his fault.

"It was nice of him to come to your performance. I really am disappointed I didn't get to know him better. Hopefully when things settle down, you can bring him by."

"Bring who by?" Mom stands in my doorway.

My heart lurches. The shock of adrenaline burns my palms. The night of the performance, after Merrit and Mom had gone to bed, I found Dad in the kitchen staring into a glass of scotch. I asked him how it had gone with Alex. Dad told me he chatted a bit with him, but that Mom didn't even really see Alex because the lights were dim and she left so abruptly. I don't know if Mom noticed Alex at all. She's never brought it up. In a lot of ways, it's a relief.

"Oh, hi, honey. How did your call with the museum board go?" Dad is an expert at diversion.

Mom trudges into my room. She's wearing an old shirt of Dad's and a pair of workout leggings that are now way too loose. "I told them I was stepping down and that I was withdrawing our pledge. You can imagine how it went." She looks at her watch. "I've got another hour before I have to make the same speech again. I'm dreading telling the Bronx kids mentorship program that I can't give them the money I promised. A lot of those kids were like me."

"I'm sorry." Dad reaches a hand for hers.

She takes it and nods. "At least I don't have to tell anyone about Merrit and Princeton." Her half-hearted attempt at laughter dissolves and then she's scrubbing at her eyes and holding a hand to her mouth. Dad rises from the floor and folds her in his arms. He whispers, "I'm sorry," and "It'll be OK," again and again.

I stare at the article I'm holding and pretend to read as Mom's sobs die. She steps away from Dad, dabbing her face with her sleeve. She looks at me, as if only just remembering why she walked into my room. "Who were you talking about a minute ago?"

Dad answers before I have to. "Oh, just a new friend of Isabelle's."

I exhale slowly. Dad's a fan of minimizing the truth to keep the peace. I learned the strategy from him.

Mom's frown takes over. "Well, now's not a good time to bring anyone around. Not when our family is going through so much."

Dad glances at me. Is that apology in his eyes?

"Of course, Mom." Not that it matters anymore. Not when Alex won't even answer my messages.

After Mom and Dad leave, I pull a shoe box out from under my bed. It was from my first pointe shoes. I decorated it with metallic markers and glitter glue years ago, coloring in the long swirls of ribbon that circled all six sides. I lift off the cover. I pass my fingers through squares of paper that have been folded and unfolded so many times their corners are curved. Most are yellow. Some are white. Two were written on pink sheets. And right on top is the envelope from the other day.

I close my eyes and dig down deep. I pull out the winner and spread it flat. I trace the creases and read. I touch the spots where my tears made the ink run. I press my thumb over the *A* that's signed at the end.

I fold it up. I put it back. I slide the box deep under the bed so no one sitting on the floor will see it.

That box gets its own pile. The "stay with me always" pile.

● ● ●

The bass coming from Merrit's room shakes the walls. I feel it in my feet as I walk barefoot down the hall. I rap on the door. I rap again. When I pound, the music lowers.

"What?!" Merrit yells.

"It's me," I say back. The music quiets more.

"What do you want?"

"Can I come in?"

"Why? Do you want to have your eardrums blown?"

I chuckle, despite myself. Things can be in shards and Merrit will find a way to make me laugh.

"No. No eardrum shattering. I thought maybe you wanted some help."

A few seconds tick by. My hands start to sweat. I don't know if he's going to let me in or not.

The door cracks. Merrit leans out. He grabs the frame with his hand.

His other arm holds the door against his chest, preventing it from opening wider. He's trying to block me from seeing inside. But the bare mattress, the tumble of sheets, and blankets on the floor, covered with books and papers, a sneaker, a broken lamp, and the familiar red rectangular shape of his chess clock is enough for me to know it's bad.

"Why do I need help?" Merrit cocks his head. He doesn't brush away the hair that falls into his eyes. Like Dad, he hasn't shaved; but on him the result is different. Uneven wisps of blond fuzz mingle with patches of blotchy skin. It's like someone affixed tape to Merrit's neck and jaw and ripped it off, only the tape was missing large chunks of stickiness.

"Um, packing?" I say.

"I'm almost done."

"Really?"

"It's easy to pack when you're not taking anything with you." A clump of greasy hair parts and a light blue eye looks out at me.

"You're not taking anything?" I put a hand on my waist.

He straightens and lifts a finger, like he's about to recite in front of an audience. "Four outfits: three everyday, one special occasion. Four pairs of underwear. Four pairs of socks, matching of course." He glances down the hall and puts a hand to his mouth. "Because you know how Mom gets." He rams his shoulders back again. "A pair of sneakers, a pair of occasion shoes"—Merrit's eyebrows jump at that—"a pair of boots for the winter. Oh, and one hat."

He's speaking like himself. Which is good. It's really good.

"Only clothes then?" I ask. "What about your computer?"

He closes his eyes as if my question requires great patience. "I consider that an extension of my personal body. It doesn't need to be packed. It goes where I go. Along with my phone, of course. My watch. And . . . yes, that's it."

I almost ask him about the aviator sunglasses we bought together after

Thanksgiving. But I don't want him to think about Samantha. "How about toiletries?" I glance at his hair. "Shampoo?" His teeth aren't looking that great either. "Toothbrush?"

He reaches out with one arm and pulls me into a hug. The other still grips the door. "That's what I have you for. I can borrow yours."

I breathe through my mouth. He doesn't smell like magnolia and poppy detergent right now. "God, Merrit." I try to pull away. "When was the last time you showered?"

He holds me tighter. He tries to push my face into his armpit. He's joking, or at least I think he is, but I can't stop the panicked *thud* of my heart.

I shriek and pull free.

He retreats into his room. The door is now only wide enough to fit his face. It's squishing his cheeks together. "Don't know. Don't care. Come back on the day we're moving. Maybe I'll shower then." He goes to slam the door.

"Wait!" I shout.

The door is an inch from closing. It widens half an inch. I'm both surprised and grateful he listened to me.

"What about your school books?" I ask. "Don't you still have final papers to write?"

He gives me six more inches. His nose and mouth pop out and he regards me with open irritation. "I'm not going back. Not after the way they treated me. And by *they*, I don't only mean the president, and the dean of the School of Engineering. I mean my so-called friends and colleagues, Larry the Louse and Derek the Dick, who sold me out and took my only umbrella when the proverbial shit hit the fan. I mean, they were right, I was the mastermind behind reMAKE, and I did accomplish virtually all the programming on my own. But they were the marketers. They introduced the app to the lacrosse team and the basketball team and the swim team. They were the ones who highlighted that you could secretly record anybody, then change what that person said to whatever you wanted. And even though I know which jocks posted that video of Dean Winters making those inappropriate sexual remarks about her students, because I traced it back to their phones, the school didn't want to hear it. They didn't want to have to suspend their star players. But someone like me? I'm expendable."

Merrit's cheeks are flushed. There's spittle on his lips.

I'm afraid to say anything. I'm afraid to move. Mom told me Merrit needed a break. I figured it was the stress of finals. Mom didn't say anything about getting kicked out or about an app where you can control what people say and do.

Merrit blinks when I blink. The fevered glaze clears from his eyes.

"Um—so it's like an app to make fake video? Like that Obama clip Jordan Peele posted online?" I ask very quietly.

My brother draws an exaggerated breath. "It was intended for self-help, to allow you to create the best, most highly polished version of yourself. For when your social media interactions really matter. Like say, you're trying to get back together with someone. Or maybe you want to put a video of yourself and all your attributes on LinkedIn. But yes, reMAKE has that same capability."

Music is still on in his room. But it's background noise. Like the rattle and hum of the subway when you're inside it.

Merrit watches me, his brow still gathered in anger. I nod and drop my gaze, trying to process all that he's told me.

He says more softly, "I'm not saying I won't go back to college. Just not that one. In light of our current familial fiscal crisis, this might not be the worst thing." His door shuts with a *click*.

I catch tears on my fingertips before they hit my cheeks. The pound of Merrit's music ratchets up. I stumble toward Mom and Dad's room, my hand leaving a damp trail across the bamboo frond wallpaper.

Dad's coming out just as I reach the door. I smile really big, pretending nothing is wrong. Dad and I, we're the ones who have to stay positive. No matter what.

Dad shakes his head. "She's sleeping."

He sees my smile wobble. We both know what that can mean.

"She's taking her pills. I counted them," he says. "She's doing what she's supposed to."

"And Merrit?" I look up and beat my lashes like the wings of butterflies. No tears will get through.

Dad sighs. "He's got an appointment this week."

"Good." I press my lips together so Dad doesn't see them tremble.

Dad touches my head. He goes into the kitchen.

I sink onto my heels, curling into a ball. Bamboo ribbing digs into my shoulders. The familiar sensation gives me the strength to make it to my room. I collapse on my bed. I hang over the side. I pull out the pointe shoe box and one of Alex's poems.

FRIDAY, MAY 5

ALEX

I lean against the kitchen counter. Empty bottles of Corona Light fill a recycling bag at my feet. Romeo Santos blasts from speakers in Julissa's room. Julissa's older sister, Ramona, is in there with her boyfriend. Bryan and Julissa are in the living room, acting like they're the ones alone. No matter that fifteen City College friends of Ramona's are standing around talking about World Cup contenders and Kwame Anthony Appiah's latest book. I don't care for soccer, but a philosopher who writes about race and identity sounds chévere. I couldn't be around Julissa and Bryan anymore though. Isa is all I see.

I take out my phone. I'm about to open Instagram when who comes into the kitchen? Danny.

"¡Dimelo, chan! Missed you at yesterday's game." I pull Danny into a hug and pat his back. He hasn't been to practice in two weeks.

Danny ducks his head. He goes to the sink. He grabs a slice of lime. Instead of a beer, he fishes a Coke out of the ice. "Coronas, eh?" He takes a long drink of soda.

"Cinco de Mayo," I respond. A tonic and lime cools my hand. Beer and me, we don't get along. I don't get along with anything that interferes with my game. Papi said girls could interfere too but being with Isa only ever made my pitches faster, my swings stronger. But now? Thinking about her and not talking to her? Not even writing poems for her? That's what's messing with me.

"So where you been?" I ask him. It's good Danny's not drinking beer. I've got worries enough.

Danny takes another slug of cola. "Around." He lets out a burp that lasts a good three seconds. Bryan would be hooting and slapping his back. Me? I stab Danny's ribs with my elbow.

"Oye, owww!" He pretends what I did hurts then gives me a grin that fades too quick.

"Seriously. You gonna tell me where you been?" I ask again.

Danny gives me a look. "Don't got to tell what you already know." He lifts the can to his mouth. "Where's Isa?"

My throat dries like a heat wave. Romeo Santos's words reach us. *Bella y sensual, sobrenatural.*

I slide my cell back in my pocket. I want a drink of my tonic. I don't let myself take one. Why is Danny asking about her?

"Thought maybe she'd be here. With you," Danny says. "Don't tell me Isa's at dance school at ten on a Friday."

I study my glass. Pinhole-size bubbles skid to the top. They gather round the wedge of green like they're attacking it. "Don't know," I answer.

Danny puts the Coke on the counter. "You think she's too good for this? For us?"

I give him a hard stare. His questions are fingers digging into a bruise he doesn't know about.

Danny keeps talking. "'Cause I think she'd like it here. With you. With us."

How does Danny know when I'm not even sure?

I down my drink. I chew the flesh off the lime, spit the peel in the trash. "I don't know where she is." I spit that too. "I haven't seen her or talked to her or . . ."

Danny jabs my arm in warning. Kiara joins us in the kitchen. "Hey, Danny. ¿Cómo tu 'ta?" She tosses her smile to him then hurls a glare at me. Neither of us says anything.

She grabs a soda and heads back out.

Danny takes another Coke. He pours tonic in my glass then points to the window next to the stove. I follow him out onto the fire escape.

We look up at a night splashed with peach-colored light, at buildings of brick winking. Danny pops open the can. He gurgles down soda. In the distance a siren cries out and is answered by another.

"It's been almost two weeks since I've seen her." I don't know why I start talking, but I do. I search for stars or the moon even. I can't see anything over the city glare. "I met her parents, at her dance performance."

Danny faces me.

"Her mom, man." I take a slow sip. "She wouldn't even shake my hand."

Danny finishes his drink. He reaches through the window, puts the can on the counter. "Oye, pana, I met her too. Esa mamá es una tigresa. I was hanging near Sixty-Sixth Street and Isa walked by. She and I, we was just talking—" He looks real quick at me and then away. "We was talking about you. Until her mamá showed up, that is." He draws a finger across his neck like someone's dying.

Danny and Isa met up? Danny met her mother? How come Isa never told me?

Danny puts a hand on my shoulder. "That mai's a piece of work. Ask me, Isa seemed kind of embarrassed. Would make sense if she never said anything to you." He bumps my foot with his clean red Nike. "Not everyone's tight with their mami like you. Anyway, you with Isa because of her mamá? Or because of her?"

"¿Todo bien?" Julissa's head pokes through the window. Behind her, Bryan's scarfing down chips. He's bragging about ball to Kiara.

Julissa scrambles onto the fire escape. She rests a hand on my other shoulder. "You OK?"

"Qué sí," I tell her. I don't want to talk about this with her.

"Sure?" she asks again.

"Yeah. Thanks for having us."

She watches me real close. "You know you could have brought her, right? Your girl? Kiara'll get over it."

I stare into my cup. I clear my throat. "Gracias."

"Next time, OK?" She climbs back inside and into Bryan's arms. All three of them leave the kitchen.

I breathe the cool outside air. I swallow my drink, bubbles and all. I think of Mami's words and Danny's words and Julissa's. I think of Isa until my worries go away.

I take out my phone. I reread Isa's messages. In the faint glow of my screen, Danny smiles.

MONDAY, MAY 8

ISA

My legs and arms ache. Even my upper back is sore. The Academy does not fool around with these evening elective classes. As we were heading out into the rain, Chrissy reminded me I've already been accepted—I've got nothing else to prove. I'll start full time once I finish at Deerwood. Merci, Monsieur Thibault. Except, I *do* have something to prove. I've got to prove they didn't make a mistake. And when I dance hard, there's no room to pay attention to anything else. Not massive moving boxes. Not brothers blasting music. Not even unanswered Instagram messages.

I reach for the shiny subway rail and rise up on my toes. I slide my foot behind me to stretch my Achilles. An argument between a man and a woman at the other end of the car filters through my earbuds. I turn up the volume, just like I do at home.

A hand takes my shoulder. My instincts kick in. I whirl, swinging my bag with me. There's a soft *oomph* as the buckle of my backpack meets flesh. I skitter away to the middle of the car, my pulse hammering in my throat. I look to make sure I'm not being followed.

Alex stands where I stood. His eyes squint. A hand covers his nose and mouth. His other lifts in a silent hello.

The pounding inside me spikes. *Alex?*

Tears fill my eyes. I blink them away as I rush back. "I'm so sorry. I didn't know it was you. Are you hurt? Did I hurt you?"

"I didn't mean to surprise you." He doesn't take his hand from his face. "I called your name."

I motion toward the earphones hanging from my pocket. "I didn't hear you!" My insides feel like jello. My head feels like a balloon escaped from a child's hand. Alex is here. I let out a little laugh because if I don't, I might actually cry. My relief at seeing him overwhelms me. "I can't believe I hit you."

Alex tilts his head at me, like he doesn't know why I'm laughing either. He pinches the bridge of his nose and winces. For some reason, this makes me double over.

"Sorry," I gasp between breaths. "This shouldn't be funny. Did I . . . ? Is your nose bleeding?" I paw through my bag for a tissue. "Can I see?"

His nose is fine. But his bottom lip is swollen and split, like the skin of a too-ripe peach.

"Oh." I inhale through my teeth and offer him the tissue. I drag my gaze from his face, to his arm lingering close to mine. I want to ask if everything is OK with him and his family. I want to ask why I haven't heard from him. But I'm afraid to speak. I'm afraid of how he'd respond.

He waves the tissue away. "I've had worse."

"Sorry," I say again.

He shakes his head. "Stop saying sorry. I'm the one who's here to say that."

The drumming in my chest quiets.

He touches his tongue to his broken lip. "I've been looking for you. I miss you. I wanted to tell you that in person. I didn't want you to read it on your phone."

I grab onto the bar and sink against it.

He waits for me to say something. He waits for me to tell him I miss him too. A tear almost gets loose, along with words my heart is trying to push out. I hold on to them. Seeing Alex—my reaction to seeing him—is scaring me.

We pull into Eighty-Sixth Street and the doors open.

Alex stares out onto the empty platform. "Do you hate me? For not answering your messages?"

"No. I don't hate you." Hatred and anger make me sad. I don't do sad. It's better to convince yourself you feel nothing.

Alex runs a hand over his head. He takes hold of the back of his neck as the train pulls out of the station. "Listen, I'm sorry. For how I left."

My eyes are getting damp. He starts to say something about my parents but I stop him.

"That night at the ballet—my parents—none of it was about you. Really. They had to leave to get my brother. He was sort of freaking out. Finals and all."

Alex watches me, like he senses the tiny lie in there. "How's he doing? Your brother?"

"Fine. He's fine." I answer too quickly. I don't want to talk about Merrit.

Alex nods. He frowns at his shoes. "Your parents—your mother—she didn't say anything about me? Afterward?"

"No. She hasn't mentioned you."

"Your mother didn't mention me," Alex repeats.

"Dad said he enjoyed meeting you. He wished he could have talked with you more."

Alex lets out a long breath. A line appears between his brows. "Even though I wasn't what he was expecting?"

"What do you mean?"

"He didn't know about my skin color."

I grit my teeth. "Alex. That doesn't matter to me. Obviously." Did he think, all those times I was with him, when I was kissing him, that I was acting? That I really wasn't into him at all?

"I'm not talking about whether it matters to you. I'm talking about your parents. You didn't tell them before. Don't you think that would have been important? So that this face and this body wouldn't be what broke it to them?" He's pointing at himself. His words are quiet. He doesn't sound angry. But his other hand is clenched in a fist, like he might use it to punch something.

I turn and walk to the end of the car. I clutch my bag to my chest. Maybe he's right. Maybe it *wasn't* fair to him that I didn't tell my parents, or at least Dad. But Dad's not like that—I didn't think it would matter. As for Mom, I was never going to tell her about Alex anyway. I know how she'd react. And I can't tell Alex any of that. I can't tell him that he's right about her.

I drop onto a bench, hugging my knees to my chest. The past weeks have been torture. I've been dreaming of this, of Alex coming back to me, since the moment he left. But maybe this is a mistake. I can't feel his wide arms around me—I can't see his intense, almost hungry gaze—if he's just going to disappear. I don't think I could stand it. I have to be strong for my family. But I'm not that strong.

Alex sits two seats away. He looks worried.

"Isa. Please. Can I touch you?"

I can't speak—by now tears are streaming down my face—so I just nod.

"I'm sorry," he says. His hand on my back is warm. I hate that it feels so good.

I shake my head. "No. I'm sorry." He can apologize for not answering my messages. But the rest of it—all of this—it started because of me. Because of my messed-up family and our complicated life. I can't be with someone, not right now. It's not fair to either of us.

"I don't think I can do this." I slide out from under his arm and move to stand by the door. Alex comes up behind me; I see his reflection in the window. I feel his hurt, like heat, steaming off him.

We're coming up on Ninety-Sixth, which is good. I don't know how much longer I can stand near him and convince myself I don't want this. Only the train isn't slowing. We push through my station. The conductor comes on and tells us that due to delays, the train is running express to 137th. For access to all bypassed stops we need to transfer to the downtown train.

Oh no.

We're rushing along so quickly I can't think.

Alex offers me his phone. "Do you need to call your mother?" He remembers.

"Thanks, but I don't need to." Mom won't be waiting for me. She's seeing her doctor tonight.

I rest my head against the bar. I don't look at Alex's face, because if you're starving, staring into a restaurant at people eating steak and lobster will just make you feel more miserable, won't it? But what if you're not starving for the food? What if you're starving for the laughter, for the hands touching across the table? It doesn't matter. I can't have any of it.

We're already passing 116th. Only two more stops to go.

A baby in a stroller starts to fuss. The mother stares out the window, her sleepy eyes widening as we shoot out onto the elevated tracks. She blinks at the twinkling lights, at the raindrops that streak the glass. A fat little hand smacks at the sippy cup lodged beside a pink blanket. I'm so distracted, I don't notice the train has stopped.

"Isa? Aren't you getting off?" Alex's voice is quiet. Almost like he doesn't want me to hear him.

"Oh!" I swing around. This is where we say goodbye. Only I can't form the words, not without crying.

The woman with the baby is pushing the stroller out. The wheels get caught in the gap. She mutters and jams at the stroller. The baby falls back against the blanket.

"Can I help you?" I grab hold of the front wheels. I lift them out of the rut. I place them down gently on the platform. "There you go," I say. Only it's not the mother's hands on the stroller. It's Alex's. The mother is behind him. He's talking to her in Spanish.

"There are a lot of stairs at this station," Alex says to me. "It'll be hard for her by herself." He motions for me to step aside. Instead, I take the front.

He lifts the stroller, taking so much of the weight, I do little more than steer. As we put it down at the top of the steps, I smile at the baby. I'm rewarded with a gurgle and a flap of a chubby arm. Alex is watching the mother slowly climb up behind us. Rain pelts us as we exit the station and cross the street.

At the top of the downtown entrance, Alex heaves the stroller up. He waits down at the platform. The mother thanks us multiple times. I give the sweet baby a wave as the mother heads to a bench.

Alex stands beside me. He stomps mud from his sneakers.

"Aren't you going uptown?" I ask, pretending to myself I don't care.

His gaze swings to the mother and the baby. "They're going to Ninety-Six. I told her that's where I'm going too." He looks at me. "Do you mind? If I ride with you?"

"Sure, anything to help the baby." I fling my arm in the air. I mean it to be funny, but it comes out as overly dramatic, like something my mom would do.

Alex takes my hand just before I slip it back in my pocket. "I'm not doing this for the baby," he says.

I look at his sneakers, white laces now stained with dirt. "I know." I don't pull my hand away. It feels too good, right where it is.

"I'm sorry," Alex says again. His thumb traces my finger, just like he did backstage. Like he's sad, like he's saying goodbye. "Your show, it shook me up. Meeting your parents, that shook me up too. But the ballet itself, the story? It made me think about us. How we're so different. Maybe too different. It made me worry we would never work. *That's* why I left."

He's comparing us to a peasant and a lord in a ballet that takes place over a thousand years ago?

Alex lifts a shoulder, even though I haven't said anything. "I know. It's ridiculous. I can't help the way I feel. I'm sorry I didn't tell you before." His hand tightens. He gives my arm a little shake. "I believe you. About your parents. Maybe I'm just too sensitive about it." His gaze lifts to mine. "Will you give me another chance? Give us another chance?"

The train comes in a rush of wind and grating steel. Alex releases my hand as we step on. I take a seat, drawing in a breath as Alex settles beside me. Our hips touch, but he angles his leg away.

Maybe I can do this. Showing everyone you're happy and excited about life is so much easier when you're truly feeling it. I want to tell him the truth. But I don't know how. Not without telling him about everything.

I think about that time on the train, when Alex asked me what type of guy I liked, and I wouldn't tell him because I was too embarrassed to admit that he's my type. He is exactly my type. And then he went and proved it by asking me about dance, about my life, and actually listening to my answers. I didn't want to get off. I wanted that ride to last forever. But I was afraid to stop talking so I introduced him to that game. He caught on without missing a step.

I clear my throat. "I've been lonely. I haven't told my family. Because they need me to be strong. They need me to be the happy one."

Alex stares at me. His dark brows are nearly touching.

I don't look at the mother with the stroller, the one we helped. I don't want to give it away. "My husband is serving overseas. I send him photos of our beautiful daughter. I write to him that she is the most wonderful baby and that I love being a mother. But I miss him. I worry because being a soldier is dangerous. And being a single mother is hard. I'm tired all the time. But I tell him I'm happy because I know that will make him feel good."

Alex's eyes dart to the baby stroller and come back to me. "This … this is that game, right?"

I attempt to lift one eyebrow. They both go up, as I knew they would. "The game's not as fun when there are only five other passengers in the car." I'm not sure if Alex understood what I was trying to tell him. Still, he reaches out. He brushes a strand of wet hair from my cheek. His mouth curves into a hopeful smile. I slide next to him. I push our legs together until I can feel his hip, his knee, and his ankle. I rest my head on his shoulder.

He takes my hand in his. He understood. I missed him so much. I missed having someone who asks about me and cares about the answers.

Alex follows me out at Ninety-Sixth Street, then waits with me for the bus. It's still raining. We back into the corner of the bus stop shelter. He wraps his sweatshirt around both of us. My hands reach for each other along his back. I was starving. For all of it. For all of him.

WEDNESDAY, MAY 17

ALEX

We're on the Great Lawn in Central Park. It's been twelve days since I stopped acting like a fool. Nine days since Isa took me back. I've managed to see her five out of the nine. At night, I'm dreaming again instead of tussling with sheets. Yaritza says my appetite's come back. My average is up to .497. Yesterday, I had five RBIs and AHH advanced to the playoffs. And we've got one more hour of this beautiful sun before it sets.

"How's it going with Robi?" Isa hands me one of the sandwiches she made for us. She reaches for sanitizer. She grins when I hold out my palm. She squirts out a big glob and massages it in. I capture her hands. I pull her toward me. My lips brush hers.

"Robi's good." I take the sandwich from her. I've told her about my little brother's dreams. About my dream to help him get Papi's attention. To get his respect and help. "Yaritza's reminding him to do his exercises every afternoon. Once I'm done with playoffs, I'll have him work on catching and hitting again."

Isa rips off a piece of bread from her own sandwich and pops it in her mouth. "He loves playing? Like you do?" Isa twists her hair over her shoulder.

"Robi's crazy about baseball. It's all he ever reads about, all he talks about. Yaritza says he doesn't even watch his regular shows anymore. Just baseball games and commentary."

Isa eyes me before taking another bite. "But *you* love it, right?"

"Yeah. Of course." I don't tell her what I love most. The respect that comes with it—Papi's and everyone else's. I push the rest of my sandwich in my mouth. It's better than from a deli. Isa puts in these tiny pickles that give it crunch. Isa's watching my face, and I smile around all the crumbs. Isa rises onto her knees. She digs in her bag and pulls out a white bundle. She unwraps the napkin. Three chocolates sit in her hand.

"I got them at dance. Someone gave our instructor a whole box because she pulled a muscle in her groin. No, not that way!" She laughs at the look I give her. "It's actually a pretty common injury for a dancer."

I consider a couple of comments, ways to offer my assistance should Isa ever need it. She pokes me like she knows where my mind's at, then offers me the chocolate shaped like lips.

"You saw that one and knew it was for me, right?" I rub my tongue over the bump on my bottom lip, the small scar from that day Isa forgave me. I hope it never fades.

"We're sharing them," she informs me. "Each one is different. I love tasting them all." She bite off half and passes the rest to me. Wow. Sweet milk chocolate blended with hazelnut. Reminds me of the flavored coffee Mami gets from Dunkin' Donuts.

There's a *clap* of a bat hitting a ball. A Little Leaguer runs to first. I lie down on my back. I stare through leaves at a sky the color of faded jeans. The air smells fresh and green, like a promise. This moment is perfect. I don't want anything about it to change.

Isa's face appears above me. Her hair, soft as feathers, brushes my cheek.

OK, I can think of a few things that would make it even better.

I take her arm.

She sinks onto her heels. "Wait. I have something else." She slips a magazine in front of her. *Northeast Lit* is sketched on the cover in purple slanted letters.

Her hands shift the magazine up to reveal her grinning mouth. "Open to where the bookmark is."

I sit up. I slide my finger between the glossy pages. I find the bookmark, but I start at the front. There are short stories, and artwork, and poems in here. I'm reading the first poem, my mind forming the sounds of the words, when Isa leans into me.

"I can't wait any longer!" She snatches the magazine, flipping back to the bookmarked page. "Read!" Her cheeks and mouth are bright pink.

I pull my gaze from her face to the page in my lap. I read the first sentence. I look up at her. She's chewing her lip. Her eyes are big and full of shine.

I start at the beginning. I read all the way through. I read it again. I read a third time. I run my finger over the words, over the name *Anonymous.*

"Well?" Isa's fingers tap her water bottle.

I take her hand to make her stop. "How?" I whisper. I don't know what this means.

"It's open submissions. I sent it a few months ago. I figured you wouldn't send it yourself. I didn't use your name. I didn't think you were ready for that."

"Did you have to pay for them to print this?"

"No!" She's shaking her head. She takes the magazine from me and turns to the last page. She shows me the submission guidelines and rules.

"But why? Why did they take it?" These poems I write, they're just for her. For me. I don't expect other people to like them. It's not about them.

"Because the poem's beautiful! See, I knew I needed to do this. You still don't think you're good. Listen, just because you're this amazing baseball player doesn't mean you can't also be an amazing poet. It's not one or the other. You could grow up and be something other than a professional ball-player, you know. You could be an architect, a doctor, an astronaut."

"You want to send me to the moon?" She's the only one who likes my jokes.

"No, of course not." She wraps her jumpy fingers around my forearm. "It's just... You've got a gift and I want you to use it."

I love that Isa thinks all her possibilities can be mine too. That she doesn't see anything holding me back. I don't correct her. She was born looking like a dancer, but she could go to school, put on a white coat, and people would call her *Doctor*. Me? I was born looking like I belong on the field. Even if I went to school for years, people wouldn't see me and think *poet*. I don't say anything. I like her dream for me, even if it's not my reality.

"Have you thought about that school I told you about? Just, because . . . you never know. What if you get a career-ending injury? You said it happened to your dad. You can't control everything, no matter how hard you train or how careful you are." She lets out a breath, draws another in. Her smile comes back, bigger than before. "This"—she waves the magazine—"would help you get into the Haeres School. They've got a champion baseball team and great college acceptances."

I hold my hand out for the magazine. She gives it back to me. I flip through the pages. I read the other poems. They're chévere.

Isa's right. The baseball program at Haeres is solid. A lot of the kids I train at the Institute apply there. It's a private Catholic high school. But it's free. So it's hard to get in. They'd never take me. And Papi would never go for it. He doesn't want me to go to college. He wants me to get drafted right out of high school, like he did.

I slide my hand behind her head and draw her close for another kiss. "Thank you." I give the magazine back.

"No, that's your copy. I have two more at home. If you want one for Yaritza or your mom—"

"Nah, this one's great." I don't want to share what I wrote with other people. Anonymous is one thing. They don't know it's me. But if Papi found out? I'd never live it down. He thinks I read too much already.

Isa comes down beside me. Her arm curls around my chest. She rests her chin on my shoulder.

"Thank you," I tell her again.

"You're welcome," she whispers.

I read the poems, mine and others, until the sun disappears.

MONDAY, MAY 22

ISA

Merrit's forehead is pressed against the glass. He stares out the window as the city goes by. It's weird to see him not on his phone. For some reason, he's angry with it today.

The bus stops. A bunch of students get on at Central Park West. Merrit glances at them, his gaze lingering on a girl with a thick cascade of blue-black hair. I rub his back but I'm not sure he can feel my hand through his winter coat. It's going to be seventy today. I reminded him of this as we were leaving but Merrit didn't want to return and find it packed away in some box, perhaps shipped to the storage facility instead of to the new apartment. I can empathize. I'm carrying a duffel even though I'm just taking him to his doctor's appointment. My pointe shoe box with Alex's poems is inside.

Merrit ignores me when I ask about the World Series of Poker—he watched it for hours last night on his laptop. He shakes his head when I suggest stopping for pizza.

As we approach Broadway, I rise to my feet. I reach for his elbow, but Merrit shrugs me off, looking all annoyed. He doesn't understand why his baby sister has to chaperone him. But if you don't show up to your appointments, if you disappear for hours and don't tell anyone where you've been . . . well, you have no choice. I offered to help after school, what with the movers around. Mom's a mess and Dad's managing everything. I don't mind missing one afternoon of dance. Dad gave me a huge hug, kissed my cheek, and whispered, "Thank you." Mom didn't even respond when I said we were going to take public transportation. Taxis are just too expensive.

Merrit stumbles off the bus. He veers in front of it to cross the street. I yank him back just as a car screeches by.

"You didn't even look!" I accuse.

Merrit scrutinizes the drain, shaking his hands up and down in his pockets, jiggling the coins inside.

The light changes. I tug him through the crosswalk, then down the steps into the subway, toward the front of the tracks, where there will be fewer people waiting.

Merrit's jiggling change again, his shoulders vibrating. A lady with a Century 21 bag glances at us.

"I wasn't watching poker last night," he says. It's jarring after his long silence. "Not all night at least. I was watching *Superman*. The one from 1978. You've seen it, right?"

I nod, too shocked to speak. He hasn't spoken more than single words to anyone in days. *Superman* is one of Dad's favorites. He used to make us all watch it together on his birthday. He'd recite the lines along with the actors. *"I'm here to fight for truth and justice and the American way."* He even got Mom to play along, calling out to her, *"Easy, miss. I've got you,"* and laughing when she'd reply, *"You—you've got me?! Who's got you?"*

Merrit grimaces. "Yeah, duh. Of course you've seen it. Anyway, I was thinking about what happened to the actor who played Superman. I mean, imagine being a superhero—sure he didn't have x-ray vision and he couldn't fly in real life—but he was this tall, good-looking guy who was one of the biggest stars in Hollywood. So imagine being that guy and then having an accident and being *paralyzed*. And then *dying*. He was only Dad's age when he died, did you know that?"

I shake my head. I'm not sure whether to be happy or nervous that Merrit's talking so much.

Merrit drags the toe of his shoe along the bumps edging the yellow line. "What does that mean about us, about our society, when the man who embodied Superman is squashed so easily? Like a mosquito."

I hope Merrit is referring to how the actor died so young, and not to the accident. It's not as if life ends just because you get a diagnosis or because you can't do something you used to be able to do. I'm about to ask when Merrit loops his hand around one of the tiled columns. He swings out over the tracks.

My heart jolts. "Merrit." By some miracle, my voice stays calm. "Merrit, what are you doing?"

Merrit peers down into the wide cavity filled with trash and rats and long pieces of metal conducting high voltage. He sways back and forth, holding on with his long arm.

"Merrit, you're making me nervous. Please step back."

A train is coming. Its horn blares out a long and angry warning.

My brother turns his head to find me. His eyes are lit with a wild gleam. "I think the message is that we're all mosquitos. Any of us can be squashed in a flash." He swings again. My heart ticks madly. I'm about to scream Merrit's name when he propels himself away from the track. He trips toward me, laughing.

The train slows to a stop in front of us. Merrit's pointing at me, his smile broad and exaggerated.

"Your expression . . ." He lets out a bark of laughter.

I smack him. Hard. "That's not funny," I growl. I can still feel the beat of my heart on my tongue.

"Sure it is." He raises a hand to his reddening cheek. I've never slapped anyone before, and I'm shaking now.

I grab Merrit's coat, dragging him onto the train with me. I don't let go until we're in the doctor's office, even though Merrit's eyes are shooting daggers at me. After I tell the doctor what happened, after I say I don't know if Merrit was clowning around or if he really was thinking of jumping onto the tracks, I sit in the waiting room, wiping tears with my sleeve. The bag with Alex's poems is on my lap. I can't even open it.

ALEX

I lean against the brick of the Sixty-Sixth station wall. Two uptown trains pass. I don't care how many others go by, I'll wait forever. Isa texted that she's coming.

Footsteps echo in the crossunder. The rhythm is heartbeat-fast. Isa soars out of the stairwell, a ball off a bat. My hands seek her, strong and sure. I catch her as if this is what my training is for.

A train flies in behind her. Wind tears my eyes. I don't close them. I don't blink. I can't. Not when she's looking at me like that.

Her hands are on my shoulders. Her chest hits up against mine.

"Thank you," she breathes.

"For catching you?"

She tips her chin to me. "For that too. I meant the poem I found yesterday. You have no idea how much I needed it."

"Why? Did something happen?" My arms tighten around her.

Her eyes go dull. Her features cloud. "No." She smiles again. "I was just missing you." An incoming train slows and stops, and she pulls me aboard.

This car, with its shaking walls and machine-pumped air, is ours. Here, on the train, with her by my side, it feels like home.

"Which one did you find?"

She recites the first line.

"You liked it?" I ask. My mouth matches her grin.

She recites the rest.

"I'll take that as a yes."

We sit in our favorite seats, beside the MTA's poem poster. I can't help but think of *Northeast Lit*, of what she did for me, of what she said months ago. Someday, maybe one of mine will be up there.

Isa burrows her head into my shoulder. I inhale the scent of her shampoo. It's different. More fruit than flower. It's still all I want to smell.

Isa goes still. I follow her gaze to a girl sitting between an older boy and a light-haired woman. The girl's holding a newspaper. She chews the eraser of a pencil and looks up at her mother. The mother tells her something and the girl writes it down. The boy takes the pencil, then writes something too. The girl kicks her feet, happy with what he's done.

Above them is a black-and-white poster of a woman in a dark room, an ad for a study at one of the city's hospitals. The woman is pressing a hand to her head like she's in pain. The words *SAD, ALONE, ANXIOUS* surround her. She looks like the mother of the kids doing the crossword.

I knock Isa's knee. "Hey, it's like a before and after."

Isa looks up. Her eyes skid from the ad to the floor.

"What do you think they gave her? Shock therapy? Or maybe happy pills?" I try nudging a grin from her. "Or maybe that research is trying to prove you don't need any of that. That you can fight the blues if you do enough crosswords with friends and family, huh?"

Isa doesn't laugh, which isn't like her. She stares at one of the doors. Her answering "Hmmm" is quiet.

I release Isa's arm, searching for something else to say. "Hey, Merrit's home from school for the summer now, right?"

She leans her head on me again and the strain across my shoulders eases. She doesn't look away from the little family. "Yup. He's home."

"Can I meet him?" I wait for her answer. I try not to think about empty seats at the ballet.

Isa laces our fingers together, turning her palm up and then down, bringing mine with it. I'm afraid of what she's going to say.

"Sure. I'll find out when he's available."

I let out my breath and lift our hands. I rest her fingers against my lips.

Her face tilts to mine. "Chrissy and Kevin are going to the Catskills again this weekend. His parents are away, visiting his grandma. Chrissy's all nervous about it."

Isa's told me about Chrissy's "dilemma." I had to swear on my mami's life I would never share what I know.

I chuckle. "She should just own up," I tell her again. "If he loves her, he'll accept the truth."

"I know how you feel, Mr. I Shall Never Tell a Lie. But what if you're wrong? What if when Kevin finds out, he freaks and ends it?"

"Then she's better off without him." If he loved her, he would accept her for who she is. Like Isa accepts me. If I said I wanted to quit baseball, she'd probably be the only one all right with it. Not that I want to quit. Not that I ever would.

Isa puts her hand on my knee. "What if it were me? What if I were the one hiding something from you?"

"Yes, I'd want to know. And yes, I'd be OK with it. I'd have to be." I exhale slow as her hand travels from my thigh down to my knee. "If you're going to tell me you're an expert en la cama because of an experience you had before you knew me, I'd be OK with that too." I know I should be, at least, even if the thought makes my gut knot up.

She massages open my clenched fist. She stretches until her lips meet mine. I cup the back of her head. We're heading home, so I don't have to worry about her bun. But still, I'm careful.

"Sorry to disappoint." She smiles against me. "But you've been my only conquest."

I sweep my mouth over hers again, not caring about the people around us.

"So when's your practice this Saturday?" I ask when I've pulled away, when my breathing's slowed enough for me to speak.

She shakes her head, rubbing the tip of her nose across mine. "I don't have any. No *class,* that is. Free, for once in my life. You have a game?"

I nod. "But it's early. Should be done by three. Mami works until eight."

Isa looks into my eyes like she's been lost at sea and she's looking for land. She spots it—what she's searching for. And grins. "Are you finally inviting me over?"

I tickle her, right under her ribs. She shrieks.

"Finally?" I say. "Finally?" I ask her all the time. She's never able to come.

"Yes! Yes! I'll come. Stop!" She's leaning all the way back. Her head is nearly touching the floor. She's balancing, her knee pinching my side, holding her in place. Coño. Her muscles are so strong. Is it weird that it makes me want her even more?

We both know what this means. We've talked about finding time alone. I pull her up. "You'll stay for dinner?" I whisper.

She nods. She's trying to control her grin. "I'm excited to meet your mom."

"Oh, is *that* what you're excited about?" I take her face. I'm about to kiss her again when the subway doors open. A cop steps in. His handcuffs smack against his baton.

I drop my hands. They're weights at my sides. Not strong. Not sure.

The cop scans the car. He frowns when he sees us.

Isa slides her arm through mine. She grips my hand so tight my fingers go numb. The cop passes us. When he's in the next car, Isa reaches for my chin. She kisses me until I forget about the cop. Until all I can think about is Saturday.

• • •

The elevator dings. The words of the poem I've been writing in my head since I kissed Isa goodbye scatter. I piece them back together as I tread the brown shag rug to my apartment. In a few days, Isa will walk over the same Hershey-chocolate carpet, drag her fingers along the peanut-butter walls. She'll laugh, remembering I told her I live down a Reese's Pieces hall.

I smell the chuletas before I open the door. Mami's voice rises from the kitchen, carrying over the hiss and spatter of oil. I poke my head in. She's got the phone wedged under her ear. She pushes thin strips of cebolla y pimientos around the frying pan, then flips pork chops with a spatula. It's after nine. She's home early.

She gives me a nod, then gestures at the meat. I bring her a plate from the counter.

"Sí, sí, mi amor . . . Entiendo . . . Lo siento," she says into the phone. She slides one of the chuletas onto the plate. The edges are golden and crisped. Just how I like them.

"¿Quién es?" I mouth the words.

She holds a finger up. Her bangle bracelets slide down her arm. Their brassy color looks good against her brown skin. Her blue scrub top is flecked with grease. A sweatshirt with rows of tiny yellow pineapples drapes over the back of a chair. The steam's still running in our fifth-floor apartment. Mami jokes that it always feels like the DR in here.

Mami points to another plate. I hold it steady as she places a pork chop in the middle, then dumps spatula after spatula of onions and peppers on top. This plate must be mine.

My stomach grumbles.

Mami puts down the phone, and we sit at the two-person table. "Sorry," she says. "That was the abuelita de Danny. Have you seen him?" She saws off a piece of chuleta. She closes her lips around the fork and groans.

I'm crunching down on meat, the sharp tang of garlic mixing with sweet onion and pepper. The words of my poem flood back, riding colors of green, gold, and red.

"¡'Pérate, la leche!" She jumps out of her chair when she sees I have nothing to drink.

I swallow. "Siéntate, Mami. I'll get it." I pour us two glasses of milk.

"¿Y Danny?" she asks, when I place the milk in front of her.

"Haven't seen him today." I try to think when he was last in school. We're not in the same classes. "Maybe Monday I saw him? In the hall?" If he hadn't dropped the team, I'd be seeing him every day. It's not the same when it's just Bryan and me. It's like I'm wearing two shoes, but forgot my belt.

Mami stabs another bite. "¿Con quién está andando? Is it a girl at least?"

A girl would be so much better for Danny than Pinchón's gang. I don't want to give her Pinchón's name. I shrug instead.

Mami shakes her head. Her fork scrapes her plate.

"Speaking of girls, I know you wanted to meet Isa. She can come this Saturday. Does that work?"

Mami's eyes widen like Sra. Hernandez just told her about a celebrity visiting the Fifth Avenue salon where she works. "¿De veras? She no has class? But what about your game?"

"I'll finish in time for dinner. We're both free for once. Can you believe it?" I scoop another forkful of peppers and onions. A line from my poem is stuck on repeat.

Mami pats at her hair. "Ay, but I need to make an appointment."

"You look beautiful," I tell her. "You don't need to do anything special. We can even go out, so you don't have to cook."

She puts down her fork. She crosses her arms. Her red-painted nails tap at her skin then point at my plate. "¿Y qué? You don't like my food?"

I stand. I plant a kiss on the top of her head. "Your cooking is the best. I just don't want you to have to work. Not unless you want to."

"This, I want to," she declares. She grabs up her fork and finishes her food. "Since when has my son brought home a girl before? Never. And I would like to thank her for that smile. You no smile like that since you was nine and your papi started taking notice of you."

"Mami—" I hate when she brings that up.

She raises her hands. "No, no. To 'ta bien. I know you love your mamá. But I can do nothing to make you look like that. Your papi? Sí. Your Isabelle? Sí. And I know *this* smile"—she squeezes my cheeks—"is not just for las chuletas. You saw her tonight, no?"

I nod. I try not to smile harder.

She nods back. "I know this Isabelle, she is special. I will make una cena especial for her. And we have something else to celebrate. They told me I can have the day shift. Starting in July."

"Really?" The nursing home's had Mami's request for five years. But it goes by seniority. Someone has to retire or leave for a day spot to open up.

I grab Mami into a hug. She squeals when I lift her off the ground. Mami owns our apartment. She bought it with her settlement from the divorce, but she still has to make the monthly maintenance. And pay bills for food and electricity. So she needs that job. One of the things I dream about if I make it to the pros, besides the look on Papi's face, is being able to care for Mami.

"Ay, ¡felicidades!" I swing her around. When I set her down, she pushes a chair to the counter. Before she can climb it, I get down the bottle of Brugal from the cabinet above the refrigerator. She side-eyes me as I hand it to her. She examines the bottle, checking to make sure I haven't taken any. As if I would ever drink her rum. That same bottle's been there forever. She only takes it out on truly special occasions.

I stamp down my smirk. "You should keep it somewhere else." I put the frying pan in the sink and start scrubbing. "I don't want you falling." Mami puts on music as I turn for the cutting board. Mami's sitting in the chair, watching me, a small glass in her hand. Her crossed leg bobs to the bachata beat. She raises the glass to me. I blow her a kiss and pick up the sponge.

Dos Locos comes on. Mami stands, smoothing out her scrubs.

"Ven, baila con tu mamá."

I dry my hands and dance with her. It's her favorite song, a slow one, about two lovers who've broken up but can't stop thinking of each other. It used to make me think she missed Papi. She never got another novio. Not that I know of, anyway. When I asked her about the song and Papi years ago, she laughed. She said it was just a good song.

"Mami? Ever heard of a school called Haeres?" Yellow dish towels with palm trees, the ones Mami got from DR, hang next to the stove.

Her hair tickles my arm as she shakes her head. "No. Tell me."

"Es better than your school now?" she asks, when I finish.

"Yes," I tell her. "Almost all the students get into good colleges."

Mami stops dancing. She lifts her face to look at me. "That's what you want? You no want to play ball?"

"I'll still play." I tell her about the Haeres team. About how they're in a different division but they're just as good as AHH.

The chorus of the song comes back on. Mami sings it, and this time her voice trembles with extra emotion. *"Estando con ella y pensando en ti."* She hugs me and sways back and forth again. I wait for the song to finish before I ask the question that will determine everything.

"Do you think Papi would let me apply?"

Mami chuckles. "He will ask which professional player graduated from there. If you can find any, he will let you."

I start to tell her about Division I schools like Vanderbilt and LSU. She holds up her hand. She moves it to the merengue beat of "La Cosquillita" and sits back down in her chair. She crosses her legs and takes a sip of her Brugal.

"What tu papi thinks isn't important," she says finally. "You do what you want."

FRIDAY, MAY 26

ISA

Dad is a bundle of blankets and mussed hair on the great room couch when I get up—a larger version of what's on the inflatable mattress beside him. Even though Merrit and I are supposed to be sharing a room, Dad insisted Merrit sleep out here. Dad's been trying to hide that he's been sleeping out here too, instead of with Mom. But this morning Mom's standing by the couch looking down at Dad, pale fingers cradling a steaming mug of tea.

What's she doing up? Mornings are easier when it's just me. There are no strained smiles or sharpening of words into knives. No sudden laughter that makes me jump. Or sobs that follow me onto the street.

Mom sees me but turns and gazes out the window onto the Metro-North tracks. Does that mean I can go? I grab my breakfast, planning to eat on the train. I'd woken in a warm bubble, dreaming about meeting Alex in his apartment. The bubble's gone; the warmth too. Sometimes I can get it back if I think hard enough. If I think only about him.

I bend for my bag but Mom walks toward me, frowning. My spark of hope winks out. Is she going to ask why I sometimes come home late? Is she going to ask who I'm with? Last week out of nowhere she brought up Danny, only to her he's just someone I should avoid. It made me wonder if one of her friends had seen me and Alex in the park.

"I want you to look at this," she whispers. Her cup clinks onto the pass-through that connects the kitchen and the only other room that's not a bedroom or a bath. She pushes a large packet toward me. The words *University Medical Center* are in the upper left corner. My throat closes. My old fears come roaring back. Last week, we met with a therapist together as a family. The doctor had us all fill out questionnaires. Are my results in that envelope? Is Mom going to tell me I'm like her and Merrit, that I've inherited what she got from her dad? This is worse. This is so much worse than demands about who I should and should not spend time with.

Mom taps the countertop. Half her unpainted nails hit the envelope, half strike the gold-and-black granite that's the reason we're in this apartment. Dad wanted the top floor that had a view and light and more space. Mom said we needed to save money, to cover the cost of medical insurance now that we've lost Dad's employer's subsidy. Mom liked this kitchen. Even though it's only the size of the bathroom, the fixtures and appliances are new. She planned to cook because ordering in costs more. Last night Mom was too tired and Dad was out meeting an old contact for drinks. So I made picadillo—Dad's favorite—following abuela's recipe. I was happy to cook. No one can be strong all the time. I told myself I can take care of Dad—of all of them—until he finds a job. Once Dad is good, he'll help me make everyone better. Then maybe, just maybe, I can bring Alex to meet them. But what if I was wrong? What if I'm sick too?

"I got this for you at the hospital last night." Mom's voice is still froggy from sleep. "It's a volunteer application for summer. You need something more than dance on your college application."

I'm too frozen with fear to be relieved. I don't want to work at a hospital. I don't want to think about college. I just want to go to school. I want to make it through this single day.

"Thanks," I whisper back. I pretend to read the return address again. "I'll fill it out later." I'm good at saying yes, when what I mean is no.

Mom brings the mug to her mouth. It shakes as she takes a sip. "It would be good to have a doctor in the family. Someone to help take care of Merrit." The mug thunks as it hits the stone. She presses her trembling hand onto the top of mine.

I take a bite of my apple. I swallow again and again to get it to go down. Still it gets stuck. My eyes tear, my body crying out for water. Only water isn't what I really need. I need to get out. I need air. I need Alex.

The blankets on the couch covering Dad shift. Merrit doesn't move. Once he's out, he can sleep through anything.

"I've got to go to class."

Mom doesn't nod. She only takes away her hand.

ISA

Alex has a view of the river. He never told me that. He's at treetop level, and the leaves outside his windows are just unfurling. His apartment is warm and inviting, like he is. It smells of cinnamon and vanilla. His mom was baking in preparation for my visit. Pictures of his family, of him as a child, decorate walls and tables. I miss that in our apartment. And there are books everywhere, whole shelves of them in the living room but also pulled out—strewn across chairs, the couch, even next to the TV.

I thought I'd be nervous, but his home, the way it feels like him, puts me at ease. Alex is nervous, though. He takes me to the kitchen, offers me milk or juice or tonic with either chocolate syrup or lemon or lime. When I don't answer right away, he opens another cabinet, takes out a bottle of rum. I'm not sure if he's kidding.

"Um, no thanks. But you can go ahead."

He puts the bottle away, not meeting my eyes. But then he turns and looks at me. "Even if I did drink, I wouldn't. Not now. I wouldn't do anything that might make me forget even a single moment of today."

I swallow hard.

"Do you have water?" Of course he does. Maybe I *am* a little nervous. A grade-school Alex grins at me from under a magnet on the fridge. His hair was super cute when it was that long. "¡Qué papichulo!" I tell him.

We drain our water in a few gulps. Alex puts out his hand for my empty. He rests our glasses in the sink. He crosses the room and kisses me. I'm suddenly aware of how alone we are. Before—on the train and in the park—we did what we wanted, but only to a point; the boundaries were invisible but always there. Now there's no one watching, no one to hold us back. The rules have changed, and I don't know what to do with myself.

I breathe in the soap and pine scent of him. He's wearing a T-shirt and I'm in a tank. The feel of our bare arms shocks me. I want—no—I *need* more of his skin on mine. I don't let go of him—I don't dare lift my mouth from his—but I pull him out of the kitchen, into the hall. I don't know where we're going so we stand in the darkness, the walls close, as if to catch us if we fall. His hands are in my hair. Mine are on his back, at his waist, on his abdomen that shivers under my touch. I gasp and Alex shudders and then we're moving into a room, his bedroom. I yank his shirt up toward his head. He eases free to shrug out of it. He gently closes the door. He studies the mass of gray cotton in his hand, like he's deciding whether to fold it. I'm staring at him, at the raw beauty of his shoulders and arms, the muscles that course over him, the subtle pound of his pulse at his neck. It brings on an ache inside me. His eyes lift and study mine. They're rainforest bright, a jungle. His chest works like he ran up five flights of stairs. But he waits. He searches my face, the question plain in his.

When it's just us, just our bodies, I've got nothing to hide, nothing to pretend. My lips, my hands, the whole of me speaks in ways my words can't. And I want this. I want him. I've wanted him since that very first kiss on the train. I've never wanted anything more.

I smile and back toward the bed. I slip a small square of foil out of my pocket and tuck it into my hand. I reach up and pull off my top.

Alex's chest halts midrise. His throat bobs.

We're both nervous, then. But we're nervous together. We're bared to each other and honest, completely honest, for the first time. That's all that matters.

ALEX

I want to remember you,
  standing by my window,
  the gray of a clouded city sky brightening as it hit your shoulder,
    your back,
        the blanket of your hair.
I couldn't breathe,
Watching you.

When you touched me,
I was blinded.

After, you sat beside mi mamá,
    You laughed at her stories of Baní,
      You wolfed down her asopado.
      You glanced at me and sideways smiled,
        reminding me who was responsible for your appetite.
Our knees kissed under the dining room table.

FRIDAY, JUNE 9

ISA

Chrissy races me down the steps. We're both shrieking. I dash out of the stairwell first. Chrissy releases a great sigh of disgust.

"Catch!" She throws her bag at me then bolts through the front doors. Outside, on the terrace, she opens her arms and does a slow twirl. Her face lifts to the sun. She fans herself, accepting her victory.

I use the revolving door like we're supposed to. "First of all, you said, and I quote, 'Race you to the bottom of the stairs.'" I pull the blue-and-red strap of her bag higher on my shoulder. "Second, even if the finish line were outside, tossing your belongings at me to slow me down is totally cheating."

Chrissy takes her bag. She unzips one of the five outer pockets and takes out two lollipops. She hands me the one with the red wrapper. I accept the peace offering. She knows cherry is my favorite. We stroll over to the fountain and sit on the wide granite bench encircling it. Neither of us minds getting wet.

"Sore loser." She snickers.

I lean over and flick water at her. She squeals, clamps down on her lollipop, and splashes me back. Our shirts are soaked by the time we call a truce. Chrissy lies down on the smooth black stone, stretches out her legs, and rests her head in my lap. I pull damp curls from her face, careful not to knock the stick protruding from her mouth.

"I'm so effed for tonight. Who ever heard of ninety-five degrees in the beginning of June? Mom asked our super, but they can't get our window units in until next week. I'm going to sweat to death."

Chrissy complains about this every year. In the past, she'd sleep over when it got too hot. Our co-op had central air. Our rental does too, but there's no extra room. Chrissy hasn't been to my new place. I haven't even told her about Merrit getting kicked out of school.

"You can always stay at Kevin's. He has AC, right?"

She slaps my leg. "I can't do that. His parents will be there. It's one thing to do a sleepover when they're out of town. It's another to do it right under their noses. Gross!"

"You told me you ran up to Kevin's place during lunch the other day."

"That's different. His mom and dad were at work. They didn't even know." Her T-shirt rides up, showing her flat, pale stomach. She pulls the lollipop out of her mouth again. Artificial orange flavor wafts up to me. "God, I wish my mom worked. It would be epic if her schedule were more predictable. My place is so much closer than Kevin's. We could probably get away two or three times a day, which, honestly, is what my body needs. I keep having to remind myself to keep it in check so I don't blow my newbie cover."

I think about telling her. About me and Alex. She'll want every detail, from the color of his walls to the feel of his sheets and what happened between them. But I'm not ready to let go of the secret of what Alex and I shared.

Chrissy stretches and groans. "But thank the gods, Kevin and I are making progress. I don't know how I lasted so long without a pe—" She snaps the orange sucker back in her mouth. She lifts her sunglasses and peers up at me all bashful.

Now even saying the p-word makes her blush?

"Were you going to say p—?"

She shrieks even before I can get it out. I wait for her to quiet, then yell, "¡Pepino!"

A few guys walking on the other side of the fountain turn to look at us. They're probably wondering why I shouted the word *cucumber* across the plaza.

Chrissy sits up and play-slaps my arms. I play-slap her back. We grin at each other around our lollipop sticks.

She slumps onto her back again. I pull down her shirt. "You're going to get burned."

She yawns, unconcerned. "How are things going with your hottie by the way? Haven't seen him in a while."

"Me neither," I admit. It's been twelve days. TWELVE. What I feel for him dwarfs everything else. I can't forget that. And I can't let anything threaten it—especially not the stress I've been feeling lately. I want to be happy when I'm with him, to make the most of our time together. I don't want to show him my cracks. Which is why I missed his game last week. Merrit had a bad night—a bad four nights, really. He hadn't slept at all, and he wound up in the hospital. The doctors kept him there for a full day to adjust his meds. He's doing better now. But I didn't want Alex to see my worry. I didn't want to risk it affecting his playing.

Chrissy knows about Mom's and Merrit's histories. I could tell her what's going on. How this college thing pushed Merrit into another rough patch and that he's having a tough time climbing out of it. How that and my dad's job and the move are sending Mom into her own tailspin. But I don't want to talk about any of that with her either. It's hard enough convincing myself everything is going to be fine. I'd rather talk to Chrissy about Kevin, about dance and kisses and cucumbers. I'd rather just talk about Alex.

"He's been messaging me a lot," I tell Chrissy. "He's amazing. His team made it to the championships—did I tell you?"

Chrissy shakes her head, grinning up at me. "Nope. You haven't gushed one bit." She winks—I've been talking about him every chance I get. Just not about being alone with him in his apartment.

"Practice for his travel team started up," I go on. "He's training long hours and heading to Brooklyn to work with his dad. And I know he feels bad that he's not spending more time with his brother. It's been hectic." I motion around us and shrug. "We've been so busy too."

Chrissy nods. We have two performances coming up, and we lost time when our Technique instructor went out with another injury. Her replacement is this killer Russian woman who holds a lot of extra rehearsals.

"So that's why I haven't seen him," I tell her. "I miss him."

"I know you do." Chrissy touches my arm. She knows exactly how I feel about Alex, how when I'm with him, everything else fades away. She gets how happy he makes me—it's the same with her and Kevin. "Wait, isn't your big date tonight?" Chrissy props herself on her elbows. "Leo Xiao at Barclays?"

I suck at the last bit of the lollipop. It's down to a tiny cherry-flavored nubbin. "You didn't notice my big bag?" I point to the pillowed duffel I dropped outside the spray of the fountain. I've been counting down the hours. I felt like I'd downed five espressos when Alex told me about the tickets. He makes fun of my pop-music obsession, but he went through a lot of trouble to get us these seats. The concert isn't what I'm most excited about, though. I'm really only excited to see him. The best part is, I'm spending the night in Brooklyn. I'll sleep in Alex's room and he'll sleep with Robi. Or at least, that's what he's told his parents. I told mine I was going to Chrissy's. I didn't want to get into it with them, with everything else that's going on. Mom said fine but asked if I could come home for a few hours this afternoon to watch Merrit. She doesn't like to leave him alone. I usually don't mind—it's not like I have to take him on the subway. Only, I don't want to take time away from being with Alex. I told Mom we had rehearsals until late. Lying doesn't bother me as much as it used to.

I don't bother telling Chrissy she's my alibi for tonight, because my parents will never check. All I do is grin and ask if I can borrow her cornflower-blue strap dress. I've got about forty-five minutes before I'm meeting Alex, so I have time to change.

Chrissy slips into her mother's southern accent. "Why hell yes, you can!" She crunches the rest of her lollipop, sits up and swings her legs off the shiny black bench.

A sharp whistle cuts through the air. Chrissy whips around. She shoots to her feet and waves. Kevin waves back, the glass door swinging shut behind him. Chrissy grand jetés across the plaza to Kevin. He drops his bags before she reaches him. He catches her then fake-falls on his butt, keeping her above him. Hoots of laughter peal across the plaza.

The sun is setting behind the opera house as I wait for my friend. Paintings more than three stories long hang behind the arched glass column windows. Their vibrant colors will be more visible once night has fallen. Even with the competing light of the sunset, the butterflies stand out. One painting has the abstract outline of a girl in a kimono.

My phone vibrates, and Mom's name appears on the screen.

"Hey, guess what I'm looking at?" I say into the phone, before she can say hello. "Puccini's the composer you like, right? He does *Madame Butterfly*? Maybe we can get half-price tickets the day of—"

"Isabelle." It's not Mom. It's Dad.

"Dad? Why are you calling from Mom's cell?"

"Isabelle." His voice breaks.

"Dad? What's wrong?" My stomach tightens, like a giant fist is closing around my middle.

"Can you meet us at the hospital?"

I know the words he's going to say before he says them.

"It's Merrit."

FRIDAY, JUNE 9

ALEX

The train rattles. My pen slips over the word I was writing. Conductors who tap the brakes are weak. They can't make a decision. Stop? Or go? ¿Cuál es? And the result is passengers twitch like fish on the end of a line.

I press my back against the seat, bracing myself with my legs. Unless the train gets held, I'll be early to Sixty-Sixth for Isa. I tap the yellow page, impatient. I've had six games and seven practices since I last saw her. I've thrown three-hundred and twelve pitches. I've hit four home runs, seven triples, eight doubles, and five singles. I can't touch another baseball or bat or glove until I see her. I post updates for her throughout the day. We talk or message every night. She's been herself, all upbeat and smiles, asking about my games and practices, telling me rehearsals are going fine. Except last Friday she was supposed to come out to Citi Field to watch me pitch in the division championship finals. At the last minute she canceled. After the game, after I had been doused in Gatorade, I called to ask how she was. Isa was screaming about my win. She apologized again about missing the game, but never told me why she couldn't come.

The door at the far end of the subway opens. The sound of churning wheels and wind enters the car. I look up from my crossed-out and rewritten word. My concentration's already broken.

I shut the notebook and sit up tall. Blue-and-yellow high-tops walk toward me. A Yankee jersey hangs over ripped jeans. The red bandana that's usually on his arm is in his fist. He's lost his hat.

Last time I saw Danny he was Pinchón's shadow. They were hanging under a street lamp outside a bodega. I was coming back from a game. I crossed the street so I wouldn't have to talk to them. Couldn't have said what I wanted to anyway with Pinchón there.

Danny looks over his shoulder. He hasn't seen me yet. His high-tops move fast. I lift my chin when Danny turns. He looks behind him again. He sits next to me.

"¿Qué lo que, montro?" His arm claps my back. He holds out his hand for me to bump. He's tucked the bandana under his leg.

The high-tops do a dance under him. Red soles hit the black floor. Red laces bounce.

"¿Cómo tu 'ta?" I ask him. It's been over a month since we talked. Since he helped me figure things out about Isa.

Drops of sweat ring his face. Danny wipes his upper lip. "Wha? Yo, I'm fine. Hey—" Danny leans in, dropping his voice. "You got an extra cap with you? A jersey or anything?" He's watching the door. His gaze skims to my bag.

I unzip the backpack. I give him my cap. And my clean jersey for tomorrow.

"Hey, can I hold that glove too?"

I hand it over.

Danny pulls my shirt over his. It's big enough you can't even tell he's wearing two of them. Danny hasn't been lifting enough. Bryan warned him that was going to happen.

Danny jumps when the end door opens. A dude comes in. His El Presidente T-shirt's torn. He's wearing real pants. He's older than us. By a lot.

I open my notebook. I don't meet his gaze. It looks too much like a cop's.

The guy who might be a detective walks by, slow and steady. I don't look up until the door at the other end closes.

Danny's hunched over, pretending to sleep. The glove is tipped against his face. His mouth and nose are covered. He lifts the brim of the cap and peers out.

"I owe you." Danny taps my shoulder with the mitt. He takes off my hat. He blows out a breath and leans over his knees. He watches the door the guy went through. "Felicidades on last week's win."

I nod my thanks. "You shoulda been there with us."

Danny doesn't say anything for a bit. He stares at his joined hands. "Heard you may be switching schools next year?"

I pretend that Pinchón knowing my business doesn't bother me. Though, man, that news traveled fast. I only got Papi to agree to it five days ago. I haven't even told Isa. I've been waiting to tell her in person. "Yeah. Haeres. Know it?"

"Nah. But I looked it up. After Bryan told me."

Bryan and Danny were talking? I slide my notebook into the bag. I look at the door too.

"He's not happy with you," Danny says.

"Lo sé. He feels we all abandoning him."

Danny sighs. "Least you be moving up. That school 'ta bacana." He touches a finger to his forehead. A straight, pink line runs down his arm. It's thinner than the scar on his lip. Dots track along it, from stitches that just came out.

Danny sees me looking. He moves the glove to cover it. He clears his throat. "How'd you get El Jefe to let you switch? He always said AHH was the best feeder for the draft."

"The coach at Haeres said they could do better. And they're going to use Papi's help for weekend practices." I don't tell him that the coach knew all Papi's stats. And that he'd recited Papi's best game, play by play.

Danny nods. "Sounds like you got a smart coach."

The coach *is* smart. He came to a few of my games. He's got a different approach than Papi and the AHH coach.

"He goes by Big Red," I tell Danny. "His real name is Tony O'Neil."

"Related to Peter O'Neil? The pitcher from Boston?"

I grin. "It's his brother." Another reason Papi agreed.

"Nice." Danny bumps my hand. We haven't talked like this for a while. But sitting next to him on the subway? It feels just like old times, heading into Brooklyn for a practice.

Danny hands back my cap, almost like he knows what I was thinking. "Bryan's saying now he might get a better chance in the draft, seeing as you might be heading to college."

I hook my hands behind my head. "Ain't nothing been decided yet. Still waiting to hear if Haeres will take me for sure." I don't like to think of me and Bryan fighting each other for the same thing. We're on the same team. Doesn't matter what colors we wear.

Danny's leg is bouncing. A small corner of red from the bandana sticks out.

"How about you?" I ask him. "Any chance you gonna play ball again? The jersey looks good on you."

That gets Danny to smile. He sits up. He punches the mitt. "I was never as good as you two. Not even close. Oyéme, I do not miss being yelled at by Coach. Or El Jefe." He digs his fist into the leather. "You know what I do miss? Hanging on the field with you and Bryan. Just having fun. No scorekeeping."

I miss that too.

"Oh, and Yaritza's cooking." Danny puts a hand on his stomach. "Her tacos son los mejores que nada."

"Yeah, I'm one lucky guy." I face him. "Hey, why don't you come by to-morrow? Papi's going to warm me up before practice. Yaritza will make lunch. And you can see Isa. She asks about you."

He grins like he doesn't care about his scar. "Isa's gonna be in Brooklyn? ¡Guay!" Danny blows air past his lips. "Is Bryan going? You know he's quillao about that too, right?"

"Yeah, I know." Whenever I see him in school, Bryan rides me, asking when he's going to get to hang out with Isa. It's just, we're so busy. I hardly have time to see her.

Danny chuckles. "La Princesa, ¿eh?"

I don't say anything. Bryan called her that the other day. Not to Isa's face. But still. I came close to punching him.

"You know Bryan's just jealous, right? He's always jealous of you," Danny says.

I look away. That's no secret.

"So, thing's are going well? ¿Eh? With Isa?" he asks.

"Yeah." I tell Danny about how Yaritza's friend who works at Barclays spoke to her boss who was able to get these seats right next to the stage for tonight. They call them partial view, because you can also see part of the backstage area. When Isa realizes where we're sitting, she's going to climb onto one of the seats, wrap her legs around my waist, and kiss me until folks yell at us to calm down.

"I'm looking forward to cheering her up," I say. I tell Danny what I haven't told anyone. "I think something's going on with Isa's brother."

"Why?" he asks.

"Her face changes when I ask about him. Her smile gets bigger. But it's forced, you know? Kind of plasticky? And she never answers. She doesn't say she doesn't want to talk about him, but we never do. And another thing... She doesn't like to talk about anything sad."

"But that's good, right? Wouldn't want a whiny girlfriend. Pinchón's always complaining about girls who don't stop complaining."

I look down at my notebook, safe in my bag. "I'd rather know what she's feeling. Instead of feeling like she's hiding from me."

"El Jefe must love her, if he's letting her spend the night."

I smile instead of telling him that Isa's only met Mami. I don't tell him what Papi said when I first brought up Haeres. That the fancy school must have been her idea. That college must have been her idea too. How he asked if I'd met her parents, if I'd shared a meal with them. He patted my cheek when I said, "Not really," and said I wouldn't until I passed her rich-white-people tests and I showed her my college acceptance.

It's harder for some people to see past what's on the outside. But that's not Isa. I told Papi so. He laughed and said I was a fool.

"Mami loves her," is what I say now.

The express doors open. We're already at Seventy-Second.

"Hey, lo siento pero I'm getting off at the next stop. I'm meeting Isa. You could come. She'd love to see you."

"Nah, it's OK." Danny gives back the glove. "Maybe I'll come by tomorrow." He takes off my jersey. He doesn't look me in the face as he hands it over. I don't think I'll be seeing him tomorrow.

I stand to get ready. "Hey, I never asked how you're doing?"

Danny smiles. But it's stiff and plasticky. "I'm doing great."

The doors open. I have to get off.

• • •

Isa doesn't come to the Sixty-Sixth Street station. I wait a full half hour later than the time we agreed on. She doesn't answer her phone. Or respond to my DMs.

It's getting hot down here. I have my big bag with me and I can't bring it in the stadium. I leave Isa another message, telling her my plan. I get on the train. I run from the station to the house and back. I make it to the Barclays Center, sweat coming through all my clothes. The show starts at seven. But the main act probably won't come on until nine.

I text Isa again. And again. I wish I had Chrissy's number. I'd call her too. Something must have happened. Isa wouldn't leave me hanging like this. She knows how hard it was to get these tickets. I didn't tell her I spent three weeks of my BI paycheck on them, but she must know they're expensive. I flip through my old texts, all the way back to the end of December. Isa used my phone to contact her mom. I find the number. I press call. It goes to a voice mail that hasn't been set up.

By eight thirty the sun is almost gone. It's cooler at least. The crowds are gone too. Almost everyone's inside catching the opening act. I'm trying to stay calm. I'm telling myself nothing bad happened to Isa. I haven't moved from the top of the steps, where she'll see me. I take out my phone and try Isa again.

"¿Ále?"

I turn around. Kiara lifts and taps the heel of her sandal. She's got a hand on her hip.

"What are you doing here?" she asks.

I show her my two tickets. My eyes feel full. I blink to clear them.

Kiara looks me up and down. "Well you're not here because you want to see Leo." She takes off the small purse draped across one shoulder. "Me and that blondie must have the same taste in music, huh?" She smacks her gum. She looks me over again, slower this time. "Don't know why I'm surprised. We have the same taste in men." She steps closer. "And you don't care you're missing the first band?"

"I don't know who's playing."

"Lena Adeyemi? Leo's former classmate who became famous after she starred in his music video? Yeah, she's cool. But I got stuck on a train. So that's why I'm late." She does a little bow.

I look to the doors of the station.

"Yeah, maybe she got stuck on my train too. What time were you and blondie supposed to meet?"

I don't want to tell her we were supposed to meet at five. "Seven."

Kiara's gaze shifts to the large digital clock above the entrance. "Damn. She late. You sure she's coming?"

I look at the clock. Mostly so I don't have to look at her anymore.

"Was this a big night or something?" She blows a bubble with her gum and pops it. "Were you gonna bring her back to your place? Have her meet your papi and Yaritza?"

I look away as another pink bubble forms.

"For real?" Kiara taps her foot. "You think she stood you up because of that? Because she didn't want to meet 'em?"

I look at her quick. I mean it to be a warning. My coño eyes well up.

I show her my back.

"You called her, right? You left her messages?" Kiara's voice is quieter. I nod. I don't turn around.

"So there's nothing more you can do." Her high heels click against the sidewalk. I smell her spicy perfume. Like rum and gingerbread. "Come on, let's go in together."

I don't say anything. What if Isa's sick? What if something really bad happened?

Kiara sighs. "Fine. But don't stay out here by yourself all night. Because you know what? If she ghosted you, you shouldn't let her ruin your night and waste the money you spent on those tickets. And if she didn't? If she just can't make it? She wouldn't want you to miss the concert. She'd want you to at least go."

Kiara walks around me. I think she's going to stop and give me that look of hers. But she keeps walking, up toward the propped glass doors of the main entrance.

My phone buzzes. It's Isa. My heart rams into my throat.

So sorry. Can't make it. Something came up.

That's it? That's all she writes? No details? No explanation?

I text back.

Are you OK?

I need to know. I can't breathe not knowing.

Yes. I'm fine. So sorry again.

My heart jerks, like I'm still on that brake-tapping train. Like I'm the fish with a hook jammed through my mouth.

Kiara's on the top step when I call out to her to wait.

SATURDAY, JUNE 10

9:03 AM @ARos0133: Aren't you going to ask me about the concert?

9:26 AM @ARos0133: Hello?

9:40 AM @ARos0133: You OK?

10:08 AM @ARos0133: You're making me worried.

11:10 AM @ARos0133: Papi's yelling at me. I'm not pitching right. Because I'm thinking about you. I'm UPSET. Please tell me what's going on with you.

11:24 AM @ARos0133: Isa?

● ● ●

1:45 PM @BalletBelleIsa: Sorry. Didn't have my phone. Sorry again about last night. How was the concert? ☺

1:46 PM @ARos0133: The concert sucked. Because you weren't there. Because I spent the whole time imagining what could have happened to make you miss it. Are you gonna tell me???

1:50 PM @ARos0133: Can you please pick up the phone?

2:10PM @ARos0133: Why won't you talk to me?

2:23PM @ARos0133: Did I do something?

2:27 PM @ARos0133: Are you angry with me?

2:38 PM @ARos0133: Are you sure you're OK?

3:14 PM @ARos0133: You didn't miss your period or anything, did you?

3:15 PM @ARos0133: If you did, I'll come find you right now. We'll figure it out. Just tell me where you are.

● ● ●

4:48 PM @BalletBelleIsa: Sorry. I'm not allowed to use my phone where I am. I'm fine. Really. (And just finished my period 2 days ago, so no worries there.) You don't need to come.

4:49 PM @ARos0133: Where are you?

5:03 PM @ARos0133: You're not at the Academy because I know you can use your phone there.

5:10 PM @ARos0133: Seriously. Where the hell are you?

5:35 PM @ARos0133: Please. Just tell me where you are. I'm dying here.

6:14 PM @ARos0133: I'm staring at a plate of Yaritza's tacos I can't eat because I feel sick. You're making me feel sick. Just tell me what's going on. Please.

● ● ●

9:06 PM @BalletBelleIsa: Sorry. Just got home. Please don't be worried. Everything's fine. I hate that I'm making you feel sick. It's just there's a lot going on right now with my family.

9:08 PM @ARos0133: Is everyone OK? Would you please pick up the phone? Why don't you answer when I call?

9:15 PM @BalletBelleIsa: Sorry. My mom's home. I can't talk.

9:16 PM @ARos0133: You mean you don't want her to know you're talking to me.

9:19 PM @ARos0133: Why don't you go into the bathroom like you usually do when we talk?

9:21 PM @ARos0133: I didn't mean what I wrote about you and your mom. Just please let me talk to you.

9:46 PM @BalletBelleIsa: I'm sorry. I'm really tired.

9:47 PM @ARos0133: I'm really tired too. Of you not telling me what's really going on.

9:48 PM @ARos0133: I didn't mean that either. Just get some sleep. We can talk tomorrow. I love you.

SUNDAY, JUNE 11

1:43 AM @BalletBelleIsa: I love you too.

1:58 AM @BalletBelleIsa: But I've been thinking. Maybe we should take a break? Things are just going really fast. And you have your travel ball coming up. And I'm starting full time at the Academy.

1:59 AM @BalletBelleIsa: And I hate that I'm making you worry.

● ● ●

6:49 AM @ARos0133: WHAT??? Are you serious? You can't be serious.

6:50 AM @ARos0133: Call me when you wake up so we can talk.

8:32 AM @BalletBelleIsa: I'm heading out and I'm leaving my phone at home. Please don't call. I just need some space right now. It's nothing you did. It has nothing to do with you. It's me. I need to slow down. I need a break. I'm sorry. I hope you can understand.

8:35 AM @ARos0133: No, I don't understand. We can slow down. We can dial it back. I'd be happy just to sit next to you on the train.

And don't blame this on baseball and ballet. We can find a way to make it work over the summer.

8:37 AM @ARos0133: Unless what you're saying is you don't want to be with me anymore.

MONDAY, JUNE 12

7:12 AM @ARos0133: I guess you not answering is my answer.

SATURDAY, SEPTEMBER 9

ALEX

"Julissa's not coming. She kicked Bryan out again." Kiara rolls her eyes as she says this. She told me last week not to count Julissa when I gave Papi the final numbers for the barbecue. But we were just at the diner, the four of us, celebrating the end of the summer. It might as well only have been the two of us. Bryan and Julissa's lips hardly ever came apart.

The train comes out of the tunnel, onto the elevated tracks of the 125th St. Station. I face the river. Habit from all those mornings heading down to the Institute. The sun peeking between those East Side buildings blinds you. The days we weren't traveling or playing ball, I was working there. Turns out, I had more time than I thought I would this summer.

I glance at Kiara. "What'd he do this time?" Poor Bryan. They made it through the whole summer together too.

"You tell me, he's your friend." Kiara slides the cross pendant along her necklace back and forth.

"Yeah, but there's so many things he could've done. Question is, which one of 'em made her angry? She's *your* friend." I nudge her arm.

She rolls her eyes again, but she's still smiling. "That boy, he don't know how to act. All that talk about the females on the road who wanted a piece of him? He should know better than to bring that up in front of her."

Yeah, Bryan has that problem. He thinks it makes him look important to say that stuff.

"You should teach him a thing or two," she tells me.

"'Cause I'm the expert?"

"You better than he is. Much better."

I squint, trying for a view of the Hudson. Sometimes, you get a glimpse of it between that old brick building and that new metal one the university put up. We stop and I can hear the hum of Kiara's pendant rubbing against the links of her chain. The doors slap open. Car brakes squealing and truck doors slamming streams in. And then there're the people, arguing, laughing, kids crying.

"So there'll be thirty-eight of us," I say. Final numbers don't matter much anyway. Yaritza's sure to have made enough for a hundred. Papi even lined up a band. Yaritza was teasing him that she wanted mariachis. Papi told her we're going bachata and merengue all the way. I'm looking forward to the party, the eating and relaxing part at least. Not so much the dancing.

"You think Bryan's gonna come? He won't be nursing his poor broken heart?" Kiara keeps yanking at that cross. But it's like someone pressed Mute 'cause I can't hear it anymore.

"He better. Else he'll have to answer to Papi." I shake my head. If Bryan doesn't show, I'm gonna have to trek back to the Heights to get him. The entire travel ball team is going to be there.

The train ducks back underground. The tunnel muffles the grinding of wheels against track.

"What about Danny?" Kiara grips the pole with both hands.

"I hope he comes." Even though he didn't travel with us this summer, I still think of him as part of the team. Ever since summer started, he's been MIA. I've been afraid to look for him. I don't want to see that red bandana on his arm.

The doors open at 116th. A guy wearing a navy shirt with a white *C* and a crown gets on the train. He's holding a clipboard. Another guy and two girls crowd around him. They're all asking questions at once. *Where do we start? What's the first clue? Where do we get off?* More college students load on through the other doors. They've got clipboards and shirts with C's and crowns on them too.

"I'm worried about Danny." My shoulder knocks the rail as the train starts to move. A couple of the students lose their footing. They bump into each other and laugh. Their shouts of "Sorry!" bounce through the car.

"Why you worried? Looks to me he's doing fine. He's got some new chévere shoes each time I see him."

"Yeah." Danny traded his blue-and-yellow ones for some crazy emerald-green high tops. "But that's what I mean," I tell her. "Where you think he's getting the money for that?"

"Maybe he's not buying them?"

I hadn't thought about that. If he's stealing them off some poor other kid that would be worse. I can't picture Danny doing that.

Kiara lets out a sharp laugh. One of the college guys almost smacked one of the girls in the face when the train braked. The girl in the cap scowls at Kiara. Kiara puts fists on her hips and glares till the girl looks away.

I pull Kiara closer. I tug her fists down. "You think he's stealing?"

She shakes her head. "Maybe they're gifts? From Pinchón."

Coño. She's right. They probably are.

I should have gone to his apartment this morning, got him out of bed, got him dressed, and made him come to celebrate with the team. Doesn't matter if he thinks he's not one of us anymore. I could show him he is. I take off my hat, punch it out, and put it back on. "He's going to end up like his brother, isn't he?"

"Nah," Kiara says. "Pinchón and his boys, they look after one another. That's the whole point of 'em. They know Danny's brother's in jail. They gonna work hard not to let Danny fall in jail too."

That's the whole point of *our* team. To look after one another. We're better when we're together. Stronger. Papi said when one teammate is letting the others down, not making practice, blowing off games, sometimes you gotta make a cut. But what if I hadn't listened to him? What if I'd gone and dragged Danny with me to all those practices and games? He'd have listened to me. He'd have come. Just like he would have come with me today to this party.

I reach for the brim of my cap, but Kiara grabs my hand. She pulls me down to her. I'm a little surprised. She doesn't like to make out on the subway. At school, yes. At the diner, yes. At the field, after a game, hell yes. In fact, the more balls I hit, the more runs I drive home, the more players I strike out, the more she wants me. But she thinks the subway's dirty. She doesn't like it when I touch her when we're riding. But instead of slapping my hand, she presses it onto the back of her jeans. I slide it up to her waist. She pushes it back down.

I try to look at her to figure out what's going on. She pulls me back, her mouth all hungry.

"Hey," I ask, my finger under her chin. "You know travel ball is finished, right? I'm not going anywhere until next summer."

"Yo sé. Now stop talking." She tugs at my shirt and kisses me again.

One of the college guys across from us elbows his friend. They're not looking at us though. They're looking over our heads. Toward the other door. I glance over my shoulder. A girl with blond hair in a bun and a black hoodie sweatshirt stares at me.

Heat drains from my face, from my fingers. It plunges down to my toes. My feet are hot. The heat must melt the bottoms of my shoes because I can't move them. My lips are cold. They refuse to move too. So do my eyes. They don't look away from her.

Coño.

That's my sweatshirt. I gave it to her that night I brought her to my apartment. She was cold on the way home.

"¡Ále!" Kiara's yanking my arms.

Isa's cheeks are white. Her eyes blink. She covers her mouth with her hands.

"¡Ále!" Kiara pinches me. "¡Ále!"

I turn to her. Flashes of heat prick at my chest.

Kiara stumbles back at the look on my face. "¿Qué what?" she says, all defensive.

The doors chime and whip open. I swing around as a streak of gold aims for them.

Doors close. The train rumbles on. The girl students are talking about tofu and seitan. The guys are talking about the beautiful dancer who ran out like she was late for her curtain. Kiara and I don't talk about anything. I can't even look at her.

When we get to Brooklyn, I wait for Kiara to help Yaritza with a platter of arroz con pollo. I take out my phone. I scroll through my old posts. A week after the Barclays, I woke from a nightmare. In my dream, Isa was calling for me. No. She was screaming for me. Something awful had happened—I didn't know what. I only knew I had to get to her. But I couldn't. No matter how much I fought and kicked and cried out, I kept being pulled away.

That night—when my hands stopped shaking—I picked up my phone. I tried calling her again. I messaged her, every way I knew how. She didn't answer. I went to her dance school and stood outside, but I didn't see her. I didn't see Chrissy either. Then our out-of-city games started up. I spent the whole summer in that dusty van, checking my phone. I took a picture of every single home plate on every field I played and posted it. In our last week of travel, I posted one of the poems I wrote her. Guess some part of me was hoping Isa was checking her accounts too, even if she didn't want me anymore.

I got back from Atlanta, from our last tournament, three weeks ago. Bryan dragged me to a party. Kiara came right on up to me. I was straight with her. I told her I'm not looking for no girlfriend. She said she didn't care. She just wanted company and what kind of man was I to refuse that? She knew I was busy and wasn't ready, but she'd be happy with whatever I could give her. When she got me alone, she put her mouth to my ear. She whispered she could help me. She could help me forget.

I wasn't prepared to see Isa just now. I wasn't prepared for it to hurt so much. Now that I've seen her, I don't know what to do.

I lean against the fence and fumble with my phone as a guitarist beside me tunes up. I snap a pic of my foot, of my sneaker. I write in brilliant blue on top of it: **I'm sorry.** I post it. I know better than to let myself hope.

SATURDAY, SEPTEMBER 30

ISA

Chrissy and Kevin are waiting on the platform. They've been doing that lately even though I never ask them to ride with me. Kevin lifts his hand to wave, then drags his wiggling fingers through the air to his pocket. I do the same to him. It's our personalized greeting, a joke from when they first started dating. Because he's a piano player and he tickles the ivories and all. He also tickles Chrissy, but only when she baits him.

Chrissy tackles me in a full body hug. "How. Are. You?" She squeezes me with each grunt.

I squeeze her back. "I. Am. Fine."

"Ready to spend your Saturday afternoon sweating it out at this awe-some workshop?" Chrissy tugs down my sweatshirt, unrolling the frayed bottom cuff that used to be black but is now more of a gray. "Martha Graham kicks butt. Literally. My butt hurts for days after running her rou-tines." Chrissy leans over to touch her toes, stretching said glutes. "The teacher they're sending us is amazing. He came last year too."

"Yeah, it's going to be great." I show them a wide smile. I was just telling Dad how much I love my new school, how I love that the Academy is chal-lenging us with different techniques. I keep telling myself the same thing, that it's exciting and that I should be loving it.

"OK, babe. You want the Summer Bowl with chicken instead of tofu, right?" Kevin leans down to kiss Chrissy. "I'm heading to Sweetgreen if you want me to get you something, Isa." Kevin doesn't have to play at the work-shop. He's just going to be a groupie today. He'll probably sneak off to one of the sound rooms to work on the jazz piece he's composing.

Chrissy grabs Kevin's hand. "If the Summer Bowl's no longer available because it's almost October and all, just ask for the Shroomami but substi-tute sweet potatoes for the beets."

"Got it," he says. "Anything?" He looks at me.

"I'm fine, thanks." I've got plenty of protein bars in my bag.

"See ya." He turns, piano fingers waving at us over his shoulder.

"So look what I just noticed." Chrissy shows me a run in her tights. "You don't have any extras, do you?"

"Sorry." My dance bag is sparse these days. I only buy the bare minimum of what I need.

Chrissy looks at her phone. "I'm going to have to get out at Seventy-Second to run to Capezio. Thank the gods, I still have time. Hey." She pokes me with a finger. "I've been meaning to ask you about Merrit." The 1 train charges into the station, pulling her words away from me.

I try to look normal. "What about him?" Chrissy and Kevin know Merrit was in the hospital, because they were with me that day. We're telling people Merrit had a bad reaction to one of his medications. The doctors say it is one explanation for what happened. Mom especially will believe anything if it means she doesn't have to accept the alternative. Chrissy knows Merrit's taking the semester off, to get back on his feet. I never told her about Merrit getting kicked out before that.

Chrissy licks her fingers and smooths a tiny curl behind her ear. She slides out a bobby pin and slips it in, holding the hair in place. "Well I called your landline the other day, since you weren't picking up your cell. Anyway, Merrit answered."

I'm careful to keep my smile steady. Merrit never mentioned that.

"He sounded good. He told me all about reMAKE, which sounds really cool, by the way. Anyway, do you know when the app is going live? I was thinking maybe I could use it."

I line up next to the correct car and the correct door. I wait for a man with a very large dirt bike to get off. Chrissy follows me in. "What, you want to become a vlogger all of a sudden?" I try to keep my tone light.

"No way. But I'm thinking I want to make a video for Kevin." She traces her hair, feeling for flyaways.

I give Chrissy a what-are-you-talking-about look.

Chrissy sits all the way back. She gazes up at the ceiling. "We still haven't, you know..." She trails off, and I feel my mouth fall open. I lean toward her.

"You haven't?" I whisper. "What about all those sleepovers?"

"They're not really sleep-with-each-other sleepovers." She covers her eyes with her arm. "I know, right? Who would have thought that I, Christianna McCallum, could have lasted ten days much less ten months without getting it on? I certainly wouldn't have." She slides forward and looks at me. "I mean, we do other stuff. He keeps me happy. I keep him happy, I think." Chrissy bites her sleeve.

"So why the video?"

"It's just... I'm worried about blowing my cover. I thought maybe a real virgin would want to wait longer before doing the deed, so I keep holding him off. The longer we wait, it just becomes a bigger deal. Now it's like this thing between us that's defining us. We're the virgin couple who's so in love and who respect each other so much we don't want to de-virginize each other. So I figured maybe I could use Merrit's app to make a video. Explain everything to Kevin. Ask him to forgive me for not telling him. I don't think I can do it in person. And I'd be too nervous to video myself actually saying all those things. Typing them would maybe be OK though."

I pull the sleeve out of her mouth. I think of her, of what she should do.

I do not think of me in that situation at all. "You don't need a video. You don't need to tell Kevin. Just make a plan. Set a date for the deed. Build up to it. It is a big deal even if it's not the first time . . ." I look at my hands as she searches my face. "Or . . . handful of times. It'll be important. Because it'll be with him." I try not to think of me and Alex. "And you love each other." I take a slow breath. My fingers are going numb. I beg my throat not to seal up. "That will be a first for you, even if it's not *the* first."

"I can't be with Kevin," she says. "Not until I come clean with him. And I certainly can't fake a first-time experience. I'm scared enough as it is."

"Scared? Why?" The words croak out of me. I reach for my water and take a long sip. I keep drinking until there's none left.

Chrissy's eyes get really big, like she's pleading with me not to laugh. "What if it's not as good as those other times? What if I only like sex when it's with semistrangers? What if that's the type of sex person I am?" She whispers all of this.

"Chrissy, you're too young to define the type of sex person you are. Anyway, people can change, right? You won't know until you try." It's what I tell myself so I don't get too depressed. I haven't thought about or even looked at anyone since Alex. All the desire, all that crazy energy my body had, it just disappeared when Alex did. Sometimes I wonder if it will ever come back. Like it clearly did for him, with Kiara.

Chrissy nods. I tickle her elbow. She starts to laugh, then stops. Her eyes balloon open again.

"What—?"

"Don't turn around." She grabs my shoulder, but it's too late.

Alex walks into our car.

I press my hand to my chest, the soft cotton of his sweatshirt flattening under my palm.

When I was in the auditorium during orientation, surrounded by students perched on the edge of their seats with perfect posture, and the dean was describing workshops and visiting professorships and travel performances, I kept waiting for the thrill my mind expected. Now I feel it, under my hand, the quick thrum of my heart.

He's in his baseball uniform. He's got a huge bag over his shoulder. It must be filled with bats and gloves and balls. The entire front of him is splattered with mud, from his shins up to his chest. Sweat stains track under his arms and around his collar. Beads of it trickle from his hat, down his cheek, to his jaw.

Alex hasn't seen me yet. He turns slightly, talking to someone behind him. I hope it's not that girl, Kiara. It's hard enough seeing him. I can't watch the two of them together.

"Come on, let's go." Chrissy takes my hand. I don't move. A young boy is standing behind Alex. He's also in a baseball outfit. Only he's not caked in mud. Alex tells him to take a seat. The boy doesn't want to go to the empty one without him. It's all the way in the middle of the car. Alex lets out a sigh. He takes the bag off his shoulder. He says excuse me as he weaves between standing passengers.

Seeing him move sends a jolt of familiarity through me. My heart stumbles, then picks up speed, like a rock crashing downhill. The boy sits down across from us. I study his face. It has to be Robi. Alex stands in front of him, his back to us.

People on either side of Alex make their way toward the door. A man in a sports coat next to Robi gets up. Alex looks down at his uniform. His back rounds, like he's trying to make himself smaller. He tells Robi to lift his feet and stashes the bag lengthwise under the seats, out of everyone's way. He stands with his arms tucked against himself. He rides the gentle swaying of the train and doesn't hold on.

Those passengers moved because of him. Either because he's so big or because of the dirt on him. That he's self-conscious about it makes it hurt to breathe.

It was my decision to walk away. If I'd been home that day, my brother wouldn't have spent two weeks in the ICU and three weeks after in the psychiatric hospital. If I'd spent more time with Merrit instead of running off to be with Alex, my brother wouldn't have almost died. And all those times I kept things from Alex? He knew. He let me. He was willing to take what I could give. But missing the concert? Not telling him why? That was too much. Alex deserved an explanation. I couldn't tell him about my brother, not without telling him everything else. Not without him knowing what a horrible sister and girlfriend—what a horrible person I am. Thinking about it all makes my stomach turn.

Chrissy doesn't know any of this. She thinks Alex is the one who broke it off. Another reason to feel guilty.

Robi peeks around Alex's side. He must have noticed me staring. His eyes aren't dark like his brother's. They're light brown, like mine. I give him a little smile, embarrassed at being caught. His return grin is blinding. There. That's the family resemblance.

A woman rises from her seat. She covers her nose as she passes Alex.

"God, ever think of taking a shower?" Chrissy snaps.

"Chrissy!" I hiss. "Don't."

Alex turns, his eyes wider than I've ever seen them. He holds my gaze for three long seconds. He tips his face to the floor and frowns.

My lips feel dry. My throat too. I wish I hadn't finished all my water. I didn't expect he'd be happy to run into me. But does he have to be so unhappy?

Chrissy looks him up and down. Her sneer would send plenty running for a cave or any other kind of shelter. "Seriously. It looks like you were wrestling in dog doo. Disgusting."

"Chrissy!" I say again.

Chrissy stands. She thrusts her chin at Alex. "We're getting off anyway." Her fingers extend for mine. "Come. You're going to the store with me."

Robi peers at me, at Chrissy, at Alex. His grin has shrunk to a hesitant smile.

I don't want to do that to Alex. I know what his brother means to him. I can ride with them for one more stop.

I take Chrissy's fingers. I squeeze her hand. "I'm fine. I'll see you at class."

She doesn't move. *You sure?* her expression says.

"Yes, thank you." I give her my stage smile, the one that shows each person in the audience, even the ones in the very back row, that I'm both overjoyed and confident.

Chrissy nods at me, glares at Alex, and marches out the door.

When the train starts up again, I lean forward. "Hi," I say to Robi.

Alex jumps back when I stand. He moves down another seat length as I come over, turning the dirt-caked part of him away from me.

"I'm Isa." I offer my hand to Robi.

Robi rips off his cap. He takes my hand and gives it a shake. "I'm Robi." He's beaming again.

"That's what I figured." I glance at Alex. He's still frowning at the floor. Is he angry that I stayed? Should I have gotten off with Chrissy?

"We were in Central Park, playing baseball. That's why we're so dirty." Robi's fingers bend the brim of the hat down and up, down and up.

"I figured that out too." I bend down to whisper. "Your uniforms gave you away."

Robi drops the cap in his lap. He holds up his hands, his eyes rounding. "Today was a special exhibition game. Each school got to send two players. Haeres sent Alex even though he's new and only a junior. It's because he's their best."

So Alex got in to Haeres. "That's wonderful," I say, and I mean it. "You must be very proud." Alex stiffens when I turn to him. His throat works as if he's swallowing down words.

"Oh, I am proud of him. And Papi is too. He's still there, helping. The younger kids, like me, are playing. But I'm not." Robi looks at his feet. "Alex is taking me home."

Alex's eyes slide almost helplessly to mine. His gaze slips away when Robi starts talking again.

"Hey, how do you know my brother?" Robi asks, as if suddenly putting it together.

"We're friends."

Alex looks up when I say that. I can still use that word, can't I? He has every reason to hate me. But I don't think I could stand it if he did.

"We actually met on the subway," I tell Robi.

Robi nods. He's looking from Alex to me. "That's so cool! Hey, Alex is taking me to the park near our house. Sunset Park. Do you know it?"

"I've heard of it. I bet it's beautiful."

"It's OK. There are some actual baseball fields near our house too, but they're probably being used by real teams now. So we're going to the park. Do you play baseball?"

"No. I don't really know how." I laugh at the face Robi makes. He adores Alex. It reminds me of how I was with Merrit at that age.

"Well, if you want to learn, Alex is the one to teach you." Robi's eyes get really big again. "Oh, you can come with us now! She can, right, Alex?"

Alex is watching me. His brow crumples. His small smile is so sad, I have to look away.

What happened to us? What did I do when I walked away?

"I wish I could," I tell Robi. "But I have a class. In fact, this is my stop." I look up at an ad for helping the homeless. I blink and blink until my eyes clear.

The train wails as it pulls into Sixty-Sixth Street.

"Oh man!" Robi slaps his leg. "Next time, then?" He scrabbles his cap back on.

"Sure. Next time," I manage to tell him.

"Bye, Isa!" Robi cries out as I bridge the gap between the train and the platform.

"Bye, Robi. It was nice to meet you," I call back. "Bye, Alex," I whisper to myself.

SATURDAY, SEPTEMBER 30

ALEX

We come up out of the subway. Afternoon sun glints off rusted rooftops. Wind blows but the yellow and orange leaves hold on tight.

We head for the park. Robi wants to carry the bag. I tell him it's too heavy. He asks why I haven't noticed how much he's grown over the summer. Fine, I say. Half a block later, I shoulder the bag again.

Some kids are playing football on the field. Another two throw a Frisbee back and forth. I lead Robi to the far corner, toward the boulder he liked to climb when he was smaller. There's enough room for us and more.

I dig out a bat Robi's size and hand it to him.

Out of nowhere he says, "Isa's really pretty. I think she's prettier than Avery Santana."

"Avery Santana?" I turn to look for his glove.

"The girl who lives next door. You've never seen her?"

The girl who was playing catch with her dad. "I've seen her." I take out two balls and put them next to the bag. Ten-year-old me would have thought Avery was cute. But she's nowhere near Isa's league. Even at ten, I bet, Isa was beautiful.

"So why was she looking at you like that?" Robi's swinging the bat. His grip is wrong.

I find Robi's mitt. I take hold of the bat. I don't let it go until Robi's moved his hands all the way down the handle. "Who?"

"Isa. You didn't see?"

I take a breath. I slide on my glove and pick up a ball.

"It's like she wanted to look at you. But instead of just facing you and saying hi, all she did was these quick looks from the side. It was kinda like how you were looking at her." Robi's stopped swinging. "And her sweatshirt. Didn't you used to have one like that?" He's waiting for my answer.

I roll my head, stretching my neck. I reach up and massage a pinched muscle. "Isa and I . . . She used to be my girlfriend." There's no harm in telling him that.

Robi's bat tips to the ground. "Shut up," Robi says. "When?"

"Last spring."

"What did you do?" he demands. "Why isn't she still your girlfriend?"

I squat and riffle through the bag. I don't need anything else out of here. I just don't want to see Robi's face. "I didn't do anything. Except walk away." What else am I going to say? I still don't know what I did wrong. And I'm not going to tell him she walked away from me. If Papi heard that? Coño. I'd never live it down. He'd be saying *Te lo dije* for the rest of my life.

Robi punches my arm as I stand. "What did you do that for? She's so nice. Nicer than Kiara. Kiara never talks to me."

I rub my shoulder and show my teeth, pretending Robi's fist hurt. I don't tell him that Kiara's different. That she's not really my girlfriend. I don't think he'd understand. "Isa is nice. But it wasn't going to work. Her parents didn't like me." This is truth.

"How could they not like you? Are they blind and deaf or something?"

I smile at his joke. "I don't know. I only ever met them once. And not for very long."

"Then how do you know they didn't like you? How did they know they didn't like you?" Robi's voice rises like it does when a game is close and we're in the last innings.

"They didn't like the idea of me."

"What does that mean?" He drops the bat and lifts his arms to the sky. It's like he's been taking lessons from Bryan.

"You'll understand when you're older." There's no way I'm explaining that. Let him enjoy not understanding for as long as he can.

Robi rolls his eyes. "Well, she liked you, right?"

I pick up the bat, flip it around, and hand it to him. "Yeah."

"And you liked her?"

Lines of dark wood course through the blond grain of the bat. They disappear under my fist. One of the poems I wrote for Isa comes back to me. About the way her hair looked against my arm.

I nod.

Robi snatches the bat. "So who cares what parents think?"

He should be right. Even if he's only in fifth grade.

"Since when do you not care what Papi thinks?" I ask him.

"Papi's different. He's not like other parents." Robi raises the bat over his shoulder. "Ezra and Seung-wong's parents are cool. They don't yell."

I tap Robi's hands, reminding him to line up his knuckles. I don't tell him I think Isa's parents are like Papi. I don't tell him that's not the only reason we're not together anymore.

I adjust the bat's angle then step back to check his form. He remembers what I taught him last week about keeping his body straight. I tell Robi I'm going to feed him twenty easy pitches. He's going to run to retrieve each ball as fast as he can. I'll time him. Just like Papi timed me. After that, we'll work on his catching.

Robi chases his first hit. I'm glad he's not asking about Isa anymore.

We walk back to the house. I tell Robi to run inside and open the basement door. I don't want to track all this dirt into Yaritza's living room. Robi grabs onto the railing like he's going to drown without it. I worked him hard today.

"Oye," I tell him. "You're getting stronger. And faster. I can see it."

He's halfway up the stoop. He turns back around.

"Thanks." His little chest is all puffed up. He takes one more step. "Hey, when did you and Isa stop being boyfriend and girlfriend?"

I scratch my chin, pretending to think. Really I'm trying to figure out why he asked. "I don't know," I tell him, even though I do. I know the exact day. "Just before school finished for the summer?"

"That's what I thought." Robi keeps climbing.

"Hey, hold up. What do you mean, 'that's what you thought'?" How would Robi know that?

Robi shrugs his bony shoulders and looks over at me. "You threw out that notebook. The one with the yellow paper. The one you carried all the time. Mami used to complain about the bits that would fall out when you tore the sheets from it, so I started picking them up for you. Don't think you noticed because you were too busy writing in it. Then one day I was throwing away the scraps in the trash and the whole notebook was in it. It still had plenty of paper. I figured something bad must have happened since you loved that notebook so much."

I rub the back of my hand across my mouth. I'm worried he's going to ask me what I was writing. I want to ask him what Yaritza thought I was writing and if she told Papi about it. I don't say anything except, "Huh."

"I saved it for you," Robi says. "In case you want it back. You know, when you wrote? You looked happy." He squints, studying my face. "I think maybe happier even than when you play."

When I get out of the shower a half hour later, the notebook with the yellow lined paper is on my bed.

FRIDAY, OCTOBER 13

ISA

I'm the second one out the door after Technique class. I've got thirty minutes before Jazz Movement.

"Excuse me. Pardon me." I dodge a beige bodysuit pirouetting in the hallway and duck under a pointed foot elevated above the dancer's head. I weave around clusters of students talking too loudly, each with limbs extending and reaching and stretching. My gaze remains focused ahead. Ever since seeing Alex and Robi on the train, I don't look at any single person's face for too long. Their smiles hurt, because they're real. They remind me what I had and what I lost, what I chose to give up. They remind me how little I have left.

The locker room is heavy with steam and the smell of damp dance clothes. I kick off my shoes and head for the showers. I stand under the jets and close my eyes, imagining heat and water peeling back layer after layer, thought after thought, discarding the sadness, finding the soft core of me underneath.

I'm out by the time Chrissy comes in, hands in her hair, adjusting her bun.

"You showered again?" She dips her chin and slides a pin through her hairnet. "Didn't you shower after Pointe?"

I ignore her and bend to wrap the long, damp mess of my hair in white terrycloth. Chrissy sits beside me as I tug on a clean pair of tights. When she's done pulling on her own, she stands, raising her arms, then drops into a deep plié. "Want to come over tonight? We're ordering in Vietnamese and watching YouTube videos. It'll be fun."

It's Friday, so I was expecting the invite. Chrissy always asks on Wednesdays and Fridays. She knows Monday and Thursday I'm either hanging with Merrit or taking extra classes until nine or ten. Tuesday is family therapy and Saturday and Sunday is family dinner.

"Thanks, but I can't." I adjust my tights, careful not to jam my ragged fingernail through the nylon.

Chrissy straightens her legs then plants her palms on the floor to stretch. "Why not?"

"I'll be at class," I tell her.

Chrissy unfolds herself, lines of confusion marring her forehead. "What class—Wait, you're not taking the enrichment session with Madame Bouchard, are you? That will be your fourth extra class this week."

It'll be my fifth, but I don't correct her.

"OK. What are you doing for Halloween then? Can we go to Lauren and Deborah's party together again? I was thinking we could be Betty and Veronica from *Riverdale*..."

"Don't you want to go with Kevin?" I ask, looking for a way out.

"Funny thing. He hates costumes. He says he'll meet us afterward. We can catch a midnight showing of *Rocky Horror*. Susan Sarandon is such a versatile actress. Hey, that's another idea! We could be Thelma and Louise, the ultimate gal pals who ditch all the men in their lives. How about it?"

I fold my wet towel and lay it on top of the others thrown in the wicker bin. I think about what I did to Alex, how he looked at me on the subway, his little brother glancing between the two of us. I did ditch him, didn't I? I don't think that's anything to celebrate. Anyway, why would Chrissy think I'd want to dress up as someone who gets back at the world by offing herself? As if that would be an answer. As if that's something anyone should ever do.

"Hey, I'm sorry," Chrissy whispers, realizing her mistake. She tries to take my hand. This time I let her. "Did, um, the psychiatrist find out what happened with Merrit and his medicines? Do we know for sure it was just an accident?"

I shake my head, my eyes smarting.

"Well have you asked him?" Chrissy asks. "Maybe he'll tell you. You've always been close." Her thumb strokes my hand. I tug it away. Alex used to do that.

"The doctor said it's best not to talk about it until he's ready," I tell her.

Chrissy nods. "OK. I guess the doctor would know. But listen, I'm worried about you. You haven't been yourself since ..." She doesn't say since Merrit or since Alex though I know that's what she's thinking. She watches me pull on my jazz shoes. "It's just, all this work and no play, it isn't good, Isa."

"I'm OK. Really. And the extra practice is good for me. I might even get a solo out of it for the spring performance. Or at least something good for *The Nutcracker.*"

"What you're going to get out of it is a sprain. Dance is an escape. I get that. It's an escape for me too. But if you don't slow down, you're going to get injured."

I undo my towel, shaking my hair loose. My smile is tight. "I'm fine," I tell her. I jam my hair into a bun. I pack my old tights and leotard into my bag, pausing when my fingers glance off a square of paper. I pull it to the mouth of my backpack. I unwrap it just enough to see Alex's handwriting.

Chrissy's staring at my back. I can feel it.

The locker room is clearing out. There's nobody else talking.

"Come on. We're going to be late," I tell her without bothering to turn around.

"You're making me nervous." Her voice sounds disant. "Kevin says I should talk to your parents."

No. I crush the poem in my fist. I shove it to the bottom of the bag. I make my smile bigger, brighter. "You don't have to worry. I would tell you if I needed help."

Chrissy scans my face. "I wish I believed you." She walks out. I reach for my lip balm. My hand comes back out with Alex's poem. His words jump out at me through my tears, words I've read a hundred times.

DREAMING

You sit on a bench
as the first batter approaches,
y te lo juro,
my chest becomes feathers
quivering
> before you.

My grip tightens and I remind myself,
my fingers know the firm curve
of this ball stitched with red,
the white skin of it soft
and smelling of earth
and grass stains
and sweat.

From my hand, this ball takes flight,
soaring toward fate,
aiming for the worn pocket of a mitt,
slipping past swinging wood,
hopefully.

The ball comes back,
thrown high in the air.
I catch it

but sink down to cradle
You,
Your foot,
the firm, soft curve of it,
the part of you that gives you flight
as you soar toward fate
across a stage of lights.

I grip this ball reverently,
tenderly.
This ball I do not want to let go
though your head tipped back in the grass,
    laughing, begs me to.

I read it three times before I cinch my backpack closed. I'll tell Chrissy I'll go to her place. I'll agree to a Halloween costume. I'll do whatever it takes, always.

TUESDAY, NOVEMBER 7

ISA

Snowflakes drift into the rose-colored halos of the street lamps below. They settle onto the dingy sidewalks and disappear. It's supposed to snow for less than an hour. There won't be much accumulation. I imagine being outside, letting the snow land on my face and my upturned palms, watching the flakes fade to nothing as if they were never there.

"Isabelle?"

I look away from the window. Dr. Patel, our family therapist, watches me. His face, as always, is kind and expectant. Dad is watching me too—only, he looks worried.

"I'm sorry. What did you say?"

"I was wondering if you would feel comfortable sharing with us how your mood's been this past week?"

Dad scratches at the stubble of his beard. Mom is looking at Merrit, who's staring into his lap, into the void left by his phone, which is on Dr. Patel's desk. Mom reaches out and presses her hand to Merrit's knee, an attempt to stop his constant jiggling. He only jiggles his leg harder, until her fingers slide off. Dad takes up Mom's hand, but his eyes stay on me.

"Fine," I tell them. I want to look out the window, at the snow.

Dr. Patel moves his head. It's not quite a nod. It's just something he does to show he's heard me. "How has it been taking the subway with your brother? I know that was a source of concern for you in the past."

"Also fine." Merrit's been so mellow these past few months. It's hard to imagine he did the things he did. I glance at my brother. He's still not looking at me.

"What has it been like taking on so much responsibility?"

"It's no problem at all." If I didn't bring Merrit with me, Mom and Dad wouldn't be able to meet with their own psychologist for couple's therapy the hour before ours. No one thought leaving Merrit alone was a good idea.

"Everyone appreciates the effort you're making for the family, Isabelle," Dad says.

I give him my own not-quite-nod to let him know I heard him. Dr. Patel asks Merrit the same question about mood he asked me. I can't help myself. I turn to look at the snow. It's my only chance to see it. By the time we go back outside it will all have melted. It will be as if it never happened.

● ● ●

Merrit and I take the subway home alone. Dad and Mom have gone out to dinner, just the two of them. We wait for the train in silence. I search the platform, half worried, half hoping to see the strings of a black hoodie or the tips of Adidas or Converse. I don't need to worry. There's hardly anyone on the platform.

Merrit's face carries a blank stare that probably mirrors my own, like he's trying not to let any emotion in or out. The train comes, sparing me from thoughts of Alex and Merrit and Chrissy's words asking me if I've talked to my brother about that day. She'd said it as if she were talking to the old Isa, the one who was close to her brother, who knew her brother better than anyone except maybe himself. I don't know if that's true anymore. I don't know why he did what he did, whether he meant it or not. That frightens me the most.

Our shoulders bump, Merrit's and mine, as the train rockets us back toward Ninety-Sixth. I turn to Merrit, desperation making me bold. "What really happened that day Dad found you? The day he had to call an ambulance?"

Merrit sinks back against the bench, arms crossed in front of him. He stares at his gangly legs, bouncing again with nervous energy. His wary glance shifts to me. "What do you want to know?"

I want to know if he meant to take those pills, if he meant to leave us, and to shout at him asking what was so horrible that it was worth doing that to Mom and Dad and me. I want to know what he remembers from the weeks that followed, being hooked up to machines in intensive care, unable to even pee on his own. I want him to tell me if it was terrible enough to make him never do it again. Mostly, I want to know if he blames me like I blame myself. I want to know that he wouldn't have done it if I had been home.

Instead I ask, "Why?"

His eyes dart back to me. His fingers dance over his thighs, playing twin imaginary keyboards. "I don't know," he says.

It's too much, not knowing.

He licks his lips when I start to cry. He throws himself back against the seat once and then again. He shoves his hands beneath him. The drumming comes out in his feet. "I—" He looks into his lap. He shakes his hair so it falls next to his face, so he doesn't have to see me. "You know I don't mind staying up all night, working on my apps or hanging with other gamers online. It's like when I was first with Samantha, like I'm on top of the world. Nothing can touch me. Nothing matters, not even getting kicked out of college. Or being twenty and living with my parents. But I know I'm weird when I'm myself. I know it's hard to put up with me." He lets out a huff. "So I took the medicines the doctor gave me. I took more when he said it wasn't working fast enough. But then, all of a sudden, it was too much. They were pulling me down like water dragging toward a drain." He nods his head. "I tried to fix it. I took a few different pills. And I went into Mom's room and took some of hers. I didn't want to feel sad. But I didn't mean for any of the other stuff to happen."

Merrit's teeth worry at his bottom lip. I wipe my face with my sleeve, then reach for his hand. The pull of sadness terrifies me too. Only, my brother is smart. He's been called a genius since he was four. He knows about side effects and drug interactions. If I can find it on the internet, it's already downloaded to the mainframe of his mind. There's no way he didn't know what he was doing, that the mix he took was dangerous.

I squeeze Merrit's hand. I press it to my cheek and lean on him. He puts his arm around me. "I'm sorry," he whispers. I start crying again. I never needed to ask him. I already knew the answer. I was just afraid he would tell me the truth.

WEDNESDAY, NOVEMBER 22

ALEX

I squint through slanted rays of sun. Men with hands shoved deep in their pockets walk beside women wearing fur-trimmed hats. Woolen scarves cover mouths. Some people carry children on their shoulders. Others push strollers with miniature faces that peek from blankets. Wind blows and people in blue jumpers holler and grab ropes to tie down cartoon characters. Next to me the foot of a purple dragon comes loose. The creature rolls as if it means to go on its back. If upright, it'd be taller than the twelve-story building behind it.

I've never done this before. I've only ever seen the parade balloons on the screen of our TV while cutting green olives and onions for Mami's special stuffing. But Haeres has off the Wednesday before Thanksgiving. I figured it would be cool to watch the setup.

My phone beeps.

I'm by Pikachu.

I turn, searching. **Coming**, I text back.

A lady knocks into me as I type. She was backing up, trying to get a picture of the Poppin' Fresh, the Pillsbury Doughboy.

"Sorry," I tell her, even though I wasn't the one moving.

She jumps when she sees me. Her hands go up like she's surrendering and her eyes search for help. Another woman in a fur hat scurries over. They link arms and move into the crowd. I shake my head and follow the mass of people down Seventy-Seventh Street, keeping an eye out for Pikachu's yellow belly and red cheeks.

Bright orange cones divide Columbus. On the other side, people huddle and bob their knees to stay warm in a different line that traces the corner of a glass-walled Shake Shack. It's so famous, not even the cold could keep them away. Smiling customers exit through windowed doors, gloved hands holding cups of thick custard. I think about grabbing us one. I'd have to jump the orange divider though.

A cop leans against the wall. He scans the crowd. I watch as he picks out a face and follows it. I keep my hands in my pockets and I'm about to duck my head when a familiar girl with red curls comes out of the store. She scoops soft ice cream while talking. The guy behind her holds the door. He pushes his glasses onto his nose.

There's no way she should see me. Not with all the people around.

I head toward the lemon-colored balloon. I pretend I don't hear anyone shouting my name. Kiara is standing below an outstretched yellow paw. I kiss her cheek and ask her where Julissa's at. She starts to tell me Julissa canceled when someone interrupts.

"Alex." Chrissy stands behind me. She must have run. I was walking pretty fast even with all the people. She had to climb over the plastic barrier. The nearby cop, a different one, isn't even looking at her. On the opposite side of the street, Kevin stands with both their shakes.

Kiara looks from Chrissy to me. "Who's she?"

"Can I talk to you?" Chrissy's focus is only on me.

I put a hand on Kiara's shoulder. "'Pérate," I tell her. "What do you want?" I ask Chrissy.

"Alone?" she asks. "It won't take long."

I bend down to Kiara. "Dame un segundito. I'll be right back."

Kiara's hands are on her hips. She shakes her head as I follow Chrissy toward Spider-Man's foot. She waits for me. Gracias a Dios, she doesn't trail us.

Chrissy walks us past Spider-Man. When we're underneath the Diary of a Wimpy Kid's diary she grabs my jacket. She spins me around.

"You should call Isa."

I check her face to see if she's joking. She's not smiling or anything.

The hot pulse of anger surprises me. "Isa and I, we're not together." I thump my chest.

Two gray-haired ladies in matching puffers look at us. No, they look at me. A mom with a stroller steers a wide circle to pass. I unclench my hands.

"I know," Chrissy says. "But still, you need to talk to her."

This girl 'ta loca. "Why would I do that? So she can throw me away again?" I didn't mean to shout. "So she can tell me I'm not good enough for her? Anyway, I'm with someone else. If you didn't notice." I jerk my head toward Pikachu.

Chrissy bunches her painted lips. She scratches at her chin like I said something that confuses her. She better not think I'm dating a balloon.

Her eyes narrow. "Wait, what do you mean, so she can throw you away? You didn't break it off?"

I give her a hard stare, the way Papi does when a player challenges his call.

She stares back. She bunches her lips more. "Well, all I know is, the only time I ever saw her happy—really happy—was when the two of you were together."

"Yeah? That's great. Thanks for your opinion. Maybe you should ask your friend what she really thinks of me though."

Chrissy shakes her head. "Listen, sometimes you don't know a person's whole story." She swats at a curl. "Sometimes we keep secrets from the people we care about. Because we're trying to protect them. Or protect ourselves."

I throw my hand up. A man and a woman duck out of the way. "What are you talking about?"

Chrissy crosses her arms. Her ruby mouth smooths to a line. "Isa told me what you thought." She shrugs a shoulder. "About me and Kevin. About me keeping stuff from him. We're good now. Isa's brother, Merrit, helped me out with that. But I should have told Kevin sooner. It would have saved us both a lot. You were right. It's not good to keep secrets from someone you love." She stares at me without looking away. Her words remind me of Mami's. It reminds me of what happened between my parents. Why Papi stopped playing ball. How he had problems with drugs and lied about it to Mami. Until it cost him his career. His marriage. He was lucky it didn't cost him his life. It's why he's so strict about it with us.

Kevin comes up behind Chrissy. He's looking up at the black squiggle of Balloon Greg's mouth. Kevin's arms are wide, holding the two shakes. I shouldn't be thinking anything funny right now. But Isa would say he looks like he's offering Chrissy a taste test.

"Hey," he says to me.

"Hey," I say back. The cop must have let him climb over the orange cone divider too.

Kevin leans down to look in Chrissy's face. "Everything all right?"

She nods. She bear-hugs him. Her hooded head burrows into his coat.

Kevin lifts his arms higher so the ice cream doesn't spill. He bends his knees to kiss her forehead.

I never told Isa about my papi. I kept waiting for her to say something, to ask me about when Papi played on the team or why he stopped. Isa never did. She was only interested in me. In my ball playing. In my poems. In making me smile or laugh. I figured it was a gift, a sign that I didn't have to tell her. Because what would she have thought of me, of my family, if I had?

Chrissy peeks up at Kevin and the way he smiles down at her makes me think maybe I was wrong. Maybe I should have said something to Isa. Sure, I know Isa was keeping things from me. But I guess I was too.

Chrissy turns back to me. Her fingers dig at her eyes. "Just think about it, OK? You need to talk to her. And you've got to get her to talk to you. Please? Just try again?"

I hold her gaze. I don't say yes. I don't say no.

She walks away.

"See ya." Kevin lifts a shake in my direction.

They're under Spider-Man's hand when Chrissy looks back. "You don't honestly believe Isa thought you weren't good enough for her, do you?" Her eyes look kind of teary, but she blinks and jams a spoon heaped with thick vanilla into her mouth. Kevin rubs her back and leads her away.

What else was I supposed to think?

Kiara's waiting right where I left her. She's watching Kevin and Chrissy stroll toward Columbus, eating their shakes.

"Wait a minute. ¿Es esa la chica que estaba en el tren en Halloween? The one who was kissing that guy?"

I put my arm around her. "No."

I tell her I know Chrissy from school. She used to date one of the other players on the Haeres team. The lie bothers me only a little. I don't want to talk about Isa. I want to forget everything Chrissy said.

I pull Kiara down Eighty-First Street, toward the Wimpy Kid, Elf on the Shelf, and the snowman from *Frozen*. Kiara doesn't ask anything more.

MONDAY, DECEMBER 4

ALEX

The fountain is drained, empty. It was like that the first time I came here with Isa. When Bryan and Danny said those things about her, and she let me walk her to class anyway.

It's late. The winter sky is so dark it could be seven o'clock or ten o'clock or one A.M. The opera house lights are on. There's no one inside except for a man with a bucket and a mop. He stops in front of a window, takes up a rag, and starts to clean. His hand passes in front of white letters that spell OTELLO against a background of black.

The past few days, I played over what Chrissy said. About secrets and not being honest. I knew Isa was keeping stuff from me—her whole family for one. I hadn't thought about what I was hiding from her. So here I am because, guess what? Isa still isn't taking my calls. She's not answering my messages either.

Students come out the glass doors of the building next door. The girls all wear buns. The guys have short hair, except for one with a ponytail. I don't see Isa. I don't see Chrissy. And I've been here since five. This time, I'll stay as long as it takes.

I sit on the granite ledge. Cold seeps through my pants to the backs of my legs. My breath makes clouds as I wait.

The janitor moves to the next window. And the next. He's on the last one in the row when the doors to the Academy open. More girls with buns exit. None of them are Isa. They walk arm in arm as if on wildflowers they don't want to crush.

I pace a circle around the fountain, then sit back down. I don't take out my notebook. I won't risk missing her.

I get up and walk to the windows. I put my hands on the glass and peer through, to see if any students are still inside. I checked the website before I came. Mondays there are no holiday performances. The dancers should be leaving after their classes. I tug on the door handle, but it's locked. A keypad flashes red at me. I go back to the fountain just as the dance school doors swing wide. A man who could be my father heads straight for me. The opera house lights glint over a brass nameplate that looks like a badge. I know it isn't one. But still, my heart knocks against me. I don't move.

"Hey." The security guard stops about fifteen feet away. "You can't be here." His hands rise to his waist. A baton hangs from his belt.

"Um . . . I'm waiting for someone."

"Who?" he asks.

"A student. A dancer." I try to look him in the eye.

"What's her or his name?"

"Isabelle Warren," I reply.

His face doesn't change. I don't know if he recognizes Isa's name.

"Is she expecting you?" he asks.

"No, I—"

The guard holds up his palm. "You need to go."

"But—"

"You're loitering. If you don't go, I'll have to call the police."

I fist my hands in my pockets. My huff of breath is like dragon smoke. "Can I at least leave a message for her?"

His squinting eyes widen. "You don't have her phone number? Now you really got to go." He shows me his thumb.

I do have her number. She just won't answer it.

I walk toward the Symphony building. I take the corner and lean up against the wall.

A couple walks by, bundled in scarves and hoods. Their laughter cuts off when they see me. I swear I see the guy draw the girl closer. They both look over their shoulders, back toward the fountain, once they've passed.

The security guard comes into view. He takes out his phone. He puts it to his ear. He watches me as he talks into it.

I'm finished here. I turn, heading for the subway.

"Alex?"

MONDAY, DECEMBER 4

ISA

Alex's eyes go round when he sees me. His hands come out of his pockets. "Hi," he says.

Freddy, the night guard, jogs over. "You know this guy? He's been hanging around for hours, looking in the windows and stuff."

I nod, studying Alex's face. The temperature's in the twenties. It's arctic out here.

"He's scared a few folks. He tried to get in the side entrance," Freddy continues. "I was about to chase him off."

Alex breaks our gaze to scowl at his feet.

The idea of anyone thinking Alex a threat is like a hand squeezing my heart. "I'm sorry." I mouth the words, but Alex doesn't see. He glares at the stone slabs beneath us, tracking the long, rigid line between light and dark. He's at the edge of one of the sand-colored spokes that radiates like a beam from the fountain. I am paces away, in the middle of a sea of black.

"You sure you're OK?" Freddy's looking from Alex to me.

"Yes, thank you." I turn to stand beside Alex, easing closer while keeping space between us. I want to show Freddy I don't need him.

Freddy nods and heads back inside.

If Alex had come on any other night, the plaza would have been filled with crowds for *The Nutcracker*. No one would have noticed him. And I would have been on stage until ten. I wonder if Alex knows that.

Alex remains motionless, his irritation not quite directed at me but near enough that it smarts. Still, my stomach quivers. Heat seeps into my hands and up my neck. My body recognizes his. It doesn't care about all that has passed.

I was planning to take the subway. I won't if it means riding with Alex.

"How's Kiara?" I don't know why I say that, of all things. It must be the part of me shouting to put distance between us. Hoping he'll leave so I can get on the subway alone.

Alex grimaces. "She's fine." He tells it to his shoes. He shakes his head and lifts his face to me once more. "She's not you, Isa. She never will be."

Wind kicks up. I shiver inside my coat. I duck behind my scarf. I should walk away but I cannot move. My feet won't obey.

"You're cold. Come on, let's get you inside." Alex's arm comes out, the other extends toward the subway.

More than anything, I want to feel the weight of that arm, the warmth of it around me. Instead I step back. "What do you want, Alex?" I mean to ask him why he's here. But also, I wonder if he wants to hold me too, if the longing for it is shaking him apart.

Alex frowns at his hand, the one reaching for me, as if it's a habit he's been meaning to break. "Your hair is wet." He says it with surprise.

Before he can move toward me, I coil the frigid, stiffening strands and tug up my hood. It's dark and the street lamp's behind me. Alex can't possibly see my face anymore. I try to back away from him. My feet have stopped listening to me. They want to know why he's here too.

Alex's frown returns as I remain silent. "Did you have a nice Thanksgiving?"

He didn't come here to ask me that. "Yes, thank you. And you?"

His hand brushes his abdomen. "Ate too many guava pastries."

I smile, safe within my hiding place.

"I had no one to share them with."

His hopeless tone springs tears from my eyes. My mood's been like this these past months, shifting from one second to the next. It terrifies me.

"I tried calling you. Over the past few days. I texted you too."

I nod even though I didn't know, because I blocked his number. I thought it would be easier that way.

"I miss you," he whispers. His hands are in front of him. His fingers open and close but he doesn't reach out this time. He gazes down at me from under thick, thick lashes.

I miss you too. I almost say it. My tongue twists, fighting to form the words. My eyes swim with tears. Thank God for my hood.

He clears his throat when I don't say anything. He looks toward the opera house. "I came because I wasn't straight with you. About my papi." He tells me his dad played pro for only a season and a half. That drugs led to an injury and then a suspension. That he was in and out of rehab and had a few arrests for possession too. One of those arrests was when Alex was with him.

Alex watches me, bare and undone. My insides ache for a five-year-old Alex who had to grow up under that shadow.

"I'm so sorry," I tell him. I'm not aware of putting my hand on his arm. The warmth of his hand covering mine makes me realize what I've done.

"I should have told you sooner," he says. "But I didn't want to give you another reason not to be with me."

"What?"

Alex shrugs. "You never met Papi or Yaritza. We set it up a few times and you never showed. And I know you didn't want me to meet your mother. Danny told me about her."

My breath catches in my throat and I fight the urge to cough. Did Danny hear what Mom said about him? Did he tell Alex that?

Alex squeezes my hand. "It's OK. Your mother's right. I'm not good enough for you. I'm just another moreno from the Heights with a papi with a record."

I feel exhausted all of a sudden. Like I could lie down on the cold stone and close my eyes.

"I would never think of you that way." He must know that, right? "You are not your dad. What he did—what he does—that's not you. It shouldn't affect how people see you or what they think of you."

"Yeah," he says, but his eyes don't meet mine. As if he knows I only partly believe what I'm saying.

"And you not being good enough for me? That's just bullshit. That's not why I needed to take a break."

His face snaps up. He watches me. He's waiting for me to give him the real reason.

Nausea clambers up my throat. I let go of his arm and step back, the hand that had been under his pressed to my mouth so I don't lose the protein bar I just ate all over his sneakers.

"Isa? Are you OK?"

I shake my head. Is this why he told me about his dad? Why he brought up my mom? He's expecting some big confession from me, isn't he?

"Chrissy told me I should come find you."

"Chrissy?" Confusion, followed by alarm, fills me. Did she tell him about Merrit? "What did she say?" I demand.

"Only that you and I should talk. I think . . ." He shifts his feet. "I think she's worried about you."

I rip off my hood. I blink into wind like ice. "I'm fine." I grit my teeth and force my face to smile. Tears stream onto my cheeks but it's from the wind and nothing more. Alex shouldn't have come. I'm glad he told me about his dad. That he trusts me enough to share that. But nothing for me has changed.

"Goodbye, Alex." I run until my feet strike the steps to Columbus Ave. I don't bother crossing to Broadway to get a taxi going uptown. I don't think of how much it will cost. I hail the first one I see.

SATURDAY, DECEMBER 9

ALEX

I run up the stairs to our apartment. Mami was expecting me sooner. One of the kids in my group didn't get picked up on time. The kid was standing by the office, his bottom lip quaking. Robi used to do that when he got upset. I sat with him out by the batting cage and we talked baseball until the nanny came.

I open our door and the smell of bacon, fried beef, garlic, and peppers hits me. Mami knows I love her sancocho. She must be trying to cheer me up.

"Lo siento," I say when I get to the kitchen. I usually cut up the onions and the vegetables.

"No te preocupes." She sticks out her lips for a kiss. When I was smaller, she'd peck the top of my head. Now I bend so she can reach my cheek. I wash my hands in the sink, careful not to let water spray the platter of tostones waiting for a final fry.

I leave my sleeves rolled up. "¿Qué hago?" I want to help.

Mami shakes her head and tuts at me. "Nada. We'll be ready to eat a las siete. Pero, go shower. Your friend, she will be here soon."

I glance at her, confused. I thought Sra. Hernandez was joining us.

Mami shrugs. "I miss seeing your smile."

I try to wash the cutting board and the pots in the sink. Mami shoos me out with a dish towel.

I go to my room and strip off my dirty clothes. Before heading to the bathroom, I take my notebook out of my bag. I open to the poem I'm working on. It's the fourth since I saw Isa outside Lincoln Center. The twelfth since I started writing again. I've been working through everything—my anger, my shame. But also there's beauty, and longing. There's Isa. I read over what I wrote, marking what doesn't sound right.

I bend my head under the shower. Water beats down on my back, almost too hot to bear. I roll my neck, loosening my muscles, relaxing my mind. Drops enter my mouth as I murmur words, shaping the poem. I crack the small window behind the showerhead, wiping condensation from the mirror. I layer on shaving cream that smells of peppermint, a birthday gift from Yaritza. With each sweep of the razor, I recite a new line.

I open the door and steam billows into my room.

Kiara's on my bed, curled on her side. Her hair is up in a bun. She never wears it like that—it's always down, a mass of dark curls. The top of her dress hugs her body. Folds the color of a tropical fruit drape her hips. She doesn't do girly outfits like that either. Frayed jeans are more her style.

I tighten the towel around me. Mami knew I was showering. There's no way she would have sent Kiara in here.

"I told your mami I needed to freshen up. She said I could use her bathroom. If she catches us, I'll tell her I got lost. I wanted to give you your Christmas present early." Kiara's ankles uncross. Her legs are covered in some sort of black lace.

Coño. Does she really think that's what I want? Does she think she owes me something?

I look away from her and my breathing cuts off. My notebook is out. I left it open to the poem.

Kiara follows my gaze. She rises onto her elbows. "Did you get me something too?" I move for my desk. Kiara's already off the bed. Her dress swishes behind her as she scoops up my writing. My back, my arms, my neck jerk tight.

"Look at you, Mr. I Don't Want a Girlfriend." Kiara's smile softens as she reads. My stomach is tangling knots. She places the notebook back on the desk. She climbs into my chair, tucking her feet under her. She turns page after page.

I slide a pair of boxers off my dresser. Kiara doesn't look up when I slip on my pants. I go to my closet. My heart drums like fists against bars.

I grab a T-shirt. I'm pulling it on when hands tipped with pointed, glittery nails stop me.

"'Pérate." Kiara presses up against my still-damp skin. She paws at my neck, draws me down to kiss her. Her fingers loop around my belt. She tugs me toward the bed.

"I didn't know you could write like that." The words are gasps in my ear.

I kiss her back even though it feels wrong, wrong, wrong. I don't see a way out of this cage.

Kiara has never made me forget. I don't think anyone can. But I don't want to hurt her.

"Tell me," she commands. She nips at my jaw. I let her put her mouth on mine. She pulls away, her smile sly. "Tell me I'm your musa."

Her body, pillowy and soft, climbs over me. But when I close my eyes, she is not who I see. I see my hand tracing the length of lean, graceful limbs. I feel muscle, taut and trembling against mine.

Kiara kisses me again, her mouth greedy. My eyes clench shut. I don't know what else to do.

My fingers drop from her waist where she put them.

She breaks away. "Tell me you wrote those poems for me." There's worry in her voice. "They're about me, aren't they?"

All I have to do is nod.

Kiara glances at my hands, fisted at my sides. I'm still not holding her. I can't.

Kiara shuffles off the bed. She snatches up the notebook and starts to read a poem out loud. The one I just wrote. Her voice catches over the last line. Her eyes lift from the wrinkled paper. They're wet, but there's challenge in her glare.

I grab another shirt from the drawer. I reach to take the notebook back.

"No!" She doesn't let it go.

I pry her fingers from pages that rip.

"Mamagüevo," she hisses, as I tear the book loose.

She slaps my chest. My cheek. I let her. I deserve it. She yanks at my shirt. She slashes at it with her nails. I deserve that too. Her groan becomes a shriek. "Maldito hijo de la porra, vete al diablo."

I hold the notebook high. It's all I care about. The only thing I won't let her get.

"Lo siento," I say even though I know it's not enough. "I didn't mean for you to find this."

Kiara scratches and slaps at me more. Her face is redder than her dress, her bun a loose tangle down her back.

"¿Ále?" Mami's concern comes through the door.

"Don't you ever—EVER—come near me again. You sorry, sorry excuse for un hombre." Kiara backs toward the hall. Her hands are shaking. "You know, I feel bad for you. She dumped you, ¿recuerdate? But you're still dreaming about your blanquita girlfriend, panting after her como un perro."

Kiara's right. Isa doesn't want me anymore. But that doesn't mean I can't still think about her. Being with Isa was the most remarkable thing that ever happened to me. I'm good at ball. I'm good at writing poems. But loving her? I was great at it.

Kiara spits out a laugh. "I was so stupid. I didn't believe what people say about you. I thought, there's no way someone so fine and so good at everything, someone who's so proud of his mami y papi, could be a hater. But apparently everyone else knows you better than me." She aims a finger at my face. "You're never gonna be one of them. You know that, right? No matter how many fancy schools or fancy teams you join. No matter how many blondies you get with. You'll always be a moreno . . . un dominicano. You got to stop hating yourself for that."

Kiara launches from my room. The front door slams like a thousand lockers.

I count to ten before I breathe. I wish she'd kept hitting me. Her hands hurt less than her words.

I love my family. I love the island they came from. I don't love that I tense up every time a cop passes. I don't love that strangers look at me like I'm someone who's going to hurt them instead of help. Do I wish I were different? Yeah, sometimes I do. And I hate myself for it. But that wasn't why I was with Isa. It's maybe why I'm not with her, though.

Mami stands in the hallway. Her eyes are so wide, the whites of them show. She glances in, sees me standing there. The notebook is still in my hand. She frowns in concern. When I shake my head slightly, she ducks her head and hurries toward the kitchen.

I want to tell her I'm OK. But I don't want to lie.

I shut my door. I put the notebook down. I pull on a new shirt and sit at my desk. I turn page after ripped page. Carefully, I tear the ruined ones from their binding. I transcribe poems until Mami calls me for dinner.

SUNDAY, DECEMBER 10

ISA

I smooth out layers of tulle and reach for my tiara, checking it's secure. The tempo of the music shifts. I extend my arms, flutter my hands like snowflakes. The first three dancers prance out. Three more come on from the other side. They leap and spin and—just as quickly—exit. I tilt my head, flicker my fingers faster, then dash on stage.

Bright lights glance off my painted cheeks, my sculpted brows. My muted lips lift into a well-rehearsed smile. My arms circle up and around my tiara. I soar into the pas de chat. I pop onto my toes, pirouette, then duck down and scurry off, lifting my pointed feet high in front of me. I've got to the count of twenty before I'm on again. I flex my foot. My left calf has been tight since I pulled it a few weeks ago. But there was no possibility of missing a *Nutcracker* performance.

"Ready?" Jane, the dancer who leads us on, shakes the hem of her sparkly skirt. Stage lighting makes it glimmer even brighter.

Chrissy stands ready behind the second curtain. She'll come on right after me. I flash her a smile to show her I'm fine. She doesn't see it, because she's frowning down at my foot.

The music fades. Notes from the harp float up from the pit as we float back out. We dip and flit and whirl, weaving circles and figure eights around one another. Sauté, assemblé, plié. I spring forward, my leg striking out in arabesque. I push off my heel, preparing for the jeté.

My ankle folds. There's a faint *pop*, like the *crack* of a toothpick.

I want to cry out. Instead, I keep smiling.

I draw myself into an exaggerated plié. I bourrée off stage, my weight on my right foot.

Bert, the props manager, catches me before I fall.

● ● ●

"Are you sure I can't help you?" It's the fourth time Dad's asked since we left the emergency room.

I shake my head. My fingers are wrapped so tightly around the crutches, there's no blood left in them.

Dad holds the door open while keeping a hand near my elbow. I pretend not to see it. He shuts the door, then kneels down and reaches for my shoe.

"I can do it." It comes out as a snap. I didn't mean that.

Dad sinks back onto his heels. He adjusts his glasses. "Sure. Of course you can." He's whispering because Merrit is asleep. Thank goodness. I was afraid he'd still be awake. Dad rises and takes off his own shoes. "I guess I'll go check on your mom."

I lean against the wall, balancing on the crutch and the plastic boot as I try to kick off my one sneaker. Pain spears my ankle. Beads of sweat pop out along my back and neck.

Dad comes out and sees what I'm trying to do. "Hold on." He carries out a desk chair and places it beside me. I slide onto it and yank off my shoe just as Mom rushes out of the bedroom. She flings herself onto me, hugging me so tight I almost can't breathe. I can't remember the last time she's held me.

"Does it hurt?" she rasps, still not letting me go.

I swallow the lump in my throat. "I'm fine, Mom. It's not that painful," I lie.

"She's OK, Elisa," Dad says. I feel the thumps of his hand on her back through my chest. Mom has gotten so skinny. She pulls away and wipes at her eyes as Dad goes to the kitchen and fills a plastic bag with ice. *The New York Times* is still unfolded on the counter. He started leaving the crossword for me this past week, when he began his new job. Dad hasn't complained about the boss who's younger than him, or his salary being so much less, or about the medical insurance that has a lower cap on mental health coverage. Mom has though.

Dad picks up the crossword and offers it again. When I was younger, Mom and I would do them together. It was one of the only times she didn't yell at me for getting something wrong.

I shake my head but Mom reaches for the newspaper.

"Maybe tomorrow you'll do it with me?" she asks.

I give her a hesitant nod, blinking when my eyes fill with tears. This whole night has been too much.

Mom stands over me, like she's waiting to see how I get up and move around. "I'm so glad nothing is broken or torn. What a relief that must have been when the doctors told you."

I try for a smile.

"But I have to say, I knew something like this was going to happen," she continues. "Overuse injuries are common in dancers. At least you don't need surgery. We have enough medical bills piling up. And your father's insurance doesn't cover physical therapy so that will be all out of pocket, which we really can't afford right now."

I bite my tongue hard, so the tears slip back. Why does she have to make me feel so guilty about it? Does she think I wanted to get injured? Even a sprain means weeks, possibly months, of no dancing. I'll miss the rest of the *Nutcracker* season. And going to Physics and World Literature with students who will be running off to Pointe and Variations will make me miss dancing even more. Not to mention I'll have nothing—*nothing*—to throw myself into to escape from everything and everyone in this apartment.

Dad puts a hand on Mom's shoulder. "Let's try not to wake Merrit," he whispers. "Do you need help getting dressed for bed?" He waits for me to say no before pushing Mom toward their room.

Dad waits while I change. He helps me into bed, props four pillows under my leg, and tucks the bag of ice around my ankle. Merrit's heavy breathing that borders on a snore filters through my open door.

"Thanks, Dad."

He rests a kiss on the top of my head, pressing it into my hair with his hand. "I don't want you to worry about the cost of any of this," he tells me. "We'll find the best physical therapist there is." He sighs. "And your mom didn't mean to upset you. It's just..." He shrugs. "She says things without thinking."

I nod, not sure I can do anything more.

"I know it's late, but is there anyone you want to call?" he asks.

"No thanks," I tell him. "Chrissy and I already talked."

He shakes his head. "That's not who I was thinking of." He looks down at his feet. "I've been meaning to ask you about Alex. Have you been able to keep up your friendship even though you're no longer at Deerwood together?"

I'd forgotten Dad thought Alex and I were classmates.

I don't meet his gaze. His concern—something I've seen a thousand times directed at my mom—will break me. "It's been hard," I tell him. "I've been pretty busy."

"Yes, I imagine so. But now..." He gestures to my ankle. "You'll have more time. Maybe you should call him. It's important to have someone to talk to. Someone to complain about your parents to." He tries to make a goofy grin, but his lopsided smile just looks sad. "Get some sleep." He reaches for the light switch.

Panic flutters inside me, pushing words into my mouth. For some reason, I want Dad to know who Alex really is.

"Hey, Dad?" My voice sounds tinny, like it's coming from a phone speaker far away. His hand pauses on the switch, and he turns to face me.

I swallow, forcing myself to press on. "Alex never went to Deerwood. He went to Alexander Hamilton High in Washington Heights. I met him on the subway. On his way to baseball practice. He's an amazing player. And an amazing poet too."

Dad leans against the wall. "Wow. He sounds like a really interesting guy. I can't wait to get to know him better." He doesn't reprimand me for not correcting him before about Deerwood. And I don't tell him that he won't get to know Alex better because we're no longer friends.

"Goodnight, sweetheart." He turns out the lights, and I lie back in my bed. The city bleeds around the edges of the shades, throwing light on the small bumps in the ceiling that look like melted rock salt on sidewalks. Outside, an angry driver leans on his horn. My foot throbs against the pressure bandage. I roll to my side, stretching for my middle drawer. My hand fumbles, finding only space where there should be the familiar edges of my pointe shoe box. It isn't there. The throbbing in my foot rises to my chest. I'm seconds from full-on hysteria when I spy the box on top of my dresser, tucked underneath the faded black hoodie. I was looking at the poems earlier in the week, after I saw Alex outside the Academy. I was so upset that night, I must have forgotten to put it away.

I reach out and run my finger over the shiny purple jewel on the box. I carefully lift the lid.

On top is a note folded in half. It's not from Alex. Not all his poems remain in the tiny square I found them in, but this one has only one crease, right down the middle. And the paper isn't lined. It's from the printer. My heart pounds. How could I have been so stupid to leave the box in full view of anyone who came into the room?

I pinch the corner of the note and ease it out. I close the box. This paper doesn't belong in there. The note springs open as soon as I release it. The shaky, slanted cursive looks nothing like Alex's; but I recognize it all the same. Merrit scolds me in that joking way of his. He even sketched a picture of himself, eyebrows a V, mouth a zigzag, finger pointing. He's glad I have someone special in my life. He hopes I know he would accept whoever loves me like those poems show. He hopes that now that I've read his note, I'll tell him about this mystery person, maybe even introduce them. He promises he'll take his medicine that day and he won't do anything awkward like stick spaghetti in his ear to make the person laugh. He signs it, *I love you. I'm sorry you have to put up with me.*

I'm crying so hard I almost can't read his P.S. He apologizes for opening the box but since I left it out, I should know it was fair game. I fold the note into a square. It ends up being even smaller than the ones from Alex. The edges aren't sharp. The paper's so damp I'm afraid it'll tear.

I open the box. I was wrong. It does belong inside.

SATURDAY, DECEMBER 16

ALEX

"So you're on second. The score is 8–7 in the eighth inning, your team's up. You've got one out and no one else on base. You gonna steal third or not?" Bryan's shoulders rock with the train. He waits for Robi's answer.

Robi stares at the space under the seats across from us. He's sucked his lips into his mouth, he's concentrating so hard. "Steal?" he answers.

"Good." Bryan knocks him with his elbow. "Now, what if you've got two outs and you're down 8–5?"

"Stay." Robi straightens. He shows Bryan a smile. "You said if we're behind more than two runs, stealing third isn't smart."

"You didn't ask about the hitter," I remind him. Papi would have hammered him if he'd given an answer without all the facts.

Bryan claps his cap to his head. "Ay, sí. Robi, what do you do if it's a left-handed hitter? Same setup."

Robi screws up his face again. He doesn't remember. I've been trying to spend more time with him but there's more homework at Haeres than there was at AHH. I've had more baseball practices too, even in the off-season. I told Papi he should bring Robi when he comes up to the school during the week to help train the team. But Papi never does. He almost didn't let Robi come today to the Institute's holiday charity drive. Gracias a Dios, Yaritza worked her magic. Papi's been setting up since six A.M., but we're only just leaving.

We get up to change trains at Forty-Second Street. Bryan's arms wave as he explains how a right-handed hitter blocks the catcher's view and stands in the way of his throw to third. He would know. Bryan's likely going to get AHH's MVP if he keeps upping his game like he has. Papi said it's because Bryan's not in my shadow no more. A star player can ruin the confidence of a solid one. I think it's because there's not as much drama between him and Julissa. Last time I saw them, they were like an old couple. I joked about it, but they've gotten pretty cute.

An express pulls away just as we reach the platform. The local's a few minutes out. No way I'm waiting for another express and getting Robi there late so we shove onto the crowded local 1 when it pulls up. Bryan asks Robi to list the nine ways you can score a run if you're on third. He turns to me as Robi's thinking about it.

"Last night Kiara texted Julissa asking after you." He nudges my shoulder. "That's good. She still be thinking about you. See? Playing it cool just drives 'em wild."

"'Cause that's what you're doing with Julissa?"

Bryan stretches back against the orange seats. His leg sways out and bumps mine. "Nah, we way beyond that. We like honeymooners now." His grin falls. "I want to tell you something, only you got to promise you ain't gonna tell no one."

I hold up my hand like I'm swearing an oath.

He bends forward, elbows on his knees. "I've been having these dreams of when I get drafted senior year."

I have those dreams too. Only, in some of them, I'm not going for the draft, I'm applying to college, and when I get in, Papi disowns me. "Yeah, so what're you worried about? That you don't get picked?"

"No, no, nothing like that." He blows out an exhale. "In my dream, I get drafted in the second round. And then I ask Julissa to come with me. She says yes."

"That's great, Bry. That's a good dream, right?" Only, he doesn't look happy.

"When I wake, my heart's racing and I'm all sweaty." He checks to make sure Robi's not listening. He leans over to me again. "You don't think I'm missing out, do you? Staying with one girl so long?"

"Don't know. You want something else? Something more than Julissa's giving you?"

His mouth twists as he considers. I can't believe he's taking so long to answer. I never wanted anyone other than Isa. She was it for me. Problem was, it wasn't the same for her.

"No. Don't think so." Bryan doesn't look at me. "I mean, sometimes I get curious, por supuesto. But never enough to wreck the good I've got going with her."

"So there's your answer."

Bryan nods. He doesn't smile. "So you don't think there's something wrong with me? That maybe I just don't got the confidence to try with some-one different? 'Cause seriously, what would the team think of me if they knew I'd only ever been with one girl?"

I can't believe he's worried about those pariguayos. "Oye, you either want to be with her, or you don't. You shouldn't worry about what other people think. What other people expect. It's just the two of you in the rela-tionship." It's like what Robi told me. And Mami too. I wish that had been the only problem Isa and I had.

Bryan straightens. He nods a couple more times. "Thanks." His leg hits mine again. "So. What about Kiara? You changed your mind about your white girl preference yet?"

The day after Kiara walked out, Bryan came over. He lit into me about letting down our people. He had a list of the Latinas who'd been crowned Miss Universe. He went on about Jennifer, and Eva, and Zoe, and Salma, saying if they were good enough for the big screen, they had to be good enough for me. I told him that's not how it was. I told him that I just still wasn't ready.

I adjust my cap. "Bry, oyeme . . ."

He holds up a hand. "I know, I know. You not ready. And you ain't got time. Pero, what you doing about your needs? A man's got to have a girl, ¿veldad?"

Robi's three seats down from Bryan with two folks between them. He's still not listening.

"No te preocupes," I tell Bryan. "I'm good."

Bryan's face breaks into a slow grin. "Ay, you got yourself another jévon, ¿sí? But I don't wanna hear it's someone from one of those Upper East Side all-girls schools." He taps my chest. "You gotta show our island women some love."

I don't answer him. He can think what he wants.

"I got your back. I won't say nothing to Julissa. Don't want Kiara finding out. You already hurt her plenty."

I don't say anything to that either. I don't like thinking about what I did to Kiara, how I wasn't fair to her, how I should've stopped what we were doing a long time ago. It's kind of like what Papi did to Mami and me, pretending for so long that everything was good even when it wasn't.

Two old ladies get on. Bryan and I stand so they can have our seats. Crowds mob the doors. I tell Robi to stay seated where he is, but Bryan and I move to the middle of the car. I lift my hand and smile at Robi from where we stand. He waves back, but it's not to say hello. He wants something. Only, it's too crowded to get to him.

"¿Qué quieres?" I call out.

He doesn't answer. He's still making weird bug eyes at me.

"What's wrong?" Bryan ducks to see around the people.

"No sé," I tell him.

I lean forward and catch Robi's face again. He's mouthing a word at me. He jerks his head toward the entryway. "¡Ále!" Robi's shouting at me now. He's pointing to the door.

A girl passes the window. She's so close to the train, all I see is blond hair reaching down her back. I can't see her face. But it doesn't matter. The way she holds her head, so straight and tall, gives her away. Only, she's moving all wrong. Her shoulder dips with each step. She's limping.

Thundering starts up in my ears. It isn't the train—we're still not moving. It's my heart, sprinting, like it's going express.

"Stand clear of the closing doors."

"Excuse me. Permiso." I throw myself toward the exit. I've got to see if she's all right.

"Hey, watch it!" A lady with a Jamaican bandana yells at me, gesturing toward a stroller.

The doors slam before I can even get near them. I crane my neck, trying to see Isa through the window as the train pulls away. All I glimpse is her coat and golden hair.

"It was her, right?" There's only two people between me and Robi now. Bryan's way back where I left him. "She was standing right over there." Robi points to where the woman steadies the stroller, her back pressed against the door. Robi frowns. "Sorry, I should have told you sooner."

●●●

"It's OK." I tell him. I look away so he can't see my face. Bryan, Robi, and I spend all afternoon at the Institute. When I'm not helping run drills or walking a kid through a better swing, I'm wrapping donated gifts for underserved communities. Robi's sixth-grade team comes in third out of four. It's not a real game, just points added up for different technical skills. But Papi's angry about it anyway. Yaritza joins us after her shift at the restaurant. She takes Robi home before Bryan and I finish up.

Bryan's no fool. He doesn't ask me anything about Isa until we're walking out of the building, heading toward the C train. I don't know what to tell him other than I wish I'd gotten to speak with her. I can't stop thinking about that limp. And how last time we talked, outside the dance school, her words and her face didn't match up—she didn't look fine at all. When our train pulls into Ninety-Sixth Street, I tell Bryan I'll catch him later. There's something I need to do.

I come out on Central Park West and jog through the park not bothering to wait for the bus. I don't slow until I reach Fifth Ave. I know better than to sprint across swept sidewalks, past sparkling glass doors Windexed every hour by men who look more like me than the people whose buildings they guard. They would draw attention too if they were running here.

I follow Ninety-Sixth until I get to Park Ave. I start on the west side of the street and walk south. Even I know north of Ninety-Sixth isn't the same. Isa never invited me over, so I never got her exact address. But I know she takes the M96 bus.

I pass green awnings and shiny brass poles strung with white Christmas lights. Underneath them, lamps radiate orange-gold heat. Trimmed evergreen shrubs flank entrances. Some have planters of stone or iron decorated with holly branches. I'm looking for statues, a pair of lions. Isa mentioned them once. I finally find the big cats on the corner of Ninety-Third.

I had pictured full-maned Mufasas, like the ones outside the Forty-Second Street public library. These don't look like anything Disney would draw. They're sitting up, not lying down, one paw on each raised in salute. A man in a pilot's hat and a matching blue-gray uniform watches me from behind the glass. He's morenito, like me. He doesn't come out and hold open the entrance. When I take a step forward, he points to the revolving door.

Inside it's almost tropical. Against the wall, a tall vase sits on a marble shelf. Orchids and lilies explode out of it. The smell reminds me of DR.

"Can I help you?" The doorman's name tag says GERALDO.

"Me gustaría hablar con Isabelle Warren, por favor."

Geraldo's uninterested gaze is meant to show me he has no clue what

I just said. That man has an accent thicker than Mami's and Papi's. If he doesn't speak Spanish, then I don't play ball.

"Excuse me?"

Geraldo wants to play games. I don't have time for games.

Maybe it's not the Spanish he doesn't understand. Maybe he doesn't recognize Isabelle's name.

"I'm looking for Isabelle Warren. Do you know her?" I wish I'd brought my Haeres ID. The folks in the fancy coffee shop near my school are nicer to me when I'm wearing it.

Geraldo looks me up and down, then breaks into a smile. "Estoy bromeando. You play beisbol?" He points to my AHH hoodie. "What position?"

I tell him and he asks me my stats. I tell him that too. He claps my back with an "Ey!" like we go way back.

Geraldo pretends to hold a bat and swings it. "My son, he's not into ball. He likes music and computers. How the team is doing this year?" He nods again to my shirt.

I tell him they're doing well. But that I don't play for AHH anymore. I play for Haeres.

He frowns and makes a gesture at the ceiling. Like maybe he's angry with God for taking the good players out of the Heights.

I ask him again about Isa.

"Claro, conozco a Miss Isabelle, pero she no live here no more. She no tell you she moved?"

She moved? "When?" The word rasps from my throat.

Geraldo presses a gloved fist to his forehead. "Seven month? En mayo fue."

In May? My hands go cold. Isa and I were together then. She never said anything about moving.

"Ay, y que triste fue todo. Miss Isabelle, I know her since chiquitica. Since she born. The brother too. Then, *shwoo.*" He waves his hand like a bird's flying away. "Se fueron."

They left?

"But why?"

Geraldo opens his hands and looks at the ceiling again.

The elevator dings. Geraldo peeks over his shoulder like a dog who's been caught eating a steak. He tugs his white gloves as an old woman in a fur comes from behind the wall with the fountain vase.

"Good evening, Mrs. Rosenbaum." He holds open the plain glass door for her. "Will you be needing a taxi tonight?"

"Hello there, Gerry," she says back to him. "Yes, I will be." She glances at me, and then stops. "Gerry? Is this that nephew you were telling me about?"

"No, Mrs. Rosenbaum. This gentleman is here asking about the Warrens."

"Hmmm, I didn't think so. He's too handsome to be from your family." She lifts her elbow and winks at Gerry. Gerry leans back and pretends to shoot her with two fingers. Mrs. Rosenbaum's chuckles die down. "It's so sad what happened to that family. Clifton was such a gentleman and seemed so smart. Well, that's how those financier jobs are. Easy come, easy go."

Isa's father . . . He lost his job?

Mrs. Rosenbaum's gaze travels down to the old dirt stains on my knees. "You must be a friend of the boy's, what was his name?"

"Merrit." Gerry and I answer at the same time.

"Actually, ma'am," I continue, "I'm a friend of Isabelle's."

"Really?" The old woman's eyes narrow. Her papery lips smile. "Well, that's nice. But you know they don't live here anymore."

"Do you know where they live?" I ask the old woman. If Gerry wouldn't tell me about Mr. Warren, I doubt he'll tell me where the family moved.

"I'm afraid I don't, young man. Even if I did, I don't think I would share that with you. If you're Isa's friend, why didn't she tell you herself?"

I don't know. I let myself out the revolving door. Isa didn't tell me a lot of things. I keep asking myself *why* the whole way home.

SATURDAY, DECEMBER 23

ALEX

I stare off at metal spearing the sky. It's the tallest spire in the western hemisphere, built above ashes of terror and destruction. It's beautiful, yet seems lonely. None of the other buildings come close to it.

I want to be that spire, rising up, despite the past. Or maybe because of it.

Only two sentences are on the yellow page in my lap. One and a half, really. I hunch forward on the bench. I try not to look at the skyline. It's hard because going back to my notebook means going back in my head where my thoughts vibrate with Isa.

I've tried calling Isa a few times since seeing her on the train. It's useless, but I can't stand not knowing if she's OK. Her Instagram account is gone, either erased or blocked. I still post to mine, every other day. I've written and hidden five poems for her on the train. They're all still there. Unclaimed. Like the child in the subway poem "Hide-and-Seek," left outside in the dark when the others gave up.

I reread the words I've written. I speak them in my head. I speak them to the squirrel looking at me from the small rock four feet away. I fold thoughts of Isa down into a tight pill-shaped packet. I tell the mouth inside my brain to open wide and swallow. My pencil bounces on my finger. I put the tip to the paper and write.

"¿Qué haces aquí?"

I look up from three pages of raw words and feelings into Papi's outraged face.

"Why your bag is thrown así en la acera? The people they can walk on it, damage your glove."

Only, it's winter. There's hardly anyone in the park. It's why I came here to write.

Behind Papi, Robi and Yaritza stroll up the sidewalk. They wave. They're too far away to hear him or see what's in my lap.

Papi snatches my notebook. "¿Qué es eso? ¿Algo para la escuela?"

I'm not going to lie and tell him it's homework. It's not. It's for me.

Robi's smile falls when he notices what Papi's holding. He breaks from Yaritza and comes running. For Christmas, Papi finally agreed to sign Robi up for a winter ball session. His practice started two hours after mine, five blocks from their house. It was the first time Papi's gone to watch Robi instead of me. Mine was just a practice, so Papi didn't miss much and Coach O'Neil promised he'd give Papi a full report. But what about Robi? How did he hit in the cage?

I study Robi's face. He's looking at Papi who's turning sheet after sheet in my notebook. Yaritza comes up behind him. Her hand touches the paper. She doesn't let him turn another page. I sit tall on the bench. My insides are as frozen as my face. I'm tired, too tired to stop them from reading. Why won't Isa respond to me?

I didn't want Papi to find out about my writing. Now that he has, I almost feel relief. His dirt-crusted nails smudge the pages. His pinched eyes rise to mine.

"You wrote all this?" His voice is neither loud nor soft.

My breath is crystals in my mouth, too sharp to take into my lungs.

Yaritza's lips still form the words I wrote. She takes the notebook from Papi's powerful hands. "Son espectaculares," she breathes.

I watch the thin line of Papi's mouth. I listen for what I know is coming. *How could you write this? This is not what a man does.*

"Es una distracción," is all Papi says. "You should be focusing on beisbol. Nada más. ¿Me entiendes?"

I bow my head. It is not a nod.

Papi tries to take the notebook from Yaritza, but she holds on too tight.

Robi is behind the bench. My bag is on his shoulder. His mouth is fighting not to smile too big. "Ále," he whispers. "I hit well! I was really driving the ball."

Papi is stalking away. Still he hears him. "It's not the same as on the field," Papi shouts back.

I stand like a tower, stiff and alone. "That's great, Robi. I'm proud of you." My hand finds his shoulder. I take back my bag. I'd expected yelling and shaming. I'd prepared for the possibility of hitting.

I wasn't prepared for disinterest.

I should have been. It hurts more.

SATURDAY, DECEMBER 23

ISA

Merrit meets my train on the platform at Ninety-Sixth Street. Mom and Dad let him take the crosstown bus by himself last week, the same time I came off crutches, as if they needed both their kids to be more independent by the holiday. Merrit lifts a hand when I stick my head out of the car. His Santa hat slides down his forehead as he jogs to my door.

He hasn't taken that hat off since Dad found it in the decorations box last weekend. Merrit didn't put a single ornament on the tree. He just sat on the couch with my foot in his lap, holding an ice pack against it, repeating the words *Ho ho ho* when Dad asked about his Christmas spirit. I handed the glass balls that were my favorites to Dad—they couldn't all fit because the tree is so small. Mom never came out of her room, so the afternoon was pretty calm. When Dad left to buy eggnog, I considered talking to Merrit about the note he left me. But part of me likes keeping our secret unspoken.

Merrit lopes onto the train. He sinks into a seat beside me and pushes the hat onto the top of his head.

"You OK?" I ask.

He nods. "Just tired." He closes his eyes. As we're pulling away from 110th, he rests his head on the side of mine, almost like he's trying for a nap. I pat his arm and shift to make myself more comfortable for him. Across from us a little boy runs a toy fireman's truck over the seats and up the wall. The red light of his truck whirls round and round and the siren's pretty loud.

His mother tells him, "Tranquilo" and points to Merrit. "Santa, pow-pow," she says. The boy stares hard at Merrit, his little mouth drawn with angry suspicion. The mom smoothes his hair, a smile on her face. He pushes her away and points the fire truck at her, the lights and sirens coming back on.

"I saw some guys using reMAKE," Merrit says.

It takes me a moment to realize he's talking about his app. It went public just before Thanksgiving. He's been staying up late, tracking the sales.

"Really? That's great. Where?"

"At Ninety-Sixth. They were waiting for the train."

"Well?" I ask. "Did they like it?"

Merrit's still leaning on me. I can't see his face, but I feel the shrug of his shoulder. "Seemed to," he says. "They were passing the phone back and forth, changing up the words in the video."

"That's great, right?" I come out from under him. I want to see his expression.

"Yeah. It is great." Only, Merrit looks sort of deflated.

"You sure you're OK?"

He shakes his head. "It's just . . . I don't feel anything. Something like this should make me feel something. Don't you think?"

"I don't know, sometimes the anticipation is greater than what you feel for the actual event. Like going on vacation, especially when it comes to *our* family." I'm trying to get him to smile but I'm not just joking. Chrissy talks about this sometimes with dance. That the lead-up to a performance is so intense that afterward you feel sort of down.

Merrit only looks away. His words make me worry. They remind me of what he said when he talked about his accident with the pills. "Maybe you should tell Dr. Peterson?" I suggest. We're on our way to meet with Merrit's psychiatrist now.

Merrit doesn't respond. He stares through the window into the darkness beyond.

The subway soars from the tunnel, rising on the elevated tracks toward the 125th Street Station. Tiny white wisps drift down around us, bright against the smudgy gray sky.

Merrit startles me by standing. He rips off his hat. The little boy's fire truck crashes to the floor. The siren whines. Merrit dashes for the doors as they open.

"Merrit!" I move as fast as I can with my limp. My heart clatters like we've jumped the tracks. This isn't our stop.

Wind dives into my eye sockets, chilling the bones of my cheeks. Merrit's running down the platform toward the back of the train. Flurries swirl wildly around him. As soon as he's out from under the rooftop shelter that spans most of the platform, he slows and opens his arms. I hobble after him, thankful he didn't take any of the exits down to the street. I couldn't have kept up on those stairs.

Merrit lifts his face to the snow as the train pulls away. He turns for the railing, the barrier that prevents passengers from falling off, down to Broadway below. I hobble faster. A small dusting of white covers the concrete, enough to leave prints. Enough for my foot, with the awkward brace, to slip. Pain, like a knife, stabs through my leg. I'm panting by the time I reach him. He's standing, hands clamped to the top of the waist-high barrier. His eyes are squeezed closed. He's leaning forward, mouth open, as if to gulp the flakes streaming by.

I grab on to the bar. Teeth of cold metal sink through my gloves. Below us, the street comes into focus. A fire truck, as small as the boy's toy, whizzes by, lights off, silent.

"Merrit—" I start.

"Just . . . just let me stand here." His hand lands on my shoulder, anchoring me to him. "You can stand with me too. It's just . . . I need to feel this. I need to feel something." He didn't see me trip. He doesn't see the tears of shock and fear running down my ice-cold face.

I press against my brother, swallowing down a sob. I don't know what to do. About Merrit or my ankle. I don't want to think about what any of it means.

The snow changes, flakes growing fatter and heavier, like enormous balls of cotton. Cold, wet clumps of it stick to my skin and melt. The droplets of soft ice come faster, rushing against my eyelids, reminding me of Alex's poem.

"His name is Alex. The boy who wrote me those notes." The words escape from my lips as though they're not mine. I don't know if Merrit turns to look at me. I don't know if what I said breaks through to him.

Merrit squeezes my shoulder. "Tell me more," he says.

● ● ●

We're back inside the train, inside the tunnel heading to 137th. I shiver against my brother, my face wet more from snow than tears. My fingers and feet, thank God, feel numb and the pain in my ankle is a distant pulse.

Merrit listens to what I tell him about Alex. He asks me questions about Alex's family, his two moms, his little brother, and his dad. He can't believe I've never been to one of Alex's games. Especially since Alex had come to see me dance. He pulls out his phone to look up the Haeres spring baseball schedule.

"I get why you were nervous to introduce him to our family," Merrit says. "Mom can be such a bitch. Samantha hated her too. Here—" He leans over to show me his phone. "Alex's first game is March twenty-third. I'm sending it to your calendar." He taps at his screen. He sets the phone on his leg, his fingers drumming his jeans. "Hey, um—I'm sorry. If I was part of the reason you kept Alex away."

I press my hand on his arm. "No, it wasn't you."

He only nods and looks away. Maybe I'm not such a good liar after all.

"Listen, I meant what I wrote." He lifts his palm, curling his thumb and pinkie together like he did when he was a Cub Scout. "I promise I'll act normal around him. I'll keep taking my medicines. I'll try really hard not to embarrass you."

Now it's my turn to rest my head on his shoulder. I don't tell him that Alex will probably never come over. I don't tell him that Alex has already moved on. Baby steps.

"You know," Merrit says. "I can help you make a video with the app. You can explain why you asked for a break and why you've been keeping so much from him. You can just send it to him on Instagram."

I think about that time Alex found me on the subway, to apologize for leaving the dance performance and to tell me he missed me. What I did to him with the concert was so much worse than that.

"Thanks," I tell Merrit. "But this is something I need to do face-to-face."

I take out my phone. I log onto the free Wi-Fi when we stop at 157th Street. I unblock Alex, then send him a message:

Can we talk? I don't know if he'll answer. He has every reason not to.

Merrit pretends he wasn't just reading my cell. He bumps my shoulder and smiles.

SATURDAY, DECEMBER 23

ALEX

The snowflake decorations strung over Broadway are all lit up. Real snow floats around them. I pull on my hood, yank the strings tight, and tilt my face skyward. My tongue tastes the tiny slivers of ice. The bakery with those carrot muffins as big as my hand is on the next block. I'll bring a whole box of them to Yaritza. Tomorrow, she'll be cooking for Nochebuena. I don't want her to have to worry about breakfast too.

At the corner, a skinny dude in a Santa outfit swings his arm up and down, jangling his bell. Only a few people drop change into his bucket. I get stuck by the light. I pull out my wallet and drop a ten-dollar bill inside. Santa tells me gracias and that God blesses me.

Someone bumps into me. He sprawls to the sidewalk, into the dust of snow.

"Ay, sorry." I put out my hand to help the guy up. Danny blinks from deep inside his jacket. "¡Oye!" I shout. I yank him to his feet. "Where you been?" I hate that he doesn't return my calls. I've got a thing about it now. "Mami invited you and your abuela to dinner para Nochebuena. Your abuela, she said she don't know your plans." I put my arm around him. "I told Mami I'd find you. You're coming, right? You don't got nowhere else to be? Not on Christmas, ¿veldad?"

Danny looks behind him. "Yeah, yeah sure. Hey, where you going now?"

I point to the bakery. He lifts a hand and follows me inside.

I ask about school and his abuela and his visit to his brother over Thanksgiving. Danny's answers are mostly nods, an occasional word. He leans against the display case as my order is wrapped. He stays facing the door, watching the sidewalk. I keep on talking like normal though I know something's up.

Outside, the snow has thickened into a screen of white. Light from lamps and Christmas bulbs stays trapped around us. Half a block up, four guys draw designs in the snow on a parked car. A flag. A gun. A face with an *X* across it. They step onto the sidewalk next to us.

Danny shoots me a look of hunger and thirst and every type of desperation there is.

"This him? ¿El Cuchillo?" one of them asks.

"Sí," says another. "But who's this?" He motions to me.

The smallest one moves forward. He's got feathers instead of a beard on his chin. "I seen him around. He's one of 'em too."

Cold locks around me like a rope wound too tight. He thinks because I'm with Danny that I'm with Pinchón too?

Feather-beard grins. He slides sharp steel from his pocket.

Danny grabs my arm. "Go!" he shouts. His voice is my coach, an ump, the *crack* of a ball on a bat.

We bolt. The cars on Broadway are driving slow. Slower than us. Still they honk with surprise. Shouts of anger rise above it. And the squealing of brakes. Wheels spin. There's a crunch and a horrible thud. The outline of a truck comes out of the falling snow. Its rear swings toward me. Hands on my back push me hard. I land on my knees in the slush.

"Come on!" Danny's fingers sink into my shoulder. He drags me up by my coat. We fly, skidding, down 165th. Danny glances behind us. He jerks his head left. We duck onto Audubon Avenue. We hug the buildings. Dive into a parking lot. Run doubled-over between cars growing fat with snow.

Danny finds a break in the chain link and slips right through. We come out onto 168th. Danny aims for St. Nicholas. His shoes kick up white clumps. I grab him and pull him into the subway.

"Come on," I grunt at him. "We can go to Brooklyn." They don't really know who I am. They don't know my papi lives there.

Danny's gasping. He can hardly breathe. He hasn't been training like me. Even with all the training, my heart is an engine, churning and burning with smoke.

I make for the A train. Danny's hand finds my arm.

"The 1," he pants. "The platform's darker. More places to hide." He takes off for the elevator. He doesn't check to see if I follow.

I tear through the tunnel behind him. I stick close to the wall. I try not to bump anyone. Still, people cry out as if I might scald them.

The elevator to the 1 is just closing. Danny sticks his hand in the gap and wrenches the doors open. We tumble inside. The few passengers scatter out of our way. Danny jams at the button until the door finally shuts. His phone is out. He texts with fury, trying to send a message before the signal is swallowed.

I tip my head against the wall. Drips patter as fast as my heartbeat into a puddle of melting snow. That guy had a knife. A really big one. They all did, I'm sure.

Danny pockets his phone. His eyes dart through the elevator then land on me. A smile ghosts over his lips. "It's OK." He says it as if it's true. I love him for trying. But those guys, they're looking for blood. I wouldn't have let Danny face them alone. I would have made myself a part of this. What scares me is they didn't give me a choice. They pushed me into it because I look the part.

The doors let us out deep underground. We take the stairs for the down-town track. I'm about to head toward the back of the train. Behind me

Danny hisses, like he's talking to a cat. He squeezes beneath the overpass to the uptown platform.

"¿Qué—?"

He waves a hand to cut me off. His eyes are white in the darkness. Across the tracks, a guy with a blue bandana paces.

I dodge under, squatting beside Danny. I fold myself into the shadows. The guy walks the length of the platform three times. He crosses back over to the downtown side. Danny creeps out as the guy heads to the rear of the train, toward the same car we wanted.

We take slow, casual steps to the uptown tracks. Danny doesn't seem worried we might get trapped on this side. There are only two ways out, two overpasses leading to the downtown trains and the elevators to the street. Danny walks to the other end of the platform, as far from the other guy as we can get. He stops at the white-tiled pillars. He slides around the edge of one, motioning for me to take another. A South Ferry–bound train rushes in. It blocks us from view. We should've stayed on the other side. We could've boarded that train, be on our way to Brooklyn.

Danny's up against a column. He stares at the tiled walls that turn to arches over our heads. He doesn't scan the rest of the station. He doesn't see the train pull away. Or the four guys rush out from the elevators, coats and pants damp with snow. They throw out their arms at the departing train. The one who was pacing the platform joins them. All five come onto the overpass. They come down to the same platform as Danny and me.

I whistle at Danny. He hears me too late. The guy who showed us the knife sees us.

The uptown train is coming. "Should we get on it?" I ask. Maybe they'll be less likely to fight with other people around. Only, I remember last year. Thanksgiving. The subway car didn't stop them then.

Danny gives a sharp shake of his head. He passes a hand over his scarred lip. "Pinchón is coming. Anyway"—he motions to the guys approaching—"they'll just follow us onto the train."

Words I do not want to hear.

The five guys who want to fight Danny, and now me, stop paces away. Waiting for the train. Waiting for no witnesses. They separate to block our path should we try to escape.

Feather-beard is chanting lyrics about hate and death and blood. His hand goes to his waist. To his pocket that's a sheath for a blade.

We can't stay here, Danny and me. We can't fight them if they've got knives. If we get on the train, maybe we can run through it to another car. If we're fast, we can jump out again closer to the overpass.

I try to tell Danny what I'm thinking without using words, without using signals they can read. I position myself in front of a door that will open. Feather-beard grins.

The train moans to a stop. Metal doors fly open like shutters.

I'm ready to dash in. To weave through people and push through cars.

The revving in my heart chokes.

Isa stands in front of me.

SATURDAY, DECEMBER 23

ISA

At 168th Street we rise from our seats. My foot is throbbing again. Merrit frowns at the effort it costs me to take the ten steps or so to the door. He swears softly as he removes his Santa hat from his pocket. He pulls it down over his wet hair.

"You hurt your ankle again, didn't you?"

When I nod, he swears once more.

He readjusts Santa's hat. "I'm so stupid," he mumbles. "I'm sorry."

"It's OK," I tell him.

"No. No, it's not. I'm selfish. I didn't think what could happen to you." His arm comes around me and his hand grips my shoulder. "I never wanted to hurt you. Yet that's all I seem to do."

"That's not true." I almost tell him how I hurt him. By not watching out for him when I was with Alex, like I should have.

Merrit stares at his reflection in the window, hat tipping again to the side. "I'll take you to urgent care before our session. Dr. Peterson can wait."

"No, he can't." Merrit staying stable is most important. "Anyway, I know what my ankle needs. We've got ice and bandages at home, plus crutches." I want to believe what I say. I don't want to think it's anything more than a sprain.

"OK. But we're taking a taxi home. I can carry you up the stairs to the elevator, even."

I'm telling him no, that I just need to lean on him, when the doors fall open.

Alex is in the doorway. His hands are clenched. The dark slash of his brow is pulled low. His body's angled forward, his knees slightly bent, like a sprinter ready to run.

An uncomfortable prickling works up my spine.

Alex straightens when he sees me. The hard determination falls from his face. His eyes widen, catching the subway's flickering light. His eyes round even more, confusion replaced by what I can only call horror. He stumbles back, out of our way.

He probably hasn't checked his phone yet. He hasn't read my message. He remembers how I ran away from him outside the Academy. How I wouldn't tell him why I left. I've become a nightmare to Alex, something for him to run from.

I was holding on to Merrit pretty hard already. Now my fingers dig into his arm so much he winces. He's looking at me and then at Alex. He saw my phone. He saw photos of me and Alex together. He isn't stupid. Please just let him not say anything. Not now.

Merrit helps me off the train, his arm still around my shoulder. I almost jump when I see Danny on our other side, his back against one of the arches. He catches my gaze, gives a faint shake of his head. He flicks two fingers as if tossing a gum wrapper. I deserve it, the look, the dismissal, all of it.

There are too many steps to the stairs for me to count. The pain in my ankle echoes like a hammer inside my head. Three other guys are in front of us. They look through us as if we're invisible. Their faces are drawn with the same cold intent I saw on Alex, their gazes locked on him and Danny. They're all here together, that's for sure.

Merrit stops when we're only halfway to the bridge. His frown has turned thoughtful. "That's him, isn't it?" he asks. "That's Alex?" Merrit snakes his arm out from under mine, and before I can tell him to wait, he's striding back toward Alex and Danny. "I'll talk to him for you."

"No—Merrit!"

Two other guys come up alongside my brother. There's a whole group of them now.

"Hey, Santa," one of them says. He says something else I can't hear that makes Merrit stop.

The train pulls out, sucking air with it down the tunnel. The last of the passengers are crossing to the elevators.

Danny and Alex have moved closer to each other. Alex's gaze sweeps from my brother to me. He looks at me like he's about to either yell or be sick.

Something's wrong. These guys, they're not friends of Danny and Alex's.

Merrit turns and looks back at me. He takes in the three guys between me and the stairs, not that I could climb them by myself. His Santa hat has fallen over one of his eyebrows. He doesn't fix it. He just moves his head, surveying the platform, taking all of us in.

"Who's this?"

I stiffen as one of the guys behind me drapes a hand across my back.

"She yours?"

I don't know who he's speaking to. The whiplash from my emotions— my relief from talking to Merrit, my shame at seeing Alex, and now my fear that something is very, very wrong—makes me dizzy. I feel like I might be sick too.

Danny puts out his hand, low, as if to block Alex or steady him somehow. Merrit raises his hand into the air, like the first-row, straight-A student he is. He doesn't wait to be called on. He shouts out, "She's mine. That's my sister. Though the implication that she's an object to be possessed by another person is not just anachronistic but also rather discourteous, to her mostly, but also to me." He steps from between the two guys as casually as if he knows them from school. One takes hold of his elbow, but Merrit shrugs it off like a suggestion he's not going to even consider. "I also object to the nature of this encounter. I mean, what is this? A game of urban chess?" Merrit's voice speeds over the words. His eyes take on the fevered glow I dread. The one that tells me he believes he can fix this. He believes he can fix anything the world throws at him.

"Who is this guy?" one of them asks. "What's he talking about?"

"Pero ese tipo está loco," another adds. They move closer to Merrit, away from me.

It's getting harder to breathe. The air seems too thin. I tell them quickly in Spanish that Merrit's not well. That he doesn't know what he's saying. I don't look at Alex as I say this.

Merrit frowns just a bit. He doesn't stop or acknowledge me or my claim. He says the next line in perfect Castellano, accentuating the accent from Madrid where he spent a summer, so different from the DR or Cuba.

"What? You guys've never heard of human chess? She is the queen." He gestures at me. "I presume he is the king." Merrit points at Alex and then at Danny. "That would make you the knight. But what would that make me?"

Four guys are closing in on Merrit. My brother's eyes are bulging out at me. He's telling me to move, to run, to get out of here. He's telling me he's acting this way on purpose, to confuse them. Only I can't run. Not with my foot.

"What did he just say? And what did you say, before?" The guy beside me jerks my arm. I fall onto my ankle and gasp. I gasp again because a knife is tucked into the waist of his pants. I tell him, in English, what we said, gritting through the pain in my leg and the alarm speeding through me. They're going to hurt us. All of us. Alex and Danny too.

Merrit races ahead, switching out of Spanish. He doesn't read the warning in my face. "I've thought about it and a bishop appeals most to me. Straight lines are really not my thing." Merrit dashes across the concrete, cutting geometric shapes over the platform. The two guys jump forward to grab him. Merrit switches direction and comes toward me.

"The rest of you are pawns!" he shouts. "And in case you don't understand the game, this label is purposeful and it is my intention to offend." He grins almost maliciously as he nears. "Ho ho ho. Merry Christmas!" Merrit slams his Santa hat onto the head of the guy beside me, covering his eyes. The guy slaps it away. But Merrit's already between us. He nudges me back even as he cackles. His laugh grows louder as another train approaches. "Check," Merrit says, triumphant. There will be more people around us soon. People means safety.

The guy throws off the Santa hat. He grabs Merrit's wrist. A blade winks in his hand.

My heart stumbles as time seems to slow.

Merrit whips his arm around, dragging the guy with him. He uses the momentum of the spin to swing the guy with the knife away from me. Only the guy doesn't let go. The guy sprawls toward the platform edge, still holding on to Merrit. They both go over. They fall onto the tracks.

I scream.

SATURDAY, DECEMBER 23

ALEX

Blood rushes like a river in my ears. It pounds. I'll use the same rhythm when beating Feather-beard for putting his hand on Isa. I'm seconds away from going for him. I'll rip him off her like a bloodsucking worm. Merrit shouts insults. He grabs the guy's attention as if he were grabbing his neck. The pendejo doesn't even get what Isa's brother is doing. When they speak Spanish, he's only more confused.

Isa watches her brother parade like a clown, working his magic of distraction. But she doesn't run. She stays where she is, her face flushed with panic and pain.

Danny and I jump the other two as soon as Merrit puts the hat on the dumbass's face. We grab their arms. They can't reach for their blades. I've got my boy on the ground, my knee in his back. Danny's scuffling a bit, but he's got this.

Isa screams. Everything else goes silent. I turn to her, ready to run and pound and rip. Seeing her step off the train, knowing she was heading straight into this mess, was a nightmare turned real. Hearing her cry out is worse.

She's standing alone. Merrit and the feather-beard guy are gone. Across the tracks, people point and take out their phones. Isa falls to her knees. She crawls toward the edge of the platform. The two guys behind her rush forward.

Understanding hits like cold water to my face.

A train horn sounds. There's a light deep in the tunnel. It's no bigger than a flashlight. It flickers and swells.

The guys pull Feather-beard up off the tracks. The three of them break for the overpass.

Isa gets to the edge. Her hand goes out, as if for a partner below. No fingers appear. No hand finds hers. She slides forward. She eases herself down onto the tracks.

NO. The fury inside me breaks.

I spring off the guy in front of me. My feet slap gray tile. My heart slaps my chest. The yellow strip is my line between second and third. I am a runner, a thief of bases.

The gold of Isa's hair bends low over the slats. Beside her, Merrit lies still, a crumple of fine clothes.

The train roars. I roar with it. And jump.

I slam onto wood and concrete. With a grunt, I grab up her brother.

Isa's face, white and tear-stained, is lit up by the flashlight that is now a flood lamp.

"Here!" Danny hauls Isa's brother out of my arms. He lays him on the platform. He glares at the other two guys running away.

I reach back for Isa. She's still on her knees. The train shoots from the tunnel. Sparks fly from its wheels.

"NO!" My shout is drowned by the blare.

Danny's eyes are caught in the gleam. "Run!" his mouth says.

I grab Isa's hands. I yank her up. I hold her against me. Our feet jam into the gaps between rails. I think of Papi's drills, of hours in biting cold, running laps and sprints and burpees. I tell myself this is nothing compared to that.

"Go, go, go!" Danny's running alongside us. The train's horn blasts.

I take Isa's weight. I shift my own. I'll throw her onto the platform, get her out.

Brakes squeal in my ear. The heat of the train's engine is at my back. The engine inside me bellows. I'm not going to make it. But at least I'll save her.

I swing Isa up and around. A bachata spin. Like in a dance, her hand wraps back around me.

"No!" she cries. She doesn't let me go. With one foot, she lauches off the track. She leaps then dives, pulling us both forward, pulling us farther ahead of the train. We smash onto wooden boards, a tangle of arms and legs.

Her hand is on the back of my head. "Down!" she screams. We're in the space between the rails. We fit, but just barely. The mass of hot metal skids to a halt inches from our feet. We made it more than three-quarters of the way down the station. Even if the train hadn't stopped, we would have been safe. Because of where we are. Because of what Isa did. The subway car would have passed over us.

"Alex?" There is so much she asks with the one word of my name.

"I'm here." It's the only answer that matters. I crush her to the ground with my arm. "Isa." The word is a croak. "Isa." I repeat it like a prayer. How did she do it? How did she know?

She trembles beside me. She's sobbing, I think. I can't see her face.

"It's OK." I'm sobbing too.

• • •

By the time I steady my nerves and help Isa up, there's a whole lot of people shouting down at us, asking if we're OK. Danny, Pinchón, and some of his boys stand near the edge. They give me a nod and some type of salute. When they see we're fine, they fade into the gathering crowd.

"I d-don't think I c-can walk." Isa's stopped crying. She's leaning against me. I don't want her to let go.

I draw Isa's arm over my shoulder. I wrap mine under her knees and lift her in front of me. Hands come down and pull her out. I climb over the side after her. Isa's swaying. I take her arm before she falls. I carry her to the wall, as far from the tracks as I can get. I sit us both down onto hard, safe stone. She's shaking all over. She's staring wide-eyed at her brother, who's lying next to an open door of the train.

"He's all right." The woman who shouts says she's a doctor. She says they're waiting for EMS to immobilize his neck.

Merrit's speaking, a long string of words garbled together. I can't understand him. The doctor quiets him and orders him not to move.

Isa's nodding. Her eyes are falling closed. "I'm sorry, I'm sorry," she chants. "I should have told you. About my brother."

"It's OK," I whisper. There'll be time for that later. I should be apologizing for getting her into this mess. "We're OK." I repeat it for her and for me.

"Don't go," Isa says. "Please, don't go."

My arms tighten around her. "I'm here," I tell her again. I'm not going anywhere. Not unless she tells me to.

I'm sitting like that, holding her, when cops rush across the overpass. A bunch of medics are behind them, gracias a Dios.

"She needs help." I'm croaking. My scream destroyed my throat.

The medics don't come near. They stay behind the cop on the staircase. The other police fan out. They stop five feet in front of me. They draw their guns.

"Hands in the air where we can see them!"

I blink, recognizing the nightmare is still going. I scan the masses of staring people for Danny and Pinchón. They're not here. They knew police would come looking for them. Did they know they'd be looking for me too?

"Alex?" Isa's voice trembles.

"Let the girl go," one of them says. His voice is slow and calm. Like he's speaking to someone unreasonable.

No. No, no, no. I think of that time in kindergarten, outside of my school, when they came and took Papi. When they took him from me though I was screaming at them not to. My heartbeat gags and starts to drown. "She's hurt," I say. "I was trying to help her. I was trying to help her brother." I rasp the words. Even if they can't hear me, they can see my face. They should understand what I'm trying to say.

Just like Feather-beard, they see what they want to see.

"You're mistaken." Isa uses her private-school voice, though it wobbles with pain. She presses against me. "He didn't do anything. The guys you should be looking for left."

"Miss, I need you to move away." The cop's pistol clicks as the firing pin slides into place. He steps closer, aiming the gun only at me. "I said, let her go."

The empty space surrounding us grows, the crowd of onlookers pushing back. None of them look me in the eye.

Inside I am fire and rage and fear. I have no choices. They've been taken from me.

I try to slide Isa away. Her hands fist my jacket. "No," she whimpers. I shake my head at her. I try to hold my lips steady. I put my hands up like they tell me to.

A cop seizes my arm. Metal rings snap onto my wrists.

"No!" Isa cries out. She rises onto one foot and launches for me. Another cop pulls her back.

The medics surround Isa. They try to tend to her leg.

Isa pushes them away. She yells after the cops. "You've got it all wrong. You have the wrong guy. Alex!"

"Is she OK?" I call out. "Is her leg OK?" A hand pushes my head down. They won't let me even look at her.

"Wait! His name is Alex Rosario. He's a baseball player at Haeres. Call the school, call his parents. He's not who you think he is." Isa hurls out the words, her voice so desperate, it cracks. I never even told her what baseball can do for someone like me. She figured it out. Only, it's too late. The cops have already decided what kind of moreno I am.

They drag me up the steps. I plead with the cops. I tell them I need to go back to Isa. I promised I'd stay. I need to stay at least until her parents arrive. My panic is claws scrambling on ice. I feel like I did in that dream, the one from the summer, when Isa cried out for me and I couldn't get to her.

"Please!" I tell them again.

A bat jabs into my gut. I fall to my knees.

"Is this the guy?" the cop next to me asks. I look up thinking maybe they found Danny. Only he's not talking to me. He's talking to a lady. She nods and says I was at the bakery. She was finishing her shift when I ran out and started that big car crash on Broadway with the others. We must have run into the subway and caused all this mess down here too. A little girl in one of those cars got hurt. Stores got smashed up. She hopes the cops teach us all a lesson.

I say I'm not part of any gang. The lady laughs like I do stand-up.

A bat strikes my back. I bite off my cry. I don't let myself fight the hands holding me. Inside, I scream. Inside, I wrestle free, I run back to Isa and hold her. I still hear her calling for me.

"¿Ále?" Kiara is a Greek goddess of anger. She's at the front of an advancing tide of folks crossing the overpass. Glares of whited eyes stab me. Shuffling feet blur. Kiara's hand is on her hip, her chin cocked.

She is an answer to my prayer.

I tell her in Spanish about Danny and the guys with the knives. I tell her about Isa and her brother and falling into the tracks. I beg her to tell these cops I'm not who they're looking for. I never was part of a gang and I never will be.

Wooden sticks meant to hit baseballs beat me instead. Shouts order me quiet.

Kiara's gaze darts to the platform, to Isa's hoarse voice repeating my name. Kiara presses her lips together. Her nostrils flare. She slides out her phone and points it at me. At the cops who are hitting me.

"He's not who you want. Unless you were looking for a pitcher with an ERA under 1 who also happens to be an incredible poet." She blinks hard, like something's in her eye, and steps back. "But I see how it is. Well, Snapchat is going to see how it is too."

The cops stop hitting me. They wrench me toward the elevators as Kiara disappears into the crowd. The doors close on Isa's cries. Just like in that messed-up dream.

WEDNESDAY, DECEMBER 27

ISA

Midmorning, our intercom rings. Mom presses the buzzer and waits by the door. I want to be the one to open it, but Mom orders me to stay on the couch. She just got me settled with my foot up on pillows.

I haven't seen Alex since that horrible afternoon when the police took him away. When I couldn't stop them from taking him away. Mom and Dad met Merrit and me in the ER. I was crying so much the doctors kept thinking I was more hurt than I was. It took me three different tries to explain to Dad what happened, how there'd been a terrible mistake.

Dad called his lawyer friend who knows one of the ADAs at the Thirty-Third Precinct. When she checked in at the station, they were already preparing Alex's release. Danny, who went straight to his abuela's to tell her he was safe, has a friend who sent a lawyer to the precinct for Alex. They released him the morning of the twenty-fourth, a few hours after Merrit and I were discharged from the hospital. They didn't end up charging him. Cameras on the street show Alex and Danny running from some guys with knives, the same ones who attacked us in the subway. One of them, the short guy, is apparently a leader of a gang from the Bronx. He must have confused Alex and Danny for someone else. It's happened before. A fifteen-year-old boy was even killed a few years ago in the Bronx due to mistaken identity. Also, there are videos from people's phones showing what happened down in the subway, how Alex jumped in to help Merrit and me. How Danny helped Merrit out. They're all over social media along with messages calling them heroes. The clip was even on one of the news websites, *"Daring Santa Rescue on the Eve of Christmas Eve."* Merrit used his app to add words to the video and posted one where Alex and Danny are narrating the rescue to the tune of Jingle Bells. That clip is trending like mad. Merrit even created a GoFundMe and tagged it to the video so people can click on it to donate to an after-school baseball program in Washington Heights that aims to keep kids out of gangs. And then there's the video Kiara posted. Merrit thought it was perfect, just the way it was. All he did was link it to his clip. When I first saw it, I had to stop halfway through. I barely made it to the bathroom before losing everything in my stomach. I don't know how Kiara did it. How she kept it together. How she even thought to do that in the first place. I DM'ed her to tell her she's a rock star. I wasn't expecting her to respond, but she sent me an emoji of a flexing bicep. A few hours later she sent me another message. She told me to take care of him. Of Alex. I lost it, reading those words. Up until that point I wasn't even sure where things stood between the two of them.

I haven't spoken with Alex, but I've talked with his mami every day since it happened. She says he's been quiet, staying mostly in his room, except for his morning runs. She had her ex-husband and Yaritza and Robi over for dinner on Christmas since Alex didn't want to ride the subway. He said he wasn't ready. I don't blame him.

But this morning—this morning he messaged me. He wanted to see me. He wanted to know if that would be all right. I texted him back asking him to please come. There's so much I need to tell him. Now he's in our building, something I once would have thought impossible.

Mom opens the door. Alex stands in the hallway. He's wearing pants and a button-down shirt, not athletic clothes, under his coat. Alex stares down at his feet—he's even wearing leather shoes, not sneakers. He glances up at my mom with a shyness I've never seen.

Mom knows Alex's parents are Dominican. But she avoided the "triggering" videos of the rescue. She hasn't seen him before. Not like this.

Mom sticks out her hand. "I'm Elisa García Warren, Isabelle's mother."

Alex takes her hand. "Hello. I'm Alex, Alex Rosario. It's good to meet you."

I fidget. I don't know what she's going to say.

"I want to thank you for everything you've done. Not just the other day with Merrit and Isa in the subway. My husband tells me—*Isa* tells me—you've been a source of support for our daughter over this past hellish year. So, for that, you have my gratitude."

Alex's tense mouth takes on the trace of a smile. It's true what Mom said; we've been talking more since the accident. She's been *listening*. Mom's still holding the door. She doesn't step back to make room for him. "And I want to apologize for my behavior back in April at Isa's dance performance. I didn't . . ." She inhales and closes her eyes, likes she's resetting herself. "I wasn't expecting to meet anyone, much less a friend of Isa's. Not that it's an excuse. But I am sorry for how I acted."

Alex watches her, his face frozen in that almost-smile.

"But before you come in," Mom continues, sounding much more like herself, "I need to ask about that friend of yours. Danny, right? What exactly is your plan with him?"

Alex frowns. "I'm sorry. I don't understand."

I don't understand either. "Mom?" I make to get up off the couch. She holds her hand up to me but doesn't look away from Alex.

"Your mother told me that Danny's gotten mixed up with the wrong people. If he's your friend, you'll want to help him. You need to tell him that either he walks away from that gang, or you walk away from him."

Wait—she called Sra. Rosario? And what is she saying about Danny? "Mom!" I shout.

It's Alex who lifts his hand this time, telling me to hold on. He licks his lips and nods at my mom. "All right. I'll talk to him. I've been planning to anyway."

Wait—it's . . . true? Danny's involved in all of that? I'm staring at Alex but he's not looking at me.

My mom lets out a breath. "Good. Because otherwise I'd have to insist that you cut off contact with my daughter. I won't allow her to be put at risk again." Mom moves into the apartment. "Oh—wait. There's one more thing." She puts her arm in front of him. "If I ever find out that you are going around with other girls behind Isa's back, I will personally make you regret it." Mom lifts her fingers into the shape of scissors and makes a cutting motion with them. "Got it?"

Alex's eyebrows shoot up, even though her threat is ridiculous. He nods again. I almost bury my red-hot cheeks in my hands, but I don't want to miss anything.

Mom gestures to the chair by the door, the one I use to get my boot off. "You can pull that over by the couch," she tells him. "I've got some work to do in my room. My husband's been looking forward to seeing you. He's still at work, but he asked if you could stay for dinner."

"Mom!" Now I do throw my arm in front of my face. That's so like her to go from terrorizing him to laying it on too thick. "Alex probably has to get back to his family."

"Do you want me to stay?" Alex's question surprises me. Those intense eyes search mine.

"Yes," I tell him, my voice very quiet. It hurts that he has to ask that, that he's not sure if I want him around. But it makes sense, because of the way I've treated him.

"Then I'll stay," he says.

"Good," Mom says. "I'll call your mother to let her know. I want to invite her too." Mom backs down the hallway, a hint of a smile replacing her typical frown. Alex and I are alone.

Alex sits on the chair. He's so tall and the chair's so tall, he towers above me. Having him close makes me self-conscious all of a sudden.

"I'm sorry," he says. "For not saying anything about Danny. I'm sorry for everything on Saturday."

"It wasn't your fault."

"But they were going after me," he says. "After me and Danny. That put you and Merrit in danger."

"Well, I'm more sorry. That they took you. That I couldn't stop them." He knows I'm talking about the police. I wish I could erase it all, everything that happened to him that hurt him. I wish it were as easy as deleting that video Kiara took. But what happened to him wasn't just a video. It was real.

Alex frowns down at his hands where they rest against his knees. He starts to speak, then stops himself. Eventually he says, "There was nothing you could have done."

"Maybe," I tell him. But I think of all those times when Alex got so tense, when he got so nervous around the police. "I never asked you about it. Before. How you felt when police officers came by. I should have." I should have found out why. I should have let him talk to me about it at least. Because now I know how stupid and naive I was. Just like I was stupid and naive about his concerns about meeting my parents. I don't have to tell him this. I don't have to tell him I saw him as this sensitive, smart, and caring person who made me laugh, and that I couldn't imagine anyone seeing him differently. But I do tell him. I don't want anything left hidden between us.

Alex only nods.

"How horrible was it?" I ask.

He closes his eyes tight, like even the memory is painful. "Bad. But I don't want to talk about that." He lets out a slow exhale. "How's your ankle?"

"I don't want to talk about that either." I don't want to tell him I likely won't dance until the spring. There's something more important I have to say.

"Alex?"

He's watching his hands again. I wait for him to look at me.

"I wasn't honest with you. About my family. Or myself." We talk about my attempt at a double life, the happy one with him and the sad one with my parents and brother. We talk about all of it—Dad's job, Merrit's suspension, the apartment. Also my fears about bipolar disorder: my mom's and Merrit's diagnoses, what that means for me. Because of the genetics. Because I might get it or pass it on.

Alex's hand closes around my fingers. He slides off the chair onto the floor beside me, pulling my palm closer so he can study it.

"I want you, Isa. All of you. That's all I've ever wanted."

He's so close I could rest my head against his shoulder.

"I want to be with you through the bad. Not just laugh next to you during the good." He tells me what his mami told him. That falling in love is easy but fighting for it is hard. "You, this." He points to the two of us. "It's worth fighting for."

I squeeze his whole hand, then every one of his fingers and then his whole hand again, this time cradled in both of mine. He smooths down the puff of my untamed hair.

I curl forward. I want to lean against him. I want to feel him next to me.

He releases my hand. He takes hold of my chin. His lips brush against mine, back and forth, as if to remind me how soft they are, how warm. As if I could forget. My heart beats like bird wings, fast and light. We're all of us safe. There are no more secrets.

He kisses me—gentle at first, then deeper, harder—all of the hurt and fear of the past days, the past weeks and months, surging between us. I don't think of anything else. I can't.

We pull away at the knock on the wall. Merrit's standing there, grinning down at us.

I draw my fingers out of Alex's hair. I grip his hands again. "Alex, I'd like you to meet my brother."

SATURDAY, JUNE 1

ALEX

Papi's behind the fence. He's yelling at Robi about a grounder up the middle that he missed. I can hear him from the rec building.

I wait for Robi to go up to bat. I don't want him or the other boys to see me. I don't want to take attention from his game.

Robi hits a single. I clap, even though I'm trying to hide. When Robi's on first, I whistle. Both Papi and Robi turn. Only Papi can come find me in the shade under the awning.

He slaps my shoulder. "Dime. ¿Cómo pasaste la mañana con Coach O'Neil?" he asks.

"Practice was fine," I tell him. He knows I'm starting in tomorrow's game against Fordham and that Isa and her brother are coming.

"Tonight you have to get good rest. Take an extra protein drink. Tomorrow is important. Oye, hay un player, a senior, up in Dutchess County at una escuela que se llama Beacon High. He doesn't pitch as well as you, but they say he'll be a second-round pick next week in the draft. We'll see." He claps me on the back again.

I lift my gaze from the grass. I look him in the face. I've been waiting for this, a moment that feels right.

"Mira, Papi. Next year? I don't want to go straight to the draft. I want to try for college. The Bigs will be there when I'm done."

Papi steps back. He turns and walks away. He comes close again and when he does, his face is the color of a Red Sox jersey.

"Estupido," he calls me. "Ingrato." He hurls spit at the ground. "After everything I did for you." His finger marks the beat of each word on my chest.

"I'm sorry I disappoint you," I tell him. "But I'll be more sorry if I disappoint myself."

After the game, Robi runs up to me. He looks like he's not going to stop. He looks like he's going to run through me or leap up for a hug. At the last moment he brakes. He blinks and grins at me, shifting from foot to foot. He's getting bigger. He's eleven now and almost up to my shoulder. I don't tell him about my decision. I need to tell Mami and Yaritza and Isa first.

Papi says not one word to me the whole walk home. That's OK. This time, I'm prepared for it.

I put my arm around Robi as we trail Papi through the park. I make a silent promise to myself that I'll always be here for him. That I won't ever leave him, even if it means staying local for college. I don't want Papi doing to him what he did to me. I don't want Robi thinking there's only one path for him, to his future or to Papi's heart. Because there's never only one path. Or at least, there never should be.

• • •

It's good to be on the 1 train again. It took a few months before I could say that. I'm still seeing the therapist Mrs. Warren found for me. I have the doc to thank for helping figure out what to do about Papi and the draft.

The rocking and the swaying of the train reminds me what I miss about this ride. I half expect to see Bryan hanging on one of the rails, begging Danny for his last taco. But Bryan's playing up in the Bronx today. AHH made the playoffs again. Danny's not in the city anymore. He's upstate at a tech school. After everything went down with me and the cops, he quit the gang. Gracias a Dios. I didn't even need to talk to him about it. He moved up near Syracuse to live with an aunt who's a principal of a middle school there. He wants to be a mechanic. Says he'll make decent money and it'll keep him out of trouble. I visited him one weekend before baseball started up. I had to thank him for getting that lawyer. I had to thank Pinchón too. Guess it makes sense that Pinchón would know an attorney, someone the cops would believe when he produced evidence that they had the wrong guy. Pinchón even offered to pay the bill, not that I let him. Those cops showed up at one of my Haeres games. I didn't pitch so well that day. And Isa had come to watch with her mother. Mrs. Warren must have sensed I was buggin'. Bottom of the third, she went right up to those cops. Few minutes later, they left. I never asked what she said, but I did thank her. I never want to see those cops again. I'm still torn up inside. I haven't been able to let it go, but I'm working on it. With the doc.

The train pulls into Sixty-Sixth Street/Lincoln Center. Mosaic stick figures leap across the tiled wall of the station. I don't see any dancers with buns. But a guy with mouse-brown hair and glasses gets on. He's carrying the case of some musical instrument, not sheets of music. I won't run into Chrissy or Kevin either, though I've seen them plenty these past months. They already left for Prague for the summer. Chrissy emailed me that the music and dance school there is mad cool.

At Seventy-Second, a man plays the trumpet for change.

At Seventy-Ninth, a guy and a girl get on. Their clasped hands remind me of me and Isa. Only, the girl looks like me and the boy doesn't have blond hair. His hair is red. The girl's even wearing a Prince Royce shirt. They sit opposite me, one row down. I can't not look at them because they can't stop looking at each other. It blows the dust off the ache inside my chest. When the girl puts her leg in his lap and tucks her shoe around his calf, my eyes get all wet.

I squeeze my lids shut. I think of my favorite poem. The one I wrote for the *San Francisco Literary Journal*. The one I dedicated to Kiara. The one about needing to really know yourself and love yourself—your inside self—before you can share that love with others. I named the poem after Merrit's new app that's number fifteen on the top 100 list, right below his companion app that allows you to know if a video's been doctored. Those apps are part of the reason Merrit got a transfer to MIT for next year. Isa's family's excited for him, but Isa and her mother are nervous. I told Isa it's OK to be worried, but that she should talk about it with her brother. Merrit suggested setting up regular times when they can video Snapchat, when Isa can see him and know he's fine.

The train doors open.

"Alex?"

My eyes are still closed. This happens sometimes. I hear her voice. I even wrote a poem about it. Only I'm not dreaming this time. I open my eyes. Isa's the one who gave me strength to talk to my papi, strength to see myself as something different from what everyone expects.

She's wearing cutoffs. She sits down next to me. Her ankle is small and perfect again. Her T-shirt is plain gray. There's no ballet shoe on it. Her irises are the exact color of the rich earth of my parents' island. Perhaps it's the same color of the earth of her mother's island too. Isa slides out the band from her ponytail. Her hair falls around her face. My jaw drops. Her hair—it's above-her-shoulders short.

"Can you even make a bun with that?" I ask.

Her lips spread wide. "Sure I can." She shows me. She doesn't stop grinning.

And I don't stop looking at her. Or listening to her as she tells me about dance. Her ankle's getting stronger every day. Then she's talking about yesterday's game and my two home runs and how Robi hugged her so hard she couldn't breathe. She can't wait to see me pitch tomorrow.

She takes my hand. She doesn't let go. Not when we get out at 168th. Not when we take the elevators up to Broadway. We walk past the hospital, past the bakery that sells muffins as big as your fist. We head toward the river. We pick our way down to the water, to empty picnic tables in the shadow of the bridge. Isa gets sandwiches out of her bag.

"I put in lots of extra pickles," she says, her voice teasing.

I kiss her. "Thank you." I kiss her again because I can. I kiss her because it's all I want to do.

A dog runs, barking, after a Frisbee. Isa pulls away, laughing. She pushes my sandwich toward me. I take an enormous bite.

"Delicious," I tell her. I thank her also for my appetite. She pinches my side. I grab her and hold her tight.

I take out my new notebook, the one Robi gave me as a gift just because. I watch the sun set behind Isa's laughing face. I put my pencil to paper and write.

ACKNOWLEDGMENTS

This book would not have been possible without the love and support of many.

To my outstanding agent, Jim McCarthy, thank you for your unwavering faith, your expertise, your wit and guidance. To my incomparable editor, Anne Heltzel, and her superb assistant, Jessica Gotz, thank you for asking all the right questions and pushing me to make Isa and Alex's story better. (You're like personal trainers—minus the whistles!) Thank you to the extremely talented Siobhán Gallagher for such an amazing cover (again!!) and to the rest of the illustrious team at Amulet, Trish McNamara-O'Neill, Jenny Choy, Mary Marolla, and Borana Greku, for getting this book into the hands of readers.

To my incredible writer friends, new and old, who are all far more accomplished and brilliant than me, Carolyn Mackler, Paul Griffin, Emmy Laybourne, Liz Acevedo, Tisha Hamilton, Stacey Lender, Mayra Cuevas, thank you for patiently listening to all my worries and even more patiently and graciously doling out advice and support. To my ever-supportive writer's group, Maria Andreu, Lisa Hansen, Gigi Collins, Hannah Lee, Betsy Voreacos, thank you for your honest but gentle critiques and for our many nights of carrots, chips, and hummus. To the gifted José Angel Araguz, thank you for lending your poet's eye. To the thoughtful Mark Oshiro, Ricardo Peralta, and Leslie Bermingham, thank you for the early reads and very beneficial comments. To my wonderful nephews, William, Connor, and

Acknowledgments

Owen, thank you for answering all my questions about baseball (an additional baseball thank-you to Betsy and my husband, Marc!). Also thank you to Lisa, Frankie and Dylan Campione, as well as Helen Poon and Laurie Rocke for NYC high school baseball insight. Thank you to Detective Isaac Moltry for answering my questions about NYC police procedures. Thank you to Lesly Torres and Albany Perez for letting me check my cubanismos against dominicanismos. Thank you to Dr. Janet Jackson and Dr. Amanda Wilson for fielding my questions about being a child of a parent with mental illness and about bipolar disorder specifically.

To my mom friends and girlfriends, Christina, Trudi, Sara, Kristin, Davina, Kennedy, Nat, Sally, Suzannah, Pilu, Amanda, Barbette, Jillian, Lucia, Jennifer (C and L), Corey, Leslie, Jane, and Rachel, thank you for long talks, laughter, and camaraderie (and for your enthusiasm and not-so-patient questions about when the next book is coming out). To my medical colleagues and friends, Guytree, Nora, Daisy, Nadine, and Daphne, thank you for supporting my medical career and helping me balance it with my writing career. To my brother and sister-in-law, Jamie and Ashley, thank you for sharing with me stories from your childhoods and for helping me understand sports team and family mentalities.

To my loving parents and abuela, thank you for the many years you drove me back and forth to ballet class and for all the recitals you had no choice but to attend! To my cariñoso abuelo, who would tell me stories deep into the night when we were supposed to be asleep, and who wrote such beautiful poetry, thank you for instilling in me a love of words and characters and plot. To Rachelle and to my brother, Curtis, and to Emma, thank you for helping out with the kids when I was pulled in five different directions. To my in-laws, thank you for your unwavering faith and support and for bragging about me to all your friends (it really is the best type of publicity). To my daughters, Auden, Amaia, and Ella, thank you for putting up with me when I disappear into my writing cave and when I emerge somewhat bearlike. Every day, your kindness, thoughtfulness, and curiosity amaze me. I am so proud to be your mother and cannot wait to see how your stories unfold! And to Marc, my Everything. Darling, I can't get enough of your love, babe.

Finally, I would like to thank each and every reader. Thank you for being interested enough in Isa and Alex to make it to this point in the book. It still astounds me that there are people in the world who are not related to me who want to read what I have written.

• • •

A note about mental illness: If you or someone you know is going through a difficult time, please don't keep it a secret. Find someone you trust to talk to. Mental health resources for patients and families can be found at the following links: childmind.org or childmind.org/audience/for-families. The National Institute of Mental Health (NIMH, at nimh.nih.gov/health/ index.shtml) and the National Alliance on Mental Health (nami.org) are also helpful resources.

• • •

A note about subway travel: The pediatrician (and mom) in me would like to remind you that what Alex and Isa and their friends do in this book is fiction. Traveling between subway cars is illegal. As Isa's mother says, the subway can be dangerous—so stay alert! Also, please don't jump onto the tracks.

ALSO BY ISMÉE WILLIAMS

Turn the page for an excerpt!

TWENTY WEEKS

"His name ain't Dr. Love. *Coño*. You're messing with me, right?"

Yaz smacks me in the shoulder. She's doubled over, fingers clamping her mouth shut. Her purple silver-studded nails press dimples into her cheek. She's trying not to laugh.

"What?" I ask her. My cell slips as I shrug my shoulders. "They expect me to believe this guy's name is Dr. Love? A heart doctor? How stupid do they think I am?" I squat and snatch the phone. I wedge it back in the crook of my neck. "Like if Toto called for a penis doctor and was told the guy's name was Dr. Weiner he would believe them?"

Toto is Abuela's boyfriend. That's not his real name. It's just what my girls call him. Because his hairline's low. And he's bulky. Like one of them fighting dogs. And he's got these small hands and feet.

Yaz is gasping, cherry lollipop–colored lips pressed almost outta sight. Teri is giggling, fingers smoothing down long strands of inky hair. Heavenly's screen is three inches from her nose. She's probably browsing posts from her favorite designers.

She doesn't respond to my joke. But she thinks it's funny. I can tell.

"Your appointment with Dr. Love is scheduled for nine thirty on Thursday, September eleventh." The lady on the phone can't wait to get rid of me.

"Nine eleven? No way, José. Give me another date."

Yaz kicks me in the thigh.

"Hey!" I circle an arm around my belly, my finger pointed, already wagging. "Watch the baby!" I catch my phone as it tries to fall again.

"Like she was anywhere near your uterus." Heavenly rolls her eyes. Thick clumps of mascaraed lashes make everyone else look like a clown doll. On Heavenly, it looks good.

Phone Lady gives me a different appointment.

I hold the phone away from my face and turn to my girls. "Does Monday, September fifteenth, at ten work for *youz* guys?" I fix each of them with my you-better-be-there glare.

"Whatever you think, Mari." Teri's smiling like I just told her I won some money off those scratch cards at the bodega and I'm takin' them all on vacay. "I'll come," she says, as if her expression ain't enough. We was all excited when I found out about the baby. But Teri was the one who went out and got a book. And read it. Teri was the one who told me when it was time for my first doctor's appointment. Found the clinic I should go to.

"*Weez* guys will be ready." Yaz strikes the air above her with her fist, like Dazzler from the X-Men. She been doing that same dumbass pose since we chased Ricky Lopez down 173rd Street all the way to Broadway for her backpack. That was in the third grade. We been besties ever since.

Heavenly's acrylics tap-tap-tap on the face of her phone. It's the second one Jo-jo's bought her. As long as it texts and is in the pocket of jeans that show off the curves of her *nalgas*, Heavenly don't care what logo it has or when it came out. But Jo-jo does. Only the best for his girl. I don't mind, seeing as I got to keep her old one. She's promised Yaz this one once it goes outta style. Heavenly's bottom lip slides out like she's gonna apply more *pinta*. But her eyes, they be smiling. "Ten on Monday? Perfect. I hate Mr. Sansone's English class."

Phone Lady's still talking. I can hear her squawks even with the phone a foot off my ear. I press it back into the space between my shoulder and cheek and catch the end of what she's sayin'. "And please arrive twenty minutes early to fill out all the necessary paperwork."

Twenty minutes? For paperwork? You gotta be kidding me. "*Coño.* Listen," I say, trying to be nice seein' as Yaz knows what I'm thinking and is giving me those lizard eyes. Like my swearin' is some bug she's fixin' to eat with that long tongue of hers. "I was just there yesterday seeing my baby doctor. She told me I had to make this appointment. Don't you have all my info in some system?" I know they do, 'cause every time I go I have to stand there and wait for them to pull it up.

Silence. Then, "You have our number if you need to reschedule. Is there anything else I can help you with, Miss Pujols?"

Miss Pujols. I've gotten over the way white folks say my last name—*Poo-joe-ells*. It's actually better than how it sounds in Spanish—*Poo-holes*. Yeah, I won the instant scratch-off lottery with that one. But what I hate most is that they always call me "miss." I know I look young. But we're on the phone. She can't see me. And I'm making a pregnant-lady appointment. Shouldn't that make me a Ms. or a Mrs.?

"No." I wanna say something else. But Yaz, with that sharp lizard tongue of hers, is staring at me hard. My upper lip itches. I scrub at it. I need a nap.

Yaz mouths something at me, pointing to her dimples. "Oh . . . And, uh, thanks."

I hang up.